BLOOD AND MEMORY

THE QUICKENING Book Two

FIONA McINTOSH

An Imprint of HarperCollins*Publishers*

This book was originally published in a mass market edition in 2003 by Voyager, an imprint of HarperCollins Publishers, Australia.

EOS
An Imprint of HarperCollins*Publishers*
10 East 53rd Street
New York, New York 10022-5299

First Eos paperback printing: July 2006
First Eos trade paperback printing: August 2005

In blood and in memory of . . .
William Richards

ACKNOWLEDGMENTS

It would be wonderful to write a simple but huge "thank you" and hope that everyone who is connected with this work somehow knows how grateful I am for their support. There are always those, however, whose contribution makes such a difference that they deserve individual recognition. That list, which grows longer with each book, includes:

Gary Havelberg and Sonya Caddy—draft readers I've now come to rely on for guidance. Then there's Robin Hobb, my long-distance friend and mentor, whose own work continues to inspire and drive me harder as does the work of Guy Gavriel Kay. . . . They both make me appreciate what a long journey is still ahead for me! My parents for looking after our childen while I roam the world for my work and for freeing me up to write without guilt.

Pip Klimentou, my good friend and early-morning caller who ensures I don't sleep in after late nights of writing. Thank you. A nod to the members of the Fab Fantasy Book Club and to all the regular visitors to my bulletin board—for your encouragement and constant support.

No thanks are complete without a mention for my wizard agent, Chris Lotts, who brought me together with the fine team at HarperUS/Eos—Kate Nintzel is a fun and generous editor to work with.

Finally, love and endless thanks to the three patient men in my life—my sons Will and Jack, and their father Ian, my rock.

BLOOD AND
MEMORY

PROLOGUE

He slid off the saddle to unsteady feet. Too flustered to tether the horse, Wyl trusted it to remain where he left it as he stumbled deeper into the copse and retched. The sickening need to be rid of the curse seemed to last an eternity as he desperately tried to yield it, rip the sorcery free from its sinister grip. At the rim of his addled mind Wyl acknowledged that this cold, moonlit night was too beautiful for death . . . once again.

He believed he could taste the taint of the magic that had claimed his body hours earlier. Wyl did not want to remember it, but it was so fresh, so horrific, so ugly in his mind, he could not banish it. Commander Liryk of Briavel has smiled when the man called Romen Koreldy, newly banished from the realm, had suggested the Forbidden Fruit for their overnight stay before leaving for whichever border he chose. He had smiled in understanding, knowing that the mercenary had decided to drown his sorrows within the soft and welcoming embrace of a whore in the region's well-known brothel. And he had smiled more widely when Romen had accepted the offer of Hildyth. The Commander had sampled her on a previous occasion and had known there could be no better place for his grieving companion to lose himself for a few hours. Wyl Thirsk, trapped in Koreldy's body, had felt the same until the stiletto had buried itself deep into his heart, trying to take his life. Except it had not. Romen's body released its trapped guest so it could travel . . . travel into Hildyth and claim her life instead.

It was not a new experience for Wyl. He had felt that same wrenching sense of despair once before and even now could hardly believe it had happened once again. He was dry-retching now; knew he must force himself to stop. He looked to where his hands—his smooth woman's hands—gripped the tree he leaned against, concentrated on the feel of the rough bark beneath his tense fingers, and forced himself to ease his convulsions of fear.

Don't think about who you've become. Remember who you are, he reminded himself. *Remember who you are!*

"I am the son of Fergys Thirsk of Argorn," he croaked through his new and strange voice.

"I am Wyl Thirsk. General of the Morgravian Legion." He spoke it more loudly this time, hating the femininity of the pitch.

"I am alive," he finally said, voice stronger and steadier, his mind accepting, his spirit resolute.

He repeated his mantra until the nausea finally subsided and his cramping muscles stopped answering the call to expel the enchantment. It was not possible anyway, he knew.

Wyl Thirsk raised his head to the starry skies and screamed his despair in the voice of the assassin . . . the woman he had become this night.

It was a cry without hope. He knew all too well that no shaking of fists or howling to the heavens could change the dark enchantment that doomed him to cheat death. He understood that his spirit was now destined to shift from one body to another, waiting for death to make another attempt to claim him.

A wave of sadness crashed against his thoughts as he remembered Romen, his first victim—if he could call him that. Now Romen's body was dead too.

Wyl felt gutted to have lost the comfort of that once-strange—now-familiar—vessel that had welcomed him, sheathed him, given succor and life. Romen's essence had lived on with him while Wyl's true body was mortifying in a tomb. The two of them were one . . . and now perhaps they must consider themselves three with this woman among them, part of them . . . one with them.

She was now their shield; they were now her secret.

Wyl limped to the narrow brook that traveled languorously nearby. It glinted in the silvery light. He threw himself down at its edge and cleansed his mouth. Now he succumbed to the tears; deep, heartfelt sobs shuddered through the body of the woman, but the grief belonged only to Wyl Thirsk.

I live, he told himself again, fumbling in his pockets for the linen that held the key to his life. In it lay the bloodied ring finger of Romen Koreldy of Grenadyn: noble, mercenary, and beloved suitor of Queen Valentyna of Briavel. Wyl had retrieved it from the chamber at the Forbidden Fruit where he had hidden it . . . and now he would use it. Use it to beguile Celimus, the treacherous King of Morgravia, into believing that Romen was dead and confirm that the mysterious assassin, known only as Hildyth and masquerading as a whore, had succeeded where others had failed.

Wyl calmed his panicked thoughts, drawing on his skills as a strategist, to think through what he must do. He would send Koreldy's finger to Celimus, precisely as Faryl had been instructed through the King's scheming chancellor, Jessom, and in doing so he would allow Morgravia's sovereign, the betrayer, to live within a false cocoon of safety.

The neighboring realm of Briavel was Celimus's main concern now and his plans to wed its queen, Valentyna, would be occupying his time. In his disguise as Romen, Wyl had aided Valentyna in hindering those marriage plans diplomatically, but Wyl knew she would not do so with ease again. He understood all too well what a tightrope of careful politics she was treading. Her own nobles and counselors were pressing for the marriage and the peace and prosperity it would bring; in fact both realms were clamoring for a royal wedding of such importance. Briavellians and Morgravians alike had become captivated by the romantic notion of their sovereigns bringing the neighbors into harmony. Both nations could almost hear the wails of an heir that would once and for all unite the realms under one sovereign.

It made political and strategic sense. Of course it did. When Celimus had first broached the subject to him, Wyl had been highly impressed by the farsighted plan the young King had devised to force these two warring realms to set aside their differences, their history of hate, once and for all. He had even agreed to help shape such a union—until his inner sense told him things were not as straightforward as the new sovereign proposed. First, the old King, Magnus, had died only hours before Celimus already had presented Wyl with a well-laid strategy and a team of foreign mercenaries hired and ready to depart. The side of Wyl that knew from bitter experience that Celimus was a traitorous snake smelled the trap. And he had been right. His decision not to support the King's wishes had led to the slaughter of his great friend, Alyd Donal, and had almost claimed the life of his sister, had he not then agreed to travel into Briavel, escorted by strangers, and win a princess for the King of Morgravia.

How could he have known—in that moment, terrified for his sister and by how close that vicious axe blade had come to ending her life in the Stoneheart courtyard—how twisted Celimus's plan actually was. Not only had the King planned to use the Thirsk name to win an audience with King Valor and then Valentyna's hand in marriage, but he had already ordered the deaths of Wyl and Valor—by different assassins—once the betrothal agreement had been made. Darker yet, Celimus had contrived to blame Wyl Thirsk for the King's death while ensuring that the executioners, one of whom was Romen Koreldy, were also killed, thus covering his trail of deception.

Celimus, however, had not reckoned on the integrity of the assassin, Koreldy, whose lifetime loyalty the King thought had been safely secured with an obscene payment of gold, or of a blood pact made between Thirsk and Koreldy for whichever one of them survived a duel to the death to reveal the King's treachery. But little did any of them know about an even greater menace that lurked mysteriously around their grand plans and lived within Wyl Thirsk himself; brutal and without loyalty to anything but itself, it was a gift from the witch Myrren to Wyl for his kindness during her trial torture. It had waited patiently for many years to wreak its havoc, and when it had finally struck, it was savage and shocking, forcing the spirit of Wyl, whose body was dying from Koreldy's sword blow, to claim Koreldy's life and body instead. Thirsk had become Koreldy and now he had become the whore Hildyth when Myrren's Gift had struck again.

Wyl surfaced from his troubled thoughts realizing his mind was rambling over old ground. He could not change what had happened; he could only move forward now and work to protect his sister—the last of the Thirsks—and somehow thwart Celimus's determined intentions to control Briavel through marriage to Valentyna. First, though, he must track down the Manwitch. He was Myrren's true father and might have answers for him.

In making the decision to let go of the past, his biggest regret was knowing that Valentyna, whom he had loved from the moment she had first breezed into his life when he was General Wyl Thirsk of the Morgravian Legion, had fallen in love with him as Romen Koreldy. His own feelings for her had only intensified during his time as Romen and he could never forgive himself for risking that love and allowing her to think that he had betrayed her when she had so relied on him.

A headache was gathering. He must find out more about who he had become before the pain and this grief over his love for the Queen claimed him completely. She could never love him now in this strange and female body. Wyl could not bring himself to look at his new body just yet or touch it. But he held no such reticence for the memories, not caring that they were not his own. What remained belonged to Wyl now. They were his to remember and use.

He leaned back exhausted against a tree and delved. Wyl learned the whore Hildyth had simply been another guise. He was in fact Faryl of Coombe—a brilliant assassin, born in the midlands, familiar with places far away from Morgravia or Briavel—and riddled with secrets.

1

THE QUEEN HAD SUFFERED A SLEEPLESS NIGHT, CHURNING over her decision to expel Romen Koreldy. Valentyna had measured the dark hours by listening to the muted noises of the guard changing. The only other distraction was the distant, infrequent howl of a dog—or was it a wolf? She wondered if it was caught in one of the traps laid by poachers . . . or more whimsically she imagined it had lost its mate and was venting its despair.

She understood such things, for the sorrowful cry only served as an echo of her own loneliness.

Valentyna asked herself yet again if she could have hung on to the man she loved and still appeased an angry king? A king, she added, with more than enough fighting power to overwhelm Briavel. The answer, whichever way she approached the problem, was no.

"Damn duty!" she murmured into her coverlets. She punched the feather pillow that brought no comfort this night.

To add to the misery, a vision of Fynch haunted her. How he had looked at her she would never forget. He too had grown to love Romen, despite his misgivings about the man. She and her young friend had shared so much in the short time they had known each other. But all of that closeness was shattered now. Fynch was avoiding her because she had so deliberately distanced herself from Romen and ordered him expelled from Briavel.

She had cast aside a man she loved over Celimus—a man they all hated. A child, not familiar with the way of politics and diplomacy, would believe her actions made no sense. But this was no ordinary child. Fynch was special in his serious, deep-thinking manner. He understood all too well, but that did not mean he felt any comfort in his understanding.

She did not want to lose his companionship, but it seemed the day just gone had risen solely to bring loss to her life.

King Celimus, she realized, kicking off her blankets with irritation, would probably be close to the border by now, possibly even crossing into Morgravia. She had no doubt spies would keep him updated on Briavel's events, and her standoff with Koreldy would be high on the list of missives. It suddenly occurred to her that the King might have Romen tracked down upon hearing this news. Surely Romen would be cautious? He had been warned that to set foot into Morgravia was to risk certain execution. Failing his own good sense, she trusted that her own Commander Liryk would counsel Romen. Hopefully they had ridden through the night and would be headed north, back to where he had come from.

"Where Cailech, King of the Mountains, awaits him," she whispered sorrowfully.

The last time Valentyna had cried passionately was over her father and the time before that when she had fallen from a horse a decade ago. She considered herself resilient, but silent, heavy tears won now as she accepted the enormity of her orders. Romen had nowhere to go. Briavel represented safety. Beyond its borders to the north and west, people wanted to kill him. The south offered only ocean, no comfort. To the east, only fear in the little-known Wild. Fynch knew it too. That was the reason for the accusation in that chilling final glance he had given her.

It spoke of betrayed friendships.

And he was right. What had Romen been thinking during that swordfight! It was clear that he had meant to kill Celimus, and then where but in intense danger would that have left Briavel?

Romen knew how precarious her predicament had been. What had been his intention? She had not had a chance to consider it, in truth. She had not had the luxury of opportunity to think it through; she had been forced to react, and swiftly, in the only way that a monarch in her situation could have done. She knew her decision was politically correct, but this reassurance was cold comfort.

Her heart ached. She loved Romen and she had sent him away . . . not just away in fact, for expulsion had more serious implications. Briavel no longer recognized him as friend. Romen Koreldy would not be permitted to set so much as a toe inside Briavel. If recognized, he would be captured and imprisoned. Her actions had trapped him. Whichever way he turned; whichever borders he finally crossed, he was as doomed as their new and fragile love.

Valentyna twisted beneath her remaining sheet, banishing thoughts of his touch, which brought a new kind of ache to her body. She would have given herself gladly to him that night before the tourney, but his was the voice of calm among the waves of passion. It was Romen who pulled back, Romen who made her see the reason for holding on to the most precious commodity for a new queen.

Virginity was wealth, he had counseled. More importantly, it was power. A virgin queen was an irresistible magnet for appropriate suitors. Except she wanted no husband . . . not unless it was Koreldy.

She rubbed her tired but stubborn eyes and sat up. This would not do. Pulling on a soft robe to ward off the chill, Valentyna moved to the window and looked out toward the dark woodland she loved so much.

"It might work," she murmured as an idea gathered resonance in her thoughts. She could meet him somewhere outside of Briavel's borders. Somewhere safe, where they could rendezvous in secret. If only she could feel his kiss just once more, it would be enough, she told herself naively, hardly believing it herself.

Her plans to meet with Romen outside of Briavel took rapid shape. She would take Fynch too. Between them they would mend friendships, renew loyalties, rekindle the flame that burned brightly between them all. She could apologize for making the hardest of decisions and she knew Romen already understood; his eyes had told her as much when they had regarded her so gently despite her harsh words. She could ask him why he had risked so much. They could set things straight between them. Her daydream had even rambled beyond to when perhaps she could find a way around the expulsion order; when time had healed and life was less precarious. Perhaps there was a chance for them in time.

"Where are you now, Romen?" the Queen of Briavel whispered toward the trees, now determined to see her lover one last time, not knowing he was at this very moment just a few miles from entering her own castle's walls.

Far sooner than she could have imagined, Valentyna would cast her eyes on Koreldy; kiss him just once more as she so desired.

Liryk's expression was grim. Beneath it anger seethed. This should not have happened. The Queen had deliberately granted life, given Koreldy the chance to make a new one elsewhere. She could have easily commanded death. There was friendship between the two, possibly more, if his intuition served him well.

He could not blame her. Who could help but fall under Koreldy's spell?

They had emerged from the cover of the woodland that surrounded the northern rim of the palace grounds. Commander Liryk glanced to his left, where the body of the man he hardly knew but comfortably called friend lay dead in a cart, wrapped in sacking. Combined sorrow and guilt threatened to take over Liryk's checked emotion, forcing him to look away and back toward the castle.

Now they had arrived at the famous Bridge of Werryl, where past sovereigns, remembered faithfully in marble, stood proudly on either side and guided visitors into the palace. Liryk raised his hand toward the ramparts, where he knew his guards saw their fellow soldiers approaching through the light mist of dawn. The gate was up, he noticed, and he grimaced. He would have to take a hard look at security again and ensure the castle remained closed to all visitors until permission was formally granted. After Valor's sudden death, everyone had been so careful, but more recently he had noticed a general slackening of the rules. With an assassin on the loose, who knew what could happen. Their queen must be better protected.

In the courtyard he wearily handed his horse's reins to the stable boy and gave orders for Koreldy to be taken to the chapel and laid out. He, like his men, was tired. They had ridden through the night, determined to bring the body back as quickly as possible to ensure that the gossip fled with the evidence. It would flare and rage for a day and then hopefully be forgotten. There was no body, no sign that the grisly death had even occurred. The Forbidden Fruit's women would be entertaining in that same chamber this very night—no sign of the recent bloodshed in evidence. His mouth twisted at the thought. Poor Koreldy. He deserved better.

Well, no matter how tired he was now, the next hour would be his most difficult. He suspected that no matter how he counseled her, their headstrong queen would want to see the corpse for herself. He shook his head, resigned. Valentyna was an early riser. Best to go see her immediately and get this ugly business done.

Liryk made his presence known to another man he liked. Krell, the Queen's chancellor and former servant to King Valor, was a calm and solid force among Valentyna's advisers.

"May I ask if it is urgent, Commander Liryk?" Krell said, shifting papers around his desk. "This is quite an irregular hour to be requesting an audience."

Liryk nodded. "Something unexpected. She must be told."

"Bad news?" the Chancellor asked. Liryk's expression was enough to foreshadow the fact that this would not be a happy meeting.

Liryk would have told him everything anyway; Krell had that way of not showing unnecessary curiosity while still finding out what he felt he should know. It was a masterful skill. He was also a man to trust.

"It is, I'm afraid. Koreldy is dead."

The Queen's servant looked up sharply from the neat piles of orderly paperwork he trawled through for his monarch. He had single-handedly eased Valentyna into her challenging role as ruler, allaying her fears, guiding her with informed skill, instinctively knowing what her father would expect. In terms of administering the realm, he was a blessing for them all and could rarely be ruffled. However, the expression on his normally well-guarded face was all shock at this moment. Liryk was convinced that Krell wanted to ask the Commander if he was quite sure but had checked himself.

Liryk confirmed it anyway. "I've had him laid out in the chapel. I imagine the Queen will want to view the body."

"Indeed. She will not be persuaded otherwise," Krell replied, distracted. He walked around from his desk. "This is dark news, Commander. I'm sorry to hear it. He was, in spite of the reason for his expulsion, a good man for Briavel . . ."

Liryk guessed that the Chancellor wanted to add that Koreldy was a good man for Valentyna as well. Instead the Chancellor held his tongue, asked him to wait. He would seek an appointment with her majesty immediately. He left Liryk alone with his bleak thoughts and fatigue.

When Liryk was shown into her study, he could see Valentyna had not slept well. Her eyes lacked their sparkle. Dark smudges beneath made them appear hollow in the much too pale skin. He wished once again he could escape this task and hoped Krell had forewarned her of the tidings.

She was wearing a satin robe and had obviously come in a hurry straight from her chambers, not caring about her state of dress, but then Valentyna never was one for vanity. He had known this fine young woman since she was newly born and she had always treated him as a kindly uncle—she still did, in fact. So the fact that she was in her night attire in his presence would not worry her one bit. He noticed she managed to muster a smile for him, rising above the reasons that had troubled her slumber.

"I'm glad to have you back, Commander Liryk," she said formally, turning from her window. She crossed the room, and after he had straightened from his bow, she fell back into her less regal manner, taking both his hands in her own. "Now, ease my worry," she said. "Tell me it all went smoothly."

Liryk glanced toward the departing Krell, who was passing behind her majesty, carrying papers. The Chancellor shook his head slightly and Liryk felt the weight of his task settle like a stone in his throat. Krell was following protocol. He had left the bad news entirely for Liryk to deliver.

Valentyna was searching his face, a confused smile on her lips now. "What is it? Krell tells me you have news that cannot wait. I presume you wish to report that Romen Koreldy was seen safely to a border. But which border? I must know," she said, her words coming out in a rush.

Liryk's eyes came back to rest sadly upon her own. "May we sit, your highness?"

"Oh, of course, how remiss of me. You've obviously been riding through the night to be back here so fast." She gestured toward one of the comfortable armchairs. "Please."

"Thank you." He sat, taking every last moment he could before he had to share his tidings with the lovely young Queen. So much grief around her. He wished Krell had remained but knew once again the man had done the right thing and given them privacy.

Valentyna joined him in the opposite chair.

"You look very pale, your highness." He blurted out his thoughts.

She nodded. "You know me too well. I did sleep badly. I've anguished over yesterday's decision, Liryk. It was the appropriate action to take for Morgravia's king and the dutiful thing for Briavel. But oh, it was a poor decision for me personally. I miss Koreldy more than most would realize."

He was shocked. He sensed the friendship had run deep but had no idea it had progressed so far and so quickly. Her carefully chosen words could not mask the true admission. Liryk leaned back in his chair and closed his eyes, risking her further confusion while he gathered up his anguished thoughts.

"My apologies, sir. I should not burden you with my heart," Valentyna said to fill the awkward pause, sorry that she had said as much as she had.

She noticed the sad expression on Liryk's face when he opened his eyes and sat forward again. He even took her hand, held it gently but firmly in his large, gnarled, soldier's hands. Liryk sighed heavily, and when he said "your majesty," as though his shoulders carried the very weight of the realm, her intuition suggested she did not want to hear whatever it was he had to report. She had to bite her lip to prevent herself from begging him to say no more.

He began to speak, his tone measured, his words carefully chosen.

Valentyna looked at Liryk's hand covering hers, trying to shut out the voice, concentrating on the gingery hair on the back of his, which made her think of Wyl Thirsk, of all people. Poor, lovely Wyl Thirsk with his thatch of orange hair and freckles. She recalled the way he blushed whenever her eyes glanced toward his, and his smile, so hard to win but bright and joyful when it came. He should never have died. He had fought courageously for a realm not his own, to save the life of his enemy. She had liked him the instant they had met, had felt a connection to him somehow that was hard to shake. Curiously the young man entered her mind at the oddest of times to this day and there were moments—none that she would admit openly to—when Fynch's suggestion, that Wyl Thirsk was still among them, rang true with her.

It was an odd situation. Normally she did not take to people so readily; she was wary of folk by nature and downright suspicious of strangers from Morgravia. But Wyl was not what she had expected. He was forthright and humble. Just a little in awe of her father, which she had appreciated because it showed respect—even between enemies. And her father had liked him and, more importantly, trusted him.

That much was obvious. She recalled how Romen had admitted that Wyl had fallen desperately in love with her on that first meeting. How shocked she had been and, strange though it sounded, how flattered she had felt. There was something about Wyl Thirsk—something special. Despite his lack of stature, which she had gently poked fun at, he certainly possessed a presence . . . and there had been a chemistry between them. Valentyna recalled how he had not felt ashamed to weep in front of them or accept her comfort. She had admired that about him.

Liryk's voice spoke on.

The Queen heard, as though from a distance, Liryk talking about a place called the Forbidden Fruit. It sounded like no establishment she would ever visit. Apparently Romen had gone with a woman. She knew what this meant but she tried to ignore it. She wanted to believe that the bathing and smoothing was an innocent activity to help ease the tension of that strange and joyless day. But it was more than a smoothing. She could read as much in the way Liryk said it.

Hildyth was her name. Hateful name. She suddenly despised the woman . . . a stranger she had never met or ever would meet. A whore.

Romen's whore.

She imagined the stranger laughing with him; unselfconscious at being naked with this private and yet playful man. The whore would feel his fingers over her body, his tongue, his lips . . . and Valentyna tried to convince herself, as these visions raged, that Romen was using the woman because he could not have his queen. His queen had banished him. Expelled him. Marked him as no friend of hers, or of Briavel's. He had to drown his sorrows somewhere and he had drowned them at the Forbidden Fruit, sheathing himself within a woman called Hildyth. Is this what Liryk seemed so hesitant to tell her . . . that Romen had spent the night with a paid woman?

It seemed not. There was more to the tale. As Liryk continued, her throat caught, and then began to close, as though it meant to stop her breathing. Liryk was speaking of being stabbed . . . something about a fingerless hand.

She looked up suddenly. He stopped speaking, disturbed by her sudden attention.

"I . . . Liryk . . . I don't understand." There was a tremor in her voice and she hated it. Hated it almost as much as she hated Hildyth for taking the pleasures of Romen's body when they were meant for a queen.

It broke every protocol but Liryk did not care for that right now. The little girl of Briavel, loved by all, needed comfort. He put his arm around his young sovereign and pulled her toward his broad chest in the manner a dear uncle might. She allowed him to because she was scared. She had heard the words but did not believe him. She would need him to say them again.

He spoke in a near whisper this time, his lips close to her hair, which smelled of fresh lavender. "Your highness," he said gently, "Romen Koreldy was murdered last night. We have nothing more than the woman's description of a man running down the hall. She was understandably distraught, so the details are vague, to say the least." He stopped, not sure of what else to say or even whether she had paid attention.

As he pulled away, her gaze was locked on his face, but her expression suggested her mind was far away.

"Dead?" she said, as though she were testing the word on her tongue. He nodded. Valentyna moved fast, leaping to her feet, grabbing her commander's shirt in her fists. "Romen's dead?"

"Yes, my queen. He was murdered," Liryk answered as gently as he could.

He was relieved when the door softly clicked open and Krell tiptoed through, something steaming from the mugs he carried. The man said nothing, walking silently across the rugs to lay down the tray nearby. Liryk caught a waft of dramona. It was a wise choice. The medicine was strong. It would help with the shock.

Valentyna became aware of Krell. His presence helped

her to compose herself as she released her grip on Liryk and felt for the chair behind her. She found herself wringing her hands and regained control of them, locked them together. The Queen took a long, deep breath. She remained silent for a moment or two longer and then lifted her chin, returning a steady dark blue gaze at the man whose news had just stuck a blade into her own heart. There was some pleasing symmetry to that notion, she thought bitterly, for if her ears had heard correctly among her frantic thoughts, a blade in the heart was the manner in which Romen had died.

"Commander Liryk. You will tell me everything once again so I understand thoroughly the events that unfolded last night."

The Queen's words fell like ice crystals now. They matched the hard and wintry expression that had frozen on her lovely face.

And so for the third time that morning Liryk told his sad tale, this time sparing her no detail. He delivered his report in the detached military manner he knew best, devoid of emotion and embellishment.

" . . . only later we discovered his ring finger had been removed," he concluded.

"Why?"

He shrugged. "A trophy perhaps, although I do believe, your highness, that this was an assassination. People who kill for money, especially if their victims are of high status, must provide proof of the death before they are paid in full. It is my belief that Koreldy was murdered on someone's order."

"Whose orders?"

One name hung silently between them. Neither dared speak it, for if they did they would both believe it, and the repercussions, should they act upon that notion, were too daunting to contemplate.

Instead Liryk chose a safer path. "We have no firm evidence as to who perpetrated this."

"Other than the blade," she replied.

"Yes, highness. Other than the weapon."

Krell took this moment to offer the mugs. They were taken silently.

"Drink it all, your majesty," he whispered before taking his leave.

She smelled the dramona, knew its intention, and put it aside. They would not sedate her. "Liryk. Did Koreldy say anything to you before he died."

The man was sipping from his mug of strong, dark tea. He nodded. "He told me that he did not kill your father. He wished you had given him a sign that you knew him to be innocent of all accusations leveled at him."

Valentyna's newly calmed expression faltered, as the words hurt. She knew Liryk had not meant to drive a further wedge of pain into her. She expected him to be truthful but could not know that he was honest only to a certain point. Liryk had told Koreldy he would not do anything to dissuade Valentyna against the marriage to Celimus even though Koreldy had begged him. As promised, he held his tongue now. For Briavel's sake, the marriage must go ahead.

It was taking every ounce of Valentyna's courage to remain composed and not crumble. That would come later. Right now she had to learn everything she could about Romen's death.

"The whore—"

"Hildyth?"

"Yes, her. Where is she now?"

"After she had told us everything she could, she asked if she could leave. She was very upset, as you can imagine."

"Had it occurred to you, Commander, that the whore was involved . . . could have given the killer entry? Could have killed Koreldy even?"

"Yes."

"And?"

She watched the color rise in her chief of security. "She could not have killed Koreldy because he would have been too strong for her. You know what an artful fighter he was. As for her being involved, yes, it had occurred to me but I decided she was innocent."

"Why?"

There it was again. The hesitancy, the embarrassment, a flush of red rising at the neck. "I have met her before. She did not strike me as either violent or anything more than a young woman trying to make the best of her situation."

"I see," said Valentyna, understanding perfectly. Romen had not been the first of her acquaintances to lie with this woman. Clearly Liryk had intimate knowledge of the whore Hildyth. "I want soldiers sent immediately to bring this woman back to the castle for questioning. Can I leave that up to you?"

Liryk nodded, embarrassed. "Of course."

"Where is Romen now?" she asked, just managing to keep her voice steady as she said his name.

"In the chapel, your highness."

"Thank you, Commander Liryk. I know you must be extremely tired. Please, rest and we shall speak again when you are refreshed. I apologize for having kept you so long"—and then miraculously her voice lightened—"and for losing myself there for a few moments. It was a shock."

She watched Liryk's expression soften at her words. Perhaps her cool detachment had unsettled him, although was this not the very quality one could admire in a queen? One not prone to shrieking hysterics but someone who could control her own emotions and deal calmly with a situation?

"I understand fully, your majesty. In truth, I don't believe I have come to terms with it myself yet."

"He died as a result of a blade through the heart, that's right, isn't it?"

He nodded. "Driven into his chest with expert precision. The killer knew what he was doing."

"So it would have been quick?"

"Dead before Koreldy even realized he'd been struck," he assured her, not quite believing it himself as he stood to bow before his sovereign.

She nodded that he might depart and he did so gladly, flooded with relief that his ugly task was done.

2

KNAVE KNEW. THE DOG HAD WOKEN HIM IN THE NIGHT WITH A howl so sorrowful it hurt Fynch to hear it. They had been sleeping rough in the woods because Fynch could not bear to be in the castle after all that had happened. Most of all he could not face the Queen. She had done something so unexpected that he had been unable to disguise his feelings over her actions, not that he had any status to disapprove. They were friends, though. Friends did not cast each other aside. She needed Romen . . . why could she not see this?

It was true that even he had been wary of Romen originally; how could he not be? It was Fynch who had overheard King Celimus plotting with Koreldy to assassinate Wyl Thirsk. But it was Fynch who had noticed the curious attachment that Knave, Wyl's dog, had shown for Koreldy when they had tracked him back to Pearlis. Fynch had been shocked to see the foreigner with Ylena and to hear that he had brought Wyl's corpse back to Stoneheart for the formal respect it was due. It was he alone who had worked it out or at least accepted that something very strange had occurred. Fynch believed in magic and so did not suffer from the same wariness of it as did most Morgravians or dismiss it like the Briavellians.

His suspicion that Wyl Thirsk was somehow still among them had been confirmed, first by Knave's uncharacteristic affection for a stranger and then by the fact that Koreldy had claimed Ylena, taking her away to safety. Furthermore, he had cleared the Thirsk family name simply by arriving in Pearlis with Wyl's body. Fynch had been relieved when Koreldy had admitted to being Wyl and explained about the frightening phenomenon that was the Quickening, which had given him life and taken the real Romen Koreldy's.

But Wyl had forbidden Fynch from sharing this knowledge. He alone knew the truth of Koreldy, which is why the Queen's decision had been so painful for him. He loved Valentyna and wished he could tell her who Romen Koreldy was, but he knew it would be in vain. How could anyone who could not conceive that sorcery existed believe such a tale?

He had hoped to see Romen before they took him away from Werryl—that way he could hear Wyl's plans, however thin they might be. It had not been permitted. Knave had wanted to follow his trace, but Fynch had exerted his own authority for once and told his companion to wait. They needed to plan their next move. The boy sensed that the dog could find its master anywhere. They could catch up with Wyl later. Instead he needed time to tidy his mind to consider all options first. So the woods had become their hiding place.

Fynch had expected to be here for a few days, but he was wrong. Outside events began to have their own crushing impact.

No amount of shushing or cajoling had prevented Knave from the sudden howling he had taken to that night. Fynch presumed it was to ward off any wolves or poachers, but it was a strange sound, one of despair. Perhaps he was missing Wyl? The dog was closed to him, so he could not work out what was troubling him. Knave did not want to be touched or spoken to and so Fynch had tossed and turned, trying to shut out the terrible keening. Before first light Knave had roused Fynch again. The boy sleepily obeyed and followed. Clearly the dog had an objective. It was still dark, so he knew they would not be seen by Valentyna. They slipped into the castle grounds, waving to guards and getting a familiar raised hand back. Knave was making for the main courtyard. Fynch had no idea why, but it became all too clear after the arrival of Commander Liryk.

They had watched him enter the bailey. He looked grave and weary. They saw him hand over the reins to the stable boy and heard him give some order to his men, although Fynch had not been able to make out the words.

As Liryk had left the courtyard and entered the castle, Fynch noticed that Knave was no longer at his side but was whining by the cart that had rolled in after Liryk. He watched with what felt like a claw around his throat, squeezing tighter and harder, as the men had struggled to lift something out of the cart. Instinctively, before he could even tell its shape, he knew they were pulling at the corpse of Romen Koreldy and his heart broke.

Relieved that they gave him permission to be present, a distraught Fynch followed them into the cool chapel. The men obviously recognized him as one of Koreldy's friends. He stood, rigid in his despair, by the side of the body, feeling disturbed by its pallor. Romen had been browned from the sun; he should not be this ghostly.

A guard, sensitive to the friendship that had existed between the dead man and the child, gently explained that a great deal of blood had drained at the time of death, which would account for its shockingly pale appearance. The boy was not so sure he had needed to hear the reasoning, but he whispered his thanks all the same and was glad when the man had stepped away.

The soldiers, all known to him, murmured their sympathies. One even apologized for not keeping Romen safe. Fynch wanted to cry out that Koreldy could take care of himself and so he had obviously been duped, then murdered— not that he knew the circumstances yet. Instead he accepted their commiserations silently and was relieved when they gradually departed.

He and Knave were alone at last with their friend and he felt it would be all right now if he cried. He reached out and smoothed back a few stray hairs from Romen's face; Wyl had adopted Koreldy's fastidiousness and would not like his hair so scruffy.

Those who had dealt with the body in Crowyll had done their best—mercifully wiping away most traces of blood and putting him in a fresh shirt. Still, he was hardly tidy and Fynch knew he would hate to be seen so disheveled. He leaned down and kissed his friend's forehead before laying his own head on Romen's cool chest and allowing his sorrow to echo through the chapel.

The dog sniffed the body long and carefully. Presumably satisfied that his master no longer breathed, he joined Fynch. Knave was patient. It was as though he understood that it was Fynch's turn now—the boy needed to grieve.

That was how Valentyna found Fynch.

She felt her composure slip as she stepped quietly into the chapel flanked by Krell and Liryk, who had insisted on accompanying her. On seeing the child draped over the corpse, she felt the sickening lurch of a cry rushing toward her throat. It was real. Death was here. It was Krell's guiding hand, a gentle, well-timed touch, steering her down the short aisle, that rescued her. She fought the grief back down and was able once again to look at the poignant scene before her. Fynch looked so small, so vulnerable. She desperately wanted to hold him; cling to the living—not allow him to hate her so.

Instead, as she silently drew up beside him, she risked taking his hand. She knew it was leaving herself open to his rebuke, for who could blame a youngster for not keeping his emotions in check? She was relieved when he did not pull away from her touch but straightened and stepped back from the corpse to stand next to her. Valentyna looked down into the tear-stained face and felt herself rewarded with a vague, watery smile. It was enough.

"We lost him," he whispered, his voice leaden with sorrow.

"Yes," she replied, now finally finding the courage to look fully upon the body of the man she had loved.

Neither Krell nor Liryk stirred and both Fynch and Knave stood like statues while she stepped around Romen, seeing nothing for the moment other than how handsome he was in such stillness. Even through her concentration, however, she was aware that one set of eyes moved with her and regarded her intently.

Knave watched. *What is he thinking?* she wondered, glad of the distraction for her mind while she absorbed this final vision of her love.

"May I?" she asked, tentatively pointing toward his shirt.

Liryk's sad eyes blinked. He nodded gently, knowing what she wished to see.

"He's so pale," she whispered.

"There was a lot of blood lost," Fynch replied, his voice coming as though from far away.

She felt herself lurch again inwardly as a picture of Romen's body spewing forth his lifeblood swam into her mind. Undoing the buttons, she revealed his chest, no longer warm and filled with love for her. Valentyna needed to see the ugly wound where the blade had been expertly driven and Romen's heart had been punctured, all of its love drained out on the floor of a brothel while a whore called Hildyth shrieked as she watched him die.

Or had she killed him? The nagging thought would not leave her.

Knowing looks passed between the two men as the Queen lingered over the corpse, an awkward silence stretching.

"Your highness," Krell uttered after clearing his throat lightly. "Don't torture yourself any further."

"But I must. I sent this man to his death."

"No, highness!" Liryk spoke up. "You gave him his life . . . and a chance to make a new one. Without you, King Celimus would surely have had him killed."

"Perhaps he did," Fynch muttered.

Valentyna tore her gaze from Romen and laid it on Fynch. "Tell us what you think."

She and Liryk held their breath. If the youngster was thinking it, then surely their unspoken yet shared conclusions could not be that far off the mark.

"Celimus wanted Romen dead. Now he is," Fynch said tonelessly.

"We cannot prove such a thing, lad," Liryk replied, voice gruff with rebuke.

"No. That's the point, though," Fynch said, staring at the corpse. As he spoke he suddenly sounded a lot older. "You need not be a scholar to see that this was an expertly achieved death. Celimus could not be seen to have bloodied hands . . ." They were impressed at his casual use of the Morgravian monarch's name.

"You sound familiar with the King, boy," Liryk said.

"I know him. Certainly enough about him to accept that Romen's death could easily be by the King's design. We already know Celimus thinks nothing of hiring mercenaries to kill sovereigns." There was a sharp intake of breath from both men, although Valentyna seemed not to react. Fynch continued as though they were discussing the weather. "What makes you think he would not order the death of a troublesome noble? Someone who knows too much about the comings and goings of Morgravia?" He stopped speaking suddenly, his look accusing, defying them to contradict him.

"I don't think that, lad," Liryk lied, impressed with Fynch's grasp of the situation. "I just can't prove the King of Morgravia is behind it."

"No, and that's why we must be very careful about what we say aloud," Valentyna warned. "Please, all of you. What has been aired here is between the five of us."

Fynch found an inward smile. It amused him that the Queen counted Knave among them, but he could not blame her. He too believed Knave heard and understood everything. The dog sidled up toward him again and he laid his hand on Knave's head, glad of the comfort.

Without warning, a familiar dizzy sensation claimed him as Valentyna opened her mouth to speak again.

"Krell, I know this is unusual but you and I will wash Koreldy's body."

"My queen! I cannot permit—"

"No, you cannot permit me anything." She said it kindly.

"This is my order, although I prefer it be a request. I am doing this so we keep Romen's death among as few people as possible."

He nodded, an unhappy expression on his face.

He is not dead! Wyl lives! a voice spoke to Fynch. The boy's world spun and his head began to throb. He saw only swirling gray mist, but he heard the words clearly. Then the mist cleared briefly and he saw a small town. At its fringe were fields and fields of hops. He had no idea what its significance was.

Find him. He walks in another body now, the voice urged.

The swirling sensation dissipated as fast as it had arrived and the voices of the people in the chapel sounded sharp again. Fynch steadied himself, the pain intense and shock reverberating through his body as he tried to think about what he had heard through Knave. He knew now the dog was the reason he could hear the voice. He just did not know why. Fynch felt distracted and nauseated.

His mind was in turmoil. If Knave's information was correct, then they were needlessly grieving over a man who was not dead. *He walks in another body now.* Had it truly happened again? Had Wyl Thirsk become the person who killed Romen Koreldy? Valentyna deserved to know but what could he say to her? She would not even hear him out. Valentyna was liberal in most ways and he would describe her as tolerant—certainly of his views on magic—but she was not a believer. The Queen would probably banish him as well if he started raging about transference into another body. No. This he would have to keep to himself for the time being.

The Queen was still speaking when the voice left him. ". . . and Liryk, I want that woman—that Hildyth creature—at the palace by sunset tomorrow. Bring her before me. Did many other people at this place know?"

Liryk was grateful for the Queen's tact at this moment. "Several. But none would know Koreldy. He was a stranger. It was not crowded either, so those to whom the gossip has spread would probably not even know his name. Simply that a man was killed."

"Good. Your men will spread the rumor that this man was Briavel's prisoner but that we had granted him a new life across our borders. So far this is true. The seed you will plant, however, is that we have no other option but to suspect a Briavellian loyalist took offense at Koreldy's actions at the tourney and took it upon himself to rid our two realms of a troublemaker. Make sure everyone understands how keen Briavel is to pursue the betrothal—no official word, mind," she cautioned, emphasizing her own quiet despair at such a thought by cutting the air with her hand as she gave her warning. "Tell the story into a few inns where loose mouths lurk. I will provide coin. Allow the story to become warped as it is retold, fret not that it comes out any which way. So long as people believe it was purely an internal problem."

"Why?" Krell asked, unable to follow his queen's rapid line of thought.

Liryk could not help but give a grim smile of appreciation. He nodded a bow. "Inspired, your highness." Then he turned to his companion. "Because, Chancellor Krell, if it's supposedly our own work, the word will die quickly. There is less intrigue to the death of a prisoner than the assassination of a noble—particularly a noble we supported. More importantly, however, in designing this, our queen has deflected any potential damage to Briavel. Whether or not the person we suspect is behind this, he can only be privately grateful to her majesty for being so without guile, accepting blame on Briavel."

"I see," the Chancellor replied, impressed. "Your majesty has inherited her father's quick mind for strategy."

Valentyna gave a brief, harsh laugh. "Oh, I do hope so. We're entering challenging waters, gentlemen, and we shall need all our wits to navigate the safest channel."

Both men nodded their agreement.

"What of the body, your highness?" Krell asked gently.

The Queen sighed, inwardly proud that she had so far held on to her grief in front of these men. They were obeying her now as they would have obeyed her father. "Liryk, for anyone who may inquire, you can say Koreldy's body was buried quickly in an unmarked grave. Make out you left it for others and so it passes down the chain of command until no one really knows who took responsibility. Give the impression that neither do we care."

"Yes, your highness."

"Krell, you and I will prepare the body. Who can we trust?"

"Father Paryn is a good man, my queen. He will help us give Koreldy some dignity."

"Dignity, yes," she said, seeing once again Hildyth enjoying her evening's work with Romen. "He will be buried at a private ceremony. No one is to speak of it with anyone other than Father Paryn. Krell, please make arrangements for a site near my father."

"In the royal plot, majesty?" His tone carried sufficient surprise that she knew he was not happy with such an arrangement.

"Yes," she said firmly, eyeing him. "He deserves as much. He fought to save my father's life. He certainly saved mine. He was also . . ." She paused, forcing herself to stop what was about to be said. She took a breath. "This is what I want."

"As you wish," Krell said, bowing.

"Liryk, what of the men who accompanied you?"

"All reliable, your highness. If you'll excuse me I shall round them up now and make our orders clear."

"Each to be promoted and paid double salary this moon cycle. They are to understand their silence is appreciated at the highest level."

He nodded and bowed before taking his leave.

"Clothes," Krell muttered. "I should organize some fresh garments for him."

Valentyna looked again at Romen's beloved body in his dusty traveling clothes.

"Please. He looks best in dark gray," she said. "It sets off his eyes," the Queen added softly, the sorrow in her voice thick.

Krell looked sharply at his sovereign and then away. The

expression of pain on her face was too raw. He knew she needed privacy.

"At once, your highness. I shall go find Father Paryn now," he murmured before leaving quietly.

Valentyna heard the door of the chapel close. "Lock it, Fynch," she begged. "I need some time," and she broke down, her soft cries heartbreaking as she bowed helplessly over the cold corpse. No longer a queen, having to follow protocol or keep her emotions in check, but a young woman grieving over the death of the man she loved.

"His killer took his bracelet as well," she said through her tears. She felt no shame with Fynch.

"Yes, highness, I noticed. But it was worth nothing. He admitted to me his sister had plaited it for him . . . the beads were hers from childhood."

"A trinket yes, but worth everything to Romen, I imagine, and still more to his killer."

"How so, my queen?"

She shrugged. "I suppose further proof that he is dead. Anyone who knew Romen would have noticed he always wore that tiny bracelet."

Fynch nodded, remained silent.

"He looks so peaceful," she admitted. He saw she had refastened the shirt buttons to hide the brutal wound.

"Asleep even," he ventured.

"Yes. Except Romen was never still, was he? He had a special energy. We shall never again hear his laugh or that way in which he mocked everyone with gentle affection."

Fynch took a chance. "If I suggested this was simply a dead body, not a real person, what would you say?"

She looked at him, disturbed, wiping away the helpless tears. "I would call you cruel. Why would you suggest such a thing when you know how I feel . . . felt about Romen?"

It was pointless pursuing this conversation, but he tried anyway. At least later he would be able to reassure himself that he had. He swallowed. "Although Romen's corpse lies here before us, I don't believe the man you knew . . . the man you loved, your highness . . . is dead."

She looked at him, aghast. "Fynch, whatever are you talking about? Stop, now. This is hurtful."

He sighed, dropped his head. "Apologies, highness."

She wanted to retain his friendship. She could not lose Fynch as well and yet here she was pushing him further away. Valentyna moved swiftly beside him and then crouched so she could look directly into his large, serious eyes.

"No, I am sorry. He is dead because I banished him. This is my cross to bear—not yours. You would never have done this to a friend, but, oh my dear Fynch, I am bound by duties and royal protocol. And I am so scared. I don't want to marry Celimus but it seems I have to. I have never loved anyone like I have loved Romen. I don't think I can bear to live without him because I know that every day I will grieve for losing him, pushing him into danger."

Fynch knew she would not have to. If only she knew it was Wyl she truly loved. "I understand. Really. I think I've got it straight in my mind why you did what you did."

"It's your forgiveness I seek. I don't want to lose you, Fynch. You and your strange dog there are my closest friends in the world. Without Romen I have no one I can trust to care about my feelings. Those who surround me are good people—don't get me wrong—but they are looking to forge a peace with Morgravia and I'm the key to that union. My needs, my desires, my hopes and dreams don't come into it. With Romen's death I feel as though I've lost all control over my own life, mad though that might sound to you."

Her words touched him. "Then you must trust me."

"I do."

"And understand what I must do," he added.

She noted the grave tone. "What must you do?" she asked, frowning.

"I'm leaving, your highness."

The shock of his words stopped her tears. "No! Why?"

"There is something I must pursue."

"Fynch, speak plainly. Tell me," she commanded, searching his open and guileless face for clues.

"You cannot understand."

"Make me."

He smiled. It was shy and rare, full of kindness. "I cannot, your highness. I have tried before."

She took a deep and audible breath, then laid her hands lightly on his shoulders. He could feel them trembling from her pent-up emotions. "Is this about Wyl Thirsk . . . and what was it? Romen taking on his duties . . . his desires—you said you felt his presence."

Fynch nodded. His expression was somber. "More than that but I cannot explain yet."

"Magic." She spoke the word as if it were poison in her mouth and felt his thin shoulders shrug beneath her hands.

"Just trust me," he repeated.

"But where will you go?" There was a plaintiveness in her voice. "Please don't leave me, Fynch."

"To track down Romen Koreldy's murderer," he said.

The Queen rubbed a hand over her face. He could not tell whether it was with frustration, anger, despair, or a combination of all three.

"But you are a child," she said, hating to state the obvious and working hard to keep her voice level.

"All the more reason I shall go unnoticed, your highness. Who would bother with a child?"

"And your purpose?" she blurted out, irritation spilling over, sarcasm evident in her tone.

If Fynch noticed he did not react. He spoke evenly. "I mean to see his killer with my own eyes." He kept as close to the truth as possible, for lies did not come naturally to him.

"And?" She stopped just short of shaking him.

Fynch was silent. She waited, knowing he was considering how best to answer her. He was always very careful with his words, rarely making a casual remark.

"I will decide, then," he answered, annoying her further with the cryptic reply.

Inside, her emotions were tumbling around. Fear and grief threatened to undo her and now Fynch's news left her numb. She did not know what to say that might stop him from leaving. So she stood and turned away, her voice harder now. "It's your decision and you will be missed. Will you remain for the burial?"

"There's no point," he said quietly, and she refused to give that notion any credibility by answering it. "No, your highness, I prefer to leave immediately, unless you wish it differently."

"I do. We must honor him."

"It's not even him anymore, your highness."

"Stop it, I beg you," she beseeched, the pain of his words cutting through her.

Fynch's gaze was unblinking and honest. "Once again I ask for your faith. I will not let you down. Neither will he," he said, nodding toward the corpse.

Valentyna wanted to scream at him, shake his bony shoulders and push some sense into his head. She did neither. "I shall spend some time with him alone, if that's all right. I insist on your presence at the burial."

He bowed but she had already turned away from him.

The burial was as raw as it was swift. The body was surrounded by small candles that would be permitted to burn themselves out. A few spoken words, a simple prayer, and Father Paryn was asking the attendees to lay their gifts in the casket so Koreldy's spirit might move beyond while his body remained surrounded by possessions from those who had cared for him. Liryk laid a blade. He now dearly wished he had given Koreldy one—perhaps he might have saved himself if he had. Krell laid a quill, the symbol of his duties for Briavel. It was all he could think to leave with a man he had not known well but had respected. Fynch cut off a twist of his own hair and one from Knave. He laid them on Koreldy's chest.

Finally, Valentyna pressed a small wreath of mint, basil, and lavender bound with one of her own ribbons and intertwined with a thong he used for his hair beneath Romen's crossed hands. That this wreath was heart-shaped was missed by no one.

May it remind you of where love's first tentative touch

embraced us, she cast silently, hoping his spirit might hear its echo.

Two soldiers, trustworthy men who had accompanied Liryk and Koreldy on their fateful trip into Crowyll, slid the heavy stone slab across the tomb in which Romen had been laid. It was unmarked.

Valentyna lifted her head. "No one is to ever speak of this." She eyed each of the men who stood with her. "Or I shall have his tongue cut out. This is a secret that Briavel holds."

They nodded as one.

"Thank you, gentlemen," she said, relieved that she could trust them.

Fynch was the last person to leave the crypt. As he stepped out into the brightness of day, he was momentarily blinded, but as his eyes adjusted he noticed a soldier making fast passage toward the small, curious group of people standing outside the chapel.

"What news?" Liryk asked, all formalities dispensed with. It was one of his most trusted men.

"Your majesty," the man said breathlessly as he went down on one knee. "Sir," he added, addressing his commander. "May I speak freely?"

"You may. Please report."

"The woman is no longer at Crowyll. She left her lodgings either during the night of the attack or possibly the next day. None of the people who live nearby remember seeing her that morning."

Liryk's face twitched in annoyance. "You checked her place of employment."

The man was sucking in air. He had obviously ridden at high speed. "Yes, sir. Everywhere that we knew she frequented as well. There is no trace."

"The plot thickens, Liryk," was all Valentyna said as she strode away, convinced now that the whore was in on the deed. "Fynch, a word."

Fynch hurried behind her. She stopped near her favorite herb garden.

"And so you leave me now?"

"Yes, your majesty. I must."

"Then I shall miss you until I see you again."

"Likewise, highness."

She pulled a pouch from one of her pockets. "I don't understand this journey of yours, Fynch, but I see I have no choice."

He shook his head sadly, unsure of what to say.

"I know," she said more quietly. "I must trust you."

When he looked up she was making an effort to smile. He knew it did not come easily to her after what they had just done. No doubt she was in some personal pain and his leaving only magnified her loneliness.

He hastened to offer some reassurance. "As soon as I have found out what I need to know, I shall return, your majesty."

"I wish I understood what it is you need to know."

Sensibly he remained silent.

"Here, Fynch. Please take this," she said, holding out the pouch. He took it; it rested heavily in his hand, suggesting gold and silver within. "No, don't fight me on this. You will have need of it."

He nodded.

"This is a dangerous person you go headlong to meet. I wish I could stop you," she said, pulling her hand away.

"You cannot. But you must be strong, my queen," Fynch replied. "Koreldy would expect it of you."

She gave him a sad smile. "Everyone expects it of me, my friend. Shar speed you safely, Fynch."

Valentyna allowed him to kiss her hand, then walked away, too fearful to hug him farewell. It made him recall how she had turned from Romen in the same manner. Now they had both hurt her. He left quietly to find Liryk, Knave padding silently behind.

Fynch refused a horse. He and Knave cut a lonely pair heading out of the castle, across its bridge, and down the long road that branched off toward Crowyll. Liryk, surprised at the boy's queries, had given him all the information he had of the murder, down to an accurate description of the woman.

"Where do you go, son?" Liryk had asked, his curiosity piqued by the boy's questions and distant manner.

"To find Hildyth," Fynch had replied.

3

CELIMUS MUNCHED ON AN ALMOND CAKE BAKED FRESH THAT morning. It mattered not to him that his pastry cook had to leave his bed many hours prior to dawn to craft the specialty. It not only meant a great deal of tedious preparation in skinning and crushing the nuts, but it also required energetic kneading and shaping of the dough into the complex designs, as well as priming the oven to the right temperature. The fiddly cakes were normally reserved for celebrations, but Celimus had a particular liking for them and so on a whim, just before midnight, had ordered that some be served with his breakfast. No one dared put forward an objection. That the fellow responsible, a man no longer young in his years, had had barely more than three bells' sleep that night would not have roamed among Celimus's selfish thoughts. He was king. Whatever he wanted—no matter the toll on someone else—he would have. When the old baker sighed at the page's news, it was as if he sighed on behalf of all Morgravians at how little the son resembled the father, their revered and well-loved King Magnus.

Celimus glanced momentarily at the second cake he held, relishing its chewy texture and delicate flavor, before looking back at the strange gift that had arrived that morning by courier. The King picked it up again; he had not been able to take his eyes from it since its arrival and unwrapping. Ce-

limus twirled its strange shape and odd feel between his own
fingers. It gave him immense satisfaction to hold it at last.
He wished he could preserve it somehow and thus hang on
to the grim pleasure of glancing at it from time to time,
knowing that once again he had triumphed.

He considered Koreldy. He had rather liked the mercenary's sardonic manner and appreciated his carrying out Wyl
Thirsk's murder, but ordering Koreldy's execution had become necessary once Celimus had realized he could not rely
on the man's loyalty.

His strange behavior in the cathedral on the day of
Thirsk's funeral was odd, to say the least, and once Koreldy had fled Stoneheart, Celimus understood he could
not take the risk of trusting the man to keep their dark secret. There was too much at stake—not just the annexing
of Briavel but also his own crown. If the Legion even suspected that he had had anything to do with Thirsk's death,
then his sovereignty was vulnerable in the extreme. The
Legion was too powerful . . . even without Thirsk it could
take over the realm.

No, he thought, flicking crumbs absently from his mouth,
ridding himself of Koreldy was regrettable but wise, especially as the man hailed from Grenadyn . . . who knew what
links he might have with the Mountain King. Secrets from
Morgravia falling into the hands of Cailech in the Razors
would be tempting fate indeed.

"Best without him," he murmured, putting Koreldy's severed ring finger back into the box.

Celimus was looking forward to showing his new prize to
Jessom, glad that he had circumvented the man's normally
thorough inspection of all deliveries into the palace. It was
purely by chance he had been talking with his personal
horse handler when the messenger had arrived. They had
been returning from the stables, the horse handler skipping
slightly to keep up with the King's long stride. Their intense
discussion about a new stallion, a warhorse Celimus was
looking forward to having delivered, had been interrupted
by the man's arrival at full gallop.

"Find out what's so urgent," the King had ordered a passing page.

The startled boy, unused to giving even eye contact to his majesty let alone service, had looked terrified, unsure whether to bow or run the errand. He had attempted both clumsily. When he returned, he stammered to his king that it was a package . . . a delivery for his majesty.

His curiosity piqued, Celimus had strolled toward his guards. "You have a delivery for me?"

"Yes, your highness," the most senior of the men had replied, nodding his head repeatedly in small bows to ensure that all the right cringing that seemed to please the King was observed.

"Well, give it to me. I can't stand around here all day."

"Er, sire. Chancellor Jessom has ordered that all—"

Celimus's anger had always been swift to stoke. He was bored too. A deadly combination for his humor. Impatient as he was for his new horse and impatient for something different to occur in the tedious days of routine that had followed his return from Briavel, his ire had sparked. The package was a small diversion but a diversion nonetheless.

"I don't give a flying fig what the Chancellor has ordered. Give it to me now or, Shar help me, you'll be cleaning the latrines for the rest of your career . . . after I've had your feet cut off!"

The man had visibly swallowed, unprepared for such an assault. He would be in serious trouble with Jessom, but it paled by comparison to his king's wrath. He had motioned the gatekeeper to pass over the seemingly inconsequential parcel, then had bowed low and handed it to Celimus, face burning from the embarrassment of being shamed in front of the other soldiers.

He had tried to salvage some small pride. "Apologies, my king. I am following orders."

"Indeed," Celimus had replied drily, his anger quieted. "It looks like something of no matter anyway. I've been expecting some new jesses for my hawk. It's most likely those," he had lied, wondering if the contents could possibly be what he dreamed of holding in his hands.

"Yes, sire," the man had said. He had bowed once again for good measure and sighed with relief as he watched the King stride away to pick up the conversation with his horse handler as though no interruption had occurred.

Celimus smiled now to himself in memory as he chewed another mouthful of his favorite cake. There was no warmth in the expression, though, only malice.

"Farewell, Koreldy," he whispered, wondering again whether the finger had been cut off before his enemy died. If so, Romen would have known it to be an assassination— and on whose orders. He certainly hoped so.

There was a knock at his chamber door. It would be Jessom. He covered Romen's finger with the linen and put down the lid of the box.

"Come," Celimus called.

Jessom arrived, his hands full of parchments. "Good morning, sire. I need you to sign some papers, if you please." He noticed the King was suppressing mirth and in fact had already heard about the parcel's delivery, but he had not yet connected the two.

"I'm rid of him, Jessom."

"Rid of whom, sire?" the man asked absently, setting down the pile of papers and shuffling them into a neat pile before the King.

"Why, Koreldy, of course. Care to take a look?" Celimus pushed the small box toward him.

Jessom felt a thrill of elation. She had done it! He contrived a brief expression of confusion for the King's benefit.

"Whatever is this, my king?" he said, staring at the proffered parcel but not yet picking it up.

"Open it."

He did as asked, lifting back the linen and pausing theatrically, knowing that not making an immediate exclamation would drive Celimus to distraction.

"Well?" the King said irritably. "Your man triumphed."

Jessom carefully re-covered the lid on the bloodied finger. "As I see."

"Are you not sharing my glee?" Celimus was indignant now.

"Of course, your highness. I am extremely gladdened we achieved your desire. It is always my aim to please, sire."

Celimus ignored the maddening obsequiousness. "Your man?"

"Hmm?" Jessom deliberately busied himself with the papers. He did not want to answer any questions about the woman he knew as Leyen and he knew she would certainly not appreciate him divulging any information about her. "These are quite urgent, my lord."

Celimus pushed them away. Some fluttered to the floor. "Jessom, are you being deliberately vague?"

"No, sire. That is not my intent."

"Then tell me his name."

"My king, we have discussed this previously. I do not wish to involve you in any matters that may incriminate you. By just knowing the name of the killer, you haplessly become part of the intrigue."

"But I am the intrigue, Jessom." The olive gaze narrowed.

Jessom knew he must never play Celimus for a fool. The King was pretentious and often petulant; he had many qualities that might cause a less perceptive person to consider him a dolt. That would be a mistake, however, for Jessom knew Celimus possessed the sharpest of minds, the cruelest of tongues, and absolutely no remorse for the suffering he caused. The King missed very little. He would have to tread carefully now.

"Bring him here to Stoneheart," the King added, reaching for his third cake.

Jessom's throat constricted. This was everything he did not want. "I'm not sure I can do that, sire."

"Why not?" Celimus asked, casually brushing almond crumbs from his shirt. He slumped farther in his chair, lifting one leg to rest on a nearby stool. "Tell me why this is impossible."

Jessom knew not to trust the relaxed stance. "This assassin is not easily contactable, I must admit."

"Then find him. I wish to meet him."

"May I ask why, my king?"

"Because, Jessom, someone who has done my bidding where others have failed rises in my esteem. This man is useful to me. I wish to know him, speak with him, perhaps even discuss further . . . tasks." He chose his words with care. "Have you paid in full?"

"The last installment on proof of death, sire," Jessom answered unhappily.

"And now you have it. Your man will have to collect that payment, and when he does, you will bring him before me. Do you understand?"

"I shall try, sire."

"No, Jessom. You will not try. You will do." The voice was no longer casual. There was clear menace despite the softly spoken tone.

The Chancellor nodded his acceptance. Keen to change the subject, he said lightly, "So you are free of the Thirsk influence, my lord king? That must make you happy."

"Not yet free."

"Oh?" Jessom said, bending to pick up the spilled papers.

"There's still the matter of the sister. Once she is dealt with, I will have rid myself entirely of all connections to the Thirsk family. So this is what I'm proposing. I want you to find out everything you can about the disappearance of the lovely Ylena. Where did Koreldy take her? He pulled the wool over my eyes on that occasion. I really believed he was going to use her and cast her aside. It suited my needs, I suppose, and I allowed myself to be duped. I shall find her, though."

Jessom was not surprised at the King's quick change in temper. Suddenly he was charged with energy, all previous threats pushed aside. Jessom fought the temptation to shake his head at the unpredictable nature of the monarch. It made him a very dangerous individual. "How much do we know of Koreldy's movements?" Jessom said.

"Nothing, in truth. He slipped out of Stoneheart on the evening of Thirsk's funeral feast. No one saw them leave, although I'm told one of my guards spoke to him earlier in the day in a little-used courtyard."

"It had a gate, I presume?"

The King nodded. "The same gate where apparently Thirsk's dog caused a commotion that night."

"Ah, that was the diversion, then. Not that I understand how one gets a dog to cooperate," the Chancellor said, picking up the King's line of thought, pleased to see Celimus nod. "Where did the closest road lead, your highness?"

The sovereign frowned. "That would be toward Farnswyth, I suppose."

"It's a start. I shall make inquiries. Did you make provision for Koreldy to have any staff during his brief stay?"

"A page, I think. I know not which one. Why?"

"It may lead nowhere but you never know what a servant overhears. I will look into it. Thank you, your highness."

"Good. Now, about my lost taxes and revenue. Any progress?"

"I have men infiltrating the entire Legion, sire."

"You remain convinced it is someone from within our own?"

"Yes, sire."

Celimus became quiet for a few moments. Jessom knew something bad was coming, although it had nothing to do with him. Tax collectors from all over the realm were being ambushed far too regularly for it to be merely random bandit raids. It had to be someone from the inside leaking information.

"In that case," the King finally said, "today and for every day that we do not know the culprit, two men from the Legion—I don't care how they are selected—will be wheeled. Take strong, healthy men. Fear will spread like the plague. They'll yield the perpetrator very quickly." He took another cake.

His servant bowed, hoping to be given permission to depart. As he moved toward the door, the King stopped him. "And Jessom?"

"Sire?"

"When you find Ylena Thirsk . . ."

"Yes, your majesty."

"I want her killed."

"Consider it done, my lord."

Jessom left the King's chambers troubled. He had not successfully deflected Celimus from his desire to meet Leyen. It was going to be hard work to persuade her to come to Stoneheart, but he had no choice now but to try. She had to be tracked down.

4

CAILECH STOOD OVER THE PRONE FIGURE THAT WAS SLUMPED amid the filthy straw of the tiny cell that saw neither day or night. Buried in the mountain out of which the fortress had been hewn, it might as well have been a tomb. Gueryn, the prisoner, hoped it would be.

"Is he dying?" the King asked, his jaw working to temper the anger he felt. Cailech rarely wasted words and the man he spoke to knew to offer the same courtesy.

The jailer nodded. "Willing himself to death, my lord. He hasn't taken food in a long time."

The jaw worked harder. "Water?"

The man shook his head. "Doesn't talk, doesn't move much either."

"I should have been told," Cailech said, disgusted. "Summon Rashlyn immediately. Leave us."

The jailer disappeared, well aware that he had not pleased his King. He called for a runner and a message was sent for the strange, dark man nobody cared for but who was barshi to the sovereign.

Inside the cell, Cailech paced as he thought. He had no idea who this man was, other than a soldier in the infamous Legion. Initially his delight in capturing the soldier had been purely because he could make an example of a Morgravian through torture and humiliation . . . salvage some sense of revenge for his people, who had lost a fresh group of their own to the cruel King from the south. The senseless slaughtering of innocent youngsters, not even warriors, offended Cailech deeply. He had planned to make the brash new King pay. Except then he had been distracted by the curious behavior of Romen Koreldy toward this same man. Why Koreldy had returned to the Razors after the intense warning he had received at the time of his previous visit remained a mystery. Romen—whom Cailech could not help but like and to some degree admire—had spun a web of excuses, none of which resonated as truth to the Mountain King, although he could not prove otherwise. Until Romen had fled the Razors, Cailech had not relished the thought of killing a Grenadyne, and the Koreldy family had already lost too many members by his hand. But now his life was forfeit. Koreldy's odd attitude to this Morgravian soldier when they had met on the night of the great feast piqued the King's attention. How and from where did they know each other? Why had Koreldy stepped in for the prisoner and argued to save his life? And why, in turn, had this man given up his own chance at living, squandered his brave escape attempt to lead mountain warriors away from the trail of the other escapees, Koreldy and the woman, Elspyth of Yentro?

And so King Cailech, who could tease at a secret as a dog gnawed at a bone, did not kill the Morgravian soldier as his heart wanted to. Instead, driven by instincts he was still unsure about, he had incarcerated him. Had even had near-fatal wounds healed and cared for to preserve the Morgravian's life, in order that he might prove useful in luring Koreldy back to the Razors and to death.

Cailech had not taken the escape of his prisoners with any grace. If not for the recapture of Gueryn le Gant, he would have had his own men executed for allowing the three

Morgravians to slip past their guard. They had had help of course, through Cailech's own second in command. Lothryn's deceit was a matter that continued to make the King's gut twist, for first and foremost they were the closest of comrades. Brothers, no less. It seemed unthinkable—even now—that Lothryn had chosen betrayal and Cailech was uncertain yet whether this was because of the woman he seemed to have developed sympathies for; or because his wife had died birthing the King's son; or, most likely, Lothryn's disapproval of Cailech's recent treatment of captured Morgravians had burgeoned into a far more damaging issue. Whatever it was, it mattered little. Loyalty had been asked, Lothryn had refused to give it, and now he had paid.

Returning his thoughts to the prisoner below him, the King felt sure that Koreldy was not finished with this one yet. He would return to rescue him and then Cailech would deal with them both. He smiled humorlessly at the thought.

His musings were disturbed by movement from Gueryn. A flicker of the prisoner's eyelids told him that the starving man was aware of the King's presence. However, he also knew the candle that the jailer had lit threw a deceptively warm pallor over the Morgravian. The chill was biting and the constant *drip, drip* of water in one corner of the cell was enough to drive anyone mad. It had created a mossy slime down one rough wall and the earthy smell from that growing mass did little to mask the stink from Gueryn, who had long ago given up caring for himself or his health. In fact, he had deliberately lain amid his own dirt, hoping infection would find his old arrow wound—a gift from Cailech—and kill him. He was clearly determined to die.

All of this enraged the King, but he held on to his famous temper now as he spoke to his prisoner. "Understand, Le Gant, that I will keep you alive. I must, for you will bring Koreldy back and not only will I have his secret but I will also take his life, which is now forfeit. I know you hear me, soldier." The man did move now, properly—enough to let Cailech know that he was paying attention.

"Why the silence, Morgravian? I would have thought you'd welcome some company by now."

"Not with you," the voice croaked, weak but still tinged with anger.

Cailech nodded, pleased to have the recognition. At least the prisoner had not lost his wits.

"We will make you well, Gueryn. And then you will return here to your dungeon."

"And I will repeat the process," Gueryn said defiantly, still not opening his eyes.

"As will I. You might crave death, soldier, but I will not grant it. Get used to the idea and make it better for yourself. Choose to live. Who knows, you might even see Koreldy before you both die at the time of my choosing and manner."

"You're so naive, Cailech," Gueryn chided, weak as he felt. "No wonder Celimus isn't worried about a threat from the north," he lied. "He knows you can be provoked into a hasty decision and your kingdom dismantled at the time of his choosing and manner."

Gueryn knew his words would enrage the man who stood over him and he waited for the kick or punch that would surely come. Instead he heard the King of the Mountains choking back his anger.

"Don't be so sure, soldier. Your king is the ruin of Morgravia and I will be its ultimate destroyer."

Gueryn had no time to respond, hearing footsteps and knowing this would be the healer arriving, the strange man who had brought him back from the brink of death once before.

"Sire," said the new voice.

"I want him made well again—no matter what it takes," the King growled.

Rashlyn nodded. "I shall see to it."

Cailech grunted. "And this time he's to be force-fed and watered daily."

"It will be done, my lord."

Gueryn was moved immediately from the dungeon to a room he recalled from his nightmares.

It was where he had watched Cailech unceremoniously execute the kind, brave woman known as Elspyth. She was a Morgravian, captured with Koreldy. How he had cheered inwardly when she had stood up to the King. And it was she who had patiently cut away the stitches that bound his eyelids together so that he could look upon his rescuers. The one he thought was Wyl—who had spoken to him as if he were Wyl—turned out to be a handsome mercenary from Grenadyn. The man had certainly known Wyl, but the disappointment had cut through Gueryn as keenly as a blade. Elspyth was as pretty as she was feisty, while his early torturer, Lothryn, who had turned friend, was, as he had imagined, a huge, dark man. His beard softened his strong jaw, while his eyes revealed a depth of kindness he could not have guessed lived in this person when he was blind. Gueryn could not imagine what fate had befallen the mountain man who had betrayed his king. No ordinary man, mind. He had been the second in command and so the defection would have been a damaging blow to Cailech. Gueryn was glad. He wished he could deal damaging blows of his own, but he was so pathetically weak that his only way of fighting back was to try to kill himself. That had been a fight in vain. The cruel healer was preparing to bring him back to full strength so they could continue laughing in his face.

Gueryn had never felt closer to tears. He was not a man given to emotional outbursts. Trained by the stoic Fergys Thirsk, he had been taught how to keep his thoughts and emotions in check. He had had many reasons to weep in his life and since adulthood had given in to none of them, but he was tempted now. He felt useless—a senior soldier of the Morgravian Legion and personal attendant to the Thirsk family, not even offering resistance to the enemy.

He spat.

"Save that," Rashlyn called over his shoulder. "No use in wasting precious liquid or I'll do just as my king asks and give you the added humiliation of having men hold you down and force food and water into your throat."

Gueryn sighed. He remembered Elspyth's sad end, how her blood had gushed from Cailech's savage cut and congealed around Gueryn's boots, marking him as her killer, all because he had refused to tell Cailech what he wanted to hear. Blackmail was only one of the King's weapons. Gueryn remembered how Rashlyn had smiled as she died, his eyes sparkling with pleasure. He would not hesitate to hurt Gueryn, if given authority. For now his job was to heal and Gueryn came to the painful realization that the King of the Mountains was right. It was pointless fighting, for they would continue the cycle that would keep him alive—if not fit—until he was of no further use. But perhaps he could still strike some damaging blows. He could not think clearly enough yet, for his mind was dulled by the starvation and thirst, but he promised himself to think on ways to hurt Cailech.

"There's no need to force me," he murmured, his voice cracking from lack of use.

"Oh?" Rashlyn said, turning now.

"I'll eat and drink."

"Good. The other method is rather messy," the strange, wild-looking man said, cackling horribly.

"I make a demand, though, for this cooperation."

"You are in no position to make demands," Rashlyn replied softly.

"Your mad king wants me well and healthy. I will make this easy for you, for all of us, if he'll allow me time outside to breathe fresh air and work my muscles. If he won't permit this, then I will fight you and I promise you that I will find a way to die and anger him. Remember whose head will be on the chopping block, Rashlyn," Gueryn warned.

There was a silence while the man he spoke to digested the import of his words.

"I shall speak to the King. But now you eat," the barshi said, "lightly at first," and he clapped his hands to summon a bearer with food.

"You will remain here until I release you. Consider yourself lucky, Morgravian. You have windows to look out of and a comfortable pallet to sleep on."

"I want to be outside for periods and for that I'll exchange your comforts for the dungeon."

Rashlyn acted as though Gueryn had said nothing. "And you will be chained for the entire time you are in my care. Have no delusions, soldier. There is no escape, not even if you breathe the outside air."

"I did it once before," Gueryn said, more out of defiance than any real threat.

"With help. It will never be offered again."

"Where is Lothryn?" he asked, and hated the sound of the other man's cruel laughter.

"Nowhere where you can help him," Rashlyn answered, delighted that he could hurt with words.

"Is he alive?"

The man barked a laugh. "Hardly," came the cold reply. "Although it was a lot of fun dealing with him."

Despite his lack of strength, Gueryn threw himself toward the small, dark man, and for the first time in his life Gueryn felt real fear, spine-tingling fright that made the hairs on his arm and at the back of his neck stand up.

Rashlyn had held his hand up the moment he heard Gueryn move and the soldier found himself pinned in midair. All of his wits were given over to the realization that something awesome and terrible had just occurred. Rashlyn was a sorcerer and had just wielded magic on him.

"I will make it hurt next time. Never try that again, Morgravian. If you've never believed, then believe it now: Magic exists. You and the rather strange position you hang in are testimony to that. Remember how this feels, Le Gant, for I can immobilize you for eternity like this if I so choose."

Rashlyn removed the spell and Gueryn crashed painfully to the ground. He groaned, final and gut-wrenching despair taking over his mind as he began to grasp the full terror of what he was up against.

5

FYNCH WAS STANDING AT THE BACK ENTRANCE TO THE FOR-
bidden Fruit. Knave had followed his friend's suggestion to remain hidden for the time being, but he had good
vision from his quiet spot and could see the boy kicking at a
stone, biding his time for someone to arrive who might
speak to him.

Several women had hurried past and into the dark opening. It mattered not to Fynch. They did not strike him as
being the sort of friendly target he was looking for. He
trusted his instincts, knew someone would come along who
would be the right one. It had been a couple of hours now.
Winter was mild this year but still cool enough to chill his
thinly covered bones. He must have looked cold, sitting on
the fence stump, when the young woman arrived. She
seemed in no rush and he had no idea if her full-length cloak
covered a revealing gown. With no firm knowledge of how
a brothel actually operated, his mind teased at such minor
detail.

"You'll catch your death out here," she said, eyeing him
from under her hood.

He recognized the Briavellian accent. So she was a
local. "Yes, it's right cold today," he replied in a strong
northern farmer's dialect he had picked up from listening
to some of the other lads at the kitchens of Stoneheart. He
could pitch it perfectly, masking his own less distinctive
southern accent.

"You're far from home, boy. Morgravia?"

Bull's-eye, he thought. "That I am, madam. How sharp
you are."

She smiled. "Are you waiting for someone?"

Fynch nodded. "My sister."

"Oh? And who might that be?"

"Her name is Hildyth. I've traveled many days to see her. Our mam's dead. I've been sent to find her."

Her expression melted, as he had anticipated it would. "You poor mite—she's not here, love. Come on inside. Let's warm you up a bit. I'm Rene."

Fynch followed, making no protestation.

"Thanks to you, Rene," he said as she pulled a chair up to the stove and sat him down.

"There, that should warm those thin bones of yours. Now, how about something to eat? You must be hungry—boys are always hungry."

He was not. Hunger rarely entered Fynch's mind. "I'm starving," he said, forcing a grin, not really enjoying beguiling this kind soul.

"I knew it. I've got a couple of young nephews and their bellies are always grinding." She ruffled his hair and set about gathering some items to tempt him.

Rene said hello to a few women who moved into and about the parlor. They ignored him and he them. Fynch stared into the flames through an opening in the stove, making sure he looked cold, scared even, and not open to conversation with others. As he sat lost in his thoughts, he realized he had already begun thinking of Romen's murderer as now being Wyl. He wondered whose shoes Wyl walked in now. Fynch had no doubt the whore was involved, even though Liryk had looked shocked at the Queen's insinuation. He intended for her to lead him to Wyl.

"There you are, sweetie," Rene said, arriving at his side and dragging his thoughts back to the warm kitchen. "Cheese and homemade chutney is the best I can do. And here's a knuckle of bread. I've left a glass of milk behind you on the table. What's your name, by the way?"

Fynch hated milk. "I'm Fynch. Rene, you're very kind."

"I just feel badly you've come so far for nothing," she said, her expression soft. "My little brother died a few years ago. He would have been a few years older than you, around ten summers now."

Inwardly he sighed. He was nine summers, knew he looked younger. "You must miss him," he said, forcing himself to munch on the food.

"So much. He was a lovely lad. Shouldn't have drowned. It was an accident but still . . ."

"I'm sorry, Rene."

Fynch noted how she forced herself to brighten. "I know. But you remind me of him a little with your coloring. Somehow I don't think he would have trekked so many miles to find me, though. You must love your sister very much to have come so far."

"I had to. We need Hildyth. Father is really sick too and there are five wee ones, the others all younger than me," he said, laying on the accent thickly, suggesting he was becoming upset. He was, in truth, for lying was not Fynch's style.

"Oh now, now. Come on. Hildyth is no longer working here—in fact I know she's left Crowyll—but let me see if I can find out any more for you."

He nodded, pushing more bread into his mouth so he would not have to lie any further to such a decent person.

She disappeared for a few minutes and returned whispering with someone. Another woman, slightly older, regarded him.

"You're Hildyth's brother?"

He nodded slowly, weighing her up, not allowing himself to fib anymore. Her eyes were narrowed.

"She never said anything about a brother."

"Hush," Rene said. "His mother's just died. There's several children. Be gentle."

The other woman shook her head. "Hildyth's gone. She left on the night of that fellow's death here—the one who got stabbed."

Fynch wrinkled his brow in confusion.

Rene rolled her eyes at her companion's heavy tongue. "We had a mishap here not so long ago. A noble. We don't know anything about him, but obviously someone wanted him dead. Hildyth was . . . looking after him at the time. I took her home."

The other woman bent down. "Do you know what your sister does for a living, boy?"

Again he nodded. "She makes men happy," he said seriously, and he watched Rene's face soften once again with affection.

"That's right, love, she did that," Rene said. "Go on, tell him." She grimaced at the woman beside her.

This time her friend sighed. "She came back much later that night. Must have been the early hours of the morning when all the fuss had died down. Everyone was asleep or gone back to their homes. I just happened to be still around and I saw her."

"What did she say?" Fynch said, listening intently now.

"Nothing, really. She looked terrified and who wouldn't be with what she'd just been through. I asked her what had happened." The woman shrugged. "She told me briefly about the man's death, said she was leaving."

"Why did she come back that night, I wonder?" Rene queried.

"She said she'd left something behind in the room, but she didn't want to see all those soldiers again, so she'd waited until the place was quiet."

"What was it?" Fynch hoped for a clue.

Irritatingly she shrugged again. "How would I know? She just stepped inside one of the chambers and was out again almost straightaway."

"Did she tell you where she was going?" Fynch held his breath.

"I didn't know she was going anywhere to even ask. She was acting really strangely, I recall . . . I mean there was something else, apart from being scared. It was as though she was drunk, but I smelled no liquor on her."

"What do you mean?" Rene asked. Fynch was glad she did.

"Well, I can't really say. You know, staggering a little, unsure of her words, couldn't hold my gaze. I figured she was just upset, but she seemed really uncomfortable around me."

Fynch tried to phrase his question differently. "Did Hildyth say anything that might help me find her?" His accent slipped in his determination to learn as much as he could, but neither of the women seemed to notice.

"No. Perhaps she decided to go home, not that I know where that is. She said a name . . . a girl's name. I didn't catch it. Miriam or something. I don't know anything else."

"Does that help you, Fynch?" Rene asked, her face filled with hope.

He hated doing it but he shook his head, adopting a glum expression. "No, but I'll just keep looking," he said, his heart lurching inside at the mention of Myrren. "Thanks rightly for the cheese and bread," he said to Rene, "and to you, miss." He nodded at the other woman.

She shrugged again and left, Fynch already forgotten.

"Can I pack you a little food?"

"No, Rene. I'll be fine."

"Good luck, then."

Fynch surprised himself by giving her a hug. After all his sadness, it was uplifting to have such a positive lead. "I'll come back and see you someday."

She smiled, knowing he would do no such thing.

Fynch found Knave and they quickly moved away from the Forbidden Fruit. Fynch's mind was racing. "I'll explain everything in a moment," he said to the dog, mainly to calm himself. "Let's just get away toward the woodland."

They loped toward the edge of the town. Later, drinking water from the same stream where Wyl had drunk, Fynch gathered his thoughts. He found it helpful to speak them aloud to his silent friend, arrange them neatly before them both so he could store his deductions tidily away.

"Wyl is alive. I'm convinced of it. The vision told me so and I have to believe it's happened again and that he now walks as his executioner, Hildyth. If I'm right, then it was Wyl who lied about the man breaking in and stabbing Romen." Fynch adjusted his seating to lean against the big dog. Knave licked him. "I suppose he discovered himself as this woman"—he shook his head unable to imagine how distressed Wyl must feel—"and disappeared from the scene as fast as he could. We have to find her."

He let his mind flow freely. When he needed to think things through, he had taught himself to let go, to stop teasing at one strand of thought and let his mind loose to roam among his wealth of gathered information. Invariably he found that clues began to show themselves as threads intertwined.

Knave wandered away. Fynch assumed the dog was hungry and would hunt down a careless rabbit. He settled back against a tree and closed his eyes to ponder. Where would Wyl go? he wondered. And then memory of his recent vision slipped into his mind. He went back over the words he had heard and then considered the town and the hops. Why had that picture been given to him? He let the thread go and allowed his thoughts to become random.

Where had Myrren come from?

Fynch sifted through his memories and recollections of overheard conversations between excited city folk about the witch trial. He relaxed, turning his face to allow the watery sunlight to fall upon it through the canopy of leaves. Where? It came to him moments later. Baelup! Could that be it? Baelup was where the realm's best ale was made. He knew this from listening to the soldiers over the years; they loved assignments that took them through the tiny town. The picture of the fields of hops came back to him. Hops were used in ale making. It was a clue.

Wyl must be going to Baelup—back to where Myrren had lived. Perhaps he was trying to track down her family.

The dog returned. He was carrying something in his mouth, but it was no creature. Knave dropped his offering into Fynch's lap. It looked like a ragged thong until Fynch realized it was the bracelet that Romen used to wear.

"It's a sign, Knave. He must have hidden here on the night he became Hildyth. Wyl left this deliberately, I'm sure. Perhaps he hoped you would find it, you clever dog." He scratched Knave's ears and hugged the animal close. "We're going to Baelup," Fynch whispered to his friend. "I

shall need a horse to do that. Valentyna's purse will be put
to good use."

Wyl had collected a tiny stash of coins from a hiding
spot in Crowyll, the whereabouts of which Faryl's
memory released. She had similar hides sensibly stashed
over both realms, he realized, so she could access money
relatively swiftly. What he had was very little—he would
need more . . . much more. He took the time to write down
the locations, just in case Faryl's essence and memories
faded as quickly as Romen's had.

He learned that her mind was tidy and her ways thorough.
He was impressed.

If you must be a woman, be glad it's this one, he reminded himself almost every hour.

Faryl was not just good at her chosen work; he discovered she was the very best. Her kills shocked him. Highly
placed or influential people from many different cities and
even realms across oceans, like Tallinor and Cipres, had
drawn their last breath as a result of her actions. She had felt
nothing for them. Faryl was cold. More than that. She was
bitter. Why? This he could not tease out from where it was
buried deep and locked away through layers of years and, he
gathered, self-torment. He sensed it was connected with her
family, but no more would come through. Wyl left it. It
might surface as had so many vague recollections of
Romen's.

He was riding toward Morgravia, destination Baelup. It
was a start. He knew that Myrren's mother had left that town
almost immediately after her husband and daughter's traumatic deaths. Back then Lymbert had reluctantly given Wyl
details of where they had found Myrren and he had immediately traveled to Baelup to collect Knave as he had promised the girl he would do. He had met the mother only
briefly—they had not even swapped names. He had tried to
explain that he was from Pearlis, a member of the Legion,
but she had hardly paid attention.

"What do you want?" she had asked, no further formalities exchanged. She had been almost out of her wits, packing frantically. He had told her in simple terms that he had promised Myrren he would pick up her pup, and the mother had been glad to hand over Knave without further questions.

There had been no additional conversation other than her bidding him good day and him thanking her, although he was not sure what the thanks were for. Where she had gone he could not guess, but it was the only lead he had to go on. With Faryl's good sense for these sorts of intrigues, he had donned a disguise. It definitely felt more comfortable to be traveling as a man. The fact that he had found some sense of calm after the despair of evenings previous was a comfort right now. Until this moment, it had been all he could ask of himself to refrain from grabbing his blade and opening his wrists.

That bleak thought had been well and truly scrutinized the night before. He had come close too. It had seemed the right answer when every demon came to haunt him as he slept rough beneath the hidden moon. Last night he had felt there was no point in trying to live on. He hated being a woman, despised the very sight of the body that had not so long ago tempted him, stirred him to thoughts of lust.

But thoughts of Valentyna had swirled in his mind and he had not been able to do it. Plus there was Ylena, Gueryn, Lothryn, as well as his noble duty to ensure he did not take his own life. He must fight on and deal with where this all began . . . with Celimus.

And so Wyl found himself on a lonely, dusty road, a man living in a woman's body, disguised as a man, dressed plainly and carrying weapons. No one who glimpsed those would make the mistake of thinking that he was a vulnerable lone traveler. He displayed his sword deliberately so that any thief who might consider tackling him would think twice. His blades were once again close to his chest, lying uncomfortably against the breasts he had bound tightly. He had not been tempted to look at his body in the mirror kept in Faryl's belongings. It would be too much for his mind to bear right now. He preferred the discomfort of the bindings to the swell and disarming weight of the breasts when they moved freely.

He had been tempted to hack off Faryl's hair too but had resisted, reasoning that he might well be grateful for the female disguise Faryl offered. So he had pushed her hair under a wig—one made by a master craftsman, he could tell—and pulled a cap down on his head. A false beard—again of such quality he knew it had been purchased at high cost from craftsmen who probably had asked no questions and accepted only gold—was his greatest comfort, together with the artful hair glued to the back of his hands. In this guise, if he did not dwell on it, he could convince himself he was a man again.

Wyl estimated he was now a day from the Morgravian border and a few days' ride then to Baelup. The trail he was hoping to pick up was almost a decade cold, and although he had no choice but to try, he quietly doubted that he could follow the scent of Myrren's mother. This made him think of Knave. He hoped his dog had sensed his death. He seemed to know when Wyl was in trouble. If he had, then perhaps Knave had already led Fynch to Crowyll and tracked down the bracelet. It should resonate in Fynch's sharp brain and set the lad thinking. Wyl felt confident his young friend would work it out and come looking for him. He would like to have both of them close when and if he finally confronted the Manwitch.

He refused to allow himself to think further about Valentyna. Did she know by now? Of course she would. Would she be grieving? He hoped so, but then again perhaps she would see it as a fitting end to a flawed relationship. He could not forget the grief that Valentyna thought she had masked but was evident to him. It spoke of perfidy, and her public accusation of his treachery was almost more than he could bear. But bear it he did, for he loved her more than he had ever loved anything or anyone, including himself. He would gladly die for her. Wished that he could do that now—leave this wretched existence of his.

The soldier in him reminded him that death was a cow-

ardly option. And where there was life, there was hope. He
might walk in Faryl's body, but he could still use his soldier's brain to wreak havoc on Celimus. He must find the
Manwitch; that was his first priority.

Wyl spurred his horse into a trot, making a promise to
himself that he would waste was no further time in sorrowful musings. He was Faryl for now and might as well get
used to it.

6

NTERING GRIMBLE TOWN, WYL KNEW HE COULD NOT STAND
the tight bindings around his chest much longer. The
temptation to spend the night at one of the two inns got the
better of him. He quickly found a stabling for his horse
where the master of the stables hardly looked twice at him,
and Wyl reminded himself to stop being quite so self-
conscious.

"Which inn do you recommend, Master Paul?" Wyl
asked in a deep voice that Faryl could adopt with ease,
adding some extra coin to the amount required. It was an
old habit, one Gueryn had drummed into him from an
early age.

"Pay well for whoever looks after your horse. His care
might save your life one day," he recalled his mentor saying.

Wyl believed such a creed should extend to all areas of
his life. A few extra coins, especially silver, in someone's
palm often made that person unwittingly yours through the
subtle bond of generosity. Thinking of Gueryn brought a
wave of sadness that he blinked back fiercely as the stable
master replied.

"Well, the Four Feathers be as good an inn as you'll find

in these parts. The ale is watered only lightly and Kidger's wife does an honest stew."

"Thank you," Wyl said. "I'll see you on the morrow."

"That you will, sir," Master Paul said, already bending toward buckets of water to wash the horse down. Wyl smiled. Gueryn had been right. His horse would be fresh for tomorrow's long ride, having been rubbed down properly and well fed.

He strolled into the town proper as late afternoon settled with the stillness that often comes as the sun lowers. At this time of year, once the sun dipped far enough, the temperature plummeted and the evening became crisp. Wyl could feel it chilling as he cast a glance about Grimble Town's main square. It was a neat, sleepy sort of place known mostly for its fields of orchards, which yielded Morgravia's tastiest almonds and prized cherries. Come early summer the town swelled as transient workers flooded in to help with the harvest. It was also handily positioned not far from one of the main routes into Pearlis, so it enjoyed valuable seasonal trade from merchants.

Right now it was quiet, which suited Wyl. He made his way toward the Four Feathers and was relieved that Kidger hardly took notice of the bearded stranger asking for a room. He had given his name as Thom Bentwood. It seemed Faryl had a skill in pitching her voice to a tone low enough to be acceptably manly, so it drew no attention. He understood from her memory that this had taken years of practice and silently thanked her for her commitment. Wyl paid for two nights as a precaution as well as for several meals. He suddenly realized how hungry he was and this revelation was in no little part brought on by the hearty smells wafting from the kitchen.

"That smells good. What's on tonight?" he asked.

"The missus has got some lamb stew simmering or there's chickens on the spit."

Both sounded delicious. "I'll have stew."

"Thank you, sir," Kidger replied. "The girls will be serving from dusk."

Wyl nodded and gratefully made his way to his room, sinking onto the bed with such pleasure it might have been down-filled and covered with fine linen rather than the worn sheets and horsehair mattress. Nevertheless the bed and room were clean, with a pleasant draft of air from the open window. He had meant to undress straightaway. Instead he dozed off immediately, the bindings forgotten as sleep claimed him.

A loud clatter of pans beneath his window woke him abruptly less than an hour later and the pain across his chest reminded him the bindings were still in place. He ordered a bath to be brought up and filled.

"The bathhouse in town is very reasonable, sir," said the sullen girl who took his request.

Wyl realized she did not fancy hauling up a tub or the water. He grinned through the beard, hoping it looked friendly. "I know but I don't feel like leaving my room. Here"—and he handed her two crowns, an exorbitant sum in her small world.

"Oh, sir! I—"

"Please. And bring my water quickly."

She grinned, tucking the money beneath her blouse. "At once, sir."

Impressive, Wyl thought. If he ever allowed himself to be seen as Faryl, he must remember that trick and practice it! True to the girl's word, hot water was soon steaming in the tub and she sent up soap as well as scented oil. He thanked the two lads who had dragged up the pails and the tub. Obviously the girl had coin enough now to pay for lackeys.

When the door closed and he was finally alone, Wyl stripped down. He struggled to untie the lengths of torn sheeting that held his breasts flat, and when they eventually loosened he sighed with relief at the wondrous sensation of being free again. He refused to look down at himself. Instead, he poured in a few drops of the musky oil to soften the water and then, after checking the latch was firmly on the door once again, he climbed into the tub, immersing his body as deeply as he could, looking away from the smoothly muscled yet clearly feminine legs that bent at well-shaped knees. He had thought to have a flask of wine sent up as well and he sampled it now, glad he had paid that little bit extra to Kidger, for the first swallow told him that it was of an acceptable quality.

He closed his eyes, blanked his mind, and focused on nothing but the soothing sensation of the water warming his tired, unfamiliar body. As the steam rose, he pulled the beard and eyebrows away from his face, the glue dissolving as Faryl's memory told him it would. Wyl placed them on a nearby chair next to the wig; these were valuable possessions now. Untying his hair, he let it fall loose, marveling at its heaviness as it dropped, its ends curling into the water. Wyl ran his hands through it to push it off his face. Gone was his coarse red hair. Gone was Romen's smoothly combed plait. In its place he found lustrous locks of a curious, darkly golden hue; he touched it, unable to resist, and was rewarded by the feel of its soft texture. He remembered the feel of Faryl's hair against his body when she had bent over him.

His eyes remained fixedly on the blank wall, below which stood a small dresser. He knew on the other side of the chamber was a table with a mirror that he had ignored and intended to continue ignoring. He still had no desire to see himself as a woman. Feeling his hair was, he was sure, as close as he would get to knowing this strange new body. Again he closed his eyes; his thoughts roamed to Myrren's mother. She had betrayed her husband. Had Myrren's father known he was raising another man's child? And had it mattered to him? Wyl remembered how it had hurt Lothryn to relinquish his newborn son to Cailech, even knowing that the boy had been sired by the King.

Remembering Lothryn's pain inevitably led him to think of the warrior's fate. *What became of you, my brave friend?* he thought. He had given Elspyth a promise, one he knew he could not break. He had given his oath that he would go back one day to find out Lothryn's fate. At the back of his mind was the thought that he must find Gueryn's body too and bring it home to Argorn.

Argorn! His eyes watered as he remembered his proud father. No, he could not kill himself. The Thirsks were a proud line and he was its last son. He must fight on and deal with the man with whom this all began . . . with Celimus.

He wondered where Elspyth was and how she would get on with Ylena and his spirits plummeted further as he thought of these two women traveling alone; frightened, despairing at the loss of loved ones, their happy lives shattered because of him. He could not even protect them; instead he needed them to be courageous and fend for themsleves until he could get to them. He sent a silent plea to Shar to unite and watch over them.

The act of prayer put him in a somber mood. He finished his soak swiftly, deliberately ignoring the chance to soap himself. He could not bring himself, just now, to touch the body he resided in. Wyl stood to reach the towel. The tub rocked on its uneven base, and in that moment of alarm, Wyl caught sight of his naked body in the mirror.

The shock was complete.

He fought back the surge as his gorge rose and opened his eyes. Reflected was the image of a striking woman. As he remembered, she was not intensely pretty like Ylena or classically beautiful like Valentyna. Faryl possessed something else that was hard to describe. It blossomed from confidence; he noticed the arrogant twitch of a smile at the neat, clearly defined lips. The eyes were feline and sensual in an oval face that was tanned lightly from the sun. Her hair, he mused, was probably her vanity. If not, she would have cut it short, for it was an encumbrance for her trade. The body itself was a marvel to his eyes. Curvy but strong. She ran to keep herself fit apparently; digging into her rapidly fading thoughts, he discovered that Faryl favored hills for her exercise because they tested her stamina but also gave her cover. He nodded. She would make the very best kind of soldier with her rigorous fitness routines and high level of fighting skills. She favored the blade but was handy with a sword and skilled with a bow.

He felt foolish but he smiled back at himself in the mir-

ror, rewarded by Faryl's normally intense or otherwise with-
ering look relaxing into a softness he had not glimpsed previously. He stared at the smile on the face that looked back
at him. It touched the feline eyes, sparking a mellowness
that changed Faryl's look. It was girlish and mischievous.
Wyl wished he could have glimpsed that smile when she
was alive. Any man could fall head over heels in love with
it. She had not smiled often, though. He tried to find the
source of her grim outlook on life, but it was still hidden
from him. He must be patient. It would yield itself to him.

Many minutes had passed. He was almost dry. And as he
stood there, feeling like a Peeping Tom stealing a look at a
naked woman, he found the disturbing memory. Faryl could
shoot an arrow with more accuracy than any of her five
brothers, but none of them ever knew it.

He shook himself clear of her memories and noticed that
her legs were long too, lean and muscled. It pleased Wyl to
remain tall; he had gotten used to towering above people as
Romen. Flat and trim though it was, his belly felt empty and
it reminded him now with a loud grind. Toweling himself
unnecessarily, he felt the somber mood dissipate slightly and
he was grateful for this, for it clouded his thinking. He was
glad his curiosity had won through. Looking at Faryl, learning about her, had put something away and turned the key on
it. He was her now. He had no choice but to use her body to
all of its best advantages to find Myrren's true father and
learn the secret of this gift of hers.

Reluctantly he lifted the strips of linen that would help to
make him look like a man again. Wyl sighed, knowing it was
only for an hour or two, and then wasted no further time
binding his breasts flat again and climbing into fresh
clothes. He swished his previous ones in the still-warm bath,
rubbing at them with soap and realizing that this simple act
brought all three of his personalities together: Faryl's dili-
gence, Romen's need to be neat and tidy, and Wyl's training
to take advantage of every opportunity. He squeezed the
clothes out and hung them to dry. Dark had fallen. He should
hurry. Checking his room for any giveaway signs of Faryl,

he was convinced all had been well hidden. He reglued the beard to his face and donned the wig, very carefully pinning his hair this time because he did not have the luxury of the hat to hold things in place. He would need to be careful tonight, even though he was not planning to do anything more than eat his meal quickly and return to his room. Tucking away the glue, he satisfied himself in the mirror that he was now Thom Bentwood again. Faryl's instincts suggested that a merchant in this town at this time of year was odd, but Wyl decided he was only passing through so quickly that it was most likely no one would notice or care.

He headed downstairs into the common dining room, marveling at how easily Faryl slipped into a masculine stride. His mind turned hungrily toward the lamb stew. With a practiced gaze he swept the chamber without being obvious, taking in that the common room was busy, particularly with a group of men, some of them Legionnaires.

Wyl's heart skipped but again he settled his nerves. None of these soldiers could possibly know him. He did recognize one, a man older than himself whom he had never had much time for when he had been general. Wyl remembered the fellow to be lazy, the sort who looked for short cuts and was always onto some form of shirking or another. He was loud of personality, though, and tended to impress the younger soldiers with his wit and confidence.

Wyl took a swallow of ale, deliberately looking away and around the room as he tried to remember the fellow's name. It came to him—the man was called Rostyr. He had always been good with the ladies, Wyl recalled as he watched the man give one of the serving girls a brash, knowing smile. Wyl busied his eyes elsewhere and fiddled with his beard as he waited, trying not to think of his breasts, which had sounded a fresh ache, threatening to ruin his appetite.

"Lamb stew, wasn't it, Master Bentwood?" a plump young girl asked, startling him, as she set down a huge clay plate. He nodded distractedly and she smiled. "I'll be right back with some bread. Can I bring some more ale, sir?"

"Please," he replied, relieved that his hunger remained intact as he eyed the deliciously rich and sticky stew. Vegetables and even some dumplings floated amid the dark gravy.

"Perfect," he said quietly, and began eating. He became lost in his pleasurable chewing and the food gave him something to focus upon . . . So focused was he, in fact, that the meal was gone very quickly. It had been a large portion and he realized he must have been extremely hungry to wolf it down so fast. He pushed his plate aside, hardly noticed when it was cleared or the new ale deposited before him. He felt sated and peaceful at last. Leaning against the wall, he surreptitiously watched the rest of the room. His attention was drawn back to the soldiers. There were only three of them, yet they sat among five civilians clearly known to them. The civilians looked dusty and road weary. They were travelers. He wondered at the easy connection between the two groups and their increasingly loud behavior. Wyl noticed there was not just ale but also wine flowing freely. Money must be plentiful. All had eaten here, and if the night wore on much longer, he believed they might even be staying here. Legionnaires did not normally stay at Grimble Town, and if they did then they would be part of a small company passing through, certainly more of them than this trio.

He puzzled at it and could come up with no answer other than a vague suspicion that the soldiers were not meant to be here and so were here in secret. Furthermore, there was no officer present, which was further damning. Three foot soldiers in a tiny town? He let it go. Right now he was Thom Bentwood and he had a mission. What these members of the Legion were up to was not his business any longer.

Wyl finished his ale. As he drained his mug he noticed one of the men in civilian clothing watching him. The man was big. Built like a bear. The man averted his eyes immediately, rejoining the merriment around the table, but he somehow did not seem to belong. Not that it mattered to Wyl. It was time to go. He stood and felt momentarily lightheaded. Too much ale on top of the wine earlier. He noticed that he had managed to down two jugs of the liquid.

I need some air, he told himself, and against his original

plan decided to step outside the inn for just a few minutes
before retiring. He waved his thanks to the girls, left some
coin at the table, and made his way to the main door. He did
not even glance toward the group that had previously held
his interest.

As he stepped outside, the freshness of the night hit him
and he felt sobered and brightened straightaway. He allowed
himself the luxury of a short stroll up the street, planning to
head back upstairs just as soon as he could settle his large
meal. Turning to walk back down the darkened street—he
was barely fifty paces from the door of the Four Feathers—
he noticed a figure. He recognized the man's hat. It was one
of the men from the group. Wyl wanted to believe the fellow
was doing the same thing as he—merely taking some fresh
air—but all his soldier's senses were on instant alert,
blended with Romen's and Faryl's ever-suspicious and
world-wary ways.

Wyl walked back briskly toward the inn. He was not
daunted by the presence of a single man and farther down
the street a few locals mingled, going about their business . . . closing up for the night, walking home, perhaps
even headed for the Four Feathers.

As he drew close, confident now that he would pass without incident, the man began to whistle tunelessly, softly. It
was too obvious, and as Wyl's body clenched in anticipation, his fears were confirmed as several more shadowy figures melted out of an alley and Wyl found himself
manhandled and bundled back into the same unlit area. They
dragged him around the corner, behind the sheds of the inn.
There would be no help here, so he allowed his body to go
limp rather than fight it—he counted five of them, one of
them Rostyr, who obliged Wyl with one of those bright, fake
smiles Wyl had hated so much. "What were you doing
watching us?"

One of the men had brought a candle. He held it close to
Wyl's face now. Wyl shook his head, faking a look of confusion. "I don't know what you mean. Get these men off

me," he said, using what he hoped sounded like the haughty tone of an offended merchant.

"Oh, yes you do, friend. You seemed far too interested in us back at the inn."

"Good fellow," Wyl spluttered, realizing he should have allowed Faryl's instincts to rule. She would not have allowed herself to be noticed. "My name is Thom Bentwood, I am a merchant, and I have never seen you or your companions before. You're a soldier, anyway. What in Shar's name could I want with you?"

"My question entirely," Rostyr said with unnerving calm. "Perhaps we should help his memory along," he added, and Wyl felt the first blow land and his breath whooshed out of himself, leaving him struggling to fill his lungs.

He coughed. The next blow, delivered with precision, doubled him over. These men, it seemed, were in no hurry. The third blow put him on his knees.

"Pick him up," Rostyr ordered.

Wyl was hauled back to his feet, where he hung between the two men who held him, sucking in air, his face battered, all of him hurting. He realized his beard had gone askew. His tormentor noticed as well; at first he looked baffled and then he began to laugh.

"It's a lad," he said, reaching low beneath Wyl's jacket. "Let's hear you squeal the truth now, boy," he added, gripping between Wyl's legs.

It would only be much later that Wyl would enjoy the memory of the look of shock on Rostyr's face. Expecting to squeeze the truth from the impostor, Rostyr found that his large hand gripped nothing.

"What the—" He jumped back. "Pull his breeches down!"

"Are you mad?" someone asked, then laughed. "Do it yourself!"

Rostyr, angry now as well as confused, reached for Wyl's waistband. "Bring the candle here."

Wyl closed his eyes. He had not thought he could despise Myrren or her gift any more deeply, but right now he was plumbing new depths of hate. His trousers were torn down to reveal the truth of what he had become.

"It's a woman," a dismayed voice said.

Rostyr's expression coalesced into something new and horrible in the glow of the candlelight.

"This bitch will give us the truth, all right. Hold her down."

Wyl watched with horror as Rostyr snarled menacingly while he freed himself from his clothes. Some internal defense forced Wyl to close his eyes. He felt the abomination of probing fingers, then something else pushing, and from deep within he began to scream. It was Faryl's true voice this time, primal and angry. A filthy hand clamped itself over his mouth. He tried to bite it and succeeded for a moment. Wyl filled Faryl's lungs to scream again, but someone hit him on the head and his world filled with sparks of light and he was plunged into her memories.

Scenes emerged from buried hurts of youthful years. Faryl's eldest brothers—twins—raped her regularly. Her father too. The younger boys knew of it but were too intimidated by their burly elders to do anything about it except come to her later when the vile couplings were done and help her to the brook nearby to wash herself clean of them. Her youngest brother, just twelve, would cry as he dabbed at her bruises and she would weep for him having to share this atrocity.

He learned that Faryl's mother also knew of the rapes but was helpless to prevent them, for she had been long cowed and battered by her brutish husband. And so the rapes continued until Faryl killed her father. She used a blade that she stuck into his stretched throat as he took his pleasure. She had relished the sight of his blood gushing over her before she pushed his corpse from between her legs. She walked to the brook, as she had done on so many previous occasions, but this time she was not weeping and she was not scared. Her twin brothers had come then, trembling in fury and fright. She had defiantly raised her catlike eyes toward the handsome, perverted pair.

"Watch your backs, boys," she had threatened. "One day I'll be coming for you."

It was her calmness and the demonic look in her eyes that stilled their tongues and rattled their minds. Neither moved, too shocked at sighting the bloodied corpse in the empty stable.

"I'm leaving now," she had said, climbing out of the water and, not even bothering to dry herself, pulled on some clothes. "You're evil, both of you. I hope Shar finds a way to take you soon," and then she spat on the ground between them.

Picking up her cleaned blade, Faryl of Coombe, just fourteen, had walked away from her life of despair, vowing never to desire a man. She had enjoyed the sensation of killing her father and in her bitterness looked forward to doing the same to other men. The smell of his blood still in her nostrils, the girl on the verge of womanhood framed her future life.

Wyl returned from the blur of Faryl's memories to an altogether different scene than what he had been expecting. Rostyr's body was arched but it was not from the anticipated release. Rather, it was because a knife had just penetrated his lung. He spasmed and then coughed, spattering Wyl's face with dark blood. His body was hauled up by a huge shadow and flung like a rag doll. Wyl looked around. The others were dead, one still dying. The candle had been extinguished. Wyl was certain he was about to be run through with the knife too.

It wouldn't be the first time, he thought darkly. The figure stepped over him and finished off the person groaning. Someone nearby was breathing short and shallow. Wyl realized it was, in fact, him.

A face appeared close to his own. "Come," the voice said, and he was lifted as if he weighed nothing.

"Who are you?" Wyl slurred.

"Aremys."

The dizzying mist returned and this time it enveloped him. Wyl blacked out.

When he woke he was in a bed. He opened his eyes slowly. The man sat in a corner watching. Wyl remembered now. It was the bear from the dining room. He realized he was naked beneath the sheets—a fact he found deeply disturbing. He dimly recalled the man's name.

"Aremys?" he said, careful to use Faryl's real voice this time. It was obvious the man knew he was a woman.

"I'm here."

"Why?"

"I don't like women being attacked."

Wyl could not have agreed more. "You were one of them, I thought. The Bear."

The man smirked as though such a title had been leveled at him often. "Not really one of them."

Wyl remembered how the huge man had seemed distant from the others. He nodded, let it pass. "All dead?"

"Yes."

"The bodies?"

"Taken care of," the bear reassured.

"Taken care of?" Wyl could not keep the incredulity from his voice. "Five corpses!"

"Seven actually."

Wyl took a sharp breath. The man had been with seven companions. He had killed them all.

"Why?"

"That seems to be a favorite question of yours," Aremys replied, a suggestion of a smile behind his words.

"It's a good question under the circumstances!" Wyl countered, a suggestion of anger behind his. He moved stiffly to sit up.

"May I have some water?"

Aremys moved smoothly for a big man. He took his time lighting a second lamp before pouring a mug of water, which Wyl gratefully swallowed before falling back on the pillows. Faryl ached everywhere.

"Tell me what happened . . . please."

Aremys gave a reluctant nod. "It's a long story."

"I'm not going anywhere."

The man's mouth twitched as if to smile, but he sighed instead. "Let me pour myself a glass of wine."

"Where are we?"

"My room. The other inn."

"I see. Whose side are you on?"

It was a loaded question. "Yours, it seems." He leaned over to pour himself a cup of the wine from a nearby carafe.

"Who undressed me?"

"I averted my eyes," Aremys said, and then a smile did ghost across his face.

Wyl could not remember a moment in his life when he had felt more embarrassed.

"You took my clothes off!" It came out with a girlish shriek attached, which he hated even more.

"You've got lovely tits," Aremys added, fueling Wyl's discomfort, making his cheeks burn.

The big man laughed. "Couldn't help myself."

It felt somehow good to share a joke, despite the awkwardness. Wyl smiled. "I'm glad you appreciate them."

The mood became serious again as Aremys attempted to apologize. "I'm sorry I didn't arrive in time to stop them . . . well, you know . . ."

Wyl closed his eyes at the distressing memory of the violation and the revelation of Faryl's early life. "I know," he said, softly now, wanting to put it behind him, wondering how women who were attacked in this way ever could. Faryl had never succeeded. She had hated men for the rest of her life. "Is that why you killed them?"

The man sipped from his cup. He looked over its rim at Wyl. "No. But your plight made it easier for me to do it."

It fell into place. "You're a mercenary?"

Aremys nodded. "Is it that obvious?"

"Let's just say I've known a few." There was a wryness in his tone, which his companion heard but did not pursue. "In whose service?" Wyl added.

"The realm's."

"Celimus?" It came out choked.

"I suppose. His monkey, Jessom, hired me. I gather royal revenue has been going missing with alarming regularity. Jessom suspects it's someone from within the Legion."

"A Legionnaire working against Celimus," Wyl murmured. "How fitting."

Aremys shrugged. "I don't care. I'm not Morgravian, but anyone who can steal back taxes has my vote. Except your king has no sense of humor," he said drily. "Jessom paid me a fortune to track down the culprits. It turned out to be three of them and I managed to infiltrate their group. It took me many weeks to find them and then most of this winter to win their trust. Their leader was a man named Rostyr. Cluey fellow too. He used bandits to do the deed, but he was the brains behind the jobs."

"I see," Wyl said, trying to straighten himself on his pillows again. "A lot of money stolen?"

"Enough to fire the King's wrath."

"Did they hurt anyone?"

"Yes. On a couple of occasions. It wasn't intentional but it happened."

"Soldiers?"

"Yes. You seem very interested in them."

"Can you blame me?" Wyl bristled. "It hurts, Aremys. I'm not sure many men realize quite how much!"

"Apologies. That was blunt of me."

Wyl accepted it graciously, although the part of him that was Faryl was angry. "And so why was tonight the night you killed them?"

"They were planning something daring. It would have meant more deaths for innocents and someone of note included. I could not allow that to happen—it was the right time to deal with them as I was instructed."

"Poison?" Faryl's senses told Wyl this would be the best mode.

Aremys nodded. "Good guess. That was my plan, until you entered the dining room and ruined things. I had to use a more messy method."

"I'm sorry to have spoiled things. What have you done with them?"

"Tomorrow they'll be carted back to Pearlis as proof. I've already sent a messenger to inform Jessom of my findings."

"Not to mention requesting final payment."

Wyl's barb had no effect on the man, who simply shrugged burly shoulders and made a deprecating sound. "And so now it's your turn." Aremys set down his mug. "I'm all ears."

"For what?"

"To hear the intriguing tale of Thom Bentwood, a woman in disguise with an unhealthy interest in the seedier sort and a sometime merchant passing through a town whose season for merchants is long gone."

Wyl mentally kicked himself. Faryl's instincts had niggled at him along these lines and he had ignored them. Aremys had him nailed good and proper.

He tried for the obvious. "It's not easy being a woman traveling alone," he replied. "The disguise helps."

"I accept that. But why do you travel alone?"

"Do I need a reason?"

Aremys fixed a dark gaze on the bruised woman before him. Secrets. That was all right. He had them too. "No, I suppose not. But will you tell me anyway?"

That was unexpected. Wyl felt flustered.

Aremys could see it. "Perhaps tomorrow. Right now I suspect sleep is what you need." He could sense the woman's relief. "Will you allow me to tend the injuries to your face?"

Wyl nodded. "Are they bad"

"I shan't be giving you a mirror tonight."

"Oh, that alarming," Wyl said, disappointment strong in his voice.

Aremys was rifling through an old leather sack. He pulled out a small, flat glass box. "It would be if I didn't have my miracle salve with me." He moved to the bed. "I'll have a bathtub brought up tomorrow," he said absently, digging a finger into the cloudy ointment. He daubed it onto Wyl's face. It soon began to tingle as he gently rubbed it into the injured spots. "The bruises will surface and disappear quickly," he reassured. "Now rest."

"Where are you going?"

"Not far. I'll be here on the floor beside you. I'll leave a fresh candle burning."

Wyl was touched. He could more than take care of himself under normal circumstances, but it felt rather comforting to have someone looking out for him. It reminded him of being a youngster again, when Gueryn had made all his decisions for him. He missed being looked after. He missed Gueryn. On that sad thought he closed his eyes and turned on his side. Sleep would come fast tonight.

He listened to the sounds of Aremys trying to make himself comfortable on the hard floorboards. Wyl was grateful to him for not pursuing the story of Thom Bentwood further tonight.

"My name is Faryl," Wyl said quietly into the darkness, surprising himself by giving the truth . . . and by finally acknowledging it to himself.

7

HE DAYS AT RITTYLWORTH HAD PASSED SLOWLY, FOLLOWING their own particular rhythm as the men of Shar kept to their routine of worship and work. For some of them their duties were in the library, poring over texts and carefully scribing passages; others spent hours in the beautiful studio where they patiently copied some of the ancient illuminations. Many toiled in the vegetable gardens or orchards, tending to the flocks of sheep and goats that kept them fed. Others looked after the few cows that sustained the gentle community with their fresh milk for drinking and that also produced the butter, rich cream, and famed cheese of the region.

Rittylworth Bruise won its name for the dark wax that the

monastery's cheesemakers dipped their proud product into for maturing and preserving. The shiny, violet rounds of hard cheese were stored in a special pantry beneath the chapel, but even this great room was not as deep into the ground as the secret grotto, which few outside of the monastic order knew about.

It was Ylena's favorite place of all. Jakub, all too aware of this visitor's grief, had suggested within the first day of meeting that she make it her own for a while. As much as she enjoyed her bedroom, with its view over the orchards, it was to the grotto that she escaped for her solitude and there, within the fizzing waters of the warm spring, she had begun her gradual healing.

In the beginning it was all physical recovery for Ylena, while the delicious monotony of daily life around the monastery was a great nourishment to her mental strength. It had not been easy and many times the grief threatened to carry her away with it, but on those occasions Ylena would remind herself of her surname and dig deeper toward the strength she knew she possessed. She could think of Alyd and his execution now without being overwhelmed by tears, and her shock at losing all of those she loved had dulled to bitter acceptance. It had left her numb, but she was learning how to put that aside too.

Wyl had once quietly spoken of how he had taught himself to deal with the death of their mother and more lately their father. She used that teaching now and had taken all of those painful emotions of hers inward, burying them in a safe, dark place where they could no longer disable her. It was Celimus, of course, who had contrived all of this death and suffering and on whose hateful name she should build her own hate.

The real catalyst that prompted her determination to be fully in charge of herself again was learning that Romen had not taken Alyd's remains away with him. At first she had been filled with wrath and it was that anger that had, in truth, brought her back to full sensibility. Jakub had counseled that Romen no doubt had good reasons for his decision and had asked that Alyd's head be preserved as proof of the abomination at Stoneheart. This had placated Ylena, who accepted that whatever those reasons were, Romen had her interests at heart.

Since that discovery, she had allowed the days to blend until her body and mind healed. One of her great friends through this process was Pil, who, Shar bless him, seemed just a little in love with her. He took his role as her caretaker very earnestly and she had to keep reminding him that she was not an invalid and preferred to do things for herself. He would smile shyly and apologize but then go right back to fussing around her. In truth, he was a very big reason for her recovery. His almost childlike desire to make her smile and see her well again was infectious.

Pil was one of a big family who hailed from the northwest. His father was a fisherman, as were his brothers, while his sisters and mother prepared and sold the catch. Everyone in their village was involved in the sea and its bounty, but Pil was the only member of his family who felt no calling for it. In fact, he would be the first to admit that he suffered the ocean sickness and hated anything to do with boats and fish. Saying such things was sacrilege in his village, so he suffered in silence, but despite trying so hard did a terrible job of mending nets. His father finally gave up on him and on one particular evening of high frustration asked a traveling monk whether he would take his youngest, good-for-nothing son with him and teach him the ways of Shar. "Perhaps he'll be some use to us then and can pray for our safety and prosperity," Pil had haltingly repeated to Ylena one day. The monk had agreed, and after traveling with the man for several months, Pil had discovered that he was good at his letters, but was also interested in doing Shar's work. The kindly guardian had contacted his old friend Jakub at Rittylworth, and by year's end, young Pil had found himself a new home and a new family, who welcomed him with love and patience. He had fit in easily and being the youngest had been spoiled with care and affection from the Brothers. Ylena could see that the love they had given him had manifested itself in Pil's ebullience and his desire to do his god's work with enthusiasm. She thanked her lucky stars that Pil had been so dreadful at fishing and had told him this not long ago, amusedly watching him blush and stammer.

And then there was Brother Jakub: calm, elderly, patient Jakub, with his searching eyes that seemed to see into the depths of her heart.

It was obvious he knew something of what had happened to her, and by whose hand, but he had never asked anything directly of her dark experiences. Perhaps Romen had given him information, but she suspected not. Her time with Romen told her that Koreldy was an intensely private man with secrets of his own, and one used to keeping them, be they his or someone else's. There were moments on their journey from Pearlis when Romen reminded her of Wyl. Just now and then there were phrases he used or a way he might hold his head or comfort her when she could almost believe Wyl was still near her. Romen had explained that he had given his word to her brother, before he died, to save her from the dungeon. But she suspected he had not shared any of their dark background with anyone else. There was no need for the kind Brother Jakub and his fellow holy men to suffer her torments. That they offered sanctuary was more than enough.

Today felt no different from the others that had gone before. Despite the bright day, winter's bite was still nipping at everyone's heels, although the buds on the fruit trees and the promise of blossom suggested that spring was not far away. Ylena pulled her soft shawl more tightly around her. The mornings were still bitterly cold this far north and even the steaming creamed oats and oozing chunk of honeycomb she had swallowed gratefully earlier had not warmed her sufficiently. She shivered, relishing the thought of her daily soak in the soothing waters in the grotto.

Crossing the main courtyard, she smiled at two Brothers who dipped their heads toward her but did not break the morning silence, held until third bell, due any moment. She wondered where Pil was. He was normally skipping around her by this time, making her laugh with his tall stories.

Truly, it felt as though she had lived here among the Brothers for an age when in fact it was barely weeks.

Her boots clicked on the flagstones of the great arched cloisters. She turned her head, knowing Brother Tomas would be in the tiny courtyard to her left, where he lovingly tended the citrus bushes. The peel of the Akin fruit had healing properties, he had explained to her, and it was curiously at its most powerful in the morning. And so each day he was here at the same time, touching the fruit, testing it for readiness. She waved and he nodded back to her, holding up one of the bluish-green spheres, grinning. It was a good one obviously. Tomas had mentioned that he was fortunate if he could coax one fruit per week from the trees in season. They were one of nature's more stubborn follies and one needed extraordinary patience to tend and harvest them. It was easy to be patient at the monastery, she thought, considering the sleepy, tranquil nature of the hamlet surrounding it.

Skipping down the few stairs from the cloisters and into a larger courtyard, Ylena realized she felt the brightest she had in a long time. "Happy" was not the word she would choose, but she felt she was almost ready to consider a life beyond Rittylworth and getting herself to Alyd's people. The powerful Duke of Felrawthy would know what to do and after learning the fate of his son would surely help her to bring down Celimus . . . she was sure of it. If she could raise her own men from Argorn on the strength of the Thirsk name, then perhaps that would be all it would take. Ylena was convinced the Legion would not take up arms against them when it learned the truth behind the deaths of its general and its popular captain.

Third bell sounded and Ylena smiled; the silence for the day was over. Soon the Brothers would pour out of prayer and commence their day's work. It occurred to her that she had meant to call in on Brother Farley and get a gargle for a gritty throat she had developed the previous night. Torn between wanting to step into the warm waters of the spring and not wanting to risk falling ill now that she felt so much better, Ylena hurriedly veered toward the old physic's rooms and ran straight into Brother Jakub.

"Ah, my girl. You are a sight to gladden the heart of an old man."

She hugged him. "Good morning, Brother Jakub. You're not at morning prayers; are you ailing?"

His face crinkled into the warmth of his gentle smile. "No, child. There are some sick children in the village and I want to speak with Brother Farley before he gets too engrossed in his day's toil. I'd like him to look in on them this morning." She nodded with understanding. "And you?"

She touched her neck. "Sore throat."

"Well, my dear mother used to say if you gad about with wet hair on cold days you're bound to catch a chill," he said, wagging a finger in what was clearly a fair imitation of an old woman. She laughed at his impression and he squeezed her hand, delighting in her joy. "How good it is to hear you laugh."

Ylena gave a rueful expression. "There are moments when I can hardly believe how fine it is to be alive. I catch myself smiling and I feel almost guilty."

"You mustn't," Jakub counseled. "This is the human spirit restoring itself, child. It is how we heal. Let your spirits soar when they're of a mind to, Ylena . . . trust them, for it means they have found hope again. Hope is a powerful weapon."

She nodded, feeling tears welling at this man's goodness and generosity.

He sensed her emotion and, not wishing to upset her bright mood, changed the subject. "Is Pil attending you well, Ylena?"

"Too well, Brother Jakub!" she replied with mock despair.

"Ah, he's a good boy and takes his role of protector very seriously."

"I know. He's been most kind . . . all of you have. But I must think of leaving."

"Not too soon, I hope," he said softly. "Take your time. Be well."

She took her chance. "I shouldn't hold you up, Brother Jakub," and he shook his head slightly to show it was of no consequence, "but I wonder if I can ask you whether you've heard from Romen?"

"I've received no word," he replied, guiding her into the warmth of the physic's chamber. The other man was busy measuring out powders and breaking chunks of dried herbs into smaller pieces. He muttered to himself, hardly noticing them.

"Then may I impose on you further by asking about that important item he left with you for safekeeping." Jakub's expression grew grave. "It's all right," she said. "I can talk about it now. I'm much stronger."

"I know you are, child. You are a marvel and it's not difficult to see that you have been grown from strong stock."

"Did you know my father?" she asked, surprised.

Jakub nodded toward his fellow brother to give them a moment. "Of him, of course. I regret I didn't have the pleasure of meeting your fine father, or brother, in person. They were good men, as I hear it."

"Thank you," she whispered. "Where is the head?"

He hugged her. "It's safe. In the grotto."

Ylena flinched at the realization that she had been sharing these weeks with Alyd. "Where?" she asked.

"There's a false back to the cupboard where we keep the candles. I hid it there. It should be well preserved as Romen requested."

She was going to say more, but the words were choked off by the sounds of men yelling. Frowning, Brother Jakub told her to remain where she was as he hurried outside the chamber to see what was happening. A few moments later he ran back in, face ashen.

He grabbed her hand. "Ylena, hide behind this counter."

"Whatever's going on?"

"Riders. King's men!" It was Pil bursting into the room, a look of terror on his face. "They're hurting the Brothers."

Her eyes widened with disbelief and rising panic gripped at the throat whose soreness she had forgotten in an instant. "What—"

"Do as I say," Jakub ordered, his voice hard now. "Hide, both of you, and as soon as you can climb out of the window here, make for the grotto. Your passage will be hidden. You know what to do, child," he said somberly to Ylena before glancing toward Pil and saying to him: "Now is when you prove your worth, lad. Keep her safe. Get her away from here as soon as you can."

"Jakub!" she began, voice trembling. "It's me they've come for, isn't it?"

"But they'll never find you, my girl. Not so long as I draw breath." He nodded at his colleague. "Come, Farley. Be brave now. We have nothing to share with these men." Jakub gave Ylena a searching look, kissed her briefly and whispered for her to be brave, and then he took the dismayed Farley's hand and together the two old men walked out into the bright day.

Ylena was too stunned to move until she heard the gruff sound of strangers' voices.

"Come on!" Pil hissed, dragging her around the counter.

They ducked behind Farley's weighing bench and climbed beneath his shelves. Ylena held her breath as she heard boots clatter into the room. Pil put his finger to his lips, more out of a need to comfort himself, she was sure, for his eyes were tightly shut.

She heard Jakub's voice. It was gentle, filled with the contrived confusion of an old man. "There's no woman in our monastery, son," he offered innocently, presumably to a soldier. "But by all means you're welcome to search . . ." His voice trailed off as they all left the chamber again. Mercifully the men had done only an initial cursory search of rooms.

"They'll be back," Pil whispered.

"I want to see what they're doing," she mouthed back.

He shook his head vehemently. "I promised Jakub."

Ylena knew he was right, just as she knew that these intruders had come for her and if they found her she might not live to enjoy her revenge. "I know you did, but if this is about me I need to know what's happening."

Pil bowed his head, beaten. "Perhaps we can see from the small tower," he suggested.

The small tower was a disused area of the monastery that had once been a special place of prayer for Brothers choosing to live for a while in Solitary. Part of the floor had collapsed a few years back and Jakub had declared it too dangerous and the tower had been closed. The lack of Brothers looking to spend time in Solitary meant that its repair had still not been attempted.

"We can get there easily enough," he added cautiously, "and the grotto can be accessed through the cheese pantry if we have to."

Pil climbed out from under the counter and motioned that the way was clear. They opened the small window—fortunately both were slight of frame—and wriggled out.

"I didn't know you could get in from there," she whispered, looking about her as they tiptoed across the small clearing toward the tower and closer to where they could now hear voices.

"Secret entrance," Pil admitted, his face a mask of worry. "Quick! Someone's coming."

The pair hurtled through the small tower's doorway with barely a moment to spare. Leaning back against the stone wall, they breathed hard and silently, fearing the sound of boots crunching on the small pebbles. The boots stopped outside the door.

"Did you check in here?" a voice asked.

Ylena held her breath now, praying to Shar to keep them hidden.

"Yes. It's a ruin anyway. No one there."

"Right. Put a bar against the door so no one gets in . . . or out. Then all our boys know this one's clear."

"At once."

Footsteps trailed off. Ylena looked toward the pale-faced Pil and appreciated for the first time how very young he was, at most fifteen. She would have to be strong now, just for him.

She took his hand and squeezed it. "We'll find a way out, Pil. Trust me," she said with such confidence that she surprised herself. Wondering where all this new courage was coming from, she remembered Jakub's words about the human spirit and hope. Not hope, she told herself, there was no hope with Alyd and Wyl dead. Just hate and revenge . . . and determination.

"Come on, lead the way," she encouraged.

Pil gave a thin, nervous smile and, holding on to her hand, began to ascend the narrow, winding staircase. Slits in the wall gave air and Ylena felt a new fear claw at her heart.

"I smell smoke, Pil."

He said nothing, just kept climbing. At the top he pointed to some of the rotten timbers.

"Be very careful," he said softly.

"Are you all right?" she ventured.

"They were beating some of the Brothers," he said, his eyes glazing with tears. "I'm not sure I want to see any more."

Ylena swallowed hard. How could she have been so insensitive? The men could not be Legionnaires. She knew the soldiers too well; they would never perform this sort of atrocity.

"But you know they're King's men?"

"They have his banner," the young man said.

"Then Celimus must have amassed a small army of paid mercenaries . . . no Legionnaire would participate in something as heinous as this," she assured. "Wait here, I'll look."

Pil did not argue. He pointed out where she must tread and she crossed the small area of floor with ease. Only now did she allow her gaze to take in what was happening below.

At her first strangled sound, Pil slumped to the floor. He did not need to see it to know the world he knew and loved was being smashed. Ylena's throat closed in terror and the wind blowing through the broken shutters of the tower confirmed that fires had been lit. The monastery was burning.

Men she recognized were lying in contorted positions in the gardens, their hoes and spades carelessly resting around them. They had died where they had been working; no warning, just a sword through the belly. Others, more bloodied, had tried to escape and been hacked down. Some had arrows protruding from their backs.

She covered her mouth with her hands when she recognized the slumped figure of Brother Farley. He was still alive, barely, but one of his hands was gone and he was looking at the bleeding stump, bewildered. *How will he measure out his powders now?* she thought idiotically, knowing he would die from shock within minutes. Others were still being interrogated and in the middle of them was the tiny figure of Brother Jakub, rallying their spirits and trying to keep his human flock—what was left of it—from fighting back or giving offense. She could see him pleading with the strangers, begging for mercy for his men of Shar.

It was when he was soon after singled out and nailed to a makeshift cross that Ylena knew if she did nothing else but kill Celimus, she would have achieved something worthwhile with her life. She choked back the scream that almost flew from her throat and watched the perpetrators throw something from a flask at Jakub. A lit torch was flung toward the frail figure and he ignited. Now she did let out a heartfelt sob.

"Jakub," she whispered.

Pil was crying, his hands covering his ears, but she knew he had seen how her lips moved and that the anguish in her expression told him all he needed to know. She did not need to see any more carnage to know that these men had not come to find her. They had come to kill her. They knew she was at Rittylworth and so they were persecuting its community to get the truth of where she was being held safe.

They would not find her. If only to avenge the deaths of these beautiful, helpless men, she would get away. She would frustrate Celimus's plans in every way she could before she worked out how to bring about his downfall.

She moved to where her young friend crouched. She pushed back her fears for his sake. He must not know how terrified she was or he would never have the courage to do what she needed of him now. Her voice was steady and deep with anger. "Come, Pil. We must go."

"Where?" he sobbed.

"To the grotto first. I have something to fetch from it and we will also be safe there. We can make our plans."

"Is everyone dead?" he mumbled.

"I don't know." It was a poor answer but was at the very least vaguely truthful. She knew it would not help their cause if she told him all that she had seen. "We must hurry."

"We can't get out," he reminded her, trying to stop his tears.

"Yes we can. We'll go out through this window behind you—they can't see us."

He looked at her as though she had lost her mind.

She stated the obvious. "We can't stay here. They've barred us in and they might come back and look through all of these places again."

"It's too dangerous across the roof."

"You know, Pil," she said as gently as she could, "you said to me when I first came here and was too frightened to be left alone that Brother Jakub had taught you how to fix your eye on the things that scare you and walk toward them—do you remember that?"

He nodded bleakly.

"Well, it was you who helped me to find myself again. You helped me to conquer my fears of what had happened to me in Stoneheart." She knew he had only scant information, but the gravity of her words was enough to suggest it had been a terrifying experience for her.

"I did?"

"Truly. And so now you have to take Jakub's advice again and stare this beast right back in its eyes and let it know you don't fear it. And I shall do the same."

"How?"

"By running across the rooftop with me and helping me to the grotto so we can make our escape."

His expression told her that he was now convinced she had lost her mind. She grinned wolfishly in the manner she had often seen Alyd and Wyl do as boys when they were up to mischief. "Trust me."

"Where are we going?" he asked, in some awe now of the woman standing before him.

"Felrawthy, to raise an army."

8

REMYS WAS TRUE TO HIS WORD. IN THE MORNING A TUB WAS brought up and filled with steaming water and fragrant oils. Once again Wyl was surprised by the thoughtfulness of this stranger.

Aremys turned at the door. "I'll go out for a while. You take your time."

"What have you told them about me?"

"Nothing. It's not their business. What they surmise is up to them," he said, and winked.

Aremys smiled at the look of dread that passed across the woman's face when she realized what that must mean. He was especially glad to note that the bruises had benefited from the salve. Even with her face injured, she was striking to look at. "Lock it behind me," he suggested, and left.

Wyl did so and for the second time in as many days slid with extraordinary relief into the comforting warmth of a tub. He gingerly touched spots that were hurt and then, avoiding them as best he could, scrubbed himself clean with the flannel and soap paste provided. It was the strangest of sensations. A woman felt completely different from how he had imagined. He did not have the courage to explore further and Faryl felt raw anyway. Another time, he decided, embarrassed.

Wyl knew he would never forget how vulnerable he had

felt. He was glad Rostyr was dead. Justice was done, thanks to Aremys and indeed to Jessom. What remained of Faryl certainly approved. He wondered what sort of penance had been meted by Celimus in the meantime. Knowing the man as he did, he had no doubt that the King would be seeking information on the thefts in far less subtle ways than his chancellor.

He did not have to wait too long to learn the answer.

Wyl had taken care with his hair this morning, brushing it until it shone before tying it back as best he could in Faryl's way. He had been alarmed to see the bruises on his face; they would attract unwanted attention. On the positive side, however, although he pained in several places, he knew his body was intact, with no bones broken.

Aremys returned later to find Faryl much refreshed and wrapped in one of his huge shirts that she must have dug into his saddlebags for. He swallowed at the sight of her. She really was a striking woman. He had never been one to fall for the breathily speaking, pretty sort who looked as though they might break if you squeezed them in a hug. Nor did he find the more obviously flirtatious kind desirable—those women were confident enough of their bodies to use their sexual attractiveness as a weapon. If he was honest he had never truly fallen for anyone unless he counted Elly from the farm next door when he was a young lad. Elly had been far more tomboy than girl, which was probably why she had been his favorite. She could run faster, shoot arrows better, and skin a rabbit quicker than he ever could. She had called him Bear too and like Faryl had not been beautiful, not even conventionally pretty. She had had a laugh, though, that could fill his heart and a wit that could cut anyone down to size.

Wyl felt instantly self-conscious at the way Aremys was staring. "I thought I'd travel as myself today."

The man nodded an approval but remained still just inside the doorway. He said nothing. An awkward silence stretched before them, neither knowing how best to handle their situation from here.

Wyl shrugged, touched a hand to a bruise on his face. "You've been extremely kind to a stranger. I'm not sure how to say appropriate thanks but consider it said and meant."

Aremys found his voice. "I've been back to the Four Feathers—picked up all your things for you. I didn't think you'd care to go back just now."

"Ah . . . I'm further in your debt, then. Thank you."

The mercenary took a step into the room and made a gesture to say it was no trouble.

Wyl struggled for something to say as his mind raced to consider his next move. "Do I owe you any money for the inn where I'd booked?"

"No. You had prepaid everything. A woman after my own heart," Aremys admitted. "I always prepay . . . er, just in case I need to leave swiftly."

It was Wyl's turn to nod. "Well," he said, with an exaggerated brightness. "Time I left you to your own business. You've done more than enough for me."

Aremys nodded. "Where are you headed?"

Wyl cringed. They had moved to small talk. "Oh, a small town a few days' ride from here."

"Family?"

"Er . . . no, well . . . in a way. I'm trying to track down a friend's mother." It was easier to stick as close to the truth as possible. "And you?" Wyl added, hating the forced politeness of their conversation.

"Nowhere really, now that I've finished my job for Jessom. I'm at a loose end, you could say." Aremys laced his large fingers together, then undid them, put them behind his back, and then hung them back at his sides.

It was time to move. "I hope our paths cross again," Wyl said, stepping forward to take the large hand in his. "I'm grateful to you, Aremys," he added, looking into the man's expressive eyes. "Shar keep you safe."

The dark eyes regarded him now with what looked like sadness. "I've fetched your horse as well."

Wyl grinned briefly. Aremys noted how that particular small expression made such a difference to Faryl's bearing.

She had a lovely smile that touched her eyes and changed a normally serious, often sad visage into something with lightness, even the suggestion of laughter lurking.

"I'm not helpless, but thank you," Wyl said.

Aremys shook his head to suggest it was no bother. "Well, I figured you might ride out as yourself and would not want to confront the stable master as Faryl demanding Thom Bentwood's horse." He was lying, decided to come clean. "But I also thought we could leave together. There's only one road and I'm guessing you're headed toward Pearlis rather than away from it—is that right?"

"Why, yes I am," Wyl replied, taken aback at the suggestion and not able to think of a reason to contradict it.

"We could ride together for a while, then?"

It was time to be more direct. "Aremys, you don't need to worry about me. Contrary to how it seems, I can fend for myself."

"I'm not worried about you. I can see from the tautness of your body and by the weapons you carry that you are not one to trifle with."

"You went through my things?" Wyl's voice sounded suddenly brittle.

"I could hardly miss them, Faryl. I told you I gathered up your stuff."

"It seems I have nothing I can hide from you! What else did you look through?"

"I give you my word I wasn't prying."

"You're a mercenary, Aremys. I'm not sure your word is worth much." He could see he had struck hard. It was not necessary and surely undeserved. Why was he so touchy? This man had probably saved his life. "I'm sorry. I'm edgy today, forgive me. It's just the aftermath of what happened, I'm sure. I have a long ride ahead and should get going. I really do owe you thanks rather than criticism."

"It's forgotten."

Wanting to salvage something for Aremys's sake, Wyl capitulated. "Look, I don't mind if we ride out together. I just want you to know that I'll be fine."

Aremys nodded. "Good," was all he said.

It was not ideal, Wyl knew, but it was only as far as the outskirts of Pearlis and then he could branch off. "Let me just climb into some clothes. I hope you didn't mind me throwing one of your shirts on."

"Not at all. I don't mind you rifling through my stuff one bit," Aremys replied, just a hint of sarcasm in his tone.

Their departure from the inn was uneventful and Wyl had to admit he felt infinitely more comfortable physically—if not emotionally—traveling as Faryl without all the painful bindings and irritating hairy disguise. He was dressed simply in loose tan trousers, soft boots, and a warm jacket over a shirt.

"You still look like a man," Aremys said, but it was meant kindly. He watched Faryl climb onto her mare with practiced ease. He could tell she was as comfortable in the saddle as she was drawing the weapon he had watched her strap on. She had let him hold the knives earlier. Such beautiful craftsmanship he had not seen before.

"Is your throw as exquisite as your blades?" he had asked facetiously back in the room.

His answer had been a knife whooshing past his cheek, only narrowly missing his ear but pinning some of his hair to a wooden beam. The speed and fluidity of her throw had left him stunned.

"Sorry . . . that was a bit theatrical of me," Wyl admitted, stifling the satisfaction he felt at unleashing Romen's skill.

Aremys needed no further convincing that this woman could, for the most part, look after herself.

They had reached a particularly pretty patch of Morgravia's southern rural region and Wyl felt himself relaxing for the first time in many days. They had been traveling in a companionable silence for a long way now, which contributed to his peace.

Aremys finally broke it with a question. "May I ask where you learned to throw knives with such deadly accuracy?"

Wyl had expected the query far sooner than this; was

ready for it. "When you grow up with only a host of brothers, you learn such skills."

"I have six brothers. None of us learned how to throw a knife."

"Six," Wyl said, impressed, keen to direct the conversation elsewhere. "I grew up with only five. Where is your family home?"

"Minlyton is the village I was raised in."

"Never heard of it," Wyl admitted.

"I'm not surprised. I'm from a small island off the far north."

Wyl felt as though every nerve was on high alert. "Oh? Which one?" He hoped his voice sounded casual and that Aremys would not say the word he feared.

"Grenadyn."

Wyl flinched at the name, and because Aremys had turned his dark gaze toward him, he attempted to cover this reaction by flicking at the few strands of hair that had escaped their bindings. "Do you know it?" Aremys inquired.

"Er . . . I've heard of it, of course."

"But never been there?"

"No," he said, grateful to answer truthfully. "Why?" He was cautious.

"Oh, it's nothing. I just . . . well, there was someone raised in Grenadyn who is as handy as you are with a knife. Actually I understate his skill. He could throw a knife with such deadly accuracy that until I saw your talent I never thought I'd ever see anyone as good as him."

Wyl's throat felt constricted. "Oh yes? What's his name?"

"Romen Koreldy. A noble. Very wealthy family."

This time Wyl could not hide the alarm. "Did he know you?" It slipped out. *What a stupid question,* he thought, cringing. "I mean, do you see him?" he corrected quickly as his mind raced to dig among whatever was left of Romen to give him information on this man.

"No. He was older than me. He used to lark around with my elder brothers, but I was too young. I did see him once, showing off for the kids. I was about five. He was so good with a knife he could split a thread from twenty-five paces when he was little more than a youth."

Something nagged at his attention, but Wyl ignored it. He was fascinated, for Romen's mind had not released any of this to him. No wonder his riding companion's name had meant nothing to him. "And?"

Aremys shrugged. "Nothing of note. Our family left Grenadyn not many years later and we came to the mainland—we didn't stay so long, a few years perhaps; we all missed home too much. In that time, Romen had gone. There was some talk of a scandal among the Koreldys, but I never found out what that was. I have not seen or heard of him since."

It was time to move away from Koreldy. "And you've never been back?" Wyl asked.

"To Minlyton?"

Wyl nodded.

"No, but now you mention it, perhaps once I collect my monies I may do just that." Aremys straightened in the saddle, stretching. "Time to break our fast, do you think?"

The mention of food ended that conversation and Wyl was relieved he had not been required to explain his skills with the knife any further. He had learned his lesson; would not show off again. They shared the hearty meal that they had asked the kitchen staff at the inn to pack. The servings of the chicken, cheese, and fruits together with dark bread were generous and both admitted afterward they could easily lie back on the soft verge and take a nap. Instead they encouraged each other to saddle up again and continued their journey in an easy silence for the next hour or so.

As they drew closer to Pearlis, Wyl had his question answered about punishment regarding the stolen taxes. Celimus had indeed been busy strong-arming the Legion for answers.

"Shar's Wrath!" he exclaimed as they came across the first tortured soul.

The body was well preserved by the cool weather as it rotted slowly on the fearsome spike on which it was impaled. The mouth was drawn back in a pose of absolute agony, the limbs strangely twisted.

"This man died slowly," Aremys commented. "You can see they broke his bones first, and expertly too."

"I've never seen such cruelty in Morgravia before," Wyl murmured, shaking with anger. "This is over the stolen taxes, isn't it?"

"I wouldn't know, Faryl. Come on, let's keep moving."

They counted a further nine corpses, all soldiers, hanging halfway down poles, who had been precisely impaled for maximum pain, while ensuring death occurred as slowly as possible. Some had deteriorated more than others, suggesting Celimus's vicious inquisition had been raging for several days.

"And these are only the bodies on this stretch of road. Shar knows how many more are rotting on the others that lead into Pearlis," Aremys commented.

The smell of putrid flesh threatened to spill their breakfast for them.

Wyl was horrified imagining these men—his men—being tortured like this over the likes of Rostyr. "I hate him," he whispered.

"Who?"

"The King," he said, trancelike, staring at the pair of bodies contorted in their death spasms.

His companion was staring at him with a guarded expression.

Wyl knew there was no point in trying to take the words back. "And if you repeat that to anyone, I won't miss with the knives next time." He sighed. "I'm going now, Aremys. Here's where we part company. My road leading into the western counties is about four miles from here. Again, I thank you for your company." He almost made the farewell sign of the Legion, stopping himself just in time. Instead he reached over and clasped the man's shoulder. It was not a particularly feminine gesture, but he had already decided that a woman who carried weapons was never going to be considered courtly.

"Faryl, please don't leave yet."

"I must. It's time I was on my way."

"What's so important?"

"Nothing. I just want to continue on my own now. I've seen enough to know I have no reason to travel through the city."

"Sounds to me like you have something to hide from."

Wyl bristled. *If only you knew,* he thought. "Only my hatred for this sort of thing," he said, pleased to hear how calm his voice was. "Just leave it, Aremys."

"All right, I understand," his friend said, then he grinned. "Look, come with me as far as Smallhampton. It's just a few miles away and you can pick up a small track to the western counties easily enough. It doesn't take you much out of your way, in fact."

"Why?"

"It's where I have a hide. I want to pick up some money."

"But you're going into Pearlis, surely, to be paid for your recent kill?"

"No. I've changed my mind—that money can be paid later. Since we began talking about Grenadyn, I've decided to go home . . . see my family before I die or they do."

Wyl was baffled. He swiped at yet more of the dark gold hairs that had loosened on the ride and were flapping around his face. It was such an annoying sensation and yet he recalled how wantonly attractive that same look had made Valentyna. "Well, that's good. But what has this to do with me?"

Aremys looked uncomfortable again. "Nothing, in truth. I just want to continue riding with you a little longer. We can—" He stopped, embarrassed by his own awkwardness. "I like you, Faryl. I just . . ." He struggled again. "That is, I enjoy your company."

Wyl did not know whether to be flattered or cornered. It was true, going to Smallhampton would not take him much out of his way at all and there would be a chance there for an ale and some food before heading out west, perhaps even being able to ride through the night. On the other hand, Aremys was sounding needy, which did not sit right with Wyl. Aremys had struck him as independent and very used to a

lonely existence. In fact, Wyl was convinced that the mercenary preferred to be remote from people. This did not add
up. There were secrets here, and just as Wyl began to feel
some previously nagging thoughts coming together, he noticed that Aremys would not meet his eyes and that, together
with the slight flush to his cheeks, gave Wyl far more information than he wanted.

Shar save us! he thought. *He's enamored of me. Not
good, Wyl. Not good at all,* he berated silently.

"Please," Aremys added softly, with perfect timing.

He wanted to kick his horse into a gallop and flee; this
was a terrible situation. But the man had saved his life and
he would probably hate himself later if he did not deal with
this now, gently.

"Aremys—"

"No, wait. I've embarrassed you," the big man said. "I
understand if you'd prefer to ride away on your own, but if
you'd keep me company just awhile longer, I'd enjoy the
conversation. No obligation, Faryl."

Wyl conceded. He felt sure Aremys was not going to try
anything—not after the previous day's traumatic events.
"All right. Smallhampton it is and then I'm going west . . .
alone."

Aremys loosed a broad smile, pleased with his win. "We
can share an ale at its inn before you go."

Wyl looked again at the pair of putrefying bodies nearby.
"Let's just get away from here," he said, and they rode.

They moved off the road onto a small track and then
flanked some deserted fields before entering a copse.

"Ever known of hides?" Aremys asked.

"No," Wyl replied, lying. Faryl had dozens all over the
realm.

"Actually, hired assassins tend to use them more than us
mercenaries, but I like to be cautious. You should follow
suit. It could save your life sometime."

"I don't live as dangerously as you. But yes, I may take
that advice."

There was an old disused hut on the edge of the copse.

"In there, is it?" Wyl asked.

"No. Too obvious—any vagabond using it for shelter could discover my cache. I use the hut as a marker. Let me show you." Aremys climbed down from his horse and pulled a small length of rope from his saddlebag.

Wyl got off his horse too. "What's the rope for?"

"Wait and see."

They approached the hut as far as its front door and then Aremys turned his back to it. "Now walk with me thirty strides."

They did.

"And ten strides to our left."

Wyl followed him toward the hollow of an old tree but hung back as Aremys glanced into it.

"Bollocks!" Aremys exclaimed.

"Gone?" Wyl said, leaning over to look in with his friend.

They were shoulder to shoulder now. Aremys turned and looked at the woman he liked very much—had even allowed himself some daydreams of bedding. He would have loved to have enjoyed her. He hated doing this.

"I'm so sorry, Faryl," he whispered into her hair. Then louder. "Forgive me."

"Forgive you? What?"

In a blink Aremys had strongly spun Wyl around and clamped his hands behind his back. Even more quickly he knocked his legs away, so Wyl slammed to the ground, old wounds protesting angrily, new bruises flaring. Aremys used the rope to bind Faryl's hands. It would have been easier if he had been required to kill her; she struggled furiously, courageously, nearly unbalancing him at one point. She was strong, far more than he had anticipated. But he was stronger and he finally managed to sit on her legs and still her.

"Aremys!" Wyl shrieked in that voice he despised. "What . . . what are you doing?"

"Apologies, Leyen," said a new voice, prompting Wyl to raise his head sharply toward the hut. "I knew you wouldn't come to me on the strength of my bidding. I had to hire in special help."

"Jessom!" Wyl spat, remembering the Chancellor who had accompanied Celimus into Briavel.

Aremys lifted Faryl to her feet, even moving to dust her clothes off.

Wyl kicked at him, his eyes burning with hatred toward the betrayer. "Shar rot your very soul, Aremys!"

Jessom made a sound of disapproval. "Dear me, Leyen. Language." He tutted. "So raw for a lady."

Wyl stopped struggling and simply glared between the two men. There were soldiers too. No point in trying to run or even fight. He was trapped.

"What do you want?" he snarled.

"Well, my dear, you did such a good job on your last . . . er, task, that you have impressed someone who wishes to meet with you."

"I'm not interested," Wyl said, every nerve on edge now. This was dangerous.

"I expected as much. You are certainly a private person. Is this a disguise you are wearing, bruises included?"

Wyl remained silent. Jessom looked toward Aremys.

"This is the real one, as far as I can tell," the mercenary mumbled.

"Not that I'm complaining, for she is far more attractive than I have ever seen. How can you be sure, though?" Jessom inquired, in no hurry.

"Does seeing her naked count?" Aremys growled, bristling now.

He did not care much for Jessom either, but the money was too good to ignore. The Chancellor had paid five times the price of a kill just for Aremys to track down and capture the woman. It had been too easy that she had stumbled into his path and he had been able to deal not only with the conspirators but the assassin as well. As soon as he saw the weapons, he knew he had been right—this was his prey. Those, together with the disguises he discovered in her belongings and all the other giveaway signs, including how well she rode, her lean, strong body, her private ways . . . it all added up that this was the woman Jessom was searching for. But as soon as she threw the knife, he had no longer had any doubts.

He hated himself for handing her over to Jessom. It was obvious Faryl had no desire to meet with the King. More secrets, he decided. *Take the money and leave. Don't get involved,* he told himself, not wanting to meet her gaze.

Jessom was laughing softly. "Ah, that's very convincing. I'm glad you were able to enjoy a dalliance with this intriguing creature . . . and get paid for it. Surely you didn't give her the bruises as well . . . tsk . . . tsk."

Wyl wished he could reach his blades. With their aid he could leave several dead men behind in the copse. He said nothing, just leveled a murderous stare at Aremys that he knew Faryl did very well.

Jessom became businesslike. "I know her as Leyen. She is a master of disguise. Has she told you any differently?"

Aremys considered. If Faryl's eyes were weapons, he would be dead thrice over. A dangerous enemy to make, as she would surely be permitted to live. Perhaps the money had not been worth it. She would probably pursue him now, come what may. And he had stupidly admitted where he came from. Strange . . . he knew she had been honest with him to a point, possibly shared things she would not with most, and that had made him truthful with her . . . to a point. It had been a mistake, though.

"Well?" Jessom prompted, irritated.

Aremys noted that she was staring intently at him. Her eyes were communicating something more than just the plain hate of earlier.

"Sorry, I was just thinking back over our conversations. No. I have known her only as Leyen," he admitted, and saw relief flit across Faryl's face. Then she looked away.

"Good, then perhaps we have her real name now. Not that we can be absolutely sure, but it will do. Come, my dear, you are to be escorted back to Pearlis."

"For whom?" Wyl said.

"For his royal highness, King Celimus, whom you have impressed with your talents."

9

ELSPYTH HAD STAYED TRUE TO HER PROMISE TO WYL. RESIST-
ing the urge to head home after their farewell, she
made her way very slowly south; accepting rides with a family, a merchant convoy, and a traveling band of musicians.
All were very kind and would accept no money for their
transport or hospitality. None were in a hurry and in truth neither was Elspyth, happy to meander at their pace, stopping
off at towns to perform or make their deliveries. The musicians helped her find some laughter again, even encouraging
her to sing with them around their campfires. They were taking a circuitous route toward Pearlis, hoping to earn good
profits in the spring months but more than happy to have her
in the group for part of their journey. She was surprised at
how much she enjoyed her time with them, quietly regretting
their parting. Between all her new friends they got her as far
as the outskirts of Rittylworth. The troupe gave her a fond
farewell and the usual expressions of hope for meeting again.

She was happy to walk the rest of the way, wondering
how Wyl's sister would react to her and what she was going
to say to this young, grieving woman. Wyl had extracted a
promise that would effectively see Elspyth telling lies from
here on in to anyone who knew him. So be it, she had decided. She and Wyl—as Romen Koreldy—had been through
too much together already to forsake each other. Furthermore, Wyl had given her his own oath and so she would keep
true to him, anticipating the same courtesy when the time
came for him to return to the Razors.

Elspyth had no idea why Wyl needed to guard his identity so keenly. She did, however, understand his reluctance

to share his tale, for people's suspicion of magic was too entrenched. This enchantment on Wyl was hardly a fairground trick—the enormity of it was too much for most to cope with. The fact that both she and Lothryn had accepted the sorcery was fortunate for Wyl but was purely because of their backgrounds.

She remembered how he had haltingly told them of the curse on his life. Myrren's Gift, he had called it, and had laughed bitterly. As much as it had sounded implausible, everything he had said had corroborated that this magic had been wielded on him. It explained her aunt's strange behavior toward him and the curious comment she had made after the Pearlis tourney that "we haven't seen the last of that one yet."

And she could see that Lothryn believed him too. Elspyth recalled how matter-of-fact the mountain man had been, not at all perturbed by the suggestion of magic. She felt the same way. Another reason to love him. Her thoughts turned to how hard and quickly she had fallen for the big man who had wrenched her from her home and, against her will, taken her into the Razors, only to risk his life for her a few days later. Her heart had fully melted for him upon seeing him weeping for his dead wife and holding his newborn son, and since that moment, their relationship had changed. Suddenly there had been a burning connection between them—but they had never so much as shared a kiss. She remembered how he had turned to fight their pursuers single-handed on that lonely escarpment, begging for her to run. Lothryn had pressed Wyl into running too. It hurt deeply to imagine what had befallen him after their escape. She had no doubt whatsoever that he would have been taken alive in order to stand before a wrathful Cailech and take whatever punishment was meted out to him. Would it have been death by some harrowing method that only the Mountain King could dream up?

Elspyth did not want to think about it. She wanted to believe that Lothryn lived and distracted herself by turning her mind to Wyl, trapped in Koreldy's body. He was trying to save the sovereign of the realm that had killed his father and been his homeland's enemy for centuries while sending her off to track down his grieving sister. *What a tragic family,* she thought . . . *so much despair in their lives.* But she had agreed to do this for him and in return he had agreed to return to the Razors as soon as he could to find out what had happened to Lothryn.

She had put her trust in Wyl Thirsk. It would be interesting to talk to him, in happier times hopefully, about what it felt like to become someone else. Wyl was lucky, she thought, that it was the darkly handsome Romen Koreldy he had become. She imagined how it might have been if he had been killed by someone who was crippled or retarded . . . perhaps someone of very lowly birth. Worse—she giggled to herself—a woman!

She found herself approaching the high ground from which she could look down into the valley and see the monastery with its village clustered nearby. Relief that she had made it this far safely coursed through her and her approach was made with a far lighter heart and in happier spirits than when she began her journey.

Still smiling from the notion that Wyl could have become a woman instead of handsome Romen, she began to rehearse what he had instructed her to say to Brother Jakub. But as Elspyth crested the hill, full of hope, she stopped in her tracks and the smile died, taking with it her good mood.

The tiny enclave of Rittylworth was in ruin, one tiny dwelling still smoking from the firebrands. The monastery to one side looked cold and silent. It was still whole, blackened in parts, but even from this distance she could sense it was deserted. What had happened here? She did not want to approach just yet, needed to gather her racing thoughts. Wyl had impressed caution upon her, but even he had assumed she would be safe here in this picturesque hamlet.

She scrutinized the area now, gathering as much information as her eyes would give her. Noticing something odd in the far distance, she squinted and then let out a sound of despair when she realized what it was. People crucified. She could not tell whether they were still alive or merely corpses.

Elspyth did not pause for further thought but picked up her skirts and began to run.

Her fears were confirmed. As she drew closer, gasping for her breath, she could see that the village itself had been torched. It was desolate. There was no sign of other bodies, much to her relief, so she suspected this attack had occurred to teach the villagers some sort of lesson . . . retribution for something. Presumably they had fled and would return to rebuild the village and their lives when they felt it was safe.

Panting now as breathing became easier, she discovered that the monks had not been so fortunate. The greater lesson had clearly been taught within the grounds of the monastery, where the smell of burned flesh was evident and cloying. The light breeze carried the stench from the host of charred corpses hanging from a hastily erected series of crosses.

She had not realized she was weeping until a gust of wind told her that her cheeks were wet with tears. It was obvious that the lesser monks had been set aflame, then left to burn and die in horrific pain wherever they writhed. She found herself stepping over the blackened remains of men . . . some boys too, from which she quickly averted her horrified gaze. It seemed that most had either been working in the gardens or had emerged into the gardens when the raid came, for that was where the greatest number of bodies lay. Elspyth had no doubt there were more inside the monastery itself, but she was not prepared to look within.

The full horror of being nailed through the wrists and then burned on the cross had been saved for selected monks—the most senior perhaps. She counted six. They all appeared dead, though she had no way of knowing how recently this outrage had occurred, particularly as decay was not so evident just yet. This made her skin prickle, for it meant the attackers were not that long gone.

Needing to do something to show her despair, while not being able to face going into the holy chapel of the monastery, she sank to her knees and began praying at the feet of one of the crucified. As she murmured her pleas to Shar, the body above her croaked something. Elspyth fell backward with fright, looking up toward the tortured, hairless head with the flesh hanging off it.

She stood, petrified yet craning her neck as close to the man's moving lips as she could.

"Find Ylena," he breathed. "She lives. Pil took her."

"Are you Jakub?" she asked, frantic.

An almost imperceptible, clearly painful nod told her he was indeed Brother Jakub.

"Let me help you," she said, desperately looking around for a tool that might loosen the nails.

"Too late," he croaked. She returned to look into his bleeding eyes and smoked flesh. "Tell Romen"—he coughed, his breath now rattling in his throat—"that this was the work of the King."

"Why?" She could see his death looming.

"Thirsk . . . he—" was all the monk could get out before he took one last agonizing breath and died.

Elspyth wept for his suffering and those of his brothers, all peaceful men of the cloth. She felt a rage surfacing at this new king, understood now why Wyl's identity should be protected. She eased the lids down gently over the staring eyes of Brother Jakub. There was nothing more she could do here, other than bear witness to the atrocity. It would stay with her forever. She touched a shaky hand to the blackened cheek of the brave monk who had stayed alive long enough to give her the information she needed before she set off, not knowing where she was headed, to find a woman being hunted by a merciless king.

She had trudged in something of a stupor for more than a day, only realizing as she heard the haunting call of an owl that dusk was darkening to night. She was exhausted. Since leaving the smoldering village of Rittylworth, she had met no travelers along the narrow roads of Morgravia's midnorth. Her mind too numb to think, she had put one foot in front of the other to gain as much distance between herself and death as she could. It had been many solitary hours.

Elspyth shivered now in the chill night air as darkness finally registered in her blurred thoughts. She burrowed into a small hollow behind a bush for safety and then collapsed, not so much from fatigue as from the emotional trauma of her morning.

She was convinced the smell of burned flesh still clung to her and she could not forget the fire-torn voice of Brother Jakub courageously using his last breath of life to warn her. Elspyth wept quietly into the silence remembering the horrific scene, but she knew her tears for the monk must be brief, for it would not do to fall apart now.

Rittylworth had been torched because of the Thirsk name. Men of holiness, of peace, of love had lost their lives in ugly fashion because of the Thirsk name. Even Lothryn had suffered because of . . . no, she must not follow that line of thought. She must put him aside in her mind or she would never survive this.

Elspyth sniffed. She dug in her cloak pocket and found some nuts and dried fruit that her traveling friends had provided. There was some hard biscuit too, but she decided to keep that for the morning when hunger seemed at its sharpest. She chewed without interest in what she ate, considering her path now. She must make some decisions, good ones and quickly.

Jakub had said Ylena had escaped. The girl would be on foot presumably and not that long away from Rittylworth herself. Elspyth wondered about Pil, whom the older man had mentioned. She presumed he was a monk as well. Either way Ylena would be confused, frightened, disoriented. The thought brought a sad smile to her face. *Much like myself,* she admitted, realizing that in addition she was penniless, having used all her money to buy Wyl a horse at Deakyn. They had assumed she would meet up with Ylena and have access to funds again, but now she had no means of getting any coin. She shook her head clear of the doubts, swallowed the last of the fruit and nuts, and settled back against a tree to sleep.

But her thoughts drifted to her journey and where she must go. Felrawthy. That was where she needed to head now. She had in her possession a letter for the Duke of Felrawthy from Wyl. She was alone and defenseless, which meant she would need to find a new method of transport, perhaps link up with another group of travelers who might be heading east—if she could meet any, perhaps find some temporary work to afford food and lodging?

Well, it was a plan. Something to wake up to. The owl hooted again, reminding Elspyth that her kind should be asleep while the creatures of the night went about their business. She wriggled into the least uncomfortable position she could find and let her last conscious thought be cast to Lothryn.

Elspyth dreamed.

Lothryn was calling to her. Crying for her, in fact. He was in pain. Drowning in it. Vast, all-encompassing, mind-altering pain. It seemed to her that he could feel her presence as strongly as she sensed his. What was causing this pain and who was inflicting it she could not tell. There was darkness. Anger too. She could feel the bitterness raging about Lothryn—it was not his own—but she could neither see him nor the person who felt this emotion. Magic swirled around her . . . wherever she was. It knew she was there also, but it could not touch her.

Did she scream or was that Lothryn again?

Lothryn! she called into the pain.

His voice, just barely there.

Tell Romen I will wait, he whispered, voice thick with agony. *I am no longer as he would expect.*

Elspyth did scream now, shrieking Lothryn's name again and again into the darkness and its foul magic, but her lover was gone. Their bond, whatever it was, viciously snapped as if the power wielder had cut through the point where their minds had touched.

She awoke, still crying out, as dawn crept through a heavy mist that had settled about her. At first Elspyth panicked amid the blindness, waving her arms and fighting the foggy swirls, but her vision cleared slightly, reassuring her of where she was, and coldly reminded her that she was alone. Shallow breaths came rapidly. She needed to slow them. Painfully she stood from her uncomfortable hollow and sucked in deep gasps of air, filling her lungs and expelling long breaths as gradually as she dared. Tears streamed down her face while a new fear gripped her . . . what had become of Lothryn?

Was he talking to her from the dead? Had he spoken at all or had she just dreamed, experiencing a nightmare of sorts? She forced herself to be practical even though she felt more fatigued now than before her distressing sleep. She wiped her eyes, relieved herself, and then sat down to slowly consume the hard biscuit. She was not hungry. The process of chewing and swallowing would help ease her alarm, she hoped, and so she forced herself to eat. Lothryn had made them eat when they were fleeing for their lives in the Razors. None of them had felt hungry and yet he had insisted and he had been right. She took the same advice now and nourished herself.

Elspyth had never felt more alone in her lonely life. Lothryn's words, real or imagined, were all she had to cling to. She must succeed in her task if Wyl Thirsk was to keep his promise.

Elspyth finally stood, brushed away the crumbs, and patted at her unruly hair as best she could. She knew she looked a fright but no longer cared. Lothryn was suffering. He had spoken from life, not death. She knew it. Knew that her own, albeit vague, susceptibility to magic, even though she could not use it or even touch it, was how she had felt him.

She had heard his voice. Lothryn needed help. Setting her jaw in a way only her aunt would recognize as the stubborn manner of her forebears, Elspyth walked, heading east toward Felrawthy.

10

AS ELSPYTH WAS DISCOVERING THE HORROR AT RITTYLWORTH, Fynch was entering the town of Baelup. He had made speedy progress from Crowyll out of Briavel and into Morgravia courtesy of a man in a hurry to make a delivery into Pearlis. Fynch had done him a good turn and the man had offered the boy a lift to his destination.

It was Knave who had done the deed, in fact, frightening off a couple of thieves who were nosing about in the man's cart while it was briefly unattended. Fynch had noticed their interest, and realizing their actions were furtive and hardly those of people with ownership of the cartload, he sent Knave in, knowing the huge dog was enough to scare most. When Knave sounded off his ferocious bark, the men scurried away, understandably terrified.

The scene had brought one of Fynch's rare smiles to his face, and as he strolled up to congratulate the dog on his performance, the owner of the cart had returned. He too looked nervously at the dog. Fynch explained what had occurred and the man's face had lit up.

"Travel with me," he had said. "I'll pay you."

Fynch was taken aback. "Why?"

"This is the second time this has happened. Two months ago I lost half of my goods to thieves. I suspect it is not the last time either and Lady Bench is waiting for her delivery. She's a new client and I daren't let her down."

"And how can I possibly help you?" Fynch asked,

amused, thinking of how slight he was. And then it dawned on him. "Oh, I see. My dog."

"Precisely," the man said. "You do have control of it, don't you?" he added nervously.

"Only when he wants me to. But fret not. He will not attack you."

"Shar's Thanks," the man replied with relief. "Is it a deal?"

"I need to get to Baelup."

"Perfect. I can take you there as soon as I make my delivery," the man had said. "Please. I have food for the journey and my intention is to ride the horses hard to Grimble Town, changing them there. We shall be in Baelup sooner than you can pick your nose. What do you say?"

Fynch liked the man and his amusing manner. He knew Hildyth's trail was cooling each day he spent on foot and he could make up valuable time if he took the man's offer. "All right."

They had experienced no further robbery attempts and it had turned out that the man, Master Rilk, was a tailor, one of the best in Briavel too, although modesty precluded him from claiming that he was in fact the most popular of all tailors with the nobles. Word had apparently spread and now various Morgravian dignitaries were securing his services. Lady Bench was the most notable to date and she had paid a veritable fortune for him to tailor her daughter's latest dancing gown. She had insisted, however, that Master Rilk personally deliver the gown just in case it required last-minute adjustments.

Rilk made pleasant, intelligent company for Fynch and had thoroughly enjoyed the serious lad, who was knowledgeable in the ways of the Morgravian court and seemed to know all of its nobles. Fynch had gladly passed on their names and dress tendencies, his attention to detail impressing the tailor. Master Rilk had plans to expand his business dealings in the Morgravian capital, so this inside information was a blessing.

They had parted company at Baelup as friends, with a promise to meet again sometime. Fynch had refused payment. He had been fed and watered well, as had Knave, at Rilk's expense, plus they had traveled swiftly and safely to their destination.

After they had waved goodbye, Knave made himself scarce and Fynch walked into the main square, wondering where to begin. Several hours later, having passed himself off as a distant member of the family bringing news of his own mother's passing, he had established that Myrren's mother—Emil—had left Baelup soon after she had learned of her daughter's ugly death. With her husband dead and daughter burned as a witch, people at the time had sympathized with her fears for her own life.

The blacksmith was the most helpful. He seemed to have known the family well but claimed to have no idea where Emil had fled to.

"I can't offer much more help. I know a young fellow came here to see her the next day after Myrren's death. He was with a tall chap, but I don't think the older one went in with him to see Emil."

"Was the youngster's name Thirsk?" Fynch had asked eagerly, and the man had jumped at the name.

"I don't know, lad. I just saw him arrive and leave with the pup. I gather Myrren had asked him to take her dog. He was here barely minutes."

"Can you remember anything about him?"

"Red hair. Does that help?"

Fynch grinned. "It does. He was probably accompanied by a man called Gueryn?"

The smith shrugged, none the wiser.

"How did you come to meet them?"

"My missus and I were helping Emil pack her things, as I recall," the man had said, scratching his head. "She was in a tearing hurry to leave. Once she had discovered of Myrren's end, she could only think of fleeing the house, the town, everything she knew. Shame. It was the second time in her life she had done this. Myrren had funny eyes, you see, and those Witch Stalkers just had to have her. Poor mite—she deserved better—was a lovely girl and a good daughter.

The old man just dropped dead in front of them. His heart gave out; he had feared such a thing for so many years."

"Yes, I see," Fynch had said, not wanting to interrupt the blacksmith's rambling account. "And then what happened?"

"Well, after the bad news from Pearlis, Emil was only too happy to hand the pup over to this redheaded chappie, for she had no idea what to do with it anyway. It belonged to Myrren. Apparently the lad had shown a small kindness to Myrren at the time of her torture and she had wanted to give him a gift in return."

If only you knew, Fynch had thought.

"And then Emil left," the man had concluded. "She never said anything more about the dog or its new owner. We didn't share her conversation with him, although I tell you it was only moments long. Emil could hardly string two sensible words together at the time."

Fynch nodded his sympathy and understanding. "She left with no mention of where she might have been headed?"

The man was still scratching his balding head and pulled a face. "Wait now . . . I do recall her saying something about a sister. Where was it? She swore me and my missus to secrecy, that's right."

"Please, it's important."

"Er . . . let me think now. It was midnorth. Perhaps Rothwell?"

"Where's that?"

"About five or six days from here. Tiny village. But I can't be sure now, lad. Truly, I can't remember what she said."

There was little choice. Fynch planned now to head north to Rothwell, just in case it led him closer to Myrren's mother or, more likely, Wyl. He found himself filling up on a sweet pastry at Baelup's bakery and a mug of apple juice before he set off. He had just begun to sip the refreshing liquid, thinking that he must purchase some meat for Knave, when it happened.

Onlookers watched in dismay as the small lad's mug crashed to the floor moments before he did, his body instantly limp amid the spilled juice. Seconds later a huge black dog entered the shop, terrifying all the bystanders with his fierce growl. The beast positioned himself above the boy, as if guarding him.

And then he waited, his head cocked as though listening.

Fynch could hear the familiar voice. It was not unkind by any means, but it was insistent.

Look at me, boy, he heard it say again.

Fynch turned. He stared at himself prone on the ground of the baker's shop, apple juice around him and people fussing nearby. To all intents and purposes, he was dead. Above him stood Knave, still as a statue, fearsome.

Am I dead? It was his voice—he could talk with his mind.

No, was the reply. *Use your power, child. Send yourself to me.*

He obeyed, shocking himself that he was able to lock onto the voice and reel in its echoes of sound as though he were pulling on rope. There was no physical sensation, save a soft tingling of awareness that magic was occurring. He was sensitive to his body while unable to move it. It was as though he had lifted completely away from himself. His mind was the power and it was reaching out as his senses devoured the sounds of the man's voice.

Fynch sent. It was such a strange sensation, for he felt insubstantial yet very much alive and aware.

Moments later he came before a figure. They faced each other through a thin glaze of something mistlike. Fynch thought he reached out to touch it, but it was as unreal as he was in this place. The face smiled, its warmth reaching through the mist to touch Fynch. But everything else was vague. Fynch surmised that the man seemed oddly short. His age and other features he could not make out other than a suggestion of dark hair.

Who are you? Fynch asked at last.

A friend. There was caution in the voice.

What are you?

Wyl Thirsk knows me as the Manwitch.

Myrren's father!

The man nodded.

Are you Knave as well?

There was the brief smile again as though he were congratulating the boy. *In a way.* He spoke softly. *But he is real enough.*

What do you want with me?

Your help, Fynch.

How?

Elysius shook his head. *Not now. Too dangerous like this. Come to me. Follow the dog. Trust him.*

But—

Go now. Send yourself back to your body. Forget Emil. We will talk soon.

Fynch did as he was told and moments later awoke. Knave had disappeared and people he recognized from the baker's shop were crowded around him. He came to his wits as if from a dream.

"What happened, lad?" someone asked.

"I'm sorry," he said. "I haven't eaten in days."

He heard them muttering about how tiny and skinny he was. He was used to this. Hands helped him stand. Others pushed food into his lap as they sat him down. People talked to him, talked around him, and worried about whether the ferocious dog might reappear.

"No," Fynch murmured. "He won't," he added, knowing Knave would be waiting for him now, ready to lead him.

There was no further need to search out Myrren's mother. He was traveling to meet Elysius, where he hoped he would be reunited with Wyl . . . or with whomever Wyl walked in, by the time he reached the Manwitch.

11

IT FELT STRANGE AND DANGEROUS TO BE ENTERING STONE-heart again. The last time he had come through its magnificent gates he had arrived as Romen, bringing the body of Wyl Thirsk back to clear his own name as well as rescue his sister. He thought of Ylena now, hoping she was safe at Felrawthy with Elspyth.

His thoughts were distracted by Aremys sidling his horse up alongside his own.

"I hope it was worth it," Wyl said bitterly. "Enjoy your money quickly, Aremys, because I shall hunt you down and kill you."

He turned toward the man who had betrayed him and noticed, for the first time, the sorrow.

"I regret it," Aremys admitted.

"Too late," Wyl replied. "You can't begin to imagine what you've done."

"I—"

But Wyl did not wait to hear what the mercenary had to say. He clicked his horse on and entered the bailey alongside Jessom.

"Be easy, Leyen," the Chancellor said. "He does not want you dead."

"What does he want?"

The Chancellor grimaced. "You achieved for him something important . . . something no one else could."

"Payment is enough thanks for me," Wyl snarled, handing his reins to the boys who had run toward the group.

"Not for him, apparently," Jessom said, climbing down

from his horse. "Oh, and by the way, he thinks you're a man."

Jessom requested that Aremys join him and Faryl in the audience with the King. It was clear the summons made Aremys feel uncomfortable, but he said nothing, simply nodded. They followed Jessom, who had learned that Celimus would be seeing them in the Orangery, an area the King had since claimed as his own. It was another stab in Wyl's heart that this part of Stoneheart, designed specifically for Ylena by her guardian, King Magnus, was now enjoyed by Celimus. He held his breath as the first waft of the orange perfume drifted by them, bringing a flood of memories of happier times spent with Alyd and Ylena.

"Let's hope the King is in good spirits today," Jessom murmured as they stepped down into the familiar sheltered courtyard, ringed by citrus trees laden with ripening fruit. "My liege," he said, bowing low.

Wyl let out his breath with hate as he saw Celimus turning toward them. The King had been staring out from the balustrades into the panoramic beauty of the meadows beyond. Wyl wished he had a knife. A swift throw and the cruel man before him would be taking his last gasp. Hanging, drawing, and quartering suddenly felt worth the pleasure of seeing Celimus dead.

Wyl bowed low, relieved that the man could not see the look on Faryl's face.

"Ah, Jessom. Welcome back and to your guests."

Even the smooth, resonant voice, so reminiscent of old King Magnus, Wyl realized, made his flesh crawl.

They straightened. Celimus stepped forward, tall and graceful, flicking an appreciative glance at the woman, but his attention was securely on Aremys. He reached out his hand for Aremys to bend over and touch to his lips, which the mercenary dutifully did.

"And you must be the one I have been looking forward to meeting. I wanted to thank you for your services in person. I trust we have rewarded you well?"

Aremys looked into the olive eyes of the stunningly handsome King he had heard so much about yet never seen for himself. Confusion passed across his face. "My lord, King. I . . . yes, the reward is ample." He looked at Jessom.

"Your highness," Jessom said softly, "this man is Aremys Farrow of Grenadyn. He has rid us of the Legionnaires responsible for stealing the royal monies."

Celimus looked sharply at Jessom. "Forgive me, Chancellor, I was under the distinct impression that you were bringing before me the person who has relieved me of a certain mercenary who threatened the Crown."

The King was displeased. His voice was suddenly hard and icy. He did not appreciate being embarrassed. The Chancellor moved smoothly on.

"I have, your majesty. May I introduce Leyen."

The olive gaze slid from Aremys to look into the face that Wyl hid behind. He held that familiar gaze steadily now despite feeling that he was being slithered over by a deadly snake. Celimus said nothing for a moment and that small silence was sizzling in its intensity.

"A woman?" he finally said.

Wyl bowed once again. He could hardly curtsy in the clothes he was wearing. He was not so sure he even knew how . . . perhaps Faryl might. These thoughts flitted through his mind as the full weight of the monarch's scrutiny rested upon him.

Close enough to kill with a single stab, Wyl thought, hoping his face was as expressionless as he was trying to make it.

"I am without words," Celimus admitted. "Once again you surprise me, Jessom."

"Your highness . . . I am your servant in all things," Jessom oozed.

Then came what Wyl dreaded. He blinked as he watched the hand of the King rise. He could not, would not ever, kiss that hand. He did not swear allegiance to this king. He would sooner die than do so. Celimus raised his hand casually, while his glance was one of almost infatuation with the woman who stood before him so proudly. Wyl bent over the hand, reaching to take it, and then exploded into a coughing fit. Celimus snatched back his hand as the woman he had been admiring suddenly erupted. He looked at Jessom, who appeared equally alarmed.

It was Aremys who rescued Wyl. "Your highness. Forgive us. We have been riding hard for a couple of days," he lied, "without adequate food or water. Leyen has suffered a vicious attack at the hands of those same men whose corpses I sent you, your majesty. That's how we came to meet. She is in need of rest and attention."

It was a long speech for Aremys. Perhaps a bit too long to be convincing, Wyl thought. Despite his misgivings about the man, he was grateful for his intervention.

"I see," Celimus said, not really seeing at all as Wyl continued to struggle with his contrived cough. "I have noted the injuries to your face, Leyen, and we will get you the attention you require. Jessom, see to it."

The Chancellor bobbed his head in agreement.

The King continued, irritation evident. "Let us meet later, then, when both of you have had sufficient time to recuperate."

He glanced toward his man with annoyance.

"Thank you, your highness," Jessom said, embarrassed.

"Have them join me for a private supper, tonight. I have things I wish to speak of to these people." He spoke as though neither of them was there. Grateful to be ignored, neither Wyl nor Aremys said anything further. They bowed and followed the Chancellor out of the courtyard.

"Not an auspicious beginning," Jessom spat as they moved out of earshot.

"My apologies," Wyl lied. "I really don't feel well."

"Be bright by tonight, Leyen," Jessom warned. "It will not go well for you to displease the King a second time." He glared. "He is unpredictable," he added, just in case either of them was not taking his advice seriously enough. "Follow me."

Aremys was housed in a separate wing of Stoneheart close to the Legion's quarters, which suited Wyl. He had no desire to have any further dealings with the man that were not absolutely necessary, such as the evening repast with the King. His own accommodations were sparse but comfortable and to his good fortune he saw Jorn racing by in one of the corridors, a worried look on his face. Wyl hailed him.

"Yes, madam," Jorn inquired, clearly in a hurry but just as keen not to offend one of the King's guests.

Wyl wished he could tell this lad the truth. "What is your name?"

"Jorn, madam. How may I serve?"

"You seem to be a little rushed just now."

"I am happy to help in any way I can," Jorn replied. He had grown up quickly, it seemed, at Stoneheart, for that sparkle in his eye and his eager manner were gone, replaced by polite language, a cautious approach, and a demeanor that suggested anything but happiness.

"Well . . . I was going to ask your advice actually, but may I request that you come by later when you are not quite so harried?"

Jorn looked surprised. "Have you no lady assigned to assist you?"

"It seems not, but then I require the advice which only a young man such as yourself could provide."

Now Jorn just looked worried. "In that case, madam, I shall return as soon as my immediate duties to his highness are complete."

"You work for the King?"

"I do. I am one of his personal messengers."

"Thank you, Jorn. I look forward to seeing you when you can spare a minute."

The lad bowed and hurried away. Wyl returned to his room to ponder this information. Jorn had personal access to the King's dealings. He could prove himself the ally he had so badly wanted to be when Wyl—as Romen—had fled Stoneheart with Ylena. How and what to tell him, though? It needed further thought. For now his immediate problem was what to wear tonight—every woman's dilemma. Wyl scowled, hating that it was as much a concern to him as it would be for any young woman having supper with a king.

He had nothing appropriate, obviously. He would have to speak with Jessom. In the meantime a bath was now very necessary and he had no choice but to make his way, grimacing, to the women's bathing pavilion.

Wyl had no idea of the drill. He was entering a mysterious world that had never previously been even remotely available to him. It was hushed and tranquil as he arrived within the special gardens that housed the pavilion. Outside the men's building, it was normally raucous, young men jostling and jockeying one another. Here women entered and exited in quiet conversation. They seemed to move in pairs, he noted, whereas the men tended to wander in as a boisterous herd. As General, he and his officers had a special area where they could go for more peaceful bathing. Nonetheless, they tended to form what was essentially just a smaller gang of the soldiers and they were as noisy and energetic. He hoped with all of his heart that Faryl's femininity would help guide him through this ordeal. She had surely visited bathhouses in the past, although there was no advice surfacing at present. He decided it was wise to opt for something as close to the truth as possible, and while he was thinking about all of this he had not realized that he was lurking rather than actually entering the pavilion.

"Are you all right?" a voice asked.

It was a middle-aged woman, one he recognized from his days at court.

"Er . . . my first time at Stoneheart. I'm a little daunted. It's very beautiful." And it was. The pavilion was delicate in design, aided by the use of beautiful glasswork of brilliant colors.

"Don't be, my dear," the woman said. "Come with me. I'll show you the ropes." She linked her arm in Wyl's. "What's your name?"

"Leyen."

"Pretty. Not from Pearlis or around here, then?"

"No." Wyl's mind raced. He had not thought about what

background to give. He wanted no link to Faryl whatsoever. "Er, I'm from a small village to the midnorth."

"Oh yes? Which one?" She was not going to be put off easily, he realized.

There was nothing for it but to lie. "Rittylworth." It was the first name that came into his head.

"Shar's Mercy. That poor place," the woman said, her voice suddenly grave.

"Pardon?"

But his companion was suddenly distracted by a group of other women arriving. *They sound like a gaggle of geese,* Wyl thought, amazed by the laughter and sudden burst of separate conversations that ensued.

"I won't desert you," his friend said, winking. "Take a towel and a robe. We undress over there." She pointed. "I'll be there in a moment."

There was nothing for it. He had to follow her instructions. He chose an elegantly shuttered cubicle for modesty, but most of the women just stripped down in the communal area. It was terrifying. Wyl felt way out of his depth now. He was going to have to walk naked to the baths.

He looked down at his full breasts; felt the familiar urge to gag and then steadied, trying to allay the fear of discovery. He took several long, shuddering breaths to compose himself.

He thought it through, berating himself in a furious whisper. *You're Leyen. No one bar Aremys knows any different and he knows nothing other than a name. They see only a woman's body. Now—*

"Leyen?" It was his friend knocking. "Are you in there?"

He closed his eyes. "Yes, I'm just coming," he said as lightly as he could, and reached for courage. Wyl opened the door and stepped out, his gaze looking at the floor.

"My, but you're a modest one," she said, and chortled softly. "Oh, my dear, with a body like yours, you have nothing to fear here other than all-consuming jealousy. I don't believe there is a flatter belly or tauter thighs among us. Now come, let me show you around."

"I don't know your name, I'm sorry," Wyl lied, still not risking a glance toward the naked woman who walked beside him arm in arm, her doughy flesh touching his own.

"Oh, how remiss of me." She chuckled. "I'm Lady Bench. But, please, as we have now strolled naked together, you must call me Helyn." She smiled warmly and Wyl blushed furiously.

"Thank you, Helyn," he said, knowing he must do his best to start acting like a woman and less like an impostor.

Wyl looked up and forward at last and was rewarded with a sight most men in the Legion would give a limb for. Perhaps fifty or sixty naked women, bathing, luxuriating, talking, some taking a smooth, others just being oiled. The atmosphere was serene yet playful—he wondered how they achieved that and his companion answered his thoughts.

"Welcome to the ladies' pavilion, Leyen," Helyn said. "All we do is gossip," she added. "We're all talking about each other, of course . . . but carefully." She winked again and her mood was infectious.

Wyl liked her. The bath was hotter than he expected as he stepped into the gently fizzing water, through which he could see a magnificent mosaic similar to the design he recalled from the men's pavilion. This building was more palatial, though. More glass, more light, paler marble, artworks adorning walls and smoothing tables made comfortable with cushions surrounding the main bathing pool. Everything just a little more luxurious, a little softer than the men enjoyed. The King, of course, had his own private villa in which to bathe and it was appreciably more decadent than this. Wyl was, in fact, one of a few people who had visited that villa but not on behalf of this king.

The chatter here was subdued—probably because of its content needing to be kept "just between us" and he grinned to himself. *So this is what Ylena used to get up to.*

"Ah, you must share the joke. Nothing is private here, Leyen," Helyn admonished in gentle fun. "Follow me—over here is my favorite spot."

The noblewoman gestured for Wyl to join her on a special seat built into the walls that allowed them to submerge themselves comfortably in the bath's warmth while still being in a position to talk with ease. Steam was rising off the surface of the water. Wyl commented on it, merely for conversation, as they settled themselves. He tried to keep his eyes occupied and his gaze not quite as lecherous as it seemed determined to be.

"They keep the temperature of the water in the ladies' pavilion warmer than the men's, I'm told. Apparently we women prefer it that way to steam our skin, keep our complexion healthy." She turned to level an inquiring gaze upon Wyl. "So, Leyen, who are you?"

"A guest," Wyl replied. "I'm handling some correspondence for the King between realms," he lied.

"No messenger I know of is accommodated as a guest of Celimus," Helyn observed.

"No messenger you know of is a special courier to Briavel," Wyl said evenly, wondering at the audacity of his own invention. He could thank Romen for the smooth way he responded . . . and lied.

"Indeed," she said, eyebrows raised, curiosity piqued. "Briavel? This can only be about the marriage."

"Press me no further, Lady Helyn. I am sworn to secrecy," he added theatrically, but hoping she might take the hint. It achieved the opposite effect, fueling her need to discover more.

This time the noblewoman's eyes narrowed. "You don't look like a simple courier."

"I am not and never will be simple, madam," Wyl replied, and laughed coquettishly. He recalled how Faryl had used this same mannerism at the Forbidden Fruit.

"I'll get to the bottom of you yet, Leyen of Rittylworth," Helyn said, enjoying the intrigue.

"Which reminds me, Lady Helyn. What did you mean earlier when you spoke of my home village?"

She looked at him sideways, confused. "Have you family?"

"No," he said carefully.

"You are fortunate, then. Little wonder you have not heard that it was torched."

Wyl felt his chest constrict. "Torched," he repeated in a small voice, the sight of naked women suddenly forgotten. "By whom?"

"They say bandits, but I have never heard of bandits who could be bothered torching a village. Ransacking it maybe, but they would not waste the time damaging it . . . for what end? You burn a village to teach its inhabitants a lesson."

An attendant arrived and squatted by them with a tray of multicolored layers.

Wyl looked confused.

"Oh dear, child. Wherever have you been hiding yourself? These are soap leaves, my girl. Take a few. Each is scented differently."

"Thank you," Wyl said, feeling like a dullard. In the men's pavilion there were merely strategically placed pots of soap paste. Nothing so dainty as these leaves. In truth, part of his confusion was that his mind was still in shock at the news. "I know only the dusty road, Lady Helyn, and inns with tin tubs they drag up the stairs to wash myself in. Forgive me my ignorance. But tell me, what of the monastery?"

Lady Helyn sighed as she began soaping herself. Wyl looked away, embarrassed, locking instead onto the sight of an attractive pair of breasts on the other side of the pool.

"Well, that was the worst part of it, Leyen. And why any fool would know this was not the work of bandits. The monks were killed, and not mercifully either. Everyone in the monastery was murdered."

Wyl must have paled because his new friend reached out to steady him.

"I'm so sorry to give you this news. You must have known many there."

"Yes . . . yes, I did. You say everyone was murdered?"

"Mmm, it's true. My husband deals with many merchants. One who passes through Rittylworth regularly said he had recognized the body of someone called Brother Jakub." She shrugged as if to say the name meant nothing to her. "The senior monks were nailed on crosses and burned.

Any visitors at the monastery were burned too . . . dreadful business."

Lady Bench continued talking, but Wyl had stopped listening. The horror of this information was too much for him to bear. Ylena dead? Her lovely face swam before him and he realized he could no longer remember her smile. His memory was of her virtually mute; her laughter gone from the moment she witnessed her husband's death, her life committed to sorrow. Perhaps she had welcomed death, he thought. His entire family was dead, including himself, in a way. The killers had not been bandits. He agreed with Lady Bench. Bandits did not bother with torching villages. Only a sadist would do such a thing. A sadist with power, that is. Celimus, who else! But how could the King possibly have known where he had taken his sister? He had covered Romen's tracks too well. He felt his whole being fighting back the urge to make his way to the King's rooms and, come what may, kill him.

And then another horrific thought occurred to him. Had Elspyth perished too?

"When did this occur?" he demanded.

"Pardon me?" Lady Bench said, turning back toward Wyl, having engaged someone passing by in a polite salutation. "Oh . . . I would guess at about three days ago." She waded off with her friend with a wink toward Wyl, as though she had latched onto some juicy gossip. "Won't be long," she mouthed.

Wyl was relieved she had given him a few moments alone. His mind felt dazed. This news was more shocking than the thought of having to sup with Celimus tonight. How could it have happened? Who knew? Who could have told the King where to go looking for Ylena? . . . They had covered their tracks so well.

If she had traveled quickly, Wyl calculated, then Elspyth would certainly have been there when the attackers came and there was no hope for either of them. He could only pray to Shar that she had reached Ylena and gotten her away to safety. And then, irrationally, he hoped that Elspyth had ignored his needs, broken her promise, and gone directly to her home. But he knew she would not have done that. Elspyth was steadfast and true; she would have kept her oath to him and walked straight into danger. Poor Ylena. Beautiful and fragile. He had failed her.

Lady Bench floated back. "My dear, you look very pale."

"I'm sorry. The news of Rittylworth has upset me."

"And I feel bad that I was the messenger of painful tidings. Come, wash yourself, and then you are to return with me."

"To where?"

"To my house."

Wyl wanted to be alone with his sorrowful thoughts, but he also did not really want to be within Stoneheart.

"It's just a spit from the palace," she urged. "We can share a light meal and you can spend some quiet time in my gardens. It will be better for you than here. I shall leave you in peace if you wish—you can even stay the night?"

"I'm having supper with the King tonight," he said distractedly.

"Shar save us, girl! You are important."

"Not really," Wyl said, wondering why he had blurted out that information. "I have nothing to wear."

"Well, I have plenty!" Helyn said, suddenly galvanized. "I'll hear no argument. You're coming with me."

Without further discussion, Wyl found himself dried, dressed, and in Lady Helyn's carriage bound for her home. She was alone right now; her husband away again and her only daughter staying with friends.

He had to admit it was good for him to be diverted in this way. His inclination was to jump on a horse and start riding for Rittylworth, but his soldier's mind told him there was little he could do. Whatever had happened would not change and his arrival would not make the carnage any less tragic. He had an appointment with the King he had to keep and he had begun to convince himself that Elspyth had gotten to the monastery in time and that both women were together and on the run to Felrawthy.

Jakub would not have allowed harm to come to Ylena. At

the first hint of trouble, he would have hidden her in that secret grotto and hopefully gotten her to safety.

Lady Bench was right. He did feel better for the solitude and she had been as good as her word, leaving him alone for a while. Wyl could tell Helyn was glad of the company and the opportunity to fuss around her new friend. He was not completely taken in by the attention, realizing that Lady Helyn was no doubt a pivotal and indeed powerful member of the nobility who sensed the chance to be in on secretive dealings of the King. She herself had mentioned to Wyl how Pearlis thrived on gossip and hearsay and that she was no different from other women, not that she had expressed as much—but a bored, wealthy woman was always going to be prey to intrigues. Wyl appreciated, however, that Lady Bench was intelligent as well as wise, for she knew when not to push for the information she so desperately craved. Instead, when she finally joined him, they talked about every subject under the sun, bar the King's marriage.

At least until it came time to help Wyl find some suitable attire for the evening.

"Leyen, we must find you an appropriate gown for your rendezvous with Celimus."

They were sipping mint tea in her exquisite gardens. Nearby her aviary of chittering canaries was a mass of color and movement. The pond around which they sat was filled with fat, flame-colored fish who occasionally broke the surface of the water around the delicate cups of water lilies. The garden was a sun trap, hanging on to every last smile from above, and so they were warm out here with the help of soft rugs that Wyl did not need but politely accepted. It was a serene place and certainly helped Wyl to take control of his churning emotions.

"Lady Helyn, I hope you won't take it as rude when I say we are not necessarily of a size. I am taller, for a start," Wyl said, feeling clumsy. Despite his best efforts, he believed he gave offense. No woman alive liked to hear about another being taller, slimmer, prettier . . . no matter how old she might be.

". . . And infinitely trimmer too," she said, laughing. She placed her glass on the small table beside her. "I was thinking about a gown from my daughter's wardrobe. Shar knows I lavish enough of my husband's fortune on that girl's back. She won't even notice one gone, my dear. Only the other day I took a delivery from Amos Rilk, master tailor of Briavel— my daughter's first formal ballgown and a small fortune in gold."

"You use a tailor from Briavel?"

"None finer. They say he dresses the Queen."

"Then he is privileged indeed," Wyl replied, wishing he could dress Briavel's queen . . . or rather undress her.

"Have you met her majesty?" Helyn inquired innocently.

"Yes."

"And?"

"She is very . . ." He wanted to say, *Easy to love, wonderful to kiss,* but he said, "Statuesque. Rilk would surely be in raptures hanging his fabrics from her shoulders."

"Hmm, I hear she is an extraordinary beauty."

"She is. But Valentyna"—he saw Helyn's eyes widen in surprise at his casual use of the monarch's name—". . . er, I mean the Queen, is not a vain woman, from what I can gather. In truth, I have seen her more comfortable in her riding breeches than in her gowns."

"You've mingled with her at formal functions, then . . . as well as less formal?"

"A couple."

"As her guest, no doubt," Helyn said, unable to hide the irony in her voice.

"Lady Helyn, forgive me. I have mentioned that much of my work is covert between the monarchs. I am not permitted to discuss it."

"I understand. My apologies. I don't mean to pry, but as you can understand, we Morgravians are all very excited about this marriage."

"Are you?"

"Of course! Aren't you? We all want peace. Valentyna brings it by marrying Celimus. Perhaps she can also temper his wayward pursuits—although if you ever repeat that, Leyen, I'll publicly denounce you!"

Wyl laughed in spite of his churning emotions. Made the gesture of locking his lips with a key. "How far have they progressed?" he asked.

"Regrettably, not far enough," she said to his relief. "I believe it will happen, though. Certainly all the nobility is pressing for it to occur by the spring equinox."

"Spring," Wyl murmured. Four moons was all he had to save Valentyna.

"So tonight, no doubt, you will be taking another message from Celimus to his beautiful Valentyna?"

"No doubt." Wyl grimaced.

"It's very clever that he uses a woman for this role. Who would suspect. Now, let us choose something from my daughter's wardrobe. We must put him in a good mood."

This was the last thing he felt like doing. His mind was fraying just thinking about Rittylworth, but Faryl and Romen's essences kept him strong.

Lady Bench led Wyl to one of the dressing chambers, chatting along the way about the type of woman Celimus usually favored. Wyl allowed her to ramble.

"I think olive green is your color, my dear, with that lovely hair. And perhaps a matching cape? Which reminds me, have they given you a maid?"

Wyl shook his head.

"Right, I'll send over one of my girls. She'll dress your hair with some flowers I'll send with her. Fresh gardenias, from my glasshouse. Hope you don't find their perfume too overwhelming?"

"No. But your generosity is, Lady Helyn."

"Don't mention it. I want to cheer you after your news, and who knows, I may be responsible for helping you find yourself in the King's bed." She winked at her friend as a co-conspirator, and was alarmed by the look of horror on Leyen's face. "Oh, my dear, just a jest . . . a little joke from a silly woman with nothing else to occupy her mind."

12

WYL LOOKED AT HIMSELF IN THE MIRROR AFTER LADY HELYN'S maid had departed. He hardly recognized this person he saw. Before him stood a tall, striking woman. Polished hair was swept up into an intricate design behind his head and interwoven with delicate, tiny gardenias. He would require no perfume tonight, as the fragrant flowers more than compensated.

Helyn had decided against the olive green in the end and chosen a soft cream gown for simplicity. It draped elegantly from his broad, square shoulders, softening the long, muscular arms. His lightly browned skin had been carefully smoothed and creamed by the maid until it too shone, and then, to Wyl's fascination, she had dusted it softly with a gold powder. The effect was to make his skin shimmer as he moved, and by lamp or candlelight it was a stunning addition for any woman looking to impress a man. For Wyl it was a fascinating insight into the female armory of allurement.

Helyn's generosity had not abated, for she had also sent one of her own items of jewelry to drape around his neck. A small ruby now hung like a drop of blood at his throat. No additional adornment was required other than a dab of soft kohl at his eyes to deepen their dark intensity and a smudge of tawny color on his lips. Wyl despised the taste and gluey heaviness but knew Leyen looked superb and he dared not wipe his lips clean of the annoying color. The maid had trimmed and buffed his nails until they too shone.

He was complete. Lady Bench had sent a beautiful indigo cape that he tried on but decided he would not need.

As he stared at his reflection, Wyl hoped that the King would not take a liking to what he saw, other than in a professional capacity. He was relying on his own knowledge that Celimus had always tended toward flaxen-haired beauties. He had once overhead Celimus admit that their fairness made his swarthiness look all the more dramatic. Wyl also knew that the new King preferred weaker women, ones he could dominate, which is why he, Wyl, must allow Faryl's strong personality to shine. It also made the match with Valentyna such a poor choice for Celimus—she did not suit his taste for golden-haired women and her feisty, regal style did not lend itself to his domineering manner.

Wyl realized, though, it was not Valentyna whom Celimus loved but the riches she brought and the peace their marriage would achieve. Should Morgravia join Briavel, the whole region could grow wealthier still and Celimus's heir would rule over two great realms. Wyl grimaced at the thought of Celimus siring an heir to Valentyna. And then it occurred to him that perhaps the King was looking even further afield. With peace achieved across the southern realms, the new union could deal with the people of the Razors and their upstart mountain king.

Spring equinox. The thought nagged repeatedly.

There was a soft knock at the door that turned out to be Jorn.

"Too late," Wyl said. "I've already chosen." He added, "Do you approve?"

"My lady," Jorn said, blushing. "What could there be to disapprove of?"

"Well-spoken, Jorn. Come in. You've been busy, I gather?"

"Yes, my lady," Jorn replied, stepping carefully into the chamber and leaving the door ajar.

"Close it, would you?" Wyl said.

The lad did so, clearly uncomfortable.

Wyl sensed this. "Jorn, let me put your mind at rest. We have a mutual acquaintance." This won the lad's attention. "I am a friend of Romen Koreldy."

At this, the young man's eyes lit up. Wyl was pleased Romen had made a sufficient impression.

"I'm honored, then, to know you. He is someone I admire."

Guilt raged through Wyl. The truth would not work, however.

"Tell me, how are you getting on here?"

"Did he ask you to inquire after me?" Jorn said, his eagerness heartbreaking.

"Yes, in a way."

"And the Lady Ylena. Tell me she is well, Madam Leyen?"

"In truth, I have not seen Ylena in a long time. I—"

Jorn cut across his words. "Because I have worried myself sick over hearing recently that Rittylworth has been ransacked, knowing she had gone there."

Wyl felt a twist in the pit of his stomach as a piece of the jigsaw slotted into place. It was Jorn who had told them. Innocent, eager Jorn had unwittingly led Celimus to Ylena like a cat to cream. He felt sick, thinking again about the kind and wise Brother Jakub, the young lad, Pil, all those monks murdered so cruelly in Celimus's pursuit of the Thirsk line.

A vision of his sister lying broken and dead somewhere hit his thoughts like a clap of thunder. *She is alive,* he told himself.

He took a steadying breath, working hard not to betray his fright. He could not blame the boy. "Jorn, did you know specifically where Koreldy was headed when he left Stoneheart?"

"Not really, madam. He mentioned something about the northwest and possibly Rittylworth, but he wasn't sure at that time, as I recall."

Wyl remembered wanting to bite out his own tongue when he had let that slip. "And did you mention this to anyone?" he asked, casually turning to look in the mirror and busy himself with checking his appearance so as not to arouse any suspicion in Jorn.

"I . . . um. I might have, yes. I think Chancellor Jessom was making some inquiries."

"Ah, yes, I know Jessom," Wyl said in a tight tone.

"Is everything all right?"

"Of course," Wyl reassured, forcing himself to keep his voice even. "In fact, I have promised Koreldy that I'll visit the Lady Ylena the next time I passed through the region."

"She's not at Argorn, then?" Jorn asked sadly.

Wyl recalled how Ylena had promised Jorn that she would send for him once she returned to her family home.

He shook his head. "I can't be sure, Jorn." Anything to keep the truth from getting out.

"Oh," the lad said, deflated. Then his eyes lit again. "You might care to try the duchy of Felrawthy, then, madam. Her husband's family are the Donals and she might well be visiting the far north. I gather it's really not that far from Rittylworth."

Damn the lad's excellent memory. Wyl's anxieties increased. How to keep this boy quiet without provoking suspicion? "Thank you. I shall make some inquiries."

Poor Jorn. He was determined that the promise not be forgotten, even if it meant chewing the ear off a visitor who might meet up with Ylena Thirsk. "Because she said she'd send for me, Madam Leyen."

Wyl put a kind smile on his face despite his fears for Ylena. "Is being in her service more important than serving the King, Jorn?"

The lad flushed scarlet. "I would die for her," he stammered.

This was a shock. Wyl's immediate reaction was to suggest that Jorn hardly knew Ylena well enough to pledge such a lofty sacrifice. But he himself had fallen in love with Valentyna within moments of her turning that direct blue gaze upon him. He sighed, noted Jorn was still blushing and uncomfortable.

Wyl found a grin for him. "Well, let's hope you never have to, Jorn," he said, praying that his sister's life was safe. "But now that you've expressed your loyalties," he added, taking advantage of the boy's weakness for Ylena, "I'd suggest you observe them as sharply as ever while not speaking of it to anyone. Do you understand?" And then he could not help but emphasize it further. "Be discreet to the point of silence."

Jorn nodded, but it was accompanied by a puzzled expression. Wyl would have to let the lad figure it out for himself. He could say nothing more direct.

"Well, I believe I'm expected in the King's suite. Thank you for coming," Wyl said.

"Call upon me anytime, Madam Leyen. Please give my regards to Romen Koreldy when you see him."

"And what shall I give of yours to the Lady Ylena should our paths cross?" Wyl said to the boy's back.

He was relieved to see Jorn grin. So the young fellow did have a sense of humor and was not all earnest effort. Wyl smiled his farewell. Jorn might yet prove useful.

It was a mild evening, made milder still by the braziers burning in a circle around yet another private courtyard in Stoneheart. The castle boasted at least a dozen such courtyards that Wyl could remember being in at one time or another as he grew up, but this one he did not recognize. It was very compact, ringed by beds of herbs and greenery, including several fine bay trees. There were none of the spectacular flowers that King Magnus had been known for, but this area was nonetheless beautiful in its simple, somewhat stark design.

Its ordered structure contrasted with the breathy fragrances of the herbs that mingled in the warmth, creating a sensuous atmosphere. In the center of the courtyard was a table, around which was placed four chairs. Once again Wyl was struck by the restraint shown in the table's setting. He had expected something more overt from Celimus. The King had excellent taste but leaned toward flashy. What he was looking upon now was far too understated, more to his own taste, in fact, and he felt instantly comfortable in this small square of Stoneheart.

Aremys was already in attendance. He had a cup of wine in his hand and was talking softly with the Chancellor, whom Wyl presumed made tonight's guest a foursome. He watched the mercenary turn, saw the breath catch in the man's throat, and he realized in that instant—perhaps for the first time—what power an attractive woman held over most men.

"Leyen, you look very lovely." Jessom gave the rare honor of a bow.

Aremys gathered his wits and inclined his head. "Leyen."

"Thank you, gentlemen," Wyl said. "One of the noblewomen took pity on me and insisted on dressing me tonight," he added, lest they hope this was part of his regular wardrobe.

"She did you proud," Aremys replied in a tight tone. He coughed softly to clear his throat then drained his cup.

Jessom held out a goblet. "May I offer you wine?"

"You may," Wyl said, graciously taking the goblet and raising it. "What shall we drink to? Forgiveness, no doubt?" The dryness of the comment was not lost on either of his dining companions.

"To duty," Aremys replied.

Jessom gave a cold smile and raised his glass.

Wyl sipped the sweetish aperitif as he looked around at the garden once again. "This is certainly a most beautiful courtyard."

"I'm glad you approve," the King responded airily as he made a majestic entry at the top of the shallow flight of stairs.

His guests bowed, Wyl forced to provide the more traditional curtsy now that he was dressed in a gown. He couldn't imagine how clumsy he must have looked. Still, Celimus seemed not to notice. Instead he was appraising the woman who stood before him. He remained on the stairs for the moment, preferring not to come down to their level, and in those few seconds Wyl was reminded that Celimus cut the most dashing of figures, resplendent in superb garments that were tailored perfectly to show off his tall, lean physique. Even bathed and groomed, Aremys looked like a scruffy bear by comparison.

Wyl felt the familiar hate curdle within. All the old feelings returned, threatening to unbalance him, but he reminded himself that he was no longer short and stocky with orange hair and freckles. He was tall and lithe, certainly not beautiful . . . not even pretty in the accepted sense of the word. Memorable, though. He had nothing to feel inferior about. He was the only woman in the company tonight. He must use that femininity wisely and negotiate his passage as far away from Stoneheart as possible.

Celimus finally descended the stairs. Instead of proffering his own, he took his guest's hand and leaned over to kiss it, shocking Wyl. He had to let it happen. The feel of those cruel lips, which had once ordered the death of Alyd, against his own flesh made it crawl. Wyl controlled his inclination to shrink away from Celimus's touch.

The dark gaze swept upward to meet his own. "I designed it myself," he said, continuing where he had left off. "In honor of my bride to be, whom I'm assured loves herb gardens and simplicity in all design. Good evening, Leyen." His eyes sparkled.

"Highness," Wyl said, bowing his head, hating the King's confidence that Valentyna was already his.

The others followed suit, bowing low once again.

"What are we drinking, Jessom?" Celimus asked, all ease and charm.

"It's the Cherenne, sire, your favorite."

"Ah, indeed. Come, let's sit," the King said, and at his nod a host of servants descended to lay platters of savories.

Small talk accompanied the food until a delicate fish course was served, after which Celimus banished the servants. None of his guests needed to be told that what the King had to say from here on was private.

"So, Leyen . . . I understand you're Morgravian?"

Wyl nodded carefully at the King, the sweet sauce that had set off the fish so magnificently suddenly souring in his mouth.

"From where exactly?"

Wyl needed to keep the truth from Celimus, but he remembered what he had told his new friend, Lady Helyn, and thought it would be best to stick to his story. "Rittylworth, your majesty." He decided not to be defensive. "Although I have heard since arriving here of its demise."

At this, the King stopped swallowing from a goblet of wine. "I'm sorry to hear that you were raised there. It was a necessary lesson."

Wyl appreciated Celimus's candor. He had expected lies. "What lesson is that, your highness?" he asked innocently, taking a small mouthful of the fish and not eyeing the King.

"That traitors and those who harbor them will be hounded down and dealt with."

Wyl simply nodded, his expression blank while his blood boiled. He knew Aremys watched him carefully too, particularly as the mercenary knew Faryl was from Coombe and not Rittylworth. Wyl had told him as much during their ride.

"Do you know of this village, Aremys?" Celimus said.

"Yes, highness. I have passed through it on occasion; but mostly around it."

"A sleepy enough place," Jessom commented, not wishing to be entirely left out of the conversation.

"And one stupid enough to protect those who would betray their sovereign," Celimus said.

"May I ask whom among my people you sought, sire?" Wyl asked as gently as he could, this time sipping from his wine so the King would not see the twist of hate on his mouth.

"Ylena Thirsk."

"A woman?" Aremys blurted out, and Jessom glared.

Celimus did not react. "Yes," he said mildly, "as Leyen here testifies, women can be so much more subtle than men in their intrigues."

Wyl smiled for the King, hating him. "How was this Ylena a problem for you, your highness?"

The King sighed. "The whole Thirsk family was traitorous, to be truthful. My father, may his soul rest in Shar's safekeeping, protected them for too long. This is all rather tedious but probably worth your knowing," he said airily, reaching for his goblet before leaning back in his chair. "Old Fergys Thirsk was my father's best friend . . . apparently," he said, loading the final word with irony. He grinned, white teeth perfect. "He was a villain of the highest order and would have stabbed my father in the back at the first chance, although I guess he found it easier to poison my father instead—metaphorically speaking, of course." Celimus chuckled softly.

Jessom gave his usual cold grimace in response, while Aremys remained motionless and watchful, unsure of his place around this table. Wyl could only hold together his own composure by clasping his hands so tight his knuckles were white. He was glad of night's darkness and he used all that was Koreldy and Faryl within to fix a tight, calm smile at his mouth.

The King continued. "I was thrilled beyond my wildest dreams when I heard old Thirsk had been cut down. He could not have died quickly enough for me." Celimus sipped the Cherenne. "I know what you're all thinking: How could a child hate so much? But I hated that man for taking all of my father's love, his friendship . . . not to mention land and wealth, while all the time working against the realm."

"Forgive me, sire," Wyl said, simply unable to remain still any longer. "I thought I had heard that General Fergys Thirsk had taken the sword slash meant for King Magnus. It was told in the taverns of the north, where I was traveling at the time, that he sacrificed his life willingly for his sovereign."

The King shrugged, a rueful smile just touching his perfectly shaped lips. "Who knows what truly happened on that battlefield, Leyen. My father might have protected Thirsk's name to the very last. For all we know, it was a conspiracy and someone from our own side killed the General for his devious ways. I would reward that man if I knew him."

Wyl let out a choked sound that he quickly checked by grabbing his glass. Celimus's contrived story was too ridiculous to cause him to feel any further insult. The King had nothing to substantiate his vile and slanderous claims, all but making up the story as he told it.

"You are amused, Leyen?" Celimus said, missing nothing. "How so?"

"Apologies, sire. Not amusement, one of these scrumptious dried figs has stuck in my throat." He swallowed several mouthfuls of the wine, his glance straying to Aremys, who was watching him carefully, one eyebrow raised in question. "Please, your highness," Wyl said, "forgive my interruption and continue."

Celimus did just that, outlining his newfound hate at the arrival of the son of Fergys Thirsk, their tumultuous childhood, and the story of the younger Thirsk's betrayal in Briavel. "Oh, how I wished we ran our army on the merit system. This tradition of handing down through a warrior family may be pleasant enough for the shrunken men of olden days, but these are modern times, and simply because the family had one hero in an ancient Thirsk does not necessarily mean it breeds them," Celimus spat.

"Hear, hear, sire," Jessom muttered, signaling to a watchful servant some distance away that the plates could now be cleared.

A magnificent spread of cheeses, glacéed fruits, and sweet fudges were laid out swiftly; once again the serving staff moving deliberately to be away from the table almost as quickly as they arrived.

When it was just the four of them again, Aremys cleared his throat. "Your majesty, I'm not sure I understand why I've been privy to this intriguing tale, but I'm wondering how a young woman, a nobleman's daughter, whose head is no doubt more filled with visions of lace and satin than politics, could be of any threat to your sovereignty."

The King nodded. "Indeed, Aremys. Well said. It is complicated and I don't wish to bore present company any further with those complexities." *I bet you don't,* Wyl thought. The King kept talking. "Suffice to say, Ylena Thirsk continues a fine family tradition of treachery. It is my belief that she is on her way now to the powerful Duke of Felrawthy to stir up trouble."

Wyl could hardly believe the joy he felt at hearing this statement. "So you didn't find her at Rittylworth, sire?"

"No, indeed we did not. Which brings me to why we are

here tonight," he said, his tone suggesting he would brook no further interruption. "I want you, Leyen, and you, Aremys, to travel to Felrawthy. Hopefully you can intercept Ylena Thirsk on her journey."

"And?" Wyl asked, hardly daring to breathe.

"Kill her," Celimus replied. "It's what you do, isn't it?"

Both Aremys and Wyl nodded, both stunned but for different reasons.

"Good," Celimus said. "Jessom, make the usual arrangements, will you? Provide them with horses, coin, whatever they need. No one, and I mean no one, is to know of this mission." He eyed each of them, a threat behind the look.

Again Aremys cleared his throat softly. He had noticed the shock pass across Faryl's face, and that she had covered herself adroitly. What was going on? he wondered.

"Any questions?" Celimus asked.

Aremys sat forward. "Your highness. May I ask why the Duke would protect her against you? Surely he would curry favor with the Crown rather than risk all for an old friend's daughter?"

"There are reasons. Please trust my judgment on this. I am hiring your services, not your understanding, mercenary."

Aremys nodded politely yet grew more bold. "Then may I inquire as to why the simple task of murder requires two of us?"

"I suspect if she has made it as far as the Duke, then it will take some extra planning, because he is well protected with his own men. One of Fergys Thirsk's cronies, I'm afraid, who grew fat and rich at the Crown's expense. I'm sending you as a special support, Aremys, should things turn ugly, although I suspect Leyen is capable of pulling this off, considering her last successful task for me." Celimus smiled slyly, the glance sliding off Aremys toward Wyl, who had composed his face into a polite mask. "I want proof of her death—more than a finger this time, Leyen," he cautioned.

Wyl's lips thinned and he stood. "Then we should make our arrangements to leave tomorrow, sire," he said, no longer able to spend another minute in the King's company.

"I accept the commission, your highness. I shall away to my rooms to make my preparations."

"So soon, Leyen. I thought we might take some more wine together," the King replied.

"Er, forgive me, highness." He could sense Aremys's scrutiny and Jessom's aghast expression at his audacity. "I need a good night's rest and a clear head. My intention is most certainly to intercept this Ylena Thirsk before she reaches Felrawthy." He became businesslike, keen to extract himself now from all these men. "How many days does she have on us, sire?"

"Three, as I understand it." Celimus looked toward Jessom, who confirmed this with a brief nod. "But I know she escaped on foot. One of the villagers saw her leave. According to this source, one of the monks helped her. One so new his pate had yet to be shaved."

Shar bless you, Pil, Wyl thought, recalling Koreldy's young friend at the monastery.

"Then we should waste no further time," Aremys said, pushing back his chair. "Leyen is right. We must leave at first light to have any chance of catching them."

Celimus shrugged. "So be it. Remember now, I want a corpse. For this I will pay you each a fortune in gold. The Chancellor will discuss terms. Perhaps that should be attended to now, Jessom, as our guests seem determined to leave Stoneheart almost as soon as they have arrived." He held up his hand. "But I understand and applaud you for it. You will be well favored by me if you rid me of the Thirsk curse."

Aremys had walked around to be at Wyl's side. He bowed, putting pressure on Wyl's arm, forcing him to follow suit. Wyl curtsied as best he could.

"Oh, and Leyen," Celimus said, an afterthought occurring. "I have another mission for you when this is done."

"Yes, sire?" Wyl said, his voice tightly controlled.

"Mmm. If you have a moment?" he said. "You may go, Aremys, Jessom."

Wyl watched Aremys leave. There was something in his expression that told Wyl to be careful. The King returned his gaze to Wyl. "When you are done with the Thirsk woman, I want you to go straight to Briavel."

Wyl could only nod, wondering what terrible deed Celimus was going to ask of him next.

"I want you to take a document to Queen Valentyna for me which I shall have delivered to you tonight. It is my proposal of marriage . . . my last, in fact, and I want you to bring back her signed agreement to wed this coming spring."

"And if she should refuse me, sire?" Wyl asked it matter-of-factly, careful to keep his voice devoid of all emotion.

The answer was delivered in an identical businesslike manner. "You will kill her and I will invade Briavel and destroy its Crown once and for all. See that you succeed with both women. You are free to go now."

Wyl fled the beautiful courtyard, his emotions ragged, all but running past a stunned Aremys and Jessom.

13

WYL HAD NO INTENTION OF WAITING FOR AREMYS OR UNTIL dawn. The three women he cared about were under threat from the same man and it was a terrible choice who to try to help first.

Ylena, it had to be.

If Aremys got to her first, then she was as good as dead. He could rely on brave Elspyth to do her best to reach Ylena, and if they had not already joined forces, then Elspyth had the werewithal to go on to Felrawthy and deliver the note. He realized she was penniless, but he also knew she was resourceful and courageous. As for Valentyna, she was the most protected, at least for now. With these thoughts cluttering his already swirling mind, he raced back to his rooms and packed his gear. Rousing a sleepy page, he asked the lad to find Jorn for him. While he impatiently waited he scribed a note to the Lady Helyn and tucked it into the pocket of the accompanying cape she had sent but he had not used. He changed out of her daughter's gown into his comfortable traveling clothes.

Jorn arrived, still rubbing his eyes awake. "Madam Leyen," he whispered, noticing her garb. "Where do you go at this time of night?"

"Hush, Jorn," Wyl whispered, dragging the lad fully into the room. "You must never mention to anyone that we had this conversation."

The boy's eyes widened now, fully awake. "Heart crossed and hope to die," Jorn said, making a sign over his chest.

Wyl mustered a smile for the lad. "Good. Now listen to me. Lady Ylena is in trouble. I leave now to find her, but I must do so in secret. I need your help."

He eyed the boy and Jorn nodded mutely.

"You must fetch my horse for me." Wyl pressed a pouch into Jorn's palm. "Here's coin to pay whomever you have to in order to get me safe passage out of Stoneheart."

Jorn, to his credit, did not even glance toward the bag of money. "But what excuse can I have?"

"You are the King's messenger. Use your status. Tell them I travel on the King's business. Everyone knows I am a guest of Celimus, some sort of courier. Be confident, they will believe you. Just use the coin to grease their palms—they will ask few questions. Offer my sincere apologies for disturbing them at this late hour."

"I'll do it, of course, but this sounds dangerous, Madam Leyen."

"No, I promise you it is not. Just irregular. If it were broad daylight no one would think twice."

"Am I to fetch Master Aremys as well?" Jorn asked.

"No! He especially must not know that I depart." Wyl gripped the lad's arm, concerned he even knew about the other guest. "Promise me."

Once again Jorn nodded, barely understanding but prepared to do what was asked of him.

Wyl pointed toward the bed. "This gown and cape. They are to be returned to Lady Helyn Bench, together with this jewelry. Please be careful with it."

Jorn was expecting something more difficult. "I can arrange that."

"Thank you."

"Do you wish to send a note with it?"

Wyl thought a moment. Truth was danger to this boy. "No," he lied. "Simply return them with my thanks for their use." He had already tucked the note inside a hidden pocket within the cape. He had to hope the Lady Helyn would find it.

"Do it as quickly as you can for me, would you?" Wyl asked, embellishing his plea with another lie: "I believe her daughter would like it returned for her own use tomorrow evening." It was a thin guise but Jorn was not really paying attention to such detail. He had his tasks now and was keen to move.

"I will fix all of this for you. Promise me, Madam Leyen . . ."

Wyl looked at him, suddenly feeling the weight of responsibility he was leaving with this innocent. "Yes?"

"Remember me kindly to the Lady Ylena. Let her know I await her summons."

Wyl felt a sharp pang of grief for Jorn. He would send for him himself as soon as he reached Felrawthy. "I will do that for you. Await her summons."

Jorn gave a dazzling smile. "Then I must hurry about my duty, madam." He bent low over Wyl's hand and, surprisingly, kissed it before turning for the door. "Leave as soon as you hear the next bell. I will have everything readied by then. Your horse will be at the southern end of the stables."

"Thank you, Jorn . . . for everything."

The lad smiled once more and left.

Wyl used the time to tie his hair back tightly and pull on a jacket. He looked around the chamber, checking that all was as it should be. Aremys would surely come looking in the morning and he wanted to leave no clues. He double-checked that the note was securely tucked inside the pocket of the cape. He grimaced. He was risking much in sending it—its contents damning if intercepted—but he hoped his judgment of the noblewoman was on the mark.

The bell sounded not long after and Wyl slipped from his room and stealthily made his way down corridors and through familiar halls. He encountered no one but a maid, who took little notice of him anyway—she was in a hurry, rushing from the scullery carrying hot water and towels. Wyl presumed a baby was about to be born somewhere in the bowels of Stoneheart. He continued on until he was outside, passing by the kitchens he had so loved as a youngster and then through a small vegetable patch reserved especially for meals served to the sovereign, before passing into a courtyard that led to the stables.

As promised, Jorn met him at the southern end. He led Leyen's horse, fully saddled.

"Any trouble?" Wyl asked, his chest tight with tension.

"None. Come, I will walk you out the gate. It will look better."

Wyl nodded. He put his foot on Jorn's linked hands and stepped up lightly onto the horse. Jorn tied on Leyen's small bag.

"Thank you again for this," Wyl uttered.

"Don't mention it, Madam Leyen. We work for the same cause."

Wyl wanted to shake his head. Such loyalty. He felt pride burst in his chest at the lad's dedication. At least the Thirsk family had one friend. Jorn led the horse slowly toward the main gates.

"Have you already spoken with the guard?" Wyl whispered.

"Yes. Fret not."

Wyl was impressed with Jorn's cool head. They approached a guard, who stopped them.

"This is an odd departure time," he commented, but with only idle interest.

"My apologies. As you know, being a servant of the King is never a predictable service," Wyl said, and risked a wink.

The man shrugged, understanding the meaning of the woman's words. "In that you are right," he admitted. "Go safely, madam."

"Are you sure you will be safe in the darkness? Felrawthy is many days away," Jorn muttered, worried.

Wyl grimaced. He did so wish the boy would learn to keep his knowledge to himself. "The dark is my friend, Jorn. It alone is my safety right now."

"I don't understand," the lad said, walking the horse out and away from the gates.

Wyl turned and waved thanks to the guard. He knew he could have overheard his destination, but hopefully he would not have digested the information. It was too late to worry; he just had to impress on the boy to keep quiet. "You will. Keep this our secret now; tell no one where I go. May Shar watch over you, Jorn."

"And you."

Wyl took the reins, ruffled the lad's hair, and clicked his horse into a fast trot. He did not risk looking back.

Aremys paced, unable to sleep. He was quartered near the Legion and he could still hear some of the men singing quietly or talking in muted tones. But it was not the men who kept him awake. It was Leyen . . . or Faryl, more to the point. Something was amiss. The speed at which she left the King's courtyard earlier this evening had come as a surprise. She had looked rattled too. The secrets he knew she kept seemed all the more potent tonight. He could see her discomfort in the way she carried herself, her stiffness around the King, and especially the way she reacted to talk of the Thirsk family.

It was obvious—to him at least—that Faryl was not happy at her task. He wondered why Celimus had held her back. Faryl had only been with the King minutes past his own departure, so talk was all that could have occurred and not much of that even. It was clear something that had passed between the King and Faryl had disturbed her.

It was none of his business, he knew. And yet he had already lied for her. Why? He liked her, that was true. But there was more. He was not sure yet what it was, but he had learned over the years to trust his instincts. They were screaming at him that Faryl was in some sort of trouble. Perhaps she could use his help?

Could he go to her? Would she answer his knock at this late hour? Probably not . . . probably never. Her coldness toward him was intense. His betrayal had shocked her.

"I would take it all back if I could, Faryl," he whispered to himself. "I'm sorry."

His mother had always told him never go to sleep on an argument with a loved one. Well, although he could hardly consider himself loved by Faryl, there had been something of a friendship between them originally. Perhaps there could be again. Maybe if he explained himself, told her how he regretted his hastiness in turning her over to Jessom, they could start again. They had a long journey ahead together and that would be difficult if they were not even talking to each other . . .

Realization suddenly hit him like a stone.

"You've gone, haven't you?"

Aremys ran from his chamber, pulling on his boots as he hopped down the hallway. He had to ask directions through the castle several times, startling maids and the odd page boy going about their late-night business. And the only reason he knew he had arrived at her guest chamber was that he saw a young man emerging from a room carrying the gown Faryl had worn earlier that evening and a dark cape. He descended on the boy, breathless and angry.

"Where do you go with that gown, boy?" he demanded.

The lad jumped, as if scalded, then composed himself quickly. "Sir?"

"Answer me!"

"I'm running an errand for Madam Leyen. Please excuse me."

"What is your name?"

The youngster told him, chin held high, adding, "I am the King's messenger."

It did not impress as intended. "Go about your business then, Jorn."

The lad looked as though he was about to ask Aremys what he was doing here, but hesitated and then decided to hold his tongue. He scurried away, grabbing at the folds of the garment so they would not trail on the flagstones.

Aremys turned to the door, feeling in the pit of his stomach that his hunch was right. Still, he knocked. When no reply came, he turned the huge metal ring that would open the door, hoping against hope it would be latched and not permit him entry. The door opened easily. Aremys closed his eyes briefly with worry.

"Leyen?"

Nothing.

"Faryl!" he said, louder now.

No reply. He stepped inside and closed the door. The chamber and adjoining room were empty. No sign of her even having been here. The gown being sent back to its owner was the only clue that she had been in this room; that and the vague perfume of gardenias he remembered wafting seductively from Faryl earlier that evening.

He felt devastated. She had gone. Fled from the Stoneheart— from the King no doubt. Or was it from him? He was too dangerous for her and he had betrayed her once. She was not giving him another chance. She had a secret and she was taking it with her. Who was she protecting? It was pointless to try to tease out answers from himself. Faryl was an enigma.

Aremys moved swiftly, giving chase to the lad, but he never did find Jorn among the twisting, confusing hallways of huge Stoneheart. Instead he angrily navigated his way back to his room, packed his garb, and somewhere between stuffing things into his saddlebags and hearing the light knock at his door, decided to set off after her immediately. It was madness, he knew. She was trouble. What he did not know was where she had gone, although he had a hunch. He discarded all the sensible objections to pursuing Faryl.

He flung open the door, expecting a messenger. He found Jessom instead.

"Leaving us already?" the Chancellor asked, eyeing the bulging saddlebags.

"I can't sleep," Aremys offered flatly. "I thought I'd make myself useful—early start and all that."

"And Leyen?" There was something sly in the voice.

He played it carefully. "What about her?"

"She's gone, did you know?"

Aremys thought quickly. However he might feel about Faryl, he certainly did not need a king for an enemy. Jessom's arrival and inquiry provided him the opportunity to appear loyal to both sides, although right now his loyalties, despite his reservations, were with the female assassin.

Aremys frowned deliberately. "What are you talking about?"

"I've just been to her rooms," the Chancellor said. "May I come in?"

Aremys stepped aside and Jessom entered his chamber.

"Close it," the Chancellor suggested. After Aremys had done so, he continued. "I wanted to talk to her about why the King kept her back from us this evening. I don't like secrets that I'm not in on and I'm a little intrigued at her behavior as she left. Are you not?"

Aremys said nothing. He raised an eyebrow, though, to show he was paying attention.

"And now I find she has gone. No sign of her in her rooms," Jessom smoothly continued.

"When was this?"

"Moments ago."

"I see," Aremys replied, thanking Shar's blessing that he had run out of Faryl's rooms as fast as he did.

"Any ideas why she may have left you behind?"

He shook his head thoughtfully for the Chancellor's benefit. "No, indeed. I thought we were supposed to leave at first light."

"Yes, that was my understanding. I'm wondering if the King gave her another special task."

Aremys shrugged this time. It was his notion too, but he certainly was not going to share this with the inquisitive Chancellor. "But why brief us on what seemed like an important task to the Crown, order us to undertake it immediately, and then turn around and give a counterorder?" he reasoned.

"My thoughts exactly," Jessom said, "though there is never any accounting for the whims or moods of Celimus. He is thoroughly unpredictable."

"I can't help, I'm sorry."

"So what will you do?"

"Carry on as instructed. I suppose I shall head off immediately, then."

"Yes, why not, there's no point in you remaining here." He handed Aremys a pouch of coins. "This should do you for expenses. I have already made arrangements for payment the usual way with regard to your capture and delivery of Leyen. Monies for the Legionnaires and their delivery are now paid in full," he said, handing a bigger sack—gold this time—to Aremys.

The mercenary grunted and nodded. Money was the last thing on his mind right now. He stepped with the Chancellor toward the door, eager for the man to leave.

"I shall get to the bottom of Leyen's mysterious departure. I wonder who might have seen her leave," Jessom mused.

Aremys held the door open, contriving a puzzled expression, eager for the man to be gone. "Well, start with the lad Jorn, perhaps. I think Leyen mentioned he was attending to her."

He knew it was a mistake the moment the words came out. He had just meant it as an offhand line, something to help the Chancellor on his way so he could grab his saddlebags and go. Aremys knew immediately from the clouded look on Jessom's face that he had just stirred more trouble.

"Jorn! The King's messenger?" the man said, aghast.

Aremys tried to recant quickly. "Oh, truly I have no idea. That's probably not even his name. I thought I heard her say that name tonight, but come to think of it, she said that some noblewoman had sent a maid . . ." His voice trailed off. It was already too late to repair the damage, for Jessom's expression had deepened in thought.

"You get going," the Chancellor said distractedly. "I must find that boy."

Aremys shrugged. Jorn probably knew less than he did anyway.

Jessom stopped him. "Report back to me, the usual way, as soon as you have news of Ylena Thirsk. We want her corpse in Stoneheart within weeks, although her head will do," and he laughed drily.

Aremys strode away, the sound of Jessom's amusement diminishing behind him. At the stable he roused a disgruntled horse master, whose temper was only marginally improved at the sight of silver. Here Aremys learned that Faryl barely had a couple of hours on him. At the gate he met the same guard she had.

"Lots of comings and goings tonight, then," the man said wearily.

"Yes, I'm afraid we're all on King's business," Aremys admitted. "In fact, I've been asked to catch up with the woman who left a little earlier."

"Ah, yes, she took off in a real hurry . . . on royal business," the man admitted, nonplussed.

"That's her. Do you know where she was headed?"

"No, sir. I think young Jorn mentioned something about Felrawthy, but I couldn't be sure. I just open and shut the gate on orders, sir."

Aremys gave an expression of contrived sympathy and understanding. "Thanks, anyway," and he tossed the man a silver coin.

He left the castle at full gallop.

The next morning Lady Helyn's servant delivered the flask of sweetened wine as asked. "A delivery came for you, my lady," he said as he poured.

"Oh? When?"

"In the early hours, madam. I thought it best not to disturb you."

"How very odd. Whatever is it?"

"Of no consequence, my lady. Curiously it was a gown, cape, and item of jewelry, brought by one of the King's pages, returned with thanks."

Lady Helyn smiled. "Ah, yes. Intrigue over, Arnyld. I lent these to one of the King's guests who was staying unexpectedly at Stoneheart without formal attire. Have the clothes cleaned, please, and returned to my daughter's rooms."

"Yes, my lady." The man bowed and withdrew.

"Oh wait, Arnyld. Check the pockets before you have the gown cleaned. My daughter's awfully forgetful."

"At once, my lady."

Lady Helyn had hardly taken a few sips of her sweet wine before the manservant was back and bowing before her.

"What is it?" she said, mildly irritated at the distraction.

"Apologies to disturb you, my lady. But I did find this in the cape. I checked as you asked and discovered this note addressed to you."

"Oh?" she said, eagerly reaching for the small roll, hoping Leyen might be giving her some titbit of gossip. "Where is my glass?"

Arnyld reached toward a small table and handed a fat disk of glass to his mistress.

"Thank you, you may go," she said.

After the servant's departure, she hurriedly unfurled the slightly rumpled paper and placed the disk over the words to magnify them.

She read it several times. Lady Helyn finally looked up from Leyen's note, her lips pursed, eyes reflecting her alarm. What she had read stunned her, and as she ran its contents over again in her mind, she crushed the note before throwing it into the nearby pond. She studiously watched its sodden mass drift gently toward the murky bottom, ensuring no other pair of eyes would ever read it contents.

14

THE PATH SHE HAD BEEN WALKING NOW FOR TWO DAYS widened into a proper road and Elspyth's prayers were answered. People moved freely along this road and two carts, obviously traveling together, almost knocked her down as she emerged somewhat wildly from the adjoining track, desperate to stop them.

Stop them she did, although she was nearly crushed by one of the startled horses.

"Shar's Wrath!" someone yelled.

She must have fainted with relief or fatigue, possibly hunger, but lost herself only for a short while. When she regained her wits, she was sitting beneath the canopy of a covered cart staring at several wide-eyed children.

"She's awake!" one of them called.

A woman, obviously the mother of the brood, hove into view. "Better?"

Elspyth grimaced and nodded. "I'm sorry."

"You gave us all a terrible fright," the woman said, a small smile at her mouth. "I'm Ruth. This is my family." She called to the front. "Ham, she's awake. Stop now."

The children grinned shyly and then lost interest in the wild woman.

Elspyth sat up as the cart lurched to a halt. "Thank you for your kindness."

Ruth smiled warmly now. "Come. It's time we broke our fast."

The mention of food made Elspyth's belly grind.

Ruth looked at her. "Time you broke yours too," she said, frowning.

It was reassuring to be among fellow travelers again. El-spyth felt her fears subsiding at the merry voices and the sudden activity to get a fire lit, water heated, food laid out. It was a humble spread, but it was a feast to her.

"Eat," Ruth encouraged. "How long since your last meal?"

"Days," Elspyth admitted. "Is there enough for all?"

"Always," the woman replied.

The men began to gather. There were two families. The second woman, Meg, had older children, two boys, old enough to sit up front with the fathers.

Ham, Ruth's husband, introduced himself first and then the others. Elspyth nodded, smiling at all.

"Again my apologies for startling everyone. I was so keen to speak to another person. It has been so long."

"Well, while you eat, let us tell you about ourselves. We always eat heartily at this time of the day," Ruth said, her kind eyes encouraging Elspyth to slice off some meat from the haunch that had been set out.

Elspyth did as bid. As she ate she learned that the fami-lies were Briavellians, providores returning home after a successful trip into Morgravia.

"What do you sell?" she asked through her contented chewing.

One of the lads spoke up. "We are honeymakers."

She looked confused now as she swallowed. "But surely Morgravia makes its own honey?"

They all grinned as though this was a regular question. The lad enlightened her. "Ah, but our bees are special. They have not been crossbred with any others. They're of the purest strain of Magurian bee from Magur, a tiny island off the southeast coast of Briavel."

Elspyth was intrigued. "But how do you stop the bees from crossbreeding?"

The honeymaker family was impressed that she was tak-ing so much interest. The father answered this time. "Well, my family has been in honey making for generations. But I'm the third son. There was not enough income in Magur for me to make a livelihood. So I moved to Briavel as soon as I was old enough to leave the nest and settled on the mainland." He sucked at a pipe now as he recalled those early days. "I fell in love with a beautiful Briavellian maiden, but I hated the honey on the mainland, of course, preferring the richer lavender-and-clover flavors of the Magur gold."

His wife smiled indulgently at his words.

He continued. "And so I suggested to my father that I might import some of our honeycomb—we had more than enough produce."

"I'll bet the Briavellians loved it!" Elspyth said, enjoying the tale.

"It helps that our dear King Valor, rest his soul, took a fancy to it, having tried it once while passing through our region," the wife said softly.

"And do you now supply your lovely young queen?" Elspyth asked.

Their son was eager to take up the story. "Yes. Apparently she eats it each day and attaches much to its health properties."

Elspyth nodded. "She is very beautiful, I hear."

The lad blushed. "She is magnificent. No one can hold a candle to her looks."

Elspyth grinned. "Then I must taste this honey of yours, for it must be her secret."

Her companions laughed and offered around more food and tea.

"And you?" Elspyth said to Ruth. "Tell me about your family."

"Ham can tell you," she said, nodding at her husband as she began to clear away some of the debris of their meal.

He obliged. "Well, we are grapegrowers and winemakers, but not just any old grapes, mind. Our vines produce the special frostfruit, harvested very late in the year when the first bite of winter is being felt. They are exquisitely sweet, very small, and produce the most lush, rich wine—"

"Also favored by royalty, no doubt," Elspyth chimed in, amusing the families.

"By your own royalty, in fact," Ham admitted, liking her cheek. "We recently made a delivery to the court of King Celimus and we've traveled in the north for a while. My son's first vintage, and a fine one it is," he said proudly, looking toward his boy, who shrugged self-consciously. "Don't be bashful," he added. "You've a better palate and nose than any member of our family I can remember."

"And so Briavellian honey and wine finds it way across the border into Morgravia regularly now?" Elspyth asked, and the adults nodded.

"That's wonderful to hear," she said, meaning it. "Trade overcoming politics."

Ham nodded. "Yes, but only because our two products have found favor with the royals."

Ruth sighed. "It will be a lot easier when your Celimus marries our Valentyna. We can all trade more freely. Worry less."

"Do you think it will happen?" Elspyth asked, thinking of Wyl.

"It has to," said the honey maker, taking a long puff on his pipe. "It is the only way our two realms can become profitable. All these wars have achieved is to beggar each realm's producers. If they marry we can forget war and our children can look forward to a better life."

Sounds of agreement came from those around her and Elspyth felt a surge of sadness for her trapped friend. Wyl loved Valentyna, but it seemed her duty to her realm would weigh heavier than their desire.

"You said you lived in the southeast of Briavel. Do you ever get to the capital?" she asked, chewing on a fat fig.

Ham nodded. "Yes, indeed. My eldest son and I travel there regularly. We were there very recently, in fact."

"Oh, so I wonder if you've heard of a nobleman called Romen Koreldy. I know him quite well and the last time we met he was on his way to Werryl. I hear through the grapevine from fellow travelers that there was some sort of duel between him and King Celimus at the Queen's tourney." It was true. She had heard as much.

"We were there," the eldest son said. "It was more than a duel."

"It felt like a fight to the death," Ham admitted. "Our queen stepped in to stop the bloodshed."

Elspyth was shocked. This was fresh news to her. She knew Wyl had many reasons to hate the King. "What happened?"

"Nothing much more there," Ham said, "although . . . I'm sorry to be the one to tell you this, young Elspyth, but Koreldy is no longer with us."

She shook her head. "No, I imagine not. He would leave Briavel after that, though I wonder where he has headed. I—"

Meg took her hand. "No, you don't understand."

Everyone looked suddenly embarrassed.

Elspyth turned to Ham.

"He's dead, child," the man said.

To her it felt like several long minutes passed before she took another breath. It was, in fact, only a few heartbeats, but the silence was painful for all of them.

"You must be mistaken," she stammered, feeling a chill pass through her.

Ham shook his head. "It happened at Crowyll. We were there the day after it took place. The town rumor has it that a whore killed him, although the Briavellian Guard is saying different. What was her name, son? Someone did tell us."

The boy stuck his chin in the air and closed his eyes. "Hilda was it?"

"No. Hildyth, that's right. According to the gossips, she's quite a striking woman. Unmistakable. Tall with golden-brown hair and feline eyes."

Elspyth began to tremble, her whole world crumbling about her. "Why?"

"No idea," Ham admitted. "The story goes that her majesty banished Koreldy from Briavel. He was being escorted to a border of his choice and he and the guard accompanying him stopped at a place in Crowyll for a smoothing and suchlike." He cleared his throat self-consciously, glad that the youngsters had already cleared off to play.

"And?" Elspyth asked, distraught now.

Ham shrugged. "It happened."

"But there's no reason for it!" she cried. "Why was he banished? Why killed?"

Ruth put her arms about her. "Oh, Elspyth, I'm so sorry it is us to break the news. He must have been a good friend." She scowled at her husband. "Ham, tell her everything you know."

Her husband blushed, distressed to be seen as the villain. "Rumors were rife while we were there. They say the whore worked for Celimus and that the King ordered Koreldy's death. No one knows the truth of it, though. And now with our own soldiers saying it was one of them who killed him, a renegade or something, it's all a bit baffling."

"The body, who saw it?" Elspyth demanded.

"I'm sorry to say that a close friend of ours helped to clean up Koreldy's corpse. His . . . his heart had been punctured." Ham stammered over the words, unsure of how much detail his wife meant for him to tell. "Um . . . my friend's from the morgue and he was called in to deal with the body before it was transported to Werryl. Very trustworthy fellow. He only told me because he was so shocked at the manner of death. He says it is the style used by a professional assassin. Apparently everything was hushed over quickly by the Queen's guard, and my friend was ordered to remain silent. I'm sure he didn't mean to tell me as much as he did. Oh, and she'd cut off his finger too—that's another indication it was a paid killing."

"What do you mean?" Elspyth said, confounded.

"The finger is proof of death. Apparently he wore a bloodred stone in a ring marked with a special family insignia."

At that Elspyth broke down. It was true, then. She knew the ring. Knew it was Wyl they spoke of. Dead. Now Lothryn would never be rescued from the dark magic and the pain.

The others moved away silently. Ham put his large, meaty hand on her shoulder. "I'm sorry, lass."

She said nothing but cried harder against Ruth's shoulder.

"Travel with us, Elspyth. You're in no state to be alone just now," the woman whispered.

Elspyth did not know how long they sat there together or at what point her sobs subsided and the tears dried against her cheeks. She could not remember when Meg and Ruth helped her back into the cart and laid her down, covering her with a blanket. But she welcomed the escape from her exhaustion and pain.

This time she dreamed of a tall woman with dark gold hair and catlike eyes who had destroyed her dream. Lothryn would never be rescued by Wyl. It was up to her, then. She would rescue the man she loved just as soon as she had delivered her message to Felrawthy and kept her promise to the dead friend who had once walked in the guise of Romen Koreldy.

15

THEY HAD RUN, TERRIFIED, NOT DARING TO LOOK BEHIND OR slow down until their legs were too weak to carry them any farther and their lungs protested loudly, burning for air.

"Please stop, my lady," Pil gasped, his body bent over. "We must catch our breath."

"No rest, Pil!" Ylena wore a deranged expression, her hair wild from snagging in overhanging branches, her garments muddied and torn. "I daren't tell you what they were doing." He heard her voice break and looked away. "Shar's Tears," she said, all strength leaving her as she crumpled to her knees, her face clasped in dirt-smeared hands. She wept, exhausted.

Pil sat down, at a loss for what to say and grateful that he was too fatigued to speak. What they had both witnessed at Rittylworth could not be comprehended. He knew Ylena was keeping the real horror from him and he was glad of it. He cast his own teary thanks to whichever angels had been guarding his own life.

Brother Jakub had asked Pil to remain close to Ylena from the beginning. He recalled Jakub's gentle words. "Because you are young, she will not feel too threatened by you. She has seen and experienced too much sorrow at the whim of powerful men."

Although he did not know the whole story, Pil gathered that Ylena had been terrorized at Stoneheart by the King and his minions. Koreldy had counseled that she was not of sound mind, warning them that Ylena had witnessed a ghoulish murder, but Pil was not familiar with the actual events. In the days he had spent in her company since, quietly escorting her, serving meals, generally being on hand to see to her needs, she had been withdrawn but polite. Her silence and sudden tears had been the only sign that she was disturbed.

Looking at her now, he could hardly recognize the fragile noblewoman who had arrived into their care. She had taken command of the situation like a battle-hardened general rallying his troops. Her father and her brother had been revered Generals of the Legion, and no doubt, Pil decided, courage ran in the Thirsk blood. The situation in which they found themselves had brought out the same qualities in Ylena. He wondered what it was that she carried in the sack, why she refused to allow him to help her with it. In truth, it frightened him and he could honestly admit that he did not need or, indeed, want to know what the mysterious sack contained.

The novice wanted to sleep, was desperate to lay his head down on the grass and drift into oblivion, but he dared not, for he was sure he would dream nightmares of burning bodies. He guessed they had been on the move for roughly an hour, perhaps almost two. He glanced toward the sky—barely midmorning, he estimated.

"Lady Ylena," he uttered gently, "I don't believe we've

been followed. I am sure we escaped notice." He hoped he might offer the right note of reassurance.

"Everyone's dead," she muttered, her voice flat and muffled, her face sunk into knees encircled by thin arms. "And they'll hunt me down until he's satisfied I'm dead too."

"Don't say that, my lady," Pil replied, fresh fright coursing through him.

She lifted her head to look at her companion. Her eyes were red from tears, but they held a wildness that unsettled Pil still further. "Who do you think they are after?"

He shrugged. "I don't even know why they came."

Ylena laughed bitterly. "It was me, Pil," she said, shaking her head. "Me and Koreldy. Where is he? He promised he would not abandon me."

Pil wanted to interject that she had not been abandoned to the monks. They all loved her. Instead he held his tongue as she continued. "My parents are dead, my brother killed, my young and beautiful new husband murdered . . . does it strike you that this monarch is determined to see the Thirsk name barely more than a memory?"

So that was the core of her pain. He knew she had seen someone killed, but Jakub had refused to say more. He had to assume then that Ylena had witnessed her husband's death. He chose his words carefully, wanting neither to inflame her temper nor risk pushing her deeper into grief. "I want to be a monk, my lady. I am not a politician. I do not understand the intrigues of court."

Her expression became sad. "It doesn't matter. I am hunted. The last of my line. You would do well to protect yourself by leaving me now."

Pil was shocked. "I cannot do that, my lady. I promised Brother Jakub that I would take care of you."

"And who was taking care of Brother Jakub and all the other brothers? You know what the soldiers were doing, Pil. Each monk deliberately cut down . . . murdered where he stood. Shar alone knows how those senior brothers suffered on the cross. How can a boy protect me when a whole community cannot?"

Pil suddenly felt all of his young years. He understood

what people meant when they used the saying of blood draining from one's face. He could feel it now, could feel a weakness moving through his body as if determined to shut down his movement, his speech, his heart. Not so long ago he had been carefree and laughing with his fellow monks, eager to become a fully fledged member of the Order. Now that Ylena had revealed the full horror, his mind was filled with the vision of the gentle holy men being stabbed, their throats slit and swords run through bellies . . . nailed to posts. The image would never leave him. He recalled the smell of smoke and realized the village must have been burning too. He wondered if the soldiers had destroyed the monastery.

Every ounce of him wanted to break down and weep, die where he sat and turn away from this ugliness. Instead he heard Jakub's comforting voice in his mind and he adopted a similar tone now.

"We have been spared, my lady. Shar protected us by placing us somewhere unexpected when the soldiers came. And almost no one outside the monastery knew of the grotto," he added as gently as he could, adding sorrowfully, "Brother Jakub was keen for you to have a private place to bathe and rest."

A wan smile ghosted across her face. "Go, Pil. By staying with me, you put yourself in danger. I'm not sure I can look after both of us. Please be safe."

"No," he said, adding firmly, "We stay together as we promised Jakub. That's my job, remember. He told me now was when I prove my worth."

It struck him that Ylena was no longer paying attention to his courageous words. A long silence followed and Pil believed she had forgotten the thread of her thought. So it made him jump when she stood and unexpectedly replied.

"Only Duke Donal might offer us protection."

"Then Felrawthy is where we must head, my lady." He tried to sound brave despite the sense of dread he felt.

I don't get your point, Jessom. Frankly, I like her dedication," Celimus said, kicking away the hand of the stable master, who was fiddling with his stirrups. "Leave it!" he scolded. The man flinched and stepped away silently from the beautiful roan mare whose saddle the King had just made himself comfortable upon. "I'll be galloping her," he warned. "You're sure her foot is fine?"

The stable master nodded. "Yes sire, all soreness gone. Enjoy your ride." He bowed and departed.

"Get on with it, Chancellor!" Celimus barked, irritated by the delay to his dawn ride. "Tell me what bothers you."

"It just strikes me as odd, sire, that Leyen would leave under cover of darkness."

"I would have thought most assassins craved the cloak of night." The sarcasm bit.

Jessom ignored it, continued smoothly. "She left without Aremys. No word as to why."

"And where is he now?"

"No longer at Stoneheart," Jessom said, deliberately brief. "Gone about your business."

"And?"

"Well, I'm just wondering what business Leyen might be about, sire. You specifically gave instructions that they were to track down the person in question together."

"Do you not trust your own people, Jessom?"

The Chancellor considered the cunning way in which Celimus always managed to turn accusation away from himself. He squinted into the dawn's sharp light toward where his king sat with a halo of sunshine about his head. "I trust no one, my king."

"Well said," Celimus admitted. "I gave her some additional instructions to take a message to Valentyna for me."

Jessom glanced around to see no one could overhear them. "I see. Did you ask that she perform this task first?"

"No. It was my understanding she would handle the business with Aremys before traveling to Briavel."

"It is strange, then, that she left so hurriedly, and may I say, she seemed rather disturbed after she left your chambers the other night, your highness."

Further irritation traced across the King's face. "Your point?"

The Chancellor shrugged. "Well, perhaps she did not like the message you asked her to pass on to Briavel," he said carefully, presuming the King would share the message with him now.

But Celimus was too shrewd. "It bears thinking about. Do we know anything about her departure?"

"Only that one of your pages, Jorn, was attending to her. He showed her out of the castle gates. He may know something."

The horse was restless to move, as was the King. "Jorn? Perhaps he delivered to Leyen the written piece I wanted her to take to Valentyna."

Jessom contrived an expression suggesting it pained him to divulge what he was about to explain. "You see, your majesty, my fear is that Jorn, who serves you and serviced Leyen—without permission I might add—also attended Koreldy when he was here."

That caught the King's attention, as Jessom knew it would. He let the notion hang between them, knowing Celimus's subtle mind would put it all together.

Anger clouded the olive gaze. "Find the boy. Keep him frightened in the dungeon for my return. Make sure he's ready to tell us everything—and I'm trusting your instincts, Jessom, that there is something here—by the time I get back."

"As you wish, sire," Jessom said, nodding low as Celimus clicked to his mare and urged her out of the courtyard.

16

ORN COWERED IN THE COLD OF THE DAMP CELL, FRIGHTENED and confused. He had been grabbed by two soldiers in one of the many castle orchards where he had been collecting some parillion fruit for the King's breakfast. Jorn had risen especially early to ensure that when his monarch returned hot and dusty from his morning ride he would have plenty of the refreshing chilled juice he favored to quench his thirst.

Now Jorn mournfully remembered the precious fruit he had dropped and ultimately stepped upon when the soldiers appeared and manhandled him roughly toward the dungeon. He shivered in the chill and looked around, his vision dulled from fear at what he might or might not have done to so anger his superiors. What had he done that warranted incarceration? He replayed the last few days over and again through his mind, wondering at what terrible mistake he had made.

It was coincidental that this happened to be the same chamber from which Myrren had been dragged by her torturers almost a decade earlier. Such information would have meant little to Jorn if he learned it, of course, and if he had studied the last block of stone of the wall behind the cell door he would have noted a curious inscription that might have meant a lot to him considering his adoration of Ylena Thirsk.

On that stone were three words. AVENGE ME WYL, they read.

Someone such as Fynch, susceptible to the ebb and flow of enchantments in a world that scorned their existence, might touch that inscription and feel the thrum of the magic used to make such a mark on stone. Jorn had no such talent and his heavyhearted gaze slid past the words without note.

The thin, dark Chancellor with hooded eyes who had recently arrived was offering no reassurance.

"Please, Chancellor Jessom, tell me what it is I've done," he begged through the bars.

The man's seal of office hung heavily from a chain, swaying as the Chancellor paced slowly, waiting for the King. "I'm sorry, my boy," Jessom said, adopting an avuncular approach. "This is all very confusing. It goes to the highest level, Jorn. Somehow you have attracted the King's attention . . . negative attention, that is."

"But, Chancellor Jessom, sir, it is my pleasure to wait loyally on the King. I would do nothing to harm him."

"Would you not?"

The boy shook his head dumbly. Even in his fright he knew he was missing something important. It was written in the Chancellor's heavy-lidded gaze.

"Ah, here is his majesty now, Jorn. Hopefully we can clear this up and you can be back at your duties by the noon bell."

"Oh yes, sir," Jorn said, feeling a surge of hope knife through him. "I'll do anything to set things right."

"Good boy. Be easy now. Your king approaches."

Jorn could hear the click of his sovereign's boots against the dull flagging of the dungeon floor. He could not make out the words but knew the King had made some remark that had amused the guards. Laughter erupted, the swaggering tread resumed, and then suddenly the familiar tall and resplendent shape of Celimus appeared beside Jessom. His face was shining with tiny beads of perspiration. He had come straight here from his ride, then, Jorn thought miserably. Whatever secret he apparently held from them was considered more important than the sovereign's comfort. The King turned a predatory gaze on Jorn, who quailed at the sight.

"Your majesty," the Chancellor said, bowing low.

Jorn, more terrified than ever, knelt immediately. "Your highness," he whispered, ready to confess to anything.

Celimus glanced toward Jessom, whose slight nod indicated the lad was so petrified he would tell them whatever they needed to know. Celimus smiled thinly. If Jorn had looked up at that moment, he would have known that his life was already forfeit, but he kept his head low to the floor, hands clasping and unclasping nervously as he awaited his king's pleasure.

"Stand up, lad." It was the dry voice of the Chancellor.

Jorn obeyed, kept his head bowed more from shame than anything else, for he realized that he had soiled his trousers in his fright.

The King finally spoke. "Look at me, boy." His voice was hard. Jorn struggled to obey and finally lifted damp eyes toward Celimus, who continued. "I shall ask you a few questions. What I require is complete honesty." He stared at the boy. "Because you have nothing to fear," he lied.

Jorn nodded, eyes wide with his intense desire to please. "Yes, your majesty. I promise to tell you whatever it is you need."

"Good. Now, do you recall a recent guest at Stoneheart, who dined with me? She arrived with a man called Aremys and—"

"Madam Leyen, yes," Jorn interrupted, anxious to impress his king.

Celimus nodded. Jessom smiled briefly.

"Is it true that you waited on her . . . without permission from either myself or your superiors?"

Jorn frowned. "I did not wait on her, your majesty."

"Oh? I hear differently."

The boy clutched at the bars. "Oh no, sire. I . . ." They watched his brow crease as he recalled what had occurred. "I was on an urgent errand for one of your secretaries, sire, which took me that morning into that wing of the castle where Madam Leyen was accommodated. I was in quite a hurry, as I recall." He watched both men nod. "Um . . . Madam Leyen hailed me as I ran past the corridor."

"And what did she want?" Celimus prompted.

"Advice, sire."

Jessom smirked. "What sort of advice, boy?"

"Well, I didn't find out until later that evening because she could tell how much of a rush I was in to be about my duties. I left straightaway, having exchanged only a handful of words with her, sire. She was a stranger to me."

Celimus was not so easily deterred. "And later?"

"Yes, later, sire, I did go back to her chamber, as she asked me to. I felt obliged, your majesty, because she was your personal guest and had no one attending her."

The King held on to his patience. "And?"

"She wanted advice on her gown."

There was an awkward silence before Celimus replied, an edge of threat to his tone. "You jest, of course?"

"No, sire," Jorn beseeched. "I would never do that, my king. Madam Leyen wanted to make the right impression on you, your majesty, for the supper she was sharing. She had no garments of her own and was in a borrowed gown. She sought my approval."

"A lad's approval?" Jessom said, his voice high with his disgust.

Jorn shrugged slightly before catching himself in the act. He turned it into an obeisance. "It's the truth, sire. Perhaps she thought I might know best, as I did mention that I was your personal messenger."

"That's it?" Celimus said, his own disbelief evident. "You expect us to accept that this . . . this . . . approval was all she asked of you?"

Jorn bobbed frantically. "My lord king. That is all she asked of me." He watched the King's hand turn to a fist as the famous anger stoked. "I did go back that night, of course," he blurted out.

"Ah . . . and why did you do that?"

"To deliver a parchment one of your secretaries bade me deliver very late. I was told it was urgent, King's business."

He watched a glance pass between his captors. And it was only then that Jorn realized where this strange conversation was leading. He had always counted himself as sharp. He made good use of that skill now to make the leap in his mind that it was not him they were after but Leyen. And even she was not the true prey. It was where her loyalties lay that they were most interested in. They were after Ylena Thirsk. Beautiful, sorrowful, badly treated Ylena, whom he would rather die than betray. And yet betrayal is precisely what they sought from him. He could see it now as clear as daylight. They wanted him to tell them where Madam Leyen had been traveling in such a hurry that night. They wanted to hurt his beloved Lady Ylena yet more.

Well, he would not permit it! He was only a messenger and thus nothing in the eyes of the King. But he, Jorn, had made a promise to a beautiful woman and she had returned his loyalty with a promise that she would send for him. Any day now he would escape Stoneheart and travel to Argorn, where Ylena would welcome him and allow him to serve her as he so dearly wished.

He would not reveal her secrets. Not through his lips, Jorn thought as a bright new sensation burst into life within him. He was not a fiery person, very rarely allowing anything to get under his skin sufficiently to make him angry. His naturally sunny personality helped him defuse most situations in which another's temper might flare. But a spark of anger had erupted and it was fueled by the look of accusation in both his monarch's expression and the carefully contrived vision of sympathy that the solicitous Chancellor had suddenly become, shaking his head sadly.

"Well?" the King demanded.

Jorn spoke with assurance. "I gave Madam Leyen the parchment and took her gown, cape, and some jewelry, as requested, back to Lady Bench's household."

"Leyen left that night, you liar, and you know it!" Celimus spat through the bars.

"I have no reason to lie to you, my lord king. I was coming to that," Jorn said, pleased that he did not flinch at the King's hostility despite the sudden watery feel to his knees.

He grasped his last sense of composure, ignored the damp reminder of his fear, and gilded the truth. "She told me she was leaving. I know not why, sire. She asked me if I would accompany her to the stables because she did not know her way around Stoneheart. It was not my place to question her actions, my king. I am a simple messenger, keen to serve you and your esteemed guests."

"And so you did," Celimus said, slyly now.

"Yes, sire."

"Did she mention where she was going?"

Jorn paused to think how to answer this. "No," he said truthfully.

"That's odd, boy, because the guard on duty that night recalls you mentioning the duchy of Felrawthy."

Jorn had never and would never again give a better performance. His expression remained impassive even though he suddenly hated the man he remembered on watch that night. He had given him much coin to keep his mouth closed. "That's right, sire, I think I might have mentioned it."

"Why?" Celimus approached the prison bars again as a hunter might, closing in for the kill.

"Because that's where I understood Madam Leyen comes from, sire," he lied.

Celimus looked toward Jessom, who blinked, slowly.

"I have no information on Leyen's history, sire," Jessom admitted, somewhat abashed. "She told us Rittylworth, but she is a mystery and likes to keep it that way. In truth, I have never seen her as plainly as I saw her at the supper. She is usually in disguise, even for our meetings."

"For all we know, she could have been in disguise at supper," the King growled, not realizing how close to the truth he was. "Did she share with you where she was headed?" Celimus demanded of Jorn.

The lad shook his head, seemingly confused. "She must have in passing, for I can't imagine how I would know such a thing. I'm sorry, sire, that I don't remember our brief conversations more clearly, but I do know she did not tell me where exactly she was going—I presumed it was to her home," Jorn replied smoothly, lying expertly for the last time in his life. *Forgive me, Shar,* he beseeched inwardly.

The handsome eyes of Celimus regarded Jorn intently now and the gaze felt suddenly too direct and intimidating. Jorn felt his resolve crack slightly, but he rallied his courage and mastered his fright, resisting the temptation to blurt out everything he knew of Leyen and her intentions—which was little enough in truth. He instinctively cast his own gaze down and this was perhaps his final undoing. It might have been that if Jorn had held his sovereign's cold and compelling look, the unpredictable nature of his king might have erred toward leniency. Instead it swung toward cruelty. The King could tell the youth knew very little and would hardly be privy to a secretive and highly qualified assassin's intentions, yet it nagged instinctively at Celimus that he was being beguiled somehow.

"He lies; wheel him!"

Jorn heard the hammer of his own heartbeat in his ears. He slid toward the floor, dazed with shock, and noticed for the first time three words scratched into the stone before he lost consciousness.

"My king, please—" Jessom attempted, alarmed himself at such needless torture.

"Don't even think to contradict me, Chancellor," Celimus warned, his voice hard, eyes glittering. "I want him wheeled. He's not strong enough to resist the pain. I will know whether Leyen is true to my cause or not."

Jessom knew that Leyen was true to no one but herself, but this was not an occasion to test his majesty's temper with the truth. He nodded in acquiescence, keeping his head bowed, so he heard rather than saw the contemptuous swagger of the King's departure.

The Chancellor motioned to the dungeon master, and when the man had listened to his grave words, Jessom turned back to Jorn. "I'm sorry, lad," he said, and meant it.

But Jorn did not hear the apology or feel the rough hands that grabbed his limp body and removed him to a part of Stoneheart he had never imagined he would have to see.

It was a genuine surprise for the skilled team of torturers Celimus had assembled since taking the Crown that the youngster lasted as long as he did. Battle-hardened soldiers facing the same breaking of limbs beneath the crushing wheel had either begged for the mercy of the sword or had simply died from the shock. Jorn sadly survived the initial smashing of his joints, expertly done by a man who asked no questions but simply went about his gruesome business with quiet expertise.

Normally he would have prolonged the session, taking his time placing the wooden block beneath the sweating, usually shrieking victims before bringing his heavy mallet down in punishment. The two pelvic joints and their subsequent breaking usually won the greatest attention from the condemned, but the man sensed this young lad did not deserve prolonged punishment and he pleased the two other onlookers by doing his job swiftly.

This meant they could get onto the second stage of pulverizing Jorn's skeleton beneath the crushing iron wheel that the men rolled slowly over his body. The pace was such not because they wanted to lengthen his suffering but because the wheel was so enormously heavy it took some doing to get it rolling. As it turned, the men openly marveled at the young fellow's capacity to withstand what was regarded by most in the profession as the most intolerable pain one could inflict on a person.

He was embarrassingly brave to the end and they felt ashamed that this was being visited on a youth, both of them wincing at the loud popping and cracking of the lad's bones until the weight reached his chest and finally stopped the faint, erratic heartbeat.

Jorn took his final agonizing breath, vague satisfaction skimming through his blurring thoughts that he had not let himself down, despite the chilling screams that escaped his throat. His last conscious thought was not of Ylena but of the three words scratched in his cell. As Jorn died he made the final connection in a fleeting moment of high clarity. He sent a dying prayer to Shar to preserve the Thirsk line and ensure his brave death was not in vain.

They were normally expected to use the crushing wheel over the entire length of the victim's body, but as soon as Jorn's eyes clouded with death, the two men rolling it stopped.

"Enough!" one said. He was good at his job but did not like hurting the innocents and there had been too many of those in recent times. "I'm not crushing this one's head for his majesty's pleasure. He's suffered enough . . . and with courage."

"Are you sure?" his companion said. "It'll be our own guts the King hangs us from if we're not careful."

"Jessom wasn't happy over it. He said to make it swift."

"Got nothing out of him, though, did we?" the other man admitted.

"Nothing to get, probably. Come on, roll it back. At least if his family collects the body, they can see his face is whole."

"Can't say the same about the rest of him," commented his fellow torturer. He whistled, looking at the state of the shattered, bloodied mess of a body before them.

Later that day, when Jessom had reason to visit the King's chambers, Jorn was the sovereign's first question. "Did the page reveal what we wanted to hear?"

"No, my lord king." Jessom did not have to work at being solemn. He was still in a distracted mood over the morning's events.

Celimus glared at his chancellor, hand poised over the parchment he was scrawling his mark upon. "Surely?"

"He took whatever secrets you feel he may have had, sire, to the grave with him."

Celimus stood, angry at being beaten by a youth. "He was wheeled as ordered?" he stated. It was just short of an accusation.

Jessom kept his voice even. "Yes, sire. Exactly as you instructed," he lied. "It seems the boy survived an interminable time. Not until the iron crushed the very beat from his heart did he relinquish his grip on this life." Inwardly the Chancellor felt proud of the boy. This was one death he did not agree with.

"He gave nothing?"

Jessom gave a deprecating gesture that suggested he did not believe there was anything to give.

"He spoke no words," Celimus qualified, ensuring his oily chancellor kept nothing from him.

Jessom kept his voice even, expression blank. "Just the usual assortment of shrieks and groans, sire. No words."

"Admirable," Celimus said, pausing by the window to consider. "For he surely withheld something. Where is the body?"

"Ready for burial, I presume, sire."

"I want you to think, Chancellor."

"Pardon, sire?"

"Think, man! I employ you for your fluid mind. What are we missing? There must be something we have overlooked. Ponder it—find the solution for me by tomorrow and report back. We shall meet in the morning after my dawn ride."

Jessom could only bow. He felt a pit open in his stomach at the thought of meeting Celimus tomorrow with no answers. The King's tantrums usually resulted in someone's death.

"By the way, no burial for Jorn. Impale him. Have it done on the main road into Felrawthy . . . just in case."

"As you wish, sire," Jessom said, weariness overcoming him. He knew there probably was not much left of Jorn to impale anyway. Was there no end to this man's brutality? He kept his voice steady. "I shall see to it now."

"And I shall see you tomorrow, Chancellor, with answers to my questions."

17

ELSPYTH HAD TAKEN THE REST OF THAT DAY AND ALL OF THE
night to surface from her bleak, virtually catatonic
state. When she did she knew it was time to leave the two
kind families who had cared for her. She could tell her
brooding presence unnerved the youngsters and the once-
lively chatter of Ruth and Meg was now guarded, the women
not wishing to impose on her sorrowful mood.

As the carts rolled to a pause at Five Ways, an aptly
named spot, where five roads led to different regions of the
realm, she took her leave, in spite of the families' protesta-
tions, which Elspyth knew were mild. She mustered a smile
for the group and hugged both the women, especially Ruth.

"I will worry after you," the kind woman admitted.

"Don't," Elspyth assured. "I'm really very capable."

"You know you are welcome to stay with us," Meg offered.

Elspyth felt a surge of gratitude. "Yes, I do. But I must
find Koreldy's sister—that's where I was headed when I
stumbled onto your path."

"I'm sorry again, lass," the still-abashed Ham said, handing her a small sack of food.

She took the sack and squeezed his hand to reassure
him that she held no grudge. "You've all been so very
good to me. Better I hear it from kind souls than from
those who might take pleasure in such news. I'll be fine,
I promise. It was just a shock, and once I deliver a message to the Koreldy family, I'll be able to get back to my
own life," she lied.

She hoped none would ask where this elusive sister might

be or indeed where Elspyth's home was. None did, and after another round of awkward farewells, the carts rolled on their way, headed east toward Briavel's border. Once they were out of sight, she took stock of her situation. She turned toward the road that led northeast—a more direct path to the duchy—and set off. She still felt as though her mind were blank; first Lothryn's plea for help and then the news of Koreldy had left her decidedly empty.

"It's up to me now," she said aloud on the lonely road.

Hearing her own voice sounding so defiant gave her courage. First she would keep her promise to Wyl and find his sister, ensuring Ylena was given the protection of the Duke of Felrawthy. That done, she would return to Yentro—perhaps Lothryn had been wrong and the old girl had survived. Once there, she could gather together whatever monies she could, perhaps even sit out spring, before heading far north and into the mountains. She did not relish the forbidding Razors at the close of their winter, but then she remembered the terror in Lothryn's voice and knew she could no more sit out the season than fly to Felrawthy. No, she would collect some fresh gear, a few funds, and leave immediately for Cailech's stronghold.

Suddenly the only thing that mattered to her was discovering Lothryn's fate, and if she died in the process, so be it. His love had offered her the first relief from loneliness in a lifetime and she was not about to relinquish it without a fight.

Once again, Elspyth found herself a lone figure on a dusty road headed toward the unknown. She squared her petite shoulders, lifted her chin, and began her long walk to fulfill a promise.

Ylena and Pil joined the straggling bunch of people and animals roaming through Dorchyster Green's town square. It was market day and the smell of newly baked bread and steaming meat pies that pervaded the air sharpened their hunger.

"When did we last eat?" Ylena asked, looking longingly at the wheels of cheese and potted meats.

Pil's belly was growling. "I can't remember, my lady," he said, avoiding the ponderous tread of a cow pushing by. "But we should move on, for I fear we have no coin."

Ylena's despair snapped to anger. "This is not right. I have money—I just don't have it with me. I'm so sorry, Pil."

"Hush now," he soothed, taking her arm. He understood. She was used to fine things in life, not having to wonder where her next meal might come from. In truth, he too had lived a comfortable existence at the monastery, where food had always been plentiful. "Come, let's continue."

They had stopped by a stall of fruit, the bright colors arresting both their gazes and their bellies groaning together as a new smell, roasting meat, seemed to mock them.

"To where?" she demanded. "We cannot go another day without eating."

She was right, but all he could do was shrug. "Short of stealing, my lady—and I could never do that—I have no solution."

"Then we shall beg!" She sounded so resolute his jaw opened to speak, but no words came out. "Yes!" she answered his unspoken question. "I shall sing. I have a comely voice, or so I'm told. So I shall sing for our food . . . and you . . . you shall dance a jig beside me," she added desperately.

"All right," he said bravely, hoping the bouncy lilt to his own voice would help her find the confidence to humiliate herself so. "Anything's worth a try and I am certainly hungry, my lady."

A smile ghosted her mouth, but there was no warmth to it. "Come, then, we shall position ourselves over there by the well."

He followed her, wondering how she fathomed she might be heard above the din of the market.

"Here," she commanded. "Lay your hat at our feet."

Pil did as asked, embarrassed. "You don't surely expect

me to dance, my lady . . . please," he beseeched, adding, "I find it hard enough to walk without tripping over."

"You don't have to," Ylena said, smoothing her tattered skirts and tucking back her untidy hair. "It was just a thought—but make sure you smile at the passersby. We need their pity. It's a shame you didn't have your pate shaved—being a monk would have helped our cause," she said distractedly, clearing her throat.

Pil said nothing. He steadied his gaze toward his feet and waited. However, when the first bright note emanated from Ylena, his eyes widened in amazement and his glance unwittingly flicked sideways to watch her.

Her voice was pure and beautiful, like a young bird released to soar toward the sky. Pil recognized the song. It was a ballad of high sorrow, telling the tale of two youngsters who had grown up together to become lovers and whose rapture for each other was blessed by the gods. As the story unwove, the man is murdered by a jealous admirer of the woman's. And so the tale went, lengthy and sad, pulling at the emotions.

Pil noticed a small crowd had begun to form. Ylena had chosen well, for the song had many verses—certainly lengthy enough to attract attention. He stepped away from her, realizing his presence was no longer needed. The gathering listeners had eyes only for the beautiful, albeit disheveled, woman and her song of grief. She hardly paid them any care, and so she did not notice the coins being dropped into the hat or how large and silent the crowd suddenly was.

Pil noticed it all, especially the emergence of a broad, older man who stepped out from the Dorchyster Arms, the town's inn.

He was clearly a wealthy noble from his garb, and even in his winter years, Pil noticed, he remained a handsome, vital man. Once-yellow hair had dulled to buttery white and it was pulled back severely from his face, accentuating the wide, square lines of his features. His beard, worn short, was a motley of yellow, silver, and even reddish hues that added to his attractiveness. Deep-set sea blue eyes regarded Ylena and he held up his gloved hand to the man beside him to stop the fellow talking. This was a man used to giving orders and being obeyed; even the set of his generous mouth suggested he was powerful, a leader of men. Pil watched him stride from the inn's entrance deeper into the square. People stepped aside, pulling their goats and donkeys out of his way.

Pil saw the noble's eyes narrow in concentration as Ylena reached the peak of the song's tragedy. Other men, the noble's own no doubt, began to gather nearby.

Ylena's song came to its heart-wrenching end and cries of appreciation went up in the crowd, people surging forward to toss coppers into the rather full-sounding hat. But it was the nobleman who shouldered through the people now and Pil took account that they all moved easily aside, some bowing, women curtsying.

This was no petty lord.

Pil approached carefully, bending to pick up his hat. Ylena had slumped to lean against the well, her eyes closed, her energies spent, and her emotions no doubt in further turmoil, as the song was so obviously about her and the man she had loved and lost. The nobleman reached for her hand. It occurred to Pil that the man had already recognized her status, despite her tattered, dusty appearance, for he was touching his lips to her limp knuckles. It must be the clothes, he realized. Only noblewomen could afford such quality garments.

"My lady." The older man spoke gently. "You sing like an angel." His voice was tender, but Pil felt sure his men rarely heard this tone.

Ylena's eyes fluttered open, but she gave no recognition other than to effect a brief curtsy of sorts. "Thank you, sir. I'm hoping my voice will feed myself and my companion tonight," she said, glancing toward Pil and then back again into eyes the color of a stormy sea.

"Shar's Wrath!" the man exclaimed. "But you need not sing for your supper, madam. Who is your family? I demand to know who leaves you in this state?"

"My family?" Ylena breathed, hardly above a whisper. "My family," she repeated, "is dead, sir." She looked up, the dirt of their travel—despite its best efforts—unable to mask the beauty beneath. "I am all that's left, my lord, and am on the run from those who would do me harm."

The noble made a sound of frustration. He looked behind and signaled to one of his men.

"She's weak, pick her up!" he commanded, taking off his cloak.

The man obeyed and his lord laid his own cloak about Ylena, at which point Pil thought it necessary to step forward.

"My lord," he said, bowing. "I am Pil."

"And?"

"Apologies," Pil offered. "I am a monk—well, novice, in truth—and have been instructed to stay close to the Lady. She is ready to faint from hunger. She has been recuperating with us for some weeks and I fear our journey across country has set her back."

He hoped he had made good account of himself. Brother Jakub had always cautioned that brevity was a desirable trait.

The man regarded him briefly before saying, "Follow me," and Pil found himself all but trotting to keep up with the elderly noble, hat in hand jangling from the coin weighing it down. They returned to the inn and were taken straight to its dining room. Their redeemer barked orders and suddenly the room was a frenzy of activity. Men appeared and disappeared, taking their instructions from their chief and going about whatever business he required.

Before long, the smell of bacon wafted toward them; it made Pil dizzy with anticipation.

"Eat first," the man commanded, "then we'll talk."

Ylena was given a posset of sweetly spiced milk, which she drank without comment, although her glance toward the girl setting it down was filled with gratitude. Pil was given the same and he swallowed the contents of the cup, feeling its healing warmth hit the spot immediately.

"Thank you, my lord," he heard himself say before the excitement of seeing slices of fresh bread smeared liberally with butter accompanied by thick rashers of sizzling bacon stopped whatever he might have said next.

He ate with gusto and in silence, his glance darting toward Ylena, who nibbled hungrily on her bread, not yet daring to touch the meat. The noble ignored them for the time being, talking quietly with the man Pil presumed was his second in command. Pil finished his meal and felt immediately drowsy, although the luxury of sleep would elude him for now.

"Now we talk," the man said, and beckoned Pil to a corner of the room where a tray of ales was set down.

"My lord," Ylena interjected. "I can account for myself, sir."

"Then tell me," the nobleman said brusquely. "You may speak freely."

She glanced at Pil and found a brief smile of sympathy for him. Both knew they would have to relive their trauma for this man. He nodded encouragingly, noticing the spark was back in her eyes and her expression had returned to its determined set. The food had already worked wonders. Ylena's voice was steady and firm as she began. "We're from Rittylworth Monastery. It's where we're fleeing from."

The old noble frowned. "Why?"

Ylena sighed. "The news has not yet traveled this far north, then?" The man glared beneath silver-peppered eyebrows, keen for her to get on with it. "It was burned. Most of the monks murdered where they stood, the senior ones singled out for special torture."

The two listeners, shocked, banged their mugs down on the table, heedlessly sloshing ale over their fists.

"What?" The noble's voice was hard, disbelieving.

"I speak the truth, sir. I watched it. We were hidden, but we saw the men, flying the King's colors, come and vandalize the village and then one by one cut down the monks. They crucified and burned the senior Brothers." Scenes flashed into her mind of that terrible morning and she felt sickened. "They arrived directly as morning silence ended and we've been on the run since."

"Well timed to ensure they got all of you," the nobleman's companion commented correctly.

Ylena looked at him for the first time and not only noticed the resemblance to his lord but also his easy smile and drape of bright, golden hair. He was so similar to her Alyd it was heartbreaking. He also wore a close beard. Were these father and son? she thought, not realizing she had spoken aloud.

"Yes, this is my son, Crys. My apologies, manners have deserted me. I am Jeryb, Duke of Felrawthy."

Now Ylena was startled, looking from Alyd's father to his equally handsome brother.

It was Pil who put it into words. "Good grief, my lord, it is to you that we flee!" he spluttered, looking toward Ylena. "She has said no one's name but yours. This is the Lady Ylena Thirsk."

More shock for the two men who sat across from him.

"Fergys Thirsk's daughter! My son's intended bride?" the older man roared.

"Yes, my lord," Ylena said, recovering herself. "I bring the gravest of news."

"I'm sorry we meet under these circumstances," Crys said, extending his hand. The smile froze on his face while puzzlement crinkled his brow. "Where is Alyd?"

The duke reached for her arm. "My son. Alyd. Why is he not with you?"

Ylena felt her world sway from the euphoria of finding the Duke to despair at knowing what she must share with him now. "No, my lord, he is not with me," she admitted carefully, the hairs tightening at the back of her head. "Forgive me, sir." She glanced toward the baffled expression on Crys's kind face. "It is why I am here. To tell you that Alyd is dead."

The silence that met this statement was vast and Ylena held her breath awaiting their reaction. Her pity for these men of Felrawthy was palpable. As much as she mourned Alyd, she had already accepted his death, knew the only way forward now was to seek vengeance. Nothing would bring him back, but satisfaction could be gained by bringing down the murderer. They had yet even to grasp the significance of her words, let alone hear the worst of it.

Jeryb stared at her, eyes much stormier now, brow furrowed and angry. "Dead, you say?" he finally asked.

She nodded. "I'm so sorry." She shook her head. "There is so much to tell, sir, I hardly know where to start. But you are all that stands between me and certain death too."

"I can't speak of this here" the Duke said, closing his eyes in tightly held grief. "I will hear it all, but not here. If we ride hard, we can make Tenterdyn by nightfall."

Crys reached over and squeezed her hand for reassurance. It was precisely the sort of mannerism that Alyd had possessed, never afraid to touch or show emotion. She hardly dared look at Crys for fear of breaking down. "That's the family home," he whispered. "You'll be safe with us. Can you ride, Pil?"

Pil nodded as Crys Donal took control; his father looked incapable of saying another word. Crys rested a hand on his father's shoulder as he sorted out arrangements.

"Good. Then go outside and tell Parks to find you a mount on my orders. I shall bring the Lady Ylena. Are you happy to ride with me, my lady?"

"Yes . . . yes of course," Ylena replied, although she dreaded being so close to the man who so resembled her dead husband.

18

WYL KNEW HE HAD PUSHED THE MARE HARD AND HAD FINALLY slowed her from a gallop to a canter, cooling her down to a trot that she would hold for a little while yet. He reached over and stroked her head in silent thanks and she tossed her mane as though in response.

The small stream he had expected to find made itself

known by a soft gurgling and he angled the chestnut mare off the road, ducking beneath the overhanging trees before emerging into a pretty glade. The horse was happy to stop now and drank greedily. Wyl nimbly alighted. He wished he could have continued on, for he was fretting for Ylena, but he knew he was well ahead of any party sent by the King. He was counting on Celimus not discovering the disappearance of Leyen until later this morning and even then the King might not sense anything untoward and thus not react at all. Perhaps Jessom and Celimus would assume she had set off about her duties. They would think it odd, of course, but might not dwell on her lack of a formal farewell. No, they were not the issue here.

The problem was Aremys, he realized, but again Wyl comforted himself that he had the whole of the night's ride and most of the morning's lead on the mercenary. By the time Aremys discovered Faryl's disappearance, Wyl could be halfway to his destination.

With this thought, he forced himself to allow the mare some rest time. He unsaddled her and gave her a bag of feed and a quick rubdown before settling himself back against a tree to think. He had not counted on falling into a doze quite so readily, and had he been awake, he would have heard the approach of the horse much earlier than he did. Leaping to his feet, he released the double blades of Romen Koreldy and moved into a fighting stance as the sound of a man and beast crashing through the undergrowth approached.

Wyl had no idea who it was, but he was determined the intruder would die. He crouched lower, ready to strike.

Aremys burst through the trees with a roar. Wyl realized who it was and in a fraction of the second he had left in the inevitable arc of his throw, he cast the knife slightly off center. The mercenary took that moment of hesitation to leap from his horse, landing heavily on his prey. Their bodies crunched and rolled and then Aremys grunted. He expelled all air from his lungs and lay still for a moment, on top of his victim, crushing much of the air from Wyl, who felt battered from the impact.

"Didn't count on the knives, Faryl." Aremys sighed and rolled off to show a dark patch of blood already enlarging on his shirt.

"You stupid fool!" Wyl shrieked in Faryl's voice.

"I asked for it." Aremys grinned and then his face contorted and he closed his eyes. "Ah, but it hurts."

"Be still!" Wyl ordered, using the knife that had not sunk into the man's flesh to cut away the shirt. "I'm glad it's your arm and not your foolhardy chest."

"And I thought you were accurate."

"I am, it's why you're not dead," Wyl growled.

"Then why did you hesitate?"

"Shut up and tell me what you're doing here," Wyl said angrily, knowing all too well. He hacked at his own shirt and dipped it into the water so he could clean the wound.

"Following you." Aremys sounded reproachful. He allowed the ministrations and, despite the pain, enjoyed Faryl's hands on his body. "Why did you leave without me?"

"I don't work with others. You know that."

"Not even on your king's instructions?"

"Especially then. He wants the job done cleanly and I don't need anyone else making errors."

"Except you're not going to do it, are you?" Aremys stated, staying her busy hands with his good arm. "Tell me the truth."

"About what?" Wyl cried, hating his screechy woman's voice and the uncomfortable closeness of the mercenary.

"About why you have no intention of killing Ylena Thirsk."

Wyl sat back and tossed the bloodied rag aside. "It's quite deep and going to need sewing up. You're fortunate nothing serious is severed. Do you want me to bind it for now?"

"Please."

Wyl began again, tying first a tourniquet to stem the bleeding and then dressing the wound with a fresh piece of linen. "It will hold only for a short while. You need to see a physic quickly."

"Forget my damn arm, woman! I want you to talk to me."

"Leave me alone."

"I can't do that. You see, we've been given a task—a paid one—by the King of Morgravia and I see no reason why I shouldn't carry it out."

"Then you're already a dead man," Wyl replied matter-of-factly in a much softer voice.

Aremys was left in no doubt that Faryl meant what she said. "Are you planning on using the other knife on me, then?"

"If I have to," Wyl said, moving a little farther away from his companion.

"So her life does mean something to you. Why are you protecting this noblewoman when Celimus assures us she is an enemy of the realm?"

Wyl laughed. It was a bitter sound and made Aremys wince. But it also seemed to open the floodgates and Wyl began talking angrily.

"She is barely eighteen years of age—she lost her mother at birth, her father when she was but an infant, and her brother—" His voice broke. Wyl cleared his throat. "Her brother, Wyl Thirsk, was murdered at the King's command because Celimus had long been jealous of him over the fact that King Magnus preferred Wyl to his own son."

He continued, his voice lower and harder, with the rage driving it. "Ylena Thirsk was widowed within hours of her wedding. She witnessed the beheading of her innocent husband, whose only crime was loving her and cheating Celimus of a bedmate. She was made to kneel upon her beloved's still-warm and gushing blood, tripping over his headless body as her own neck was laid on the block."

Aremys looked understandably shocked. "How can you know this?"

"Because I was forced to watch it!" The words rushed out now, angry, bewildered, not permitting Aremys the immediate question that sprang to his lips. "Her life was saved only because I agreed to the blackmail. I had to—it was either that or forfeit her life before my very eyes."

"What was the blackmail?" Aremys muttered, entirely

confused, not sure whether Faryl was speaking of herself or someone else.

"To contrive a king's death. At the time it was meant to be a meeting between Valor and Wyl Thirsk—that name of Thirsk meant something to Valor; he respected my father even though they were lifetime enemies. It's the only reason he agreed to allow a Morgravian into his palace."

Aremys shook his head, not comprehending the twist in the conversation—why was Faryl speaking as if she were Wyl Thirsk? She was staring ahead now, talking in a single, flat tone and he was loath to stop her now that she was finally talking.

"Celimus used Wyl Thirsk to get the audience with the King to discuss his daughter's hand in marriage and lure the Briavellian Crown into a sense of security. Meanwhile he had ordered not only the death of King Valor but the slaying of myself, both of which were achieved in the King's study as I negotiated for his daughter's betrothal to Celimus."

Now Wyl fell quiet, his head moving in a sad shake as he recalled the events once again. Aremys held his breath, remained silent. He desperately wanted to hear the end of this chilling tale.

"You mentioned a man named Koreldy?" Wyl suddenly said, looking up.

Aremys nodded.

"I lied. I do know him . . . did know him. He was a member of that party to Briavel and saved Thirsk's life, you could say. Together they certainly saved Princess Valentyna, now Queen of Briavel."

Again Aremys was lost. He knew Thirsk was dead, so how could his life have been saved? Sensibly he maintained his silence, allowing Faryl to speak on.

"Koreldy took Thirsk's body back to Pearlis to make sure the name was cleared of any traitorous act that Celimus might suggest to cover up the ambush.

"Because of Koreldy's actions, Celimus was forced to give General Thirsk a full ceremonial burial and his name remains unsullied. Romen Koreldy had also made a promise to the dying Thirsk that he would rescue and protect his sister, Ylena, from Celimus."

Aremys nodded as the broader picture became more clear, grateful that Faryl was telling the tale now without her own involvement. It was so odd that she had referred to Thirsk in the first person.

"When Koreldy tracked her down she was imprisoned in the dungeons of the castle. This is a noblewoman, Aremys, who grew up in the corridors of Stoneheart, was ward of the King." Wyl sighed. "He loved her as a daughter. She was treated like a princess. What Celimus perpetrated on that young woman during her incarceration is unspeakable. He surely damaged her mind. My sister is no longer the same sunny child I knew."

There it is again, Aremys thought. *What does she mean?*

"Koreldy did rescue her, under the guise of wanting her for himself. Celimus trusted him, believing it was Koreldy who had slain Thirsk. I suspect Celimus enjoyed the irony of knowing Thirsk's killer would also rape his sister. It has the cruel twist his mind would love," Wyl said bitterly.

"So you are now trying to protect her? Why?" Aremys ventured.

"Because she is innocent. Because I hate Celimus. Because she is the last of our line and I have sworn my own life to protect her."

Aremys again ignored the first-person reference. He was completely confused, but still he tried to make some sense of the tale, if just for Faryl's sake. "Where is Koreldy—is he with her?"

"He's dead," Wyl said, finally moving to stand.

"How?"

"I killed him," Wyl replied, moving toward his horse and beginning to resaddle her.

Aremys struggled to sit up. "Help me, damn it!" he yelled.

"No. You're on your own now. Go get yourself fixed up. I've told you all I'm going to. I'm asking you to leave me in peace. I suggest you head home to Grenadyn, as was your original plan." He watched Aremys twitch with regret. "Don't go near Ylena Thirsk or I promise I will finish what I began."

"Then you'll have to kill me, for until I have the truth, Faryl, I have no reason not to pursue my prey. I am not involved in the Thirsk woman's sorrows, no matter how sad her tale is."

"Well, you've been warned. I will not hesitate next time." The green eyes glittered with menace.

"Then answer me this. Why did you say Fergys Thirsk was your father?" He watched Faryl become very still. Her back was to him, but she was no longer interested in her horse. Her long arms dropped to her side. "And you said you were blackmailed by the King, you witnessed the death of Ylena's husband—yet it was clear when he met us that Celimus had never clapped eyes on you before! Which one of us is going mad here?"

Now Faryl turned and he felt the full weight of her glare.

Aremys was not to be deterred. "You make it sound like she is your sister—but how can that be, Faryl? How can that be?" he shouted, equally angry and bewildered now, determined to have an answer.

The movement was so fluid and so fast he could not have avoided her lunge even if he had had full use of his arm and half a day's warning. He had neither and within a blink the assassin had a knife at his throat and had spitefully twisted his injured arm back behind himself. She pushed him up against a tree. The pain was agonizing—Aremys knew his wound was bleeding fast again. He was amazed at her strength; he struggled but it was useless in his state and he felt the blade slice into the skin at his throat . . . more blood, he assumed, and he fell still in her grip.

She growled now into his ear. "Because, damn you, Aremys of Grenadyn and your constant interference, I am Wyl Thirsk." Wyl shoved the burly man away.

Aremys staggered forward, clutching his arm, but managed to turn and face his companion. Faryl looked like a wild animal—he half expected her to pounce again and felt sure that if she did it would be for the last time—he would take his final breath on this earth as she slashed her knife across his throat.

She was breathing hard and there were tears in her eyes. "Leave me, Aremys!"

But he could not. He was too shocked. Stupefied by her whispered words, he risked her wrath still further. "Faryl . . . please?" His voice was gruff, thick with alarm and emotion.

"My name is Wyl," came the bitter reply, and he watched Faryl turn away to hide her grief.

He left her alone for a few minutes so that both of them might steady themselves. Finally he walked toward her, clutching at the wound in his arm, which was really protesting now.

"Please explain it to me." He was begging, he realized, adding, "I want to help."

"Help?" she said sadly. "All I ask is that you leave Ylena be."

Aremys swallowed. "I promise you I will not permit a hair on her head to be harmed—not as long as I can draw breath to protect it."

He watched Faryl or Wyl—whoever it was—turn slowly and he saw a new gleam in the feline eyes. He read it as hope.

"On your honor?"

He nodded wearily. "I'll make a blood oath if you wish it."

"And in return?"

"Your whole story." He held up his hand at the retort he could see coming. "And I will help you to achieve whatever it is you are setting out to do."

"Why?"

He shrugged, too confused. "Because it was wrong of me to turn you over to Jessom."

"You owed me nothing. I'm sure he paid well."

"Not enough for my loyalty. You have that—not that I really understand who it is I pledge such loyalty to."

Wyl reached for the bladder of water and handed it to Aremys. "Here, drink some. Then you had better sit down and listen well."

If Aremys thought he was a man who had seen and heard it all, he was sorely mistaken. As the full tale of Wyl Thirsk unfolded, the mercenary felt his head begin to spin with the startling notion that he was now in the company of three people.

It was done. Both sat within a post-cathartic silence and watched the bees buzz merrily about them, crawling into and out of the bright yellow and orange wildflowers at the edge of the stream. Sparrows chittered overhead and a frantic blackbird, clearly with a new nest of fledglings to fatten up, busied himself nearby.

Spring is here, Aremys realized absently. "Thank you," he murmured, not trusting himself to say much more.

"Now I will definitely kill you if you betray me," Wyl threatened, feeling similarly awkward yet vaguely relieved that the story had been shared.

Aremys breathed deeply. "I have pledged my loyalty to you. It is not given lightly—no man has ever had it before."

"I'm grateful that you consider me a man," Wyl said with relief.

The mercenary snorted. "And I wanted to sleep with you."

Wyl was lost for a response and they both laughed, embarrassed, which surprisingly helped diffuse the awkwardness.

Aremys did not want to let the laughter go. "You know you've got the greatest tits?"

Wyl lifted one of Faryl's eyebrows. "Apparently."

"I don't suppose—"

"Certainly not!" came the indignant reply and more healing laughter. "I don't own them—I'm . . . er . . . I'm simply the caretaker."

"Who else knows?"

"A boy called Fynch, whom I trust implicitly. An old woman—a seer—who first sensed I possessed this strange magic within me. Mind you, I don't know if she still lives. Her niece, Elspyth, who I hope has already found Ylena," he said wistfully before adding, "and a brave warrior from the Razors."

"A mountain dweller?"

"His name is Lothryn and I believe he gave his life to save mine."

"You believe? You don't know if he's dead?"

Wyl shrugged. "I hope he is."

Aremys eyed his companion with a look of surprise.

"I suspect death is far preferable to his probable fate at the hands of Cailech," Wyl answered, obvious sadness in his voice.

Aremys did not push. "So Queen Valentyna thinks you're dead?"

Wyl smiled wryly. "Well, I am really. Her friendship was with Romen Koreldy. Faryl of Coombe is his murderer."

"And the Queen knows nothing of this enchantment or the magic that has touched your life?"

Wyl shook his head. "I believe Fynch has tried to talk to her about it, but Briavellians are even more closed to magic than Morgravians. It was not so long we ago that we still hunted down, tortured, and burned suspected witches. Briavel simply doesn't accept that such power exists. No, I don't think she could comprehend the truth."

"I'm finding it pretty hard myself," Aremys admitted. "But I believe you—there is too much that was odd about you not to believe it." He was still trying to come to terms with the fact that the person sitting before him had inhabited the body of the infamous Romen Koreldy from his own island.

"Do you ever feel them?" he asked.

Wyl looked up at him. "Romen and Faryl?"

"No, your tits."

At this Wyl exploded into laughter. Aremys took immense pleasure at this, for in Wyl's strange existence, there seemed little, if anything, to smile about.

"It's good to hear you laugh," the big man said.

"Haven't had much to laugh about in recent weeks."

"I did mean the others," Aremys admitted sheepishly.

"Yes. They are always present, but more as a spiritual remnant of themselves. I can tap into some of their memories, although those fade very fast, but strangely I possess their skills and much of their learned knowledge. Still there is plenty that is lost to me. Wyl Thirsk just takes over."

"So what do we do now?"

"Get your arm stitched."

"Wait. Before I turned you over to Jessom, you were headed for Baelup. What was there?"

"Ah, yes," Wyl said, sighing. "I was trying to track down Myrren's mother. I still will once Ylena is safe. I'm hoping the mother may shed some light on my situation or lead me to where I might find out more."

"You're hiding something," Aremys said. "Remember, the whole tale, you promised."

Wyl nodded, struggling against his reluctance. "I've learned that the man Myrren's mother was married to was not Myrren's true father. I need to find her blood father. The old seer from Yentro I spoke of—Elspyth's aunt—said he would tell me more about this so-called gift I've been given."

"Is it dangerous for you to travel to Felrawthy?"

Wyl shrugged. "No more so than to Baelup."

"But you'd rather be tracking down Myrren's father than chasing across the realm for your sister, who you already admit may well be in safe hands."

"I can't be sure about that, not with Celimus hunting her down."

"But he's not. I am. Celimus is under the presumption that he's already sent off his agents and I suspect he will not dwell on it further for now."

Wyl looked puzzled. "What's your point?"

"I'll go after Ylena. You find Myrren's father." There was a silence and Aremys knew what Wyl was thinking. "You can trust me. I will protect her with my life." Then he unexpectedly added, "I had a sister but she died in an accident. My father had left her in my care. I was the youngest of the brothers, so it was my job. But I wanted to go hunting with my father and the rest of the boys, so I left Serah in what I thought was a safe place in the woods."

Wyl was listening intently now—so it was not just he who had secrets. "Go on."

"She was killed. A wild pig gored her. I'm not sure it wouldn't have killed both of us, but I have still never forgiven myself for deserting her. I'm not sure my family ever did either," he added quietly.

"Forgive me, Aremys. That's a shocking story. But I'm still uncertain of why you feel obliged to fight my battle," Wyl admitted.

"Perhaps if I shared the whole truth with you, it might be more clear," the mercenary replied. "My father is a noble. We were visiting Pearlis many years ago as a family. I would have been around ten, my sister just four summers old. Celimus was perhaps eight."

"Celimus!"

"Yes, I'm afraid we both have reason to hate the King of Morgravia."

"And?" Wyl encouraged, mindful of Aremys's saturated sleeve. Thankfully the bleeding had been stanched again.

"My father and brothers were invited to hunt with the royal party. My mother, bless her, was asked to bathe with the court ladies. Coming from Grenadyn, none of us had seen such resplendence as Stoneheart offered, so she asked me to look after Serah for a couple of hours. Play with her, she said. Keep her safe." Aremys looked to the sky and grunted. "As soon as mother's back was turned I took Serah to the woods where I wanted to be. I was furious that I couldn't go on the hunt and blamed Serah. Along came Celimus and his friends. They told me they were going to beat sticks in the woods higher up where the wild pigs roamed and see if they couldn't coax out their own game to hunt." Aremys shook his head. "It was stupid but we were just boys, eager to be grown-up and keen for our fathers' respect. It didn't occur to me that Serah wasn't safe. I joined the trio of friends and suffice to say we not only flushed out a pig but we also made him angry enough to stampede straight into Serah's path."

"Shar's Wrath, man! And Celimus doesn't know who you are?"

Aremys shook his head. "I wasn't important enough to remember, and besides, at that age my parents called me Remy. He hasn't made the connection. I spent years planning how I was going to kill him. I blamed him, you see. When I was old enough, I realized the folly of youth. I was not going to kill the heir to Morgravia and I am certainly not going to kill its new king. Instead I bleed him of the money he loves so much."

It all fell into place now for Wyl. "You!"

Aremys looked abashed. "I'm afraid so."

"You told them where the taxes would be coming from," Wyl stammered. "You guided Rostyr and his men."

"It's true. And I'll continue to find ways to make the King's life miserable while all the time helping myself to his coffers doing some of his dirty work."

"But those seven men?"

"All deserved to die. They were corrupt."

Wyl could barely mask the sarcasm. "A selective assassin."

"You could say."

Wyl smiled grimly. "Well, I'm not so forgiving as you, Aremys. I aim to bring about Celimus's downfall."

Aremys grinned back. "And I will help you. I hate him as much as you. Do you believe my loyalty now?"

Wyl nodded. "Let's get you sewn up and then go find my sister. Both of us."

19

DUKE JERYB'S ESTATE WAS A SERIES OF ELEGANT BUILDINGS, running off the main two-story house. It sprawled amid a glen, protected on all sides by picturesque hills, flanked on its north by a small forest.

The family had a long and close history with the Crown and a reputation as fearless defenders of the north. In days gone by, previous Briavellian Kings had thought to storm Morgravia through its north but had met solid, tireless resistance from Felrawthy. And like the Thirsks to the south, this family boasted an impeccable bloodline of warriors. It had not been a fertile family, however, until Jeryb had assumed the mantle as Duke quite late in his life. Although his wife had already given him a son, Crys, he had no intention of following in the family tradition of siring a single heir.

It had become a joke in the early days of their marriage. "It just takes practice, my love," Jeryb had said, a sparkle in his eye.

And the young Aleda had smiled forthrightly back and replied that they would just have to practice each evening.

The twins, Daryn and Jorge, followed this rigorous routine, with young Alyd arriving as a special surprise five years later. By that time Aleda had suggested to the man she loved that they practice a little less.

"I think we've got the hang of it now," she had declared one night, to Jeryb's high amusement.

Jeryb had fought alongside Fergys Thirsk as a trusted leader. Not only had their two wives found a common enjoyment in each other, but the two heads of the families knew they could trust each other . . . and in battle, trust was the most precious of commodities.

Fergys relied entirely on Jeryb to hold the north in the increasing agitation between Morgravia and the mountain people. He knew of no other soldier he could trust as much, other than Gueryn le Gant, or a more loyal noble to the Crown. Although Jeryb rarely managed to come south other than on highly formal occasions, his relationship with King Magnus was strong. They had talked once over a warmed ale on a frigid night on yet another battlefield, of their sons holding the realm as strongly as they had done over the years.

Ylena looked out now across the glen to the elegant manor that she had previously dreamed of visiting with her new husband. A fresh wave of sorrow bit at her heart as she accepted that she was here without him, clinging to the waist of a kind, bright-eyed stranger who reminded her too much of that same man she had loved. She and Crys had ridden as fast as the horse could go carrying two people. Crys had left instructions with his men to make their way back to the duchy; in the meantime his father had left with just a couple of his men as escort, riding at breakneck speed to reach Tenterdyn first.

"To safety, my lady," Crys said gently over his shoulder. "Welcome to our home."

His voice was so kind and so reminiscent of another that she smiled and no one watching her could have failed to be arrested by her beauty despite the days' worth of traveling grime.

"Are you all right?" he asked.

"Are you?" she replied.

"Too shocked and distraught at your news to think," he admitted, and she appreciated his candor. "The worst is yet to come, I fear. Telling my mother will not be easy, although hopefully my father has already prepared her. Alyd was the favorite, you see." He looked around and chanced a thin smile. "Not because he liked it that way." He shrugged. "He was the youngest . . . the last. Everyone spoiled him and adored him, and as you know, it was easy to do both."

She forced back the tears that had sprung to her eyes. "I'm ready. I've not come here to hide, Crys. I've come here to ask your father to help me fight the person who brought this atrocity about."

"You'll find willing warriors, my lady, for Alyd's sake."

"Wait until you learn who our enemy is, sir," she said, more bitterly than she had meant it to sound.

He kicked the horse into a trot down the hill, raising a hand to his father, who had emerged from the house.

Jeryb's wife, Aleda, met them alongside her husband. Her face was pale and lined with building grief, but she found a brief smile of courtesy as their guest arrived.

"Welcome, child," she said bravely, reaching to hug Ylena, whom she had only known previously as an infant.

Both women felt the gravity of the moment, the rush of emotion that cared not for circumstance or timing. It boiled over and they gave in to it, sobbing in each other's arms, two strangers linked by the love of a young man whom they had lost. They remained like that for long enough that the men could no longer bear to watch the upsetting scene and disappeared into the house.

Finally Aleda pulled away. "I'm glad you came here, Ylena."

"I have nowhere else to go, Duchess. Forgive me, but my story is more sordid and upsetting than you can possibly imagine."

"We shall hear it all, child, in all its painful, unmasked truth. But now come, I want you to first bathe and rest."

Ylena looked at the handsome older woman with disbelief.

"You will tell your torrid tale more succinctly if you are refreshed and rested. I can certainly wait a little longer to hear your news."

Ylena liked Alyd's mother immediately, admiring the strength she sensed the woman possessed. It must have taken much courage to have greeted her son's bride so graciously, knowing what she had come to explain to them.

They entered the double doors of the mansion known as Tenterdyn, arm in arm, drying the tears from their cheeks.

Aleda, noticing that Jeryb was nowhere to be seen, looked toward her eldest child and watched him grin crookedly. She saw not only her husband reflected back but the youngest son she suddenly ached to hold again. She nodded, tight-lipped. "This girl needs a bath and a rest and then we will all talk." Her glance brooked no argument. "Let your father know, please, and call the boys in," she added, referring to his brothers. "We'll sit down in an hour or so."

With Ylena settled privately in a chamber and left to her toilet, Crys followed his aristocratic mother down the stairs and into her private reading room. It was her escape from her brood of lively sons and booming father. Here she did indeed read, but also did her quiet thinking. A servant stepped in with a tray and then left, having poured them each a goblet of the promised sweet wine.

"You look tired, son," Aleda said, before sipping.

"Has she told you anything yet?"

Aleda shook her head. "I don't want to hear it anyway."

Crys watched the pain flicker across his mother's face before she checked and masked it. He knew all too well how she did not like anyone to read her thoughts.

Here, my dear. Come and sit down. Aleda said to Ylena when she finally emerged and joined the gathered family in their main chamber. The gown she wore was loose on her—it was one of Aleda's—but she suddenly looked every bit the noblewoman she was. "Crys, call for some spiced ale."

Her son, entranced by the woman his brother had chosen to marry, moved swiftly. Aleda gestured her guest toward a comfortable armchair. The room felt suddenly crowded.

"Thank you," Ylena said, mustering her courage. "Let me tell you everything."

"Let's wait for Crys," the older woman said gently, squeezing Ylena's hand. "He must hear this too."

A ghost of a smile flicked across Ylena's hauntingly beautiful face. "Yes, of course," she said, "for I fear I will not want to tell it again."

Crys returned, his expression grim. He glanced at his still-shocked father, who caught the look and roused himself from his own silent stupor in the corner.

"Tell us, my girl," he commanded in his deep voice. "Tell us everything."

She spared them none of the horror of their son's death or of her own traumas. No one interrupted her, and by the time she finished speaking, a frigid silence had gripped the room. The room's atmosphere chilled still further as they heard how his head had been left to rot nearby his wife in the dungeon. The silence that followed her final word was like death itself.

"Alyd was formally executed, you say?" Crys asked, his voice hollow with disbelief.

His father, normally bluff and hale, looked suddenly every one of his threescore years and ten. His mother, pale and rigid, bit her lip, the only indication that she was fighting her own demons. Alyd's two other brothers stood by, stunned into silence.

Ylena swallowed. "Alyd was killed before my eyes." She fought the tears for their sake. "They used an axe," she added bitterly. "Didn't even give him a noble death."

Aleda pushed aside her despair. She felt sick to the marrow of her bones, but she wanted to hear it all before she began to grieve. "And you were married?" Aleda asked.

Their guest nodded. "As I explained, it was the only way we could outwit Celimus. He planned to bed me, claiming Virgin's Blood. His intention was to hurt Alyd and, in doing so, draw Wyl into the confrontation he needed to start dismantling Wyl's power over the Legion and his standing."

She looked steadily toward Jeryb. "I will rally men from Argorn, sir, if you wish it," she said, and he knew now why she had come to Tenterdyn.

"We will avenge Alyd and Wyl Thirsk for this atrocity," boomed the Duke, looking toward his eldest son, in whose handsome face he saw a painful echo of his youngest, now headless and rotting in an unmarked grave in Pearlis.

At his words, Ylena's tightly held composure crumbled

and she began to sob helplessly in exhausted relief. Aleda suggested a rest and called for a mild soporific to be made up and administered. The Duchess decided only a blanketing sleep would offer the release this young woman needed from having been made to relive her ugly memories. The others had no such relief and had been left to pick over the horrific account of how Alyd had been so brutally beheaded . . . without trial, without even so much as conviction of a crime. Even armed with proof of a crime, most noble families would have been petitioned by the Crown before any further action was taken.

The agony of looking upon the remains of their loved one shattered everyone. It had been left to Crys to withdraw Alyd from the sack. Aleda privately wished she did not have to see what was left of her son, preferring to remember the sunny, generous boy as he had been when he had left Tenterdyn for the last time.

The viewing left each of the Donal family shaken and withdrawn. Jeryb finally took his leave to shut himself away in his study, where he mentioned he would be considering the right path for retaliation. His words, though carefully chosen and delivered, left his family in no doubt that Felrawthy would shortly provoke civil war against the Crown.

20

AROUND THE TIME YLENA AND PIL ENTERED DORCHYSTER Green, Jessom was standing in a courtyard sharing with his king the new information on Leyen he had been able to unearth. Deep down he knew he was reaching with this, but Celimus had threatened him and Jessom knew it was easier to appease the King with some pretense at intrigue than to say he had nothing further to impart. This was all about survival now and better a busybody noblewoman's back be flayed than his own.

"And you think the Lady Helyn could be a traitor?" Celimus spun around, somewhat aghast at even the intimation.

"Not at all, sire!" Jessom replied smoothly. "I think she may be an unwitting accomplice—if indeed there is a crime that Leyen should answer for. We still have no confirmation that Leyen is working against the Crown."

The King made a clicking noise with his tongue. "But still I'm suspicious. Until we hear differently from Aremys, I am obliged to consider Leyen's actions curious."

Jessom merely nodded.

"Tell me again. Leave out nothing."

The Chancellor began once more. It was no use protesting. "On your advice, your majesty"—he started diplomatically—"I began some inquiries into Jorn's activities on the night in question. It turns out that after escorting Leyen to the gatehouse, he returned to her rooms and gathered up the gown she had worn that night."

Celimus stopped him with a finger in the air. "How do you know this?"

"He was seen leaving the castle and heading into Pearlis, majesty."

The King's alert mind was in full swing. "Was he acting in a guarded manner?"

"No, sire. Some of our own men, returning from an evening in the city, met Jorn, recognized him, and teased him—as soldiers are wont to do."

"And?"

"The lad seemed in no particular hurry and in fact he mentioned to them that he was making a delivery to Lady Helyn."

"All right. Go on," the King replied, seemingly feeling no remorse at the boy's death.

"I checked with Lady Helyn's manservant, who concurs that the delivery of a gown and cape with an item of jewelry was certainly made in the early hours of the morning following our supper. The man, Arnyld, said Jorn did not tarry at the house. He apparently handed over the garments with a simple thank-you from Leyen, then left immediately."

Celimus had already heard the account to this point. but he hoped interrogation might reveal more. "No other detours or errands?"

"Not that I can track down, sire, but . . ." The Chancellor hesitated and there was something in his sudden frown that piqued at the King's interest.

"Ah," Celimus said, leaning forward, "Now we come to it."

Jessom had primed the King perfectly. Now he would lay the trap and lure Celimus toward it. He knew his red herring led nowhere. Still, anything to divert the King from blaming him for things not going the way he wanted. "It seems Leyen did not entirely finalize her thanks verbally. Arnyld mentioned that the note was found in the pocket of the cape, almost by chance, much later."

"You see," Celimus said, pacing now. "It's the wording, almost by chance, that pricks my curiosity. Do you think it was deliberately hidden?"

Jessom shrugged slightly. "I can't guess, sire. Leyen may not have wanted to ask Jorn to try remembering anything more detailed than a courteous thank-you."

"So what did that note contain?" the King asked eagerly.

The chancellor shook his head. "According to the Lady Helyn, nothing of any consequence. She said it was merely a polite courtesy and she believes she must have sent it out with the day's rubbish."

"And you believe her?"

"She very kindly spent some time hunting for the note in my presence, just in case her memory had not served her right, sire. She called Arnyld to task over it and he too searched. There was no sign of it."

"Hmm, perfectly plausible, I suppose."

"As I thought too, sire, which is why I have not pushed any further."

"How was she when you spoke with her?"

"Charming. As I said, keen to help and apologetic for her

hasty action in ridding herself of the note. I sensed no guile, sire."

"I'd still like to speak with her."

"I anticipated as much, my lord. She awaits your pleasure."

Celimus smiled thinly at Jessom's smooth anticipation. "Show her in."

Lady Helyn moved gracefully for her size. She sketched a perfect curtsy to her sovereign. "Your majesty, this is indeed a rare pleasure."

"Come, Lady Helyn, walk a short way with me. Let me show you my new floriana garden."

Clever, she thought. *He knows how much I appreciate nature's gifts.* "Of course, highness. I would be honored," she replied, thanking Shar she had had such practice at concealing her emotions from the ladies at court. She took his proffered arm and allowed the King to guide her out of the courtyard and into an exquisitely perfumed area of a new garden. "Oh, sire, this is magnificent," she breathed, genuinely impressed.

Celimus turned on a dazzling smile for this important lady of his court. He knew he must tread carefully. Her wealthy, influential husband would not take kindly to his wife being browbeaten for seemingly inconsequential information. "It's not yet nearly finished, of course, but I'm glad someone who loves the work of Shar can see it at such an early stage." He led her toward a superb rotunda. A small stone table and benches sat within. "I have ordered some parillion juice, which I hope you'll enjoy."

"A favorite of mine, thank you." She inhaled the perfume about her. "The floriana display is magical, sire. Such colors! My, my."

Celimus was nothing but charm. "Thank you, Lady Helyn. My gardeners tell me they are the most stubborn of plants. What was it one of them said now . . . ?"

He cocked his head in thought just so and she was instantly reminded of his mother. All cold beauty, she recalled; not a skerrick of warmth helped that woman's heart to beat.

But stunning she had certainly been. No woman in Pearlis—or indeed the realm—could hold a candle to her. And the son carried all that grace and poise, the heart-stopping looks. Yet it was an eternal pity that he possessed so little of his father.

"Pardon?" Celimus said. "I missed that."

Lady Helyn flinched. Had she spoken aloud? "Your highness. My apology. I was thinking how you resemble your beautiful mother . . . may Shar bless her."

He smiled at her. "That's generous, my lady. I am reminded often of how special she was."

His companion nodded her head graciously, relief coursing through her.

The King continued. "Ah, yes, it comes to me now. The head gardener calls these flowers Shar's Folly."

"Oh, and I can understand why, my lord," Lady Helyn gushed. "They are impossible to grow—and yet look at your glorious display. I'll admit I did not realize you cared for such things."

Now his expression became soft, almost apologetic. He sighed. "It's true, my lady, that my passion runs to the hunt, my horses, and my realm, of course."

"And your people, sire," Lady Helyn added sagely.

"That goes without saying," he replied evenly. "But more recently I have developed a new passion . . . for a certain woman, my lady, who makes my heart burn with desire. It is she who has made me appreciate some of the more genteel aspects of life," he admitted. "This new garden is for her. It is one of several I am creating in her honor."

There was no avoiding the issue. "You speak of Queen Valentyna, my lord?"

"Indeed. I hope we will be married by the spring's close; I know the union will bring great joy to both realms, Lady Helyn, which brings me to why I wished to see you today."

She was heartily glad they were interrupted by the arrival of the fruit juice, perfectly chilled, the beautifully crafted silver goblets dripping with icy water like dewdrops.

"So cool and refreshing, your highness," Lady Helyn

admitted, eager for a last chance to delay the inevitable conversation.

Leyen's note had been shocking, to say the least. If what the young woman claimed was true, then she was indeed sitting with a madman. According to Leyen, Celimus had plotted the assassination of King Valor of Briavel, leaving his daughter vulnerable. Leyen had further claimed that Celimus also contrived the murder of that fine young man, Wyl Thirsk, who had been set not only to follow his illustrious father's footsteps but to fill his shoes. When his life had been taken so early, so brutally, it was a matter of sincere grief for all Morgravians, but to learn that his death might have been deliberately achieved by his own sovereign had left the Lady Helyn shaken. And Leyen had kept the frightening news coming. Now Celimus was after the sister, the beautiful Ylena. Helyn had barely been able to believe the written accusation that the young woman had not only witnessed her husband's murder but had been incarcerated in Stoneheart's dungeon. Leyen's message had been too brief—like a soldier's—yet detailed. She had summarized that it was the King's intention to marry and then destroy Valentyna, and Briavel with her. Leyen claimed that she, who knew the truth, was the only person who stood in his way.

Should the King ask questions of you, my lady, please be assured that I am a friend to you and a loyal servant of Morgravia.

The note went on to ask her to be watchful and warned that one day the realm she loved might ask her family to make difficult choices, in which case Leyen pleaded that Lady Helyn remember the secret information she had been furnished with.

There had been moments since she had read the note when Lady Bench had despaired, thinking that it was all some sort of terrible hoax. Was it truly credible? Yet her shrewd judgment of character had told her that the Leyen she had met had been honest. Furthermore Helyn Bench could not fathom what Leyen might gain by fashioning such a complex web of lies.

She swallowed another gulp of her delicious juice, not tasting it.

"Not too sweet?" Celimus inquired, dragging her thoughts back to the present.

"It's perfect, my lord. Where were we?"

"Mmm, yes," the King replied, deliberately distractedly, as if this visit were not the major topic on his mind right now. "I believe we were talking about why I asked you to come today."

"That's right, we were, my lord. How may I serve you?"

"Well, you see, it's a matter of security. For the realm."

"Good grief. I can't imagine any of my petty gossip or court knowledge might assist in something so lofty, your highness," she said, laughing gently.

"You lent a gown to a guest of the palace," Celimus began, and she realized he meant to parry no further.

She nodded. "Yes, a lovely woman by the name of Leyen."

He smiled in agreement. "That's her. Did you spend any time with her, madam?"

"Indeed. A few hours. We met at the bathing pavilion. I can't resist a new face in the palace, your highness. I pride myself on knowing all newcomers within hours of their arrival." She tittered, affecting the gossipy voice she used with her ladies.

"What did you learn?" he asked, ignoring the affectation.

She stopped her chuckling and allowed a frown of puzzlement to take its place. "About Leyen? Not a lot, your highness. She struck me as a particularly private person. I did learn that she was supping with you that evening and had nothing suitable to wear."

"Yes, the gown you lent was most becoming."

"My daughter's. I also sent around my maid that evening to dress her hair. There was a cape and an item of jewelry sent to Leyen. A messenger returned the garments and jewelry hours later with thanks." She decided to take a risk and lead this conversation toward its end, not sure her nerves could withstand the King's penetrating gaze much longer. "I know that Chancellor Jessom seemed especially interested in a note we found in the cape much later the following day."

"That's right, we are."

"Do you have reason to suspect Leyen of something, my lord?"

"I do, Lady Helyn. I have reason to believe she may be plotting against the Crown."

She knew contrived shock would not work now. This situation required the most delicate of navigation.

Instead she looked at him quizzically, deliberately pausing as if to consider before speaking. Finally: "No, sire," she soothed. Here it was. Everything depended on how she carried herself in the next few moments. Either he would accept her explanation or she would find herself a guest of his majesty's dungeon. "That young woman had nothing but good things to say of you, my lord. She expressed her wish that you would marry Queen Valentyna and admitted only to being a courier of messages between the two realms. She would not say more—in fact, she admonished me for my curiosity with a reminder that as your private agent, she was not permitted to reveal anything further."

"She did?"

"On my word, my king." *Shar forgive me,* she thought.

The gaze did not falter, although she sensed he did not disbelieve her.

"And you trust her?"

"I have no reason not to, sire. I found her to be direct in her manner, determined to serve you well."

"Did she say farewell?"

"Not in person, sire. It was all in that brief note of thanks—I do wish I'd kept it just to reassure you that it held nothing more than polite courtesies. If that young woman has any grudge against you, I did not pick it up, and if you'll permit me to say so, your highness, there are few with sharper instincts than I."

Please believe me, she begged inwardly as she waited for his response.

He took his time, leveling a narrowed gaze as if into her soul. She resisted the urge to squirm beneath it. Finally he blinked, graciously took her hand, and kissed it. "Thank you, Lady Helyn. You have put my mind at rest. Jessom here will see you out."

The Chancellor materialized from behind them, smiling obsequiously in that oily manner of his. Her knees felt weak with relief. She was glad she was still seated. "I'm pleased, your highness, to have eased your mind," she said, finding the courage to test her knees and stand. "We all look forward to the nuptials, my lord," she added.

The King gave her a wolfish grin before permitting her leave. Lady Helyn left the palace, fighting the urge to run as she kept an unhurried pace, smiling at people she knew, even stopping once and, to the Chancellor's annoyance, passing on a new tidbit of gossip to a person she had not seen in a while.

Only when she was alone in her carriage did she feel her heartbeat begin to slow and she permitted herself the first tentative congratulations on the fine performance she had given to her king. She realized suddenly that she was now officially a traitor to Morgravia—in lying to her sovereign, she was now no longer loyal to the Crown.

Not to this man's Crown, she thought, *but to Morgravia I remain loyal.* She would need to talk this over with her husband, whenever he deigned to return home. Until then, she would take Leyen's advice and remain watchful.

Lady Helyn Bench was not a lover of traveling as her husband was. Most of the time she felt sure Eryd contrived reasons to be gone from Pearlis; not that she minded, having known from their first meeting that at heart he was a solitary figure who far preferred the open road and his own company to the crush of people and his wife's gossipy intrigues in the capital. Eryd was wealthy, and powerful indeed. His voice was respected at court—notably with the King, both old and new—and his weight, when put behind a particular matter, was considered worth taking note of. Moreover, the other nobles listened to him and took guidance from the steadfast, seemingly incorruptible Lord Bench.

He had made his riches from buying and selling exotic spices and magnificent gems from the northern islands. He could, in truth, procure virtually any merchandise from anywhere, ranging from high-quality tobacco to a magnificent horse.

Eryd was the complete opposite of his plump, stay-at-home wife, who enjoyed spending his wealth on everything from lavish parties to her prized pond fish. They were an oddly matched yet loving couple whose affection for each other had never waned. Her constant chittering might drive most men of his ilk to their grave and yet Eryd rather enjoyed Helyn's comforting noise when he returned home. Likewise, Helyn did not mind her partner being so elusive; she was more than capable of handling the most formal of occasions without a husband's support and she relished the time alone to pursue her own interests.

And so the Bench household, when the family was together, was one filled with love and laughter, music and reading, intrigue and storytelling. Power throbbed through the Bench family, which was as generous with its money as it was with its time for friends and acquaintances. The couple seemed to want for nothing and they were very much envied, as much for their secure relationship as for their wealth.

However, anyone passing beneath Lady Helyn's window on that particular evening might have told a different story at the bathing pavilion the next day. Raised voices carried through the still night, thankfully unintelligibly, for the argument had occurred in Helyn's dressing room, which was well cocooned by dozens and dozens of gowns and wraps, skirts and coats.

"This is sheer madness," Eryd roared. "I've never heard of such folly."

"Haven't you, darling?" Helyn responded in the otherwise busy voice she reserved just for him. Realizing he was not to be put off quite so easily, she stopped searching through her clothes and looked at him, exasperated. "Don't wave that pipe at me, Eryd. I'm not one of your workers to do your bidding."

"No," he said, less loudly. "But you are my wife and you will listen to me."

"Of course I'll listen. But I don't have to do what you want." She flounced out of the dressing room into her chamber.

Eryd had returned only that afternoon and was still shocked at the news of her meeting with the King and her explanation that she had lied to their sovereign solely on the advice of a stranger called Leyen. He tried a less dictatorial approach. "Helyn . . . my love. I beg you not to meddle in the politics of this realm."

"Why not? You do!"

He looked at her with a pained expression. "That's not fair, my love."

She made a sound of disgust, cutting across whatever martyrlike statement was coming.

"But this is madness," he repeated, feeling suddenly helpless.

"I agree. I will do no more than keep my ear to the ground for information that might assist."

"Toward bringing down your king," he said, aghast.

"Hush!" she cautioned, speaking more quietly now. "You of all people should grasp the import of what we've been told."

"If it's true," he countered, frustrated by her easy acceptance of the words of a stranger.

"Yes," Helyn answered. "If it's true. That's what I'm going to find out, because if it is, oh Eryd, what will become of our realm?"

He sighed and sat on the bed next to her. "Civil war."

"That's right. I believe Leyen is trying to prevent it."

"Working against the Crown," he said sadly. "It's treachery, Helyn."

"So is the murder of innocent, high-ranking nobles—not to mention the King of Briavel," she hissed. "I can't stand by with this information and not do anything."

"And you don't think this could be some sort of horrible mistake."

She smiled sadly. "I hope it is."

"How can you trust a stranger?"

She shrugged. "Years of experience with liars, my love. Call it intuition, my very own and particular talent. Leyen struck me as very direct, nothing dishonest about her. Secretive perhaps, but not dishonest. There was something very vulnerable about that woman. She knows things. Is scared by them. And I know she's working for the King and I also know, following what just stopped short of an interrogation, that he is determined to find out what she might have told me. Now, firstly, why would she tell me anything—a complete stranger, as you say—unless it was true? Why would she risk writing something so damning—it could easily have her executed—if she didn't know it to be true? And, even more intriguing, why would Celimus have me especially called in on the pretext of a chat when really he was fishing for information on Leyen? Make no mistake, he wanted to know what she knew, what she shared with me. His behavior virtually attests to his guilt."

"Why indeed," Eryd muttered, beaten by her logic. "This is dangerous, my love."

She nodded. "I do know it." Helyn leaned over and kissed her husband. "Thank you for listening."

"Do you think he still believes you are involved?"

She shook her head. "No. I was at my sparkling best. But you're right, I must tread with great care."

"Let's say you do find it's all true—" He stopped. It was a question he was not ready to ask.

Helyn said nothing, all but holding her breath; wondering if her husband's heart could stand the shock of what she was thinking.

Eryd answered his own question. "Betray Morgravia?" His voice was leaden with the fear she also felt.

She had neither an explanation nor any soft speech of comfort. She too was reeling beneath her seemingly calm exterior. But Leyen's intense note was irresistible. She could not ignore it.

"I could never betray Morgravia, my darling," she said,

eyes misting as she stroked his stubbled, much-loved cheek. "But this new King of ours . . . I just don't know. If any of what Leyen entrusted me with has an ounce of truth to it, then he is no King we would want to be loyal to."

Eryd took his wife's chubby hands and stared at her intently. "He may be new and young, but he is not to be trifled with. Beneath the vain, seemingly shallow veneer lurks a mind sharp enough to cut and bright enough to blind. You did well throwing him off your scent but don't be fooled by his outward appearance . . . not ever."

21

LSPYTH ARRIVED ON THE OUTSKIRTS OF THE DUCHY BY DUSK that same evening. A middle-aged traveling monk with a donkey in tow took pity on the lone, clearly exhausted woman and suggested she ride the beast alongside him into the town of Brynt, the largest in Felrawthy. She gladly accepted his generous offer, believing the monk to be a gift from Shar. She enjoyed his thoughtful company and regretted when they crested a rise all too soon and he pointed out Brynt to the west and the sprawling pastures of the Duke's private lands to the north.

"That's where you're headed, my girl," the monk said, "although you are most welcome to travel into Brynt with me if you care to."

She smiled wearily. "I must keep moving, Father, but I do thank you for your company and my fine steed." Elspyth climbed off the mule and patted its coarse hair, marveling at the serenity in its large, dark eyes. *I'd give anything right now for your simple life, my friend,* she thought.

Turning, she looked into a genial pair of gray eyes sitting

amid a gently frowning face. "I shouldn't miss him for a day or so, you know," her companion said. "Why don't you take him? I imagine the Duke will have opportunity enough to have the little fellow returned to me. I'll be at Brynt for several days yet."

Elspyth felt her heart fill. Perhaps there was hope for Morgravia with people like this in it. She could hardly refuse, knowing she was in no state to walk many more steps. "I'm surely blessed to have met you, Father. Thank you for this. I'll ensure he's well fed, watered, and returned tomorrow."

"Oh, no hurry, child. He certainly doesn't hurry for anyone," he said, face crinkling into the merriest of smiles. "Shar guide you in your travels."

And so it was with some surprise that the noble family of Felrawthy welcomed another bedraggled and fatigued young woman. Crys was at the guardhouse briefing the man on duty regarding new security and the locking of Tenterdyn's gates. He looked up to see the woman slip off her donkey and land unceremoniously on her backside outside the gates of Tenterdyn. It was the first time since hearing the shocking news of his brother's untimely death that he had any reason to smile.

"A theatrical arrival," he commented. He helped her to her feet.

"Apologies, sir," Elspyth replied, a little fractious, "I've been traveling a long time." She disengaged herself from his arms.

"So I can see," he said, taking in her ragged appearance. "Please forgive my poor manners. I am Crys, eldest son of the Duke of Felrawthy."

"Oh," she said, disarmed slightly as she looked at him properly and appreciated his handsome looks and quality clothes. They were a handsome family, she realized as more people resembling her greeter emerged from the house and crossed the courtyard. No one looked especially pleased to see her. In fact, everyone looked downright miserable.

"Crys?" said the tall, regal-looking woman. "Where are your manners?"

"Yes, I was just apologizing for the loss of same, Mother. I'd introduce you if I knew who was paying us a visit."

Elspyth blushed and smoothed her grubby garments with dusty hands. "I'm sorry. My name is Elspyth. I am a friend of . . ." She was momentarily confused. Wyl was the friend but Romen was the man. She chose. ". . . of Wyl Thirsk," she said firmly and watched as alarm spread across the faces of the people before her. "Have I said something wrong?" she whispered to Crys.

He shook his head sadly. "No. Just more shock for an already distraught family. Elspyth, may I introduce Duchess Aleda, my mother. My father, Duke Jeryb . . ." Elspyth curtsied as the Duke regarded her. "And this is one of my three brothers, Daryn," Crys said.

Elspyth smiled tentatively toward the young man.

"The other, Jorge, is with his beloved horses, I presume, and my youngest brother," Crys added in a different tone, "we have only learned today is dead. Forgive us the lack of a more effusive welcome."

The Duke took charge. "But perhaps you already know of this if Wyl Thirsk is your friend?"

She looked at him directly, sensed his keen pain, and softened her tone. "I do, sir. I am deeply regretful for your family. Your youngest must be Alyd."

He nodded.

"Did you know him?" the Duchess asked, and Elspyth could see her eyes, though red from tears, were not puffy. She sensed this was a strong woman.

"I didn't, my lady, only of him." The Duchess nodded, her hands gripping each other until the knuckles turned white. "Er, may I ask, please, if Ylena Thirsk has made any contact with your family?"

It was Crys who answered. "We met her by chance at a town about half a day's ride from the estate."

"So . . . she's here?" Elspyth could hardly believe her good fortune.

Aleda nodded. "Exhausted and mercifully sleeping upstairs. Please come inside. You look very travel weary, my dear—let us organize some immediate refreshment."

Crisp orders were given, and before Elspyth knew it, she was luxuriating in a bath with scented oils. It felt like a healing—not just the opportunity to clean away the grime but also to cleanse her wrecked emotions and focus her thoughts. On the road, fatigue and hunger had sharpened her sense of rage at all that had happened to her and those she loved. Now, though, immersed in the fragranced water among the soft, comfortable surrounds of the beautiful chamber, she felt some of that anger float away. What remained was a crystallized intention to somehow track down this woman, Hildyth. But first, she was not to be deterred in her determination to return to the Razors and find Lothryn. Nothing else mattered but him, now that she knew Ylena was safe with this family. Her only path from here on would be to keep to her own oaths, but she hated that this assassin, in killing Koreldy, had murdered her friend Wyl, and thus her only ally in her efforts to rescuing Lothryn. Dealing with Hildyth, if she ever could, would give her satisfaction.

Despite the dozens of questions she could sense they wanted to ask, the Duke and his family were gracious enough to allow her this comfort time as soon as she arrived. In truth, it had been the Duchess who would not hear of any discussion until Elspyth had enjoyed the opportunity to bathe and feel like a woman again. She liked Aleda very much, even though she hardly knew her; smiled now remembering the glare the Duchess had given her men when the interrogation began as soon as Elspyth had stepped into the house.

There was a soft knock at the door. Aleda entered. "Is everything to your satisfaction, my dear?"

"Oh yes, thank you," Elspyth said. "I've never felt more spoiled."

The older woman gave a sad smile. "You've probably never felt more tired or tested," she said softly, setting down a lamp to brighten the rapidly darkening chamber.

Elspyth nodded, felt the tears burning. "It hasn't been easy."

"I gather as much and apologize now for my husband's gruff manner. He is suffering, you know . . . we all are." Then she snapped herself from her bleak tone. "Will you be up to talking with us later?"

"Of course, my lady. It's why I've traveled this far."

"Good girl. I shall make arrangements. Perhaps you can rest now for a while. Ylena, as I mentioned, has been forced to sleep too. She'll be up and around shortly. You'll like her. We all do," and Elspyth saw the Duchess grit her teeth to stop the emotion flowing over.

"How is she?"

"She's rather amazing, to tell the truth. Very strong. Very much a Thirsk."

Elspyth smiled. "I know what you mean. If she's anything like her brother, then she'll be looking for Celimus to pay."

Aleda frowned. "You speak of Wyl as though he lives. You do know what's happened to him, don't you?" she offered hesitantly.

Elspyth felt trapped. She nodded, not knowing how to answer the Duchess truthfully, and changed the subject quickly. "I'm so sorry about Alyd, Duchess." She did not know what else to say, even though the little she had said sounded like hollow comfort.

The Duchess forced a shaky smile. "I can't bear to think about it just yet. Now, you must call me Aleda." The aristocratic woman nodded and stood. "Rest, my dear. We shall see you later."

Later came all too soon for her, but Elspyth felt a lot stronger for the peace and quiet she had been able to enjoy. Aleda had arranged for clothes and other toilet requisites, and for the first time in a very long time, Elspyth felt her old, resilient self.

Three members of the family were gathered in the reception room. A fire added some much-needed cheer, nearby sat a novice monk. She learned through Crys, who showed a new appreciation for his freshly bathed and rested guest, that it was this monk, Pil, who had been Ylena's companion both at Rittylworth and in her harrowing journey to Tenterdyn.

"And what will you do now, Pil?" she asked, a kindness in her voice as she recognized a fellow sufferer, unwittingly trapped in the Witch Myrren's strange web.

The young monk shrugged. "I have no idea. I could not think beyond bringing the Lady Ylena to Felrawthy. I would like to return to my order, but there is nothing at Rittylworth to return to," he said, sadness evident.

Elspyth nodded, knowing all too well about the state of Rittylworth. She took the proffered goblet of wine from Crys.

"Drink it. It will help," he whispered, and she smiled at him before looking back to the novice.

"Pil, I hope it's not out of place for me to mention this, but I met a wonderful man on my way here. A monk, like yourself, who travels, spreading the word and doing the work of Shar as best he can from town to village, county to duchy. It was his kindness that saw me reach Tenterdyn as swiftly as I have. I've promised to return the mule he lent me—perhaps you might take the beast into Brynt, where Brother Tewk is staying for a few days. You may find that the two of you have something in common."

Pil's eyes shone; he understood her meaning instantly. "Would he allow it?"

She grinned at his pleasure. "You mean for you to accompany him in his work?" He nodded. "Why should he refuse you, Pil? He's not a young man, I might add, but he's learned and wise. I suspect both of you could do far worse for traveling companions."

And now the young man beamed. Having viewed the smoldering remains of Rittylworth herself, Elspyth imagined he had not had much to be bright about. "Oh, I shall definitely seek him out, Elspyth. I do thank you."

Elspyth enjoyed the warmth it put into her heart, amid all the grief, to be able to help someone with a few simple words. She sipped her wine and felt a new sort of warmth slip down her throat. Raising her glass to Crys, she saw his eyes sparkle over his own glass and realized he was flirting with her. She hurriedly looked aside. If the younger brother was anything like him, she had little doubt as to why Ylena had been in such a rush to marry him. Just as she was thinking all this, those about her suddenly stiffened, their gazes moving to the doorway, where a glorious young woman stood.

"Ah, Ylena, my dear," said the Duchess, and she moved elegantly across the room and, putting an arm around her guest's shoulders, guided her in. "We want you to meet someone . . . a friend." She led Ylena in. "This is Elspyth. She is a companion of your brother and has traveled a long way to meet you."

Ylena's gaze shifted and settled on Elspyth, who felt suddenly plain and awkward among such noble company. Ylena was most certainly a rare beauty and not at all what she had expected. Wyl had mentioned his sister's beauty, but this poised young woman was exceptional.

"How good of you to come all this way," Ylena said, and curtsied to Elspyth.

"My lady." Elspyth followed suit, not quite so elegantly. "I'm so glad you're safe. Wyl sent me to ensure that you reached Felrawthy."

Ylena's brow creased with a frown. "When did he do that?"

And so Elspyth took a deep breath. Ylena's simple question had cut through all the hesitant politeness and niceties. The time had arrived. She must tell them. Wyl had asked her to keep his secret from Ylena, but considering all the young woman had been through, Elspyth had decided his sister needed to hear the truth.

She gathered everyone's attention with her grave look. "Please. I have a long story to tell you all—and not an easy one. It will shock and perhaps even frighten, but I must share it so you understand my reason for being among you and why Ylena must have your protection."

She watched them steal alarmed glances at one another and then the Duke nodded. Servants topped up glasses and were then asked to leave.

Pil cleared his throat. "Should I remain for this?" he asked, uncertain of his place.

"Not if you are horrified by the notion of magic," Elspyth said cryptically, and began retelling her long story from the moment a young soldier, a general, in fact, had stepped into a seer's tent one night with his friend Alyd of Felrawthy.

The Duke rose imperiously. "You expect us to believe that Wyl Thirsk was killed by magic?" he blustered.

"Forgive me, sir," Elspyth said calmly. "Perhaps I haven't explained it well. Wyl Thirsk was struck down by a man called Romen Koreldy, who—"

"Yes, yes! Whom Thirsk apparently became—I hear quite well," the Duke retorted, angry and disturbed by the stranger's news.

Elspyth opened her mouth to reply and closed it again. A brittle retort would not aid understanding here.

"Father, please!" Crys said from the fireplace.

"Jeryb." It was Aleda's placating tone. "I can't imagine this young woman has trekked from the far north of Deakyn to Felrawthy in order to make some jest at your expense."

The Duke muttered something beneath his breath.

Pil's complexion had paled. "This is mystifying," he murmured.

"Yes, it is," Elspyth replied softly, eyeing each in turn. "It is, however, the truth."

Her gaze came to rest on Ylena, who, so far, had made no comment.

Now she did. "My brother is alive?" Everyone could hear the muted shock in her tone.

Elspyth could feel her heart pounding, suddenly hoping it had been a good idea to contradict Wyl's instructions. She nodded slowly, watching Ylena carefully.

"And you say your aunt saw this . . . this affliction in him?"

Elspyth nodded. "She is a seer. She called it the Quickening."

Ylena looked thoughtful. "Do you know I can remember the night you speak of. It was after the tournament . . . the day following my marriage to Alyd."

Her listeners tensed at the mention of his name, but

Ylena's voice was steady and Aleda was proud to see the young woman so in control of her emotions. She alone knew how much her son had loved Ylena, having read his gushing letters many times. And Alyd had impressed upon his parents her devotion to him. They had had plans to set up their estate near to Tenterdyn. That would not happen now, Aleda thought, sorrow knifing through her once again.

Nevertheless she was impressed with Ylena and could only imagine how much suffering the young woman had already endured. She was remarkably composed, considering she was now learning more painful news of her brother. Aleda returned her thoughts to Ylena's voice.

"They went into Sideshow Alley. Young men, letting off steam . . . celebrating. Alyd was drunk." At this she laughed bitterly. "Poor fool. I believe he was more intoxicated with life than ale. Wyl brought him back to my chambers, and after settling my brand-new husband, we talked, late into the night. My brother told me of what had occurred in the tent that night. If I recall correctly"—she screwed her face in thought—"her name was Widow Ilyk."

Elspyth nodded so that everyone could see their two stories matched.

Ylena continued. "Wyl was disturbed. Very unsettled by what she had said. Neither of us had forgotten the episode with Myrren," she explained. "Although I was not present, I did hear of it. He collapsed at her death and Gueryn—that's our guardian—the man you met in the Mountain Kingdom—he admitted to me that Wyl's eyes had changed color. It had frightened him at the time because it smacked of things magical and sinister, but he forgot about it eventually and frankly so had I until this moment." She stopped speaking as she looked around at everyone.

The silence was heavy.

Crys broke it, gazing somewhat helplessly toward Ylena. "And this Romen Koreldy is now . . ."

"Dead . . . and dear Wyl with him," Elspyth answered with feeling. Her audience gasped. "A woman apparently, a hired killer. Goes by the name of Hildyth, although I suspect that's a false one. I have her description."

"Then detail it. We shall circulate her description." He shrugged, feeling helpless but obviously keen to show his determination to help Thirsk's sister. "All of Felrawthy's loyal should be on alert. We don't know if she might strike again or who hired her."

"Oh, I think we can safely guess." Aleda's tone was acid and she glanced at Ylena, who appeared dumbstruck by Elspyth's revelations.

Elspyth obliged. "She is described as not beautiful but an intensely striking woman. Unmistakable. Tall with golden-brown hair and feline eyes apparently."

"Sounds hard to miss," Crys commented to no one in particular.

"Koreldy is dead?" Ylena suddenly asked, as if she were returning from faraway thoughts. "But he saved my life."

Elspyth turned sadly toward her and once again took her hands. "Wyl saved your life, Ylena. He was Romen."

Ylena's eyes watered and no one could blame her. "I can't believe any of it," she whispered.

"Brother Jakub said there was something different about Romen this time," Pil said, eyes shining with awe. "I noticed it too. If you weren't speaking of magic, Elspyth, I'd know you were talking truth."

"I am. You all have to trust me now. Wyl, moving in Romen's body, escaped with me from Cailech's clutches across the Razors. It was during our journey in the mountains that he admitted all of this. It was no jest. He spoke like a man beaten."

The Duke looked sharply at Elspyth. "Wait a minute. What are you talking about? Escaping from Cailech? The King of the Mountain Kingdom?"

"Yes, my lord. I told you none of this would be easy to hear. I understand how much of a shock it is. I will explain everything, but it means nothing now that Wyl is dead. Romen is no more."

"Then I have an axe to grind for both King Celimus and

now this Hildyth," Ylena said angrily, and no one in the room doubted her intention.

Aleda took a breath. "I think we should eat and then we can hear more of what Elspyth has to tell us. Come, Ylena, dear. You look pale, child."

Surprisingly, Ylena did as she was asked. As the two women left the room, Crys shook his head. "She's Alyd's widow, we'll look after her now, Elspyth," he reassured. "What about you?"

She sighed. "Oh, I think now that I've fulfilled my promise to Wyl to see his sister to safety, I shall travel home."

"To Yentro?" he ask.

She nodded. No one needed to know her intentions from thereon. Too many would try to talk her out of it. "My lord?" she said, addressing the Duke.

The gaze was direct and bright when it was leveled at her. "Yes?"

"Wyl sent this." She hesitated momentarily before handing the Duke the crushed letter she had dug from her pocket.

He took it and both she and Crys all but held their breath as he broke the seal and held the parchment to the candlelight.

"Father?"

The Duke looked contemplative. "He confirms the death of Alyd but speaks of none of this magic. He signs off as Thirsk, asks that we don't rush into any revenge. He wants us to hold until he comes. But he's dead now—or this Romen fellow is. You told us yourself," the Duke answered, turning on Elspyth.

"But I heard that news from strangers. We can't be absolutely sure it is reliable information. I would urge you to wait."

"For what?" he asked, voice struggling against his own emotion. "My son has been murdered. An innocent. Don't ask me to stand by and not take action."

Elspyth held her hands up in a warding motion against his anger. It was a gesture loaded with sorrow that echoed his own grief. "I've passed on Wyl's caution, my lord. It is not my place to suggest anything further."

He grunted and Crys caught her glance with a shrug of apology. But none was required. Elspyth, given the chance, would suggest Felrawthy rise up and storm Pearlis this night if it could. She had good reason to hate Celimus herself and could think of nothing better than riding alongside this powerful Duke to overthrow the hated sovereign. She did not begrudge Jeryb his anger.

Crys did, however. Rage helped nothing, particularly leveled against this plucky woman who had suffered plenty. "Perhaps you'd like to join my mother in the parlor," Crys suggested diplomatically. He alone knew how deeply the news of Alyd's death had cut his father.

Elspyth accepted his gracious release and left the Duke alone to brood on the letter from a dead man.

22

THE FAMILY AND THEIR GUESTS SHARED A MEAL DURING which Elspyth shared her impressions of Cailech's fortress and answered their questions about the daring escape. It was accompanied by much muttering and shaking of his head by the Duke. Only Ylena's eyes shone and Elspyth guessed this was with pride for Gueryn's steadfastness and ultimate sacrifice, but also for Wyl. She did not enlighten them on her feelings for Lothryn; that was her secret and was of no consequence to anyone in the room.

The Duchess had suggested their food be kept simple. No one's appetite was keen anyway. Duke Jeryb would not be drawn out about his plans, not even by his patient wife. Inevitably a bleakness settled once again across the household, sucking Elspyth into its maw too, driving the last of the conversation toward the inconsequential and ultimately to quiet.

It was no wonder then that when the sound of horses' hooves echoed into the still night, the men leapt to their feet. Jeryb quietened the alarmed women and motioned for Crys to find out from the duty guards who had just arrived at Tenterdyn. Swords were drawn in the dining chamber—just in case—and Aleda muttered at her husband that they should have taken the precaution of raising more men at arms when Ylena had first arrived.

They waited, the other brothers watching through the windows as Crys strode across the main courtyard just ahead of his father. His path was lit by torches. The Duchess had earlier considered it a shame that Tenterdyn's gates had been locked for the first time in the family's history but now thanked Shar's wisdom for suggesting to her husband that he do just that.

"He's coming back," one of the boys said over his shoulder, and everyone held their breath.

Crys reentered the chamber, a blast of cool air whirling about him. He looked flushed and appeared startled. His attention was riveted on Elspyth. "You're not going to believe this, but I think that the Hildyth you spoke of is at the gate literally begging to be admitted."

Elspyth could see he was not making a jest.

Crys qualified his claim. "Golden-brown hair. Tall. Dressed like a man. Eyes unmistakably like a cat. It's her all right."

Elspyth shuddered and was not the only one to do so in the room. Ylena fairly blazed with a still, silent anger.

"Alone?" the Duke demanded.

"No, sir," his son replied. "She is accompanied by a very big man . . . just short of a giant, he looks. He goes by the name of Aremys."

"And their reason for coming here?" Aleda joined in.

"She says she wants to see Ylena."

"Of course she does!" Elspyth said, heart pounding. "She'll have orders to kill her too! Are we safe? Are there enough guards?"

"No one can enter Tenterdyn, child, who doesn't win my

permission. We are safe and well guarded," the Duke replied with calm. "My love," he said, looking toward his wife now, "I did take the precaution you spoke of. We have fifty men riding toward us now."

Aleda felt no little relief. "What do we do until then?"

"I shall see her," Ylena said calmly.

Pil's expression was a mask of terror. "Sir, I beg you," he whispered.

The Duke came to his rescue in a deep and very firm tone. "No, Ylena, you will do no such thing. You came here seeking my protection and I am compelled to provide it, not only because of who you are and who you married, but because of whose daughter you are as well. You will do as I say. We need cool heads now. I shall speak with these people. Come, boys," he said, and his three sons fell into step with him.

"Be careful, husband," the Duchess called after him, but there was no response.

The women waited, fidgeting at the window. Pil stood with them and they watched the four remaining men of Felrawthy walk toward the gates with purpose. Aleda was relieved that her husband led the boys up the small tower at the gatehouse.

"Ah, good. He's being careful."

"Your husband would not risk any of them." Pil knew he was reassuring himself.

There was a protracted wait before they saw the four reemerge from the tower. The Duke must have given an order, for the two younger lads hurried to lift the heavy timbers that barred the gate.

"What's he doing?" Elspyth cried.

"Give me a sword, damn it," Ylena called, looking around for a weapon and grabbing a carving knife from the table. She stepped toward the door and hid behind it.

"Shar preserve us!" Pil swore as they watched the heavy gates swing back.

"Wait," Aleda cautioned, fighting back her own fears. "Jeryb must have learned something."

Twilight had given way to full nightfall and they watched

by burning torchlight as a giant of a man strode into the courtyard. In his wake walked another. Man or woman they could not tell, but this person was smaller, leaner, with a purposeful stride. This must be the cat-eyed woman Crys had spoken of. Aleda watched, stunned, as the second figure clasped her husband's hand.

Aleda calmed her companions with a look. They must trust Jeryb. She nodded encouragingly at Elspyth, who was clearly fretting, and then heard voices talking over one another as their latest guests entered the house. She looked toward the door at the sound of her husband's tread.

"Aleda," he said, shaking his head. "I have the most curious news."

He could share nothing further as a tall, striking woman stepped into the chamber and took off her hat. Auburn hair tumbled to her shoulders.

"Elspyth!" Wyl cried, and strode toward his shocked, confused friend. "It's me!" He laughed.

Suddenly Ylena leapt from behind the door. She had one intention on her mind and that was to kill this woman who had murdered Koreldy and apparently also her brother. All she could see in her rage was the wide mouth and feline eyes.

"Ylena, no!" Elspyth screamed.

Aremys launched himself toward Wyl as the Duke shot out his own arm to prevent the blow reaching the stranger.

All to no avail. Ylena was fast. She had been raised in a warrior family, and although she had been a pampered, demure noblewoman, she had never forgotten the lessons Wyl had taught her growing up in Argorn. She saw them all moving, avoided their reaching arms, and struck.

"Murderer!" Ylena cried, and with the full force her body could inflict, she threw herself forward and punched the knife into the neck of the smiling assassin.

Voices yelled "no!" and men leapt toward her. The assassin, she noted, had not even had time to shield herself.

"Oh, my precious, what have you done?" the woman called Faryl cried as she clutched her neck, which was hopelessly spraying blood.

Ylena heard screams around her and cries of dismay, but she felt only triumph looking into the shocked green eyes of the dying woman.

Elspyth had cradled the body as it fell and was instantly drenched in blood. Crys and Daryn had grabbed Ylena's arms, but she had tossed the knife aside and become limp, breathing deep gasps, determined to watch the light flicker and die in the woman's hated eyes.

Except it did not.

With horror, Elspyth, who was holding Faryl's head on her lap, watched the assassin's green eyes turn momentarily ill-matched and yet somehow wondrous sky gray and deep greenish brown. Beautiful individually, shocking as a pair.

And then she felt the woman's body stiffen in its final death throes, the back bending impossibly. She guessed what was happening, could almost feel it with her intuition for magic. She wanted to scream.

Ylena did it for her. Huge, gut-twisting shrieks escaped the former wife of Alyd of Felrawthy, now nothing more than a shell. Inside Faryl's body, the spirit of her brother fought the transference with all he had, somehow hoping he could save his beloved sister—but it was not enough. Myrren's Gift was too powerful.

It was Wyl, bellowing his rage at taking the life of his own sister, who gave voice to the deranged shrieks of Ylena. Crys and Daryn held on to Ylena's body strongly. Confusion reigned. Jeryb was yelling orders for calm while Aleda's horror at the brutal death scene, completed by the grisly rivulets of Faryl's blood on her cheeks, left her too shocked to move or speak.

Aremys had silently knelt in disbelief by his friend Faryl.

"Let her go!" Elspyth shouted above the din.

Crys looked even further confused at this order.

"Leave him! It's not Ylena anymore!" she screamed now, tears streaming down her bloodstained face. "It's Wyl!"

The brothers stood back, thunderstruck by her words.

This time Wyl arched his back, not from physical pain but from the greatest pain he would ever feel. He had killed his sister . . . taken the life of the very person he had striven so hard to protect. Swirling into her body, he glimpsed Ylena's confusion, tasted her hollow triumph, sensed her surprise at a sudden yet somehow welcome death.

He threw back his head and the keening sound chilled each to their core before Wyl pushed away Elspyth's outstretched hands and fled the house.

He moved blindly. Once through the gates, he ran toward the inky darkness of the moors, a demented female figure in a blood-spattered silk robe with nothing on her feet. Wyl hurled himself higher up the hills and deeper into their oblivion, consumed by hatred and grief, his own wrath mixing with Ylena's well of despair. Tears and curses raged for what seemed endlessly until he realized his throat was raw.

His new body trembled. He was not sure whether it was from shock or the cold night. He did not care. Nothing mattered anymore. The last of the Thirsks had lost the fight. He wanted to die too. It would have to be by his own hand; he could not risk another's life.

"I'm sorry," a voice said gently. There was not even the faintest of moonlight this night. Heavy clouds scudded darkly across the heavens, obliterating all illumination. But Wyl knew the voice. "I just wasn't quick enough," Aremys added, his words laden with regret.

Apart from his involuntary trembling, Wyl could not move . . . did not want to, ever. "She was so bright. Like one of Shar's own stars. She deserved none of this," he croaked in his new, all-too-achingly-familiar voice.

"The innocent never do, Wyl. Yet they always seem to suffer."

"What was it?"

Aremys knew what he referred to. "A carving knife."

Wyl nodded but his companion could not see it. "A lucky thrust," he said ruefully.

"But just as deadly as Faryl's stiletto."

There was a bitter laugh as Wyl accepted this notion.

228 + FIONA MCINTOSH

"What possessed her?" he asked, voicing his private thoughts aloud. He required no answer, but Aremys still replied.

"Fear of Celimus sending people to kill her."

"I shouldn't have come. You were right. I should have let you find her and I should have gone on to find Myrren's mother. I should never have declared myself. How did they know of me in this form?"

"Your friend Elspyth—she heard of Koreldy's death on her travels. Pieced events together and told the family. She blames herself for not considering that Myrren's Gift had permanence."

Again the deriding laugh. Wyl realized he had not sufficiently impressed secrecy on Elspyth. "It's no one else's fault," he said softly. "The errors are all mine. I was reckless. I should have let you enter first, tell everyone what had occurred . . . prepared them."

"For whatever it's worth, Wyl, I'm not sure anyone would have believed it."

"Elspyth would have. Ylena maybe . . . given time."

Wyl heard the big man shift, could make out a bulky shadow move out of a small clump of slender trees.

"You cannot undo what is done," Aremys offered, his voice gentle. He waited for an angry rebuke.

It came. "My sister is dead, Aremys!" Wyl yelled. "And yet she lives. All of my family dead. Plus Alyd, Gueryn, Lothryn . . . even Koreldy—dead. All because of me."

The big man grabbed Wyl and pulled him to his feet. He had not counted on Ylena being so light. Faryl's body had been much weightier. She all but flew up into his arms. He settled Wyl down and knew he was lucky that he could not see the anger he was sure was blazing in her eyes.

Still he pursued it. "There is nothing you can do about what's done. Nothing! But you can go to this Manwitch fellow and learn about his daughter's gift. Perhaps it can be reversed, perhaps it can be stopped."

"Will it ever stop?" Wyl asked, a pleading note in his sister's voice.

"I don't know, my friend. But I promise you, here and now, that I will help you in any way I can. You must help yourself, though. None of us understand this magic. The only way forward is to discover its secrets. And the Manwitch is the only lead you have. Go to him."

"Where do I go?"

"Find the mother, as you had planned. Start there."

They heard heavy footsteps and looked around to see the Duke approaching, breathing hard.

"Are you all right?" he wheezed, knowing it was an absurd question under the circumstances. He raked a hand through his silvered hair. "I'm sorry." He shrugged. "We're all worried about you. Coming to terms with the shock of all that's happened, especially this foul magic upon you, is more than I can bear. What's more, my good wife has taken charge of proceedings and can be quite terrifying. It was my chance to escape."

Wyl stepped forward and took the old man's hand in the Legion's way. "This is the hardest one, sir. Giving up my own body was a hundred times easier than taking this one."

"I'm sorry, son. I . . . I really am at a loss for words—I must accept this tale because I do trust that this is really you, but I understand none of it."

Wyl shook his head. "I've had more time to get used to the curse."

The Duke sat down heavily. "Forgive me, this has been a trying couple of days."

"It is I who seeks your forgiveness," Wyl said, seating himself next to the Duke. "I know your whole family is suffering, sir. Alyd was the best of men. His loss is a constant pain in my heart."

The old man nodded in the dark. "We will grieve later, Wyl, for your sister and for my son. The King is my concern right now. May we speak freely?"

Wyl nodded. "Aremys is as much a part of this as I, sir."

Aremys felt relieved to hear it and joined them, seating himself uncomfortably atop the heather.

"Tell me everything," the Duke commanded, "from the beginning."

Later, seated around the scrubbed parlor table, Wyl faced the rest of the family, so shocked still that their faces were devoid of expression. Blank, disbelieving stares had greeted Wyl when he returned with Aremys and the Duke. He could hear the two younger sons in the dining room, cleaning up as best they could.

Elspyth was trembling. She would not permit him to touch her, but her hands instinctively flew to her mouth as he arrived, her eyes betraying all the emotion of these days past. She began to weep and the sound quickly turned to heartfelt sobs, her small frame lurching with each one. She knew she had caused this trauma to Wyl by revealing his secret. She was unable to speak now, though, to offer her apologies. There was a thick silence in the room as everyone felt her grief, and much as Crys would have liked to put his arms around her, Wyl enclosed Elspyth in Ylena's own embrace, holding her tight and kissing her hair.

"It's all right, Elspyth," they heard Ylena say soothingly. "I'll explain everything."

Behind them Aremys had bowed in awkward silence to the Duchess and she smiled just as awkwardly back. That was the most either could do without formal introduction. Aremys moved to stand beside Pil.

"I'm Aremys," he whispered, for want of anything better to say into the uncomfortable atmosphere.

"Pil," came the reply. "I came with . . ." He hesitated, not sure if he could still call her Ylena.

The big man nodded. "With the sister?"

Pil nodded, too distressed to say any more.

"I'll brew some tea," Aleda said. "It's good for shock," she admitted, but only got as far as the hearth, where she sat down on a small sofa, stupefied by the night's events.

Elspyth finally pulled away from Wyl to gaze into Ylena's face. "Is it really you? It happened again?"

He nodded. "She killed Romen as instructed. Little did she know he was cursed."

"I'm going to insist you prove who you are," she replied, suddenly cautious.

"He already has, my girl," the Duke said, standing near to his wife. "Only a Thirsk would know what he told me at the gatehouse and since on the moors." He scratched his head. "I think what we all need is not tea but a sherlac, my dear," he said to his wife. "This is all very confusing, and too wild for my old mind."

The Duchess found a wan smile for her husband. She did not feel like she could ever be happy again, but in looking at him she decided that perhaps love alone would get her through this nightmare of death, deception, and magic. She signaled to Crys to fetch the decanter and glasses.

Wyl looked back at Elspyth. "No, you're quite right. What can I tell you that only Wyl Thirsk could know?"

She thought a moment. "When we escaped from the mountains . . ." She had meant to go on, but a smile crossed Ylena's face.

". . . we had no money. Or so I thought," Wyl continued. "But you had a purse that you had hidden beneath your skirts. We stayed at the Penny Whistle in Deakyn and you bought me a horse with all that was left of your money. I left you to somehow make your way to Rittylworth, your heart bursting for a good man, a brave man we had to leave behind. I am so, so sorry."

Her smile of elation dissolved to tears. "Oh, Wyl—so much to tell."

Aleda decided it was time to take hold of the emotionally charged situation once again. "You are most welcome in our home . . . er, Wyl Thirsk. I hardly understand any of this. It's too horrific to contemplate but . . ."

Wyl bowed formally to the Duchess, a woman he had admired since childhood. "I remember my father telling me how generous you were to my mother when they were first married, Duchess. He never forgot how you helped her choose a gown for a summer ball when she was feeling es-

pecially young and daunted, having married the man who
called our king his closest friend. She knew how the Queen
laughed at her. You reminded her that she was the reason
Fergys Thirsk never lost a battle. You told her, my lady,
that he could not bear the thought of not coming home to
the most beautiful and cherished woman in the world."

Wyl cleared his throat. "I wish we could have met in less
confusing circumstances, my lady, so I could thank you for
your kindness."

Now it was Aleda's turn to feel betrayed by her eyes. She
returned a gracious curtsy. "I would like to have met you as
yourself, Wyl Thirsk. I think I need to lie down for a bit."
She thought she might weep at her next thought but voiced
it anyway. "Our son Alyd worshiped you."

"He was the best friend anyone could ever have asked for,
my lady. I am so much less for losing him," Wyl replied. "I
shall avenge his death," he added softly, but the coldness in
his voice left no one in any doubt.

23

AT THE INSISTENCE OF A FUSSING ALEDA, EVERYONE TOOK TO
their beds. They would make decisions in the morning. Aleda insisted that they leave Wyl alone with his
thoughts and despite his protests she won. His sister's body
climbed back into the bed she had left just hours earlier, but
it was now Wyl who agreed to swallow the proffered cup of
warmed, sweetened milk.

"What have you put in this?"

"Something to help you sleep," Aleda said kindly, fluff-
ing a coverlet about him.

It felt similar to how his own mother used to tuck him in

at night. "I wish I could wake up and discover it's all been a nightmare," he admitted.

She nodded. "So do I."

He knew she spoke of her adored son. Wyl took her hand. "I'm sorry I could not save him."

Aleda's eyes watered, but she did not give in to the sorrow—not yet. "He worshiped both you and Ylena. I know his years at Stoneheart were happy because of the Thirsks and I thank you for that. But listen to me, Wyl." He noticed she did not hesitate to call him by his real name and he loved her for it. Believers in magic or not, some Morgravians— like these people—put life and duty ahead of superstition. "We cannot bring them back through our tears, but we can make ourselves worthy of them by avenging their early deaths. You may blame this Myrren person for your despair, but there is one true villain here." She jabbed her finger in the air toward him.

"Celimus," he breathed, beginning to feel the drowsy effects of Aleda's drug.

"Let us never forget it," she said, her defiance infectious.

"I will kill him, Duchess." His words in Ylena's voice sounded as cold as the snow that fell on the moors in winter.

"You do that, and may you feel the weight of my hand behind the blade you wield . . . and Alyd's, and Ylena's, and all those other people you have spoken of . . . even that woman Faryl."

It was his turn to feel his eyes brim and Aleda was well aware these tears welled for Ylena Thirsk alone.

"She was a brave young woman, son, although I'm not sure whether she would ever have come back to being the person you remembered. She had been hurt too much. Ylena was filled with hate and need for revenge. And, frankly, who could blame her? She showed courage and tenacity in just escaping Rittylworth and getting herself here on foot. She was every bit a Thirsk and a sister to be proud of. I shall mourn her as the daughter I lost. Even in the short time we knew each other, we shared enough to have formed a special bond."

Wyl did not want to cry. He looked away. "Do you believe in life after death, Aleda?"

She smiled bravely. "I do. And they're together now, Wyl, with Shar. We'll continue the fight."

"Thank you for all your kindness," he said, slipping away toward sleep. "What about Faryl's body?" he murmured.

"We'll take care of it," she assured. "Dream peacefully, Wyl Thirsk," she added, and kissed him softly.

Wyl's dreams were anything but peaceful.

He saw a barn. Its doors were closed. And from behind those doors came the fearful noise of a man screaming. His demented shrieks sounded as though they were filled with gut-wrenching pain.

Then the thought *Help me* came crashing into Wyl's mind.

Wyl did not know how to cast a message back. He tried, begging the man to tell him who he was, where he was. But try though he might, he could not respond in the same manner. The terrible wail continued, and the more Wyl tried to escape it, the louder it became, until it filled every recess of his head, every ounce of his being. He ran—or thought he did—but it followed. When he stopped and tried to face it, he found he had run nowhere and was still looking at the barn and the dark magics he now realized must be at practice behind those barred doors.

A new voice urged at him. A mellow, kind voice. It sounded to be coming from far away. *Turn toward me, son.*

I can't, Wyl thought he might have said, straining against the first man's screams.

Be strong. Turn away from it and look toward me.

It took all of his will and courage to do so, but as soon as he tore his eyes away from the barn doors, the shrieking ceased.

He felt his body go limp with relief, realized he was breathing hard. *Who are you?*

I am whom you seek, the voice said gently.

Myrren's father?

Yes.

Where are you?

Come to me.

How? I don't know where you are.

You will find me. There was a pause. He heard the man mutter something unintelligible, then: *I am where no one else dare go.*

Why can't you tell me?

Trust the dog, Elysius said, his voice fading.

Come back! Wyl cried, but the speaker had gone. Wyl had wanted to ask who had been screaming, but it was too late. He had not even asked Myrren's father for his name.

His dreams continued.

Now a new vision swirled before him. He saw Valentyna. She was approaching him and his heart leapt. She looked as exquisite as ever in a bloodred gown and yet her expression was haunted. He tried to smile, wanted to reach out his hands toward her, but he could not.

Forgive me, she whispered, and then he screamed but could not remember why when he woke with a start, his mind blank. What had frightened him? His nightshirt was damp and his eyelids were sticky. He pulled his legs from beneath the sheets and felt the touch of the rug beneath his feet. Looking down, he saw Ylena's shapely feet. The night's events came back to him and he felt a wave of dizziness and disappointment.

Shivering, he moved unsteadily toward the basin of water left on the sideboard and splashed his face, taking care to gently rub his eyes. Ylena's face felt completely unlike Faryl's had. Ylena's cheekbones were rounder, her forehead narrower. Wyl moved the nearby softly burning candle to the mirror, where he stood and stared at the illuminated reflection that looked back at him. He noticed how similar her mouth was to his own. He could not understand how he had missed this previously. It reassured him.

"I failed you," he whispered. "Forgive me," he added, echoing his words from the dream he only now recalled. Who had been seeking absolution in that vision? He could

not recall now. He thought it might have been a woman . . .
no doubt Ylena.

The face looking back at him was sad but beautiful despite the sorrow. She looked too thin, so wan. All that had
made Ylena such a sparkling person, jubilant with the joy of
life, had been buried. What remained was barely a shade of
the young, vibrant woman he had known and loved.

He grasped within himself for anything left of the Ylena
he had so loved. Wyl wanted to find what was left of her
more than he had wanted this with any of his other victims.
It took some time and required his patience, but he finally
coaxed her essence free and felt it fill him with its warmth.

"I knew you couldn't leave me completely." He spoke to
his reflection as memories came roaring back. Childhood
memories and great joy in life. Loving him, Magnus, and
Gueryn . . . and then later Alyd. Wyl cherished the moment
of feeling her love for him and then locked away the
swirling thoughts of Alyd. Those were private and belonged
to her alone.

Darker images of death and blood, burning and crucifix-
ion, coalesced too. He felt savaged by their intensity and
gripped the dresser in anger for what she had witnessed and
endured. Rittylworth was his final punishment; he had
brought destruction to the gentle community.

"I shall kill the King for you alone, beloved," he whispered to what was left of Ylena. "Be at peace now."

He felt stronger for saying the threat aloud. Tying his
now-grubby robe back around himself, feeling awkward in
Ylena's body, he let himself out of the bedroom and crept
down the stone stairway.

In the scullery he found a familiar figure hunched over a
steaming mug of strong, dark tea.

"Can't sleep?" he said, startling Aremys.

The big man looked up. "No, no chance of that. Want
some?" he asked, eyeing the new Wyl carefully.

"I like honey in it," Wyl replied, and from somewhere
found a thin smile as he sat.

The mercenary nodded and was glad for the activity. He

moved around Wyl's new slim shoulders, pouring another mug.

"Am I that hard to look upon, Aremys?"

"No," his friend replied, not turning from his task. "I just liked Faryl. I have to get used to you as your sister." Now he did glance around and a look of sympathy for each other passed between them.

"How are the others taking it?"

Aremys shrugged. "The Duchess is extraordinary. I gather they've only today learned about their son's demise and here she is fretting over you. The Duke is angry, confused. I don't know about the lads."

"They do believe me, though."

"Oh, no doubt," Aremys assured, handing Wyl a mug. "It takes some getting used to."

"As if I didn't know it," Wyl shot back.

"I mean, understand their position as they come to terms with it. Even witnessing it doesn't make it any easier to believe or understand. Shar knows I'm struggling."

Wyl did not answer immediately. Then he rested his chin in the cup of his hands and shook his head slowly. "So how will anyone trust me?"

"Well, your friend Elspyth believes and the mountain man, Lothryn, you said, did. Fynch, the seer." He was holding fingers up in the air as he listed them. "And you convinced me to follow you and I'm a cynic, Wyl. All of us trust you."

"Why did you believe me before seeing it happen for yourself?" Wyl persisted.

"Because of the knives. No one throws like Koreldy, to my knowledge. And because of your strange behavior toward the King. There were other things." He shrugged and then grinned. "The mere fact that you could resist me confirmed you were a man." Wyl guffawed. As always Aremys's timing was perfect. "So you've just got to believe that they'll trust you."

"All right," Wyl said, blowing on his tea.

"I'm sorry it had to be her, Wyl," the big man finally found the courage to say.

"Me too," and a glance to his friend said that he did not wish to talk about it anymore.

They brooded over their drinks in a companionable silence. The soft crackle and spit of the fire Aremys had kindled felt safe and comforting. Wyl warmed Ylena's elegant fingers around the hot mug, fighting the revulsion he felt at seeing them.

"What now?" Aremys finally asked.

"Like you said, I must find Myrren's father."

Aremys sipped and nodded. "I've been thinking . . ."

"Dangerous," Wyl commented, and returned the relieved grin that played around his friend's mouth. Perhaps they would survive this.

"You cannot travel alone."

"Oh no. You don't want to sleep with Ylena as well!" Wyl said in mock horror.

The bearlike man's amusement rumbled deep in his throat. It was reassuring to hear mirth after so much ugliness. "Well, I wouldn't say no, of course, if you're offering . . ." He caught Wyl's glare on the sister's lovely face. "I think you need a companion, is what I meant."

"You don't think I can take care of myself in this guise?"

"I know you can, but you will still be a target. If I were to travel with you, it will prevent the unnecessary interest that will be leveled at a young noblewoman alone and abroad."

Wyl considered it. Aremys was right; he might well be vulnerable as Ylena. And in truth, he could use the quiet company of the big man.

"I agree," he finally replied.

Aremys looked up in surprise. "What, not even going to fight me on it? Throw some knives at me or something?"

"No. You're definitely right. I don't have time for the obstacle of unhealthy interest some might take."

"Well, that's that, then," Aremys growled, relieved. "Where are we going?"

"I had a dream last night."

"Oh?" his friend said, lifting an eyebrow.

"A vision perhaps." Wyl sighed and pulled at his ear. Aremys had seen him make this identical gesture as Faryl and realized it was probably Wyl Thirsk's trait. That felt reassuring, for some reason.

"There's too much talk of magic, I know, but this was real . . . it felt that way at least."

"Tell me," Aremys said.

"A voice told me to go where no one else goes."

"Well, that's certainly specific. We'll find him easily, then."

Wyl gave him a gentle glare. "It's what I was told."

"All right, where could that be?"

"Across the oceans?" Wyl hazarded.

"Which one?"

Wyl shrugged. "All right, the Razors. Most wouldn't think to be heading into the mountains, especially not in this climate with war brewing."

"This was a man's voice?"

Wyl nodded. "His accent didn't suggest he was a northerner, if that's what you're getting around to. He sounded Morgravian if anything—like I used to. A southerner."

"For a Morgravian, Briavel is somewhere they don't trespass."

"Except there's been trade between the two realms for many years now." Wyl shook his head. "No, I don't think it's Briavel."

Aremys stood and stretched. "Well, there's always the Wild."

"The Wild? To the east of Briavel, you mean? There's nothing there."

"How do you know? None of us have visited."

"But isn't it supposed to have some curse on it?" Wyl added. "That you can't return from it?"

Aremys nodded slyly. "They say it's enchanted. Sounds like the sort of place cursed people go."

"That's not funny." Wyl bristled.

"It wasn't meant to be," his companion said evenly. "Sounds like a neat match to me, though. An enchanted place where a warlock might live?"

Wyl closed his eyes and breathed hard, trying to find some sense of ease. "Well, I have no better idea."

"Then we'll go take a look."

"How do we get there?"

"You're not going anywhere without me," Elspyth said, arriving at the doorway. She shrugged at them. "I couldn't sleep. I heard voices." Then she hesitated, looking at Wyl, emotions marching across her face unconcealed.

Wyl stood, walked around the scrubbed table, and he hugged his good friend. She wept a little, but he had finished with tears. His eyes remained dry. "Don't cry, Elspyth. We do them no good with tears."

"I know," she said. "This is all my fault, though. You told me not to reveal the truth. I should have stayed quiet, should have kept your secret . . ."

He hushed her mouth with his soft, female hand. "Don't. Ylena would have killed Faryl anyway. I was the one who failed. I should have seen it coming, reacted faster . . . still, I should have sent Aremys in first to explain that I was not coming to kill her."

"It's just so much sadness rolling into one huge sorrow," she admitted.

He hugged her hard again, wanted her to accept his forgiveness. "Did anyone bother to introduce you to my friend Aremys, by the way? He knows everything."

"I'm sorry, Aremys, we did meet under difficult circumstances," she said, holding out her hand.

The big man took her small hand in his and squeezed gently. "I understand from Wyl how lucky he is to have you for a friend," he said, pleasing her with his gentle words, "even though you are a blabbermouth," and watched the look of hurt cross Elspyth's face.

"Take no notice," Wyl assured. "Aremys loves to tease."

She narrowed her eyes at the big man, saw the levity in his expression, and accepted the jest with some grace. "May I have some of that?" she asked, nodding toward his tea.

"Surely," Aremys said, smiling back to reassure her that he had not meant to hurt. He was glad to busy himself once again.

"So where are you going now?" Elspyth said to the angelic-looking woman before her, an accusing tone in her voice.

"I have to find Myrren's real father, Elspyth, before I can tackle anything. I have to know more about this magic within me."

"I understand," she replied tightly.

"It does not change the oath I swore to you. I will return to the Razors and find him."

"He spoke to me, Wyl," she admitted, a tremor in her voice. "There was pain and darkness around him. He was frightened. There was someone else too, but I couldn't see him"—she shrugged—"or her. There was magic somewhere, I'm sure."

"What did he say?" Elspyth's words had jogged his memory of his own dark dream.

"He called to me," she said wistfully, remembering his sadness.

"That's all?"

She frowned in thought. "No. There was more. He said something along the lines of to tell Romen he will wait. And then he added something strange, cryptic—I can't fathom it."

"Go on," Wyl urged.

"He said to tell you that he is no longer as you would expect." She watched Ylena's face frown.

"That's it?" Wyl said.

"Mmm." She nodded, smiling fleetingly in thanks to Aremys as he set the tea down before her. "What could that mean?"

Wyl stood gracefully and began to pace. If any in the room had known Fergys Thirsk, they would have realized Wyl had caught his father's habit of movement when in thought. "I have no idea, but strangely I too dreamed tonight—well, I think I did. You've just reminded me of it and I don't know who spoke to me, but whoever it was seemed to be in terrible pain, screaming for deliverance. A man."

"He's torturing him," she said bleakly.

They both knew the torturer to whom she referred.

"If it's him trying to reach us, then at least we know he's alive," Wyl reassured.

Aremys joined them at the table. "Is this the Lothryn you have spoken of?"

They both nodded.

"I've never given up the hope that Cailech has kept him alive," Wyl said.

"But you also believed torture would not be enough for Cailech. Not his style, you said," Elspyth countered.

"That's true. The pain could be something else, of course."

"Like what?" Aremys queried.

"Magic," Elspyth murmured, and Wyl shot a glance toward her. He had not wanted to say it himself. "Why not?" she demanded, angry now as she allowed the thought to take shape. "Cailech has that evil Rashlyn hovering around him. Isn't he a practitioner of magic? Just looking at his wild appearance and mad eyes made me go cold."

"Among other nasty things, yes," Wyl admitted. He drained his mug. "I don't want you rushing off into the Razors on your own, Elspyth . . . I know it's crossed your mind," he added.

She blushed. "I cannot sit by and do nothing."

"Cailech will kill you. No parley, no niceties at all. Trust me on this."

"And you would know?"

Wyl nodded, wondering at the tension between them. It had felt different when he was Koreldy. More comfortable. Perhaps his being Ylena was driving a wedge between them. Elspyth would probably have felt less awkward if he had changed again into a man rather than this fragile beauty who was his sister. "Yes, I would. Cailech is ruthless. He will have you killed on sight."

"Then what makes you think you can get through his defenses, Wyl Thirsk?"

"Because I am no longer Romen Koreldy, that's why! He doesn't know Ylena Thirsk, but he knows you. Moreover, I'm hardly intimidating with my long golden tresses and my silk gowns and soft hands." Dawning swept across her face. "It's our only weapon. You have to trust me and be patient . . . trust Lothryn to hang on."

Aleda swept into the scullery. "I heard voices," she said matter-of-factly. "No matter the hour, let's get some food going. How are you, my dear?" she asked, looking in her kind way at Wyl.

"Stronger, thank you," he admitted, and she smiled back at him.

"That's the Thirsk in you, child. I told Jeryb you'd find your grit before morning."

Wyl stood alone with the Duke. He had diluted Ylena's femininity with riding trews and tied her hair almost viciously into a single plait. Try though he might, he could not make her feel as it had felt to be Faryl. He could neither hide her ethereal beauty nor make her movements any less elegant. It pained him on a number of levels, but he would just have to get used to being Ylena.

Aleda had given him a purse containing a small fortune. "Buy yourself some clothes and provisions. You must keep up the noble guise," she had said. "Forgive us all that has happened, Wyl. I feel somehow responsible."

"Don't," he had assured, wanting to refuse the money. He knew he could visit any one of Faryl's many hides. However, he realized Aleda was trying to help in the only practical way she could and so he had accepted her gift with grace. "You do believe me, then?"

She nodded. "What other choice have we? We watched two people suffer and one die, but we have to trust that the Ylena we met is no longer her. You tell us things only Wyl Thirsk could know; you no longer even sound like Ylena in the way you talk, and with all the other terrible things happening right now, we have to believe in this frightening magic."

"You've been a rock of strength, Aleda," he said as he hugged her goodbye. "Thank you for believing me in the midst of all the nonsensical magic."

"You are living proof of it, son. I'll try to make sense of it in weeks to come, I'm sure. In the meantime, I'll trust you now to keep your promise and help give us revenge for Alyd and Ylena." No tears now; Aleda was the bedrock of the family and she would not succumb to weakening emotions when there was a fight to be fought. She turned and left him with her husband.

"Crys will see her safely to the border," the Duke said, nodding toward the place where Elspyth sat talking with Pil.

"I know she will be safe once she crosses into Briavel," Wyl replied.

Crys strolled up.

"Perhaps we need a password . . . er, just in case the curse happens again," Jeryb suggested.

Wyl held the Duke's gaze. He was right. "What would suit you, sir?"

The tall man looked toward the sky in thought. " 'Carving knife'—innocuous enough and I'm sure none of us could forget that?"

"I know I won't, sir," Wyl said, eyes darkening at the memory.

"Are you sure you don't want me to take Elspyth all the way to Werryl?" Crys offered.

"No. Too many spies, Crys. Your name, your family cannot risk being linked to Briavel openly. Just see her safely to the border. The letter I've given her will take care of the rest."

Crys nodded. "Shar keep you safe."

Wyl shook the young man's hand, once again struck by the keen likeness to his dead brother. Crys left them while he gave some instructions to his siblings.

The old man shook his head. "After all these years of fighting. Now Felrawthy conspires with the enemy." His voice was thick.

"Briavel's not the enemy, my lord," Wyl reassured. "Our own king is the enemy. Valentyna and Briavel are, in fact, our only allies."

"Fergys Thirsk would turn in his tomb," the Duke said, disgusted.

"No, sir, he would not. My father would agree with our strategy."

"Are you quite sure of that?"

"As sure as I stand here," and they both smiled wryly. "Everyone here has agreed on the story. Ylena was not here, and although Faryl visited, she left immediately. It leaves Tenterdyn free of suspicion. In the meantime, you mustn't give Celimus any hint that you suspect him. I know you're expecting your mustered men soon, but make an excuse if questions are asked. Whatever lies he tells you, sir, accept them for what they are. Show him nothing—no emotion. He will surely concoct some fabrication to explain the disappearance of your son."

"Why can't I just kill him?" and now the Duke's voice cracked.

"Because you or whomever you give the job to, sir, will never get out of Stoneheart alive. Legionnaires are sworn to die for their king . . . and they will. You and your family will be tracked down and slaughtered . . . and then he'll go after your men. Please believe me when I say he's ruthless. You have no idea of his ambition, sir—you have been away from the capital too long."

"Fighting the Crown's battles!" the Duke growled, but his roar had no bite to it.

Wyl continued. "He has amassed a private guard of mercenaries, too. He is well protected. No, Duke, trust my counsel that it is far better you play Celimus at his own game. I have much less to lose than you. Leave the killing for me."

"So I must sit tight and not raise my hand."

"As we agreed this morning, sir. Assemble a guard around Tenterdyn, by all means, but keep it as innocent looking as possible. Parley with him. See what he has to say. And if you can infiltrate the Legion in the meantime and spread the word, all the better. Work out who is loyal to our cause. And, sir, beware of Cailech. He is unpredictable and far stronger than most of us have realized."

"You really believe he'll raid?"

"Not yet. But he's capable of anything. Be warned, he is cunning and highly intelligent. He won't do anything obvious and perhaps he may not do anything at all, but you need to keep your men alert. In fact, you might use Cailech as your excuse for assembling men at Felrawthy. Celimus will agree with it."

"And I should offer my services to the King?" Jeryb asked, as though tasting something bitter.

"Reinforce your services to him. It will throw him off your scent, sir."

The old man sighed, heavy with his troubles. "What happened to good old-fashioned war?"

Wyl extended his sister's milky white hand. "We fight a different war now, sir. We do it with intrigue . . . and magic."

Jeryb grimaced at its mention. "Shar's guidance over you and your strange, impossible life, Wyl," the Duke said. "I'll wait for word."

"Be strong, sir," Wyl said, feeling the old man's need for revenge. "You'll hear from me."

He crossed the elegant courtyard to where Elspyth stood by her horse. The Duke had provided all his guests with good horses for their various journeys.

"Are you all right?" Wyl asked her as he drew close.

She nodded. "Angry."

"Trust me. I'll get word to you."

"You know how I want to head back to Yentro."

"Don't lie to me. I know how you want to go straight into the Razors."

She pursed her lips. "You don't own me, Wyl. I'll do as I please if it comes to it. I'm feeling sick over what's happened to you, but you're going your way—where you know you must. What about me?"

He bowed his head. "I'm sorry, Elspyth, you're right. But I can't lose you too. Don't you see, this is about keeping you safe, not ignoring your needs."

"And Briavel is all you can offer?"

"For now, yes. It's important. Important for your safety and important for our cause. You want Celimus to pay too. Do this.

Go to Valentyna and live under her protection. I will come and then I'll work out what we're going to do about Lothryn."

Elspyth glared, knowing what he said made sense, hating him momentarily for being right and for caring enough about her. Too few people had cared for her as much as he did. "And I can tell her nothing."

"Nothing! And you need to keep my secret this time. She won't understand anyway. Just be her friend, if she'll permit it. You know what to say. You'll be safe there until I come for you."

"You will come?" She took his arm to reinforce her query.

Wyl nodded, feeling Ylena's plait bounce at his back. "I promise you. It seems I can't die no matter how hard I try," he said half jokingly, but there was too much grief in his tone for Elspyth to smile. "Not yet anyway," he added, and squeezed her shoulder.

He looked now to Pil. "I don't think in all the whirl and drama of last night that I got the chance to thank you for all you've done for my family."

Pil regarded him shyly. "I wish I'd done so much more, kept her safe."

Wyl took the young novice monk's hand. "You did plenty. I was the one who failed her, not you."

"I still don't understand," Pil admitted. "You were Koreldy when you came to Rittylworth?"

"I'm afraid so. Forgive me for the duplicity."

Pil shook his head. "I thought he was different. I was much younger, of course, when he first came to us, so I put it down to my being more grown-up, seeing him through more adult eyes."

"I would appreciate it, Pil, if you would keep this to yourself."

"I think I'd be locked up as a half-wit if I told this tale," the novice admitted. "Your secret's safe with me."

Wyl changed the subject. "You are clear on the story we are all sticking to?"

Pil looked unhappy but nodded. "The woman, Faryl, visited but left soon after."

"Good." Wyl could see the youngster was not comfortable with the falsehood. "We lie for good reason, Pil. And you will now seek the monk in Brynt?"

"Take his mule back, yes. The monk's name is Brother Tewk. If you ever have need of my help, it's yours, although I don't know how we'll find each other," Pil said, shrugging a shoulder, embarrassed.

"Who knows, our paths may yet cross again. Be safe, Pil. Shar's light upon you always."

Elspyth hugged the young man and watched him pay his respects to the family before climbing on the patient mule.

"So we must part again, Wyl," Elspyth said, determined not to show her fear or grief.

"Once again I ask another journey, another favor," he said, putting his arms around her. "Thank you for believing in me."

She pulled out of his embrace to regard him in his new, far prettier body. "I'm trusting you. Don't let me down."

"I won't. We're using a code, by the way." She frowned. Wyl told her the Duke's idea.

"Oh, so we know it's really you and won't kill you if you approach us in the guise of our enemy."

"Precisely. The code is 'carving knife.' I think the Duke has a sense of humor in spite of himself."

Elspyth gave him a thin smile. "Take care, Wyl. I'll look after your queen for you," she said, and liked that her comment made him look sharply back toward her. His queen. Even in Ylena's body his care and love for Valentyna was written all over his face.

Aremys had sidled up. "We'd best be going," he said, rescuing Wyl from Elspyth's prolonged farewell.

"Where are you going?" Elspyth asked.

"Where most don't go, apparently," Aremys admitted, giving her a look that suggested he had no idea. He reached around her tiny frame and dared a hug. "Be safe, blabbermouth."

They had decided that Wyl would travel as the Lady Rachyl Farrow from Grenadyn and hope to Shar that

King Celimus did no thorough investigation should her name ever make itself known to him.

"That's your family name, right?" Wyl asked as Aremys sipped a decent ale, and he had to make do with a very watery version. They had stopped at an inn in Brynt befitting a noble lady.

Aremys nodded. "At least I can give you all the background information you need."

"You're sure Celimus would not know."

"Our families go back, but he was too young, as was I. You could simply be a baby sister."

"After your own true one, you mean."

The big man sipped. "Or another one. Stop worrying. The Crown has had nothing to do with Grenadyn most of its life. It's just that our fathers fought together, got to know one another. To Celimus, Grenadyn's a backwater where he gets his good horses from—that's about all he'll know of it."

"So, do I look all right, then?" Wyl asked, straightening the bodice of the gown he'd changed into at the inn.

"Every bit the noble lady," Aremys admitted, looking at Wyl's new clothes.

"I can't wait to get out of these skirts and into my riding trousers tomorrow."

"Well, suffer now for all our sakes."

"What happened to Faryl's body, by the way?"

"The boys buried it somewhere remote."

"Good, so if the King's men come looking . . ."

"They'll find no trace and suspect she's on her way to Briavel or whatever. Who cares."

Wyl stared into his mug. "Pil might yet undo us."

"You think so?"

"He's a man of Shar. The lie about Ylena and Faryl does not sit easily."

"I wonder how easily he'd sit in the King's dungeon."

Wyl grimaced. "No point worrying, I suppose. It's out of our control now. I wonder why the Manwitch wouldn't tell me where we have to go."

"Perhaps he couldn't." Aremys shrugged.

Wyl frowned. "I don't see why not, although now that I try to remember, he wasn't exactly forthcoming with much information at all. I've been thinking it has to be the Wild."

"It's certainly where no one goes."

"Do you know much about it?"

Aremys sighed. "Not really. They say it's haunted, alive in some way. You know how superstitious Morgravians and Briavellians have been in the past."

"Ah, the old stories. And you believe them?"

" 'Enchanted' is probably the better word."

"They say many have tried to learn more, but no one returns from it."

"I've heard that. I believe it could be true, don't you?"

Wyl shook his head sadly. "Until I became Koreldy, I would have scoffed at the notion. But I have to believe in magic now. I always thought the Wild was just a fable for an uninhabitable wilderness."

Aremys drained his cup and stretched. "If it were harmless, it would already be a part of Briavel. Whatever it is, it's managed to keep all the hungry land ravagers at bay."

"There's something else," Wyl said, draining his own cup more delicately than he preferred to.

"Tell me."

"Knave."

"The dog you spoke of, so?"

"Well, I suspect he'll find me, guide us."

"Stranger and stranger," Aremys admitted, wiping his mouth dry of the ale. "Do we just wait, then?"

"No, we keep moving. He'll find us."

"Can you trust Elspyth?"

"Yes," Wyl said emphatically.

"I didn't mean it that way. I meant will her love for this Lothryn get in the way?"

Wyl shook his head, sipped his watered ale, and tried not to pull a face again. "The worst of this is having to rely on others, Aremys. I'm relying on Elspyth to get word to the Queen, and I'm relying on the Duke, in all his pain and anger, to stay firm and hold the north . . . act loyal to the King when all he wants to do is gallop with his army toward Pearlis. I'm relying on Valentyna to keep her nerve and not capitulate to Celimus while hoping Cailech does nothing rash." He made a sound of agony.

"Then don't," the mercenary said, his gaze firm over the rim of his cup. "Rely on no one, Wyl. That's my creed. You can't orchestrate the lives of others. Do what you must do and deal with the problems as they unfold. I don't trust that Elspyth will be able to wait if you take too long; I don't trust that your queen will be able to stave off Celimus for very much longer or that Cailech won't take matters into his own hands. Who couldn't forgive Felrawthy for doing something vengeful? All you can do right now is concentrate on one priority—you can't be everywhere at once. You want answers to this curse of yours—then let's go find those answers."

"Why are you doing this for me, Aremys?"

The big man drained his cup. "Because frankly I have nothing better to do."

24

KING CAILECH TOOK THE BABY WITH A RUSH OF SUCH AFFECTION that he felt his breath catch. He hushed its soft whimpering, admiring that the boy was long limbed and healthy. He had seen the child kick his legs furiously when happy or distressed and had laughed joyously at his son's lusty cry.

He would be a strong king one day, his father thought with pride.

Cailech stroked the child's downy golden hair and smiled indulgently at the dimple in his cheek that marked him so clearly the son of a King, for Cailech's own dimple had been cherished as precious when he himself was an infant. His mother had told him it was a sign from their god. Haldor had blessed him. He would lead a special life.

"Aydrech," he cooed. Cailech had never felt such intense love for anyone. This sense of ownership, this bonding with a helpless infant created from his own seed, was so powerful it threatened to overcome him. "My son," he whispered, and kissed the baby softly, his heart smitten. He knew in that instant of tenderness that he would never, indeed could never, love anyone as much as Aydrech. His heir.

Voices pulled him from his adoration. He looked into the child's still-dark eyes, which he anticipated might lighten to green to match his own. "Come and meet my new stallion, child," he added, reluctantly handing the baby back to its wet nurse as the wild-looking Rashlyn approached.

"Ready?" the King asked.

The barshi simply nodded.

"Bring the boy," Cailech ordered to the woman, and she fell in step.

They approached a dusty area surrounded by wooden palings, known as the breaking ring. Cailech climbed up the trio of stairs to a raised platform. His son was carried behind and promptly suckled contentedly at the woman's concealed breast.

The King's attention was diverted now; his eyes hungrily sought his prized new beast, whose brilliantly shiny black coat twitched in the harsh sunlight of the Razors winter. The wild stallion snorted, nostrils flaring in warning, and stamped its feet angrily.

"He's magnificent," Cailech breathed, inspired at the sight. "Truly magnificent." It was far more than he had dared imagine.

A special horse breaker, one of the best—if not the best—in the mountains, bowed and approached. "Sire, would you like me to begin?"

"No. He's all mine," Cailech said, leaping down lightly

from the platform and glancing toward Rashlyn, who barely smiled.

"As you wish," the horse handler replied. "A word of warning, my lord," he risked. "This is a very aggressive beast. He will take some special handling."

Cailech nodded and took the proffered gloves and the rope. "We won't be using the hobbling and beating method, Maegryn."

The man immediately looked worried. "Please, my lord king. It's all this one will understand." When he saw the immovable set of his leader's jaw, he nodded. "At least allow me to take the first session."

Cailech put his hand on the man's shoulder. He towered over him. "Be easy. This one will not hurt me. And I do not wish to win him through pain. We will break him the old way—we will do it by trust. He and I must trust each other. He must know what it is to fear me, but without pain. That is the greatest conquering of all, don't you think?"

It made no sense to the man. "Sire, you—"

"Hush, Maegryn. I know best," Cailech assured as he entered the breaking ring.

There were several onlookers and word was already spreading that the King was personally breaking in a new stallion, a fiery one. Cailech slapped the rope against his thigh and the horse looked at him with a wild and angry look in its dark eyes. It had been kept inside and isolated for days, and now that it was outside in the fresh mountain air, it was brimming with unspent energy and fury. The King could see the whites of the beast's eyes—a sure sign that the creature was just short of demented at being penned in.

It snorted. Cailech knew this was a threat, knew he must answer it.

"Ha!" he yelled, and slapped the rope again, making a loud noise against his soft leather riding trews.

The horse began to paw the ground. Another sign. Dangerous this time.

Maegryn tipped his head toward some helpers, who pre-

pared to leap into the ring and distract the angry animal
should it charge their king.

They watched Cailech raise his chin high and stand to his
full height. He had inherited the talents of his father, who
had been a skilled breaker of horses, and those skilled
enough to understand would know that Cailech was, in this
simple move, throwing down the gauntlet to the horse, inviting it to test its nerve and resilience against him. This was a
fight of stamina and mental strength—male against male;
the different species hardly mattered. The horse knew exactly what was being offered and knew only one of them
could win leadership.

The King took a short, aggressive step toward the stallion, holding the rope aloft. It held its ground, but it flinched
momentarily, which to Maegryn's experienced eye was an
indication that it was unsure about this challenge. It would
proceed with caution, he realized with relief.

Cailech slapped the rope, outward this time, toward the
horse's rump. Incensed, it snorted fiercely and reared up.
Again Cailech shouted, distracting it with his voice and
diverting its attention with the rope, which licked at its
back. The animal screamed, not from pain but anger and
no little confusion. It moved toward the King. The han-
dlers tensed. One even raised a bow, its arrow tipped with
the sap of the falava bush. A skilled shot to the rump
would sedate the horse, although it was not instant. They
would need to get the King out of the ring immediately if
the scene turned ugly.

Once more Cailech stood his ground and repeated the
process.

This time the horse reared, and although Cailech stepped
back, he also yelled loudly, whacking the animal hard on
the rump with the rope. It hurt. Was meant to. Stung, the
beast backed off. Man and horse regarded each other. It was
as if no one else were present. Cailech could hear nothing
but the angry breathing of the beast. He slapped his thigh
with the rope once more. The horse reluctantly moved
around the ring.

Those watching let out their collectively held breath. It was a start.

The breaking continued relentlessly over the next few days. Four suns later the stallion stood sweating and trembling. The wildness was still in its eyes, but it respected the man who stood tall before it. He too was perspiring, but his cold green gaze never left the horse's majestic face.

Now, sire! Maegryn thought, filled with admiration. As if the King could hear his private thoughts, Cailech suddenly rounded his shoulders, in the language of horses conveying safety and companionship. The stallion whinnied softly. Until now Cailech had forced domination and the horse had always faced away from its adversary, preferring little or no eye contact. Now it turned directly toward him and eyed him. Still rather magnificent, it defiantly glared at Cailech, but its body language told Maegryn that the King had been accepted.

The rounded silhouette Cailech had adopted put the horse at ease; invited it to rub its shoulders with a creature who was no longer its challenger or even its equal but its leader. Another long day of this routine continued before finally the stallion, nicknamed Proud by the mountain dwellers who stopped by over the week to watch the exciting drama unfold, lowered its defiant head in deference to its breaker, walked over to Cailech, and nuzzled at his shoulder.

As soon as this happened, Cailech straightened and gave orders. "Tie him to the snubbing post and fetch a saddle," he said, not prepared to lose the moment.

"Perhaps we should wait, my lord," Maegryn ventured.

"Now!" Cailech replied. He left no room for argument.

Rashlyn approached his friend as the men moved in cautiously to halter the horse. He handed Cailech a skin of water. "Well?"

"Impressive."

"Thank you."

"Now we make him fully trusting," Cailech said, taking another long swig and handing back the skin. "I'll be riding him by this afternoon," he said fiercely.

Rashlyn nodded, the sly grin evident once again beneath the flurry of hair.

"Ready, my lord," Maegryn called.

Cailech stepped toward the disturbed black horse. It was blowing and trembling, angry and confused again, this time at being restrained to the fence.

"Put on the saddle," Cailech said.

This was easier said than achieved, but the men working the horse were swift and experienced. Cailech carefully approached the stallion, continuously murmuring soothing words. And then at the right moment, in one smooth movement, Cailech landed nimbly on the horse's back, at the same moment Maegryn untied the animal. Alarmed, it instantly began to buck and jump, squealing and angry, as determined to unseat its guest as Cailech was to remain in place.

The athleticism and strength required to keep his balance for any length of time was unimaginable for the inexperienced breakers watching. Cailech hung on grimly, determined he would best the horse's most fearsome bucking. The stallion finally calmed, too spent for even for one more effort. The King could feel its entire body shaking with despair as well as fatigue.

It had done its utmost. It had failed.

As Cailech slid from the saddle, the horse turned its head. He was ready for it, ready for the bite—one last-ditch effort to inflict pain on the victor. The King backhanded the horse in the face with all the strength he himself had left and the horse squealed in obvious shock and agony.

"Unsaddle him!" Cailech commanded, rubbing his hand. He had not wanted to do that to this horse, but it was necessary, and only he and Rashlyn knew how much emotion was driving that blow.

Maegryn was shocked at his sovereign's aggressiveness, but he was also relieved. King and horse had been trying to outdo each other for too many days, both aiming to conquer the other. The horse had lost the battle—which was as it should be but still the horse handler was keen for the beast to have some rest from its exertions. In truth, he believed this strange horse would prefer death to subservience.

"I will ride him this afternoon. Have him readied."

"Sire?" Maegryn asked, shocked for the second time in as many minutes.

"His name is Galapek, by the way. I will ride him without a saddle."

Maegryn dared not contradict. "As you command," was all he permitted himself to say.

Cailech strode away, Rashlyn at his side.

"Have you roused the wet nurse?" the King asked.

"Yes, she will be ready when you want her."

"I will be taking my son out alone this afternoon."

"On him?" Rashlyn asked, surprised.

"Have Aydrech brought to me at the edge of the lake directly after the midday meal. I want him to know this horse."

"Is that wise, my lord?"

"He'll be fine. He won't hurt Aydrech," Cailech replied, his stride lengthening, forcing the barshi to all but skip alongside.

"I don't recognize the name you've given the beast."

"It's in the old language of our forefathers."

The sorcerer was not of the mountains. "Oh? What does it mean?"

"Traitor," the King snarled, and left the practitioner of magic in his wake.

Maegryn brought the stallion to the King. "My lord, please let me saddle him," he beseeched, fearful of what the proud beast might do.

"Take off the halter. I ride with the child, and bareback."

Maegryn blinked. He must not contradict the King, even though he knew his leader was wrong. This huge horse was more than capable of killing. But the handler wisely understood that so was his king, and it would be his own neck at the end of a noose if he risked angering Cailech.

"I'll mount him first, then you're to remove all restraints," Cailech instructed.

Maegryn gave the King a leg up and was relieved that the

horse protested only slightly. Then it settled. He held his breath and looked toward his sovereign, who nodded. The horseman removed all the tackle and the stallion shook its head at the sense of freedom.

"Leave us," the King said, and Maegryn departed, albeit reluctantly.

The wet nurse, waiting nearby, was also banished once she had handed Cailech the whimpering bundle she had brought. Once the King was alone, Cailech leaned over, laid his head against the strong neck of the horse, and as he stroked the beast he whispered to it.

"Now you are mine for good. Come, my friend, let us ride together."

And the man once known as Lothryn, now called Galapek the traitor, took his first unhappy steps as King Cailech's enchanted four-legged servant.

Watching from the shadows, Rashlyn smiled thinly, admiring his work.

Gueryn lay on the pallet in his dungeon space and faced away from the door. He had adopted this pose since Cailech had seen him fit and returned to his cell. He had spoken to no one in that time. Guards came and went about their business; the dungeoner was a nice enough fellow who regularly changed the straw and brought fresh food and water. He had tried talking with the prisoner, but Gueryn had pointedly refused to respond. Nowadays the man entered and left the cell in silence.

Today was different, though. When the man arrived he walked straight over to Gueryn and prodded him. "Come on, we've got orders to exercise you."

Gueryn stirred. No amount of pride would permit him to resist the opportunity to walk in daylight and breathe fresh air—Cailech had promised neither during his incarceration, so this was quite a development. Obviously the King had paid attention to Gueryn's threat and was as determined to preserve Gueryn's life as Gueryn was to end it. Starving himself had not worked. Rashlyn had ordered him force-fed, and the starvation felt worse than dying because his body fought him all the way.

It was more logical, then, to cooperate with food and try a different tactic, for it was now very obvious that Cailech wanted him kept alive, if not comfortable. And so his only protest was silence. They would get nothing from him. More recently he realized that deep down he wanted to live too . . . if just to hear news of Wyl—if he still lived—and Ylena. He would stay alive and alert until he could somehow contribute toward bringing this Mountain Kingdom down.

Walking, after so long without exercise, sounded easier than it was and it took two men to support him. When they emerged from the dungeon, it was not into broad daylight, as Gueryn had imagined, but into the inkiness of night. An unbelievably beautiful starry sky greeted Gueryn's return to real life and he inhaled the piercingly cold but most welcome night air and immediately began to cough.

"Take it easy, old man," one of his aides murmured.

Gueryn growled something unintelligible through the cough.

"What was that?" the mountain man inquired, amused.

"I think he's telling you your fortune, Myrt," the man on the other side of Gueryn replied, and laughed.

Gueryn cleared his throat. "I said I'll knock you senseless next time you call me old."

Both men laughed and Gueryn chuckled deeply too. It felt suddenly permissible and even rather empowering to share a jest with others, even if they were the enemy.

"How old are you?" Myrt asked.

"Twoscore and five," he replied, shuffling awkwardly between them.

"Then you'd better start acting like it," Myrt replied. "The King wants you fit and healthy, not dying in his dungeon."

"I gathered. How thoughtful of him."

"Well, now that your wound has fully healed, it's time you got your body well."

"I'll do it, just so that I can enjoy fighting some of you when my chance comes again."

Myrt chuckled. "That's the spirit. Can you manage on your own now?"

"Let me try," Gueryn replied gruffly.

He doubled up to cough again but soon enough was able to totter more freely, if laboriously.

"Don't worry, I'm not going anywhere," he said to his captors, who smiled back.

"Dyx up there will see to it you have another nasty wound to live through if you try," Myrt warned, his jaw jutting toward where an archer watched from a higher vantage than they.

Gueryn nodded. They probably knew he hardly had the strength to hold himself upright. In that moment he decided he would work his body hard from now on and would regain his former strength. He had to make himself useful to Morgravia . . . if only as a rather pitiful and captive spy.

As he passed by the two men on another agonizingly slow round, he heard the name Lothryn and his attention was immediately caught. He circled in a more shallow rotation so he could eavesdrop, turning his head away and casting a blank expression so he did not appear to be listening.

". . . so have you seen him?"

"No," Myrt replied. "And he's not in the dungeon. I've checked."

"So where?"

Gueryn, unable to see the men as he shuffled by again, assumed Myrt must have shrugged.

"Not dead, surely?" the companion queried, bewilderment evident in his tone.

"Loth always warned us that the King is unpredictable. No one, not even Loth, could gauge his moods, but he was the only one who seemed able to talk to Cailech when he was dark of spirit."

"But they're so close, as good as brothers," the man qualified, aghast.

"Loth betrayed us, Byl. Don't you understand? That's about the worst sin he could have perpetrated on the King. Cailech demands loyalty above all else."

His younger, less experienced companion grunted. "Seems odd then that he's permitted to summarily execute one of our best."

"They're the rules. Loth would have known the penalty even as he broke them," Myrt said unhappily.

Gueryn was thanking his stars for his keen hearing when a third voice broke out of nowhere.

"He's not dead," the new voice said, and Gueryn had to work hard to keep his face devoid of all expression as a figure melted out of the shadows.

It was the hideous medicine man who had saved his life but watched with bright eyes as they took Elspyth's. "He is among you," Rashlyn said with a trace of glee.

Out of the corner of his eye Gueryn could see both mountain men bristle at the approach of the wild-looking Rashlyn. It seemed only Cailech suffered the fellow gladly.

"I haven't noticed him," Myrt replied carefully.

"Oh, indeed you have, you're just not realizing it," Rashlyn said, glancing Gueryn's way and changing the subject. "I see he can walk unaided now."

Gueryn turned his back and imagined the two men nodding.

"This is good. We need him healthy," Rashlyn said.

"Why?" Myrt asked, desperately wanting to know more about Lothryn.

"Ah, that I can't divulge. But your king has plans for him."

Gueryn felt his stomach clench. He despised the secretive nature of this man.

"Can you get a message to Loth for me?" Myrt asked, ignoring the sorcerer's evasiveness.

Rashlyn laughed; it was a snigger filled with guile and knowing. "No, I can't do that. Have you admired the King's magnificent new stallion, by the way?"

"The best I've ever seen," Myrt agreed, disappointed by the barshi's lack of interest and annoyed by his irritating leaps from topic to topic.

"And do you know what Galapek means in the old language?"

"No."

"Perhaps you should learn more of your ancestors' tongue," Rashlyn answered, and walked away smiling.

"Now what's that all supposed to mean?" Byl asked.

"Search me," Myrt replied. "His mind is as frenzied and unreliable as his appearance. He makes my flesh crawl. Superstitious or not, I don't know how Cailech can stand him to be near."

"Looks like our prisoner has had enough," Byl suggested, noticing that Gueryn had stopped pacing.

"Come on, then," Myrt called to Gueryn. "Let's get you back to your cozy guest room."

Gueryn said nothing more, other than to thank the men for the rare treat of being outside.

"Don't mention it," Myrt replied. "We'll force you to do it each evening until you feel fit again."

After the men had left, Gueryn allowed his mind to embrace the disturbing nature of what he had overheard from Rashlyn. Myrt and his friend might not have understood the sly message underlying the confusing words of the medicine man but Gueryn was classically trained. His great-grandmother, originally from the Outer Isles of the north, had been married off to a Morgravian noble. Although she had accepted her new life, she never fully relinquished her cultural background, particularly its language, and she had religiously taught it to her daughter, who had in turn instructed her own son.

Gueryn knew all too well what the word "galapek" meant in the old language of the north. It meant traitor! An odd name for a stallion.

He shivered in the damp of his cell and pulled the blanket tighter about him. What was the medicine man implying . . . that Cailech had named his new stallion after his best friend? Or was it more convoluted than that?

Rashlyn had said Lothryn was alive, roaming among them. And yet neither of those men, presumably friends of Lothryn and close enough to the King to be familiar with him, had seen the courageous mountain man. Yet Rashlyn had sniggered and intimidated about things none of them could understand. What was the link between the horse and Lothryn?

Gueryn drifted off into unhappy sleep pondering this, promising himself he would make more effort to talk with his guards tomorrow night. Now he too wanted to know where Lothryn was.

Meanwhile, in the stable, a man trapped and lost in the powerful shapechanging magic of Rashlyn threw his magnificently sculpted new body angrily against the timber doors of the barn and screamed for deliverance.

25

K NAVE COULD FEEL THE PULL OF WYL'S THOUGHTS. HE ALREADY knew the Quickening had happened again and he had startled his companion the night before with a terrible howling. Fynch was far too sharp not to recognize this keening for what it might be. He recalled the last time Knave had made that sound. It gnawed away inside him that Wyl might have died once more and come back to life again—that he was now walking in a new body. But Fynch was too distracted by his own fear to allow that notion to gain too much space in his mind.

They were sitting at the edge of a dense brush on the northern rim of Briavel, known aptly as the Thicket. For most, it was simply the barrier that discouraged any unsuspecting traveler from heading into the famed and sinister Wild. Beyond the Thicket was the small tributary joining the major River Eyle, which all but bisected Morgravia and Briavel. This rivulet, ominously known as the Darkstream, was the only access into the region known as the Wild.

"Are you sure, Knave?" Fynch whispered once again.

The dog nuzzled his face. It was answer enough. Knave would not let anything bad happen to him. As it was, the dog had somehow managed to get them from Baelup to the north of Briavel with dazzling speed. Fynch knew Knave used magic; accepted it now. All that mattered was finding his way to Elysius, and although they had begun using traditional means of travel such as accepting transport with friendly tinkers and merchants, Fynch had soon come to realize that they covered a lot more distance when they traveled alone. It occurred at night, while he slept.

"How do you do it?" he asked his friend, who stared back at him with liquid, dark eyes. "I mean, I curl up with you in one spot and I wake up in another. Do you carry me," he wondered aloud, scratching gently at the dog's ears, "or do you just 'send' us from one place to another, like I did with Elysius?"

Knave groaned with pleasure. It was the only answer Fynch was going to get. Even he estimated that traveling from Baelup to this northern point in Briavel at the foothills of the Razors should take weeks. They had been traveling for just a few days and were already at the Darkstream's mouth.

"I guess I shouldn't put it off any longer," Fynch said, hoping to find some comfort in the rallying words. Knave nudged him. He wanted Fynch to move. "I'm frightened," the boy admitted.

He knew the tall tales of the Wild from his mother's stories. She had terrified him with dark notions of what must happen to the intrepid explorers who took fate in their hands. All travelers choosing to use this tributary had to register, he remembered. It was how the authorities monitored who had gone missing over the years. Fynch felt his legs go watery at the thought. What if he were never seen or heard from again? How would Wyl know where to find his body? What would happen to Valentyna?

Knave growled softly, reminding him to move. Fynch unraveled the thong of Romen's he had taken to wearing about his own tiny wrist. He tied it now to a branch, casting a prayer to Shar that someone might find it—someone being Wyl—not that Wyl even knew to come looking here!

Fynch took a steadying breath, summoned his courage, and stepped into the Thicket. It was dusk outside, but beneath the tangle of yews it was brooding enough to make the surrounds look and feel as dark as the night. Was it his imagination, or did the branches bend, as if to touch him? He kept his eyes fixed on Knave, who led the way through shrub and foliage with seeming ease. There were no birdcalls, no animal sounds. Not even an insect chirped. The silence was heavy enough to make Fynch curve his shoulders inward and wrap his thin arms about his body. He could hear the rush of the river somewhere nearby, keeping close to their path. He broke into a trot to stay up with Knave, who was pushing them more quickly now.

Fynch suddenly realized he was casting a repetitive thought. *I mean no harm,* he mentally repeated again and again. Perhaps it was his susceptibility to magical elements that convinced Fynch that the Thicket answered him, although he could no more articulate exactly what was said than sprout wings and fly.

After he had cast his mantra for some time, the Thicket no longer felt threatening. The whispers—which was the only way Fynch could describe the sensation—felt increasingly gentle and warm. What had initially struck him as sinister now felt oddly friendly. Leaves softly trailed against his face no matter how agilely he ducked and weaved. With each brush of a leaf or twig, he felt a tingle of something pass through him. There was no time to stop and consider it, though. He was all but running after Knave.

Finally they emerged on the other side. It had felt like it had taken an age to cross from boundary to boundary, yet Fynch understood—now that the weight of the Thicket's presence had lifted somewhat—that they had traveled barely minutes through the gloomy denseness.

Fynch experienced a curious tingling in his body, but its strange presence was quickly forgotten as his glance fell upon the Darkstream, which had indeed kept them company through the trees, but only now did they see it properly. It did not move as fast as Fynch had suspected, nor was it nearly as wide as it had sounded. It was sinister, though, its waters inky and intimidating. Across a small wooden bridge, surrounded by the first rocky mounds that would become the Razors, stood a hut from which an oddly cheerful column of smoke rose. A path led down to a jetty nearby, attached to which bobbed a trio of small rowboats, neatly tied to wooden poles. It was an unexpectedly comforting scene and yet the gurgle of the deep waters that passed by warned Fynch that this was not a safe place.

Knave walked a few paces across the bridge and then looked back at Fynch. Again the boy became aware of the tingling and realized it was connected to Knave. They were somehow linked via this sensation. Once more his awareness of it was diverted as he gathered that he was supposed to follow the dog across the bridge. He questioned for a moment whether he might be imagining the tingle, for it passed as quickly as it arrived and Fynch was left wondering what his fears were doing to him. He stepped forward, finding grim amusement in the thought that the bridge should yell out "friend or foe?" as it might have done in the old fairy tales. And then behind the door of the hut should be a troll.

He knocked at that same door now. No troll. It was the normal voice of a man, friendly enough, suggesting he was coming as fast as he could.

"Now then," the man said, pulling open the door, "Shar strike me down, look at the size of that thing."

"He won't hurt you, sir. He's just big," Fynch reassured, relieved the person was far from threatening and appeared nothing like a troll.

The man looked at him somewhat quizzically. He was pudgy and the action made the flesh of his face pucker in a genial manner. His ruddy complexion only added to Fynch's notion that this was a good-natured soul who enjoyed a tipple and perhaps some company on the rare occasion it presented itself.

"Come in, then, boy. Your . . . beast can wait outside."

"He's a dog, sir."

"Whatever he is, don't dawdle and let the cold air in, child."

Fynch glanced toward Knave, who had already settled on his haunches. The dog knew what to do, so Fynch followed the man's large backside into the hut. The smell of soup reminded him that he had not eaten in a long time, despite the freshly killed rabbits Knave had brought to him most evenings. He imagined it was about now that the seemingly friendly soul he sat with would throw him into a cupboard and fatten him up for cooking in the soup pot later. He shook his head free of the silly childhood stories.

"Well, now, lad, what brings you through the Thicket?"

Another deep breath. "I must travel into the Wild, sir. I need to hire one of your boats."

"I see. And why do you need to do this?"

"Is it by law that I have to answer your questions, sir, no offense meant?" Fynch asked earnestly.

"That you do, son. Without my approval, you'll be heading straight back through those trees."

"It was my impression, sir," Fynch began carefully and seriously, as was his way, "that the Boatkeeper could not refuse anyone to journey on the stream."

The man sighed and his gray eyes gleamed from deep within his face. "This is true. You are well informed."

"So you can't deny me passage?" Fynch qualified.

"Not if you have coin to pay, no. I can, however, do whatever I can think of to dissuade you from the journey, young man. You are so young to be here."

"I seek someone," Fynch replied, in answer to the original question.

"Someone lost?"

Fynch nodded. This was not strictly true and he hated to tell lies. Somehow not speaking made it easier to approve the lie.

"Family?"

"Possibly."

"How old are you?"

"Old enough."

It was obvious the man did not believe him. "You understand how perilous this place is, boy?"

"I do. I have my dog to protect me."

At this, the man laughed. "Priceless. Come and sit by the fire, lad. Let me fetch my ledger."

Fynch did as he was told, relishing the warmth. "Do you live here alone?" he called to the man, who was rifling through a chest.

"Yes. Have done all my life."

"No family?"

"Not since my parents took the fever and died." The man grumbled to himself, looking beneath books and cloths. "Raised myself in the foothills . . . a traveling monk taught me my letters. He stayed awhile and left when he felt I knew enough to get by."

"How long have you been the Boatkeeper?"

"I've always been the Boatkeeper. Ah, here it is," he said, blowing dust off the large black book he had pulled from the bottom of the chest. He carried it to a desk. "Can I interest you in a bowl of soup, child? I've more than enough for myself."

Fynch grinned awkwardly. He could use some hot food. "Thank you, sir." He wondered if it was poisoned, considered that this might be the way the seemingly friendly man entrapped his unwitting guests. He shook his head. He had to stop this.

"Polite one, aren't you? There's a bowl on that shelf. Help yourself while I find my place in this book."

The soup was simple vegetable broth, but it pleased Fynch greatly and it was far from poisonous. He ladled a small bowlful and sat at the rickety table to enjoy it.

"Bread?" the man asked, not looking up.

"This is more than enough."

The Boatkeeper grunted as if to suggest it was hardly anything. "Right then, lad." He cleared his throat as he began his official speech, fixing Fynch with a steely gaze. "I am obliged to tell you that the Law of the Wild was set two centuries back or so. Both Morgravia and Briavel agreed upon it.

All their peoples have access to the Darkstream, but no rescue parties would ever, have ever, or will ever be sent in search of the missing. They are always presumed dead. Do you understand?"

Fynch looked up from his food, his brow furrowed. "I understand, sir, but if no one ever returns from the Wild, sir, how come you always have boats. They don't look new to me."

"A sharp lad you are too—what's your name?"

It could not hurt, he figured. Celimus was hardly going to check the records out here. "Fynch."

"Mine's Samm. Pleased to meet you, young Fynch." Fynch nodded, unable to do much else with a spoonful of soup in his mouth. "Now to answer your clever question . . . the boats always find their way back." He regarded his guest and smiled. "Upstream and against the current."

Fynch was wide-eyed now. "Magic," he said, with reverence.

"I'm not saying one way or another," the Boatkeeper added. "My job is to record who sets off from here and charge the fee."

"Taxes on death," Fynch mused, taking the last spoonful.

"Hardly . . . more a formality really. Not much money to be made from here. The last person who took the Darkstream registered more than two decades ago—probably closer to a quarter of a century, if my memory serves me. A woman, it was, and her fee is the same as yours."

It fired Fynch's imagination to think of some lone, brave woman facing the Wild. "I wonder what or whom she sought."

Samm cocked his head to one side in thought. "They never say—just like you. Oh, but she was lovely. Such a waste. I nearly talked myself hoarse trying to convince her to stay. But she would not be persuaded otherwise."

"She obviously needed badly to go there."

"Broken heart perhaps."

"What happened?"

Samm sighed. "The pretty lady never returned, of course, but her boat did. Ah, here's her name. Emil, that's right.

Never heard that name before. Her hair was as dark as the stream."

The soup soured instantly in Fynch's belly. "Did you say Emil?"

The Boatkeeper nodded. "Aye. Odd one, isn't it?" He looked up. "Why?"

"Oh, nothing," Fynch followed up hastily. He felt light-headed. Emil had been the name of Myrren's mother . . . it could be coincidence, even though it was far from a common name.

"Was she from Morgravia?" he asked as casually as he could, setting down his spoon.

"Er . . . yes. Pearlis, it says here."

Too much of a coincidence, then. Myrren's mother had originally been from Pearlis and the timing fit too neatly. Myrren had been around eighteen years when she died. Her death had occurred six years ago. No, much too coincidental for his liking. So at least one person had returned from the Wild—Emil had made it back and raised her child. There was hope for him yet.

"Is something wrong, lad?"

"No. Your soup is delicious, sir. I was contemplating a second bowl," he said honestly. "But I won't, thank you."

"You eat like a bird!"

He was glad to have thrown Samm off his scent. "So I'm told," and he grinned. "Can I travel at night?"

"I wouldn't advise it. Best leave at first light. It also gives you the night to think on it."

"I won't change my mind."

Samm smiled kindly. "I understand. Have a good night's rest. You're most welcome to bunk down here with me. It will be dark in moments, anyway."

"Can I pay you now?"

"Tomorrow's soon enough."

"I will be going, Samm," Fynch said firmly.

The man grinned. "Is your dog all right out there?"

"Nothing bothers Knave. Thank you for your hospitality."

"Don't mention it. I don't get conversation often—no

human company around here," he admitted. "Settle yourself in then, lad."

Fynch did not sleep well. He woke at first light, glad to be awake and moving, although his mind felt dull while his body fidgeted in nervous anticipation of the journey ahead. He roused Samm, put on a pot of water, and politely shared some porridge with his host. In answer to Samm's gentle questions, none of which Fynch considered too pointed, he slid around the truth and gave the impression he was from Briavel and had on occasion worked at the castle.

"Will you give me no reason for your journey, son? It seems such a waste."

"Maybe I'll return, Samm," Fynch said brightly, trying to avoid the question.

"I must ask again that you understand the terms of your departure. There is no rescue party once you step into the boat and leave the jetty."

"Truly, I understand," Fynch said, very seriously.

"Then you owe me a crown."

Fynch handed over the coin. "I'm ready. Thank you again."

Samm neatly recorded the details in his ledger. "I've put your home as Werryl—would that be right?"

Once again Fynch nodded, loath to speak a lie.

"I've put together a small sack of food for you and a rug for the cold. You look too scrawny to last a day," Samm grunted, embarrassed. He pointed toward a small table by the door.

"Can I pay—"

"No. It's nothing. I have plenty. Go on with you, then, boy. And may Shar and that black beast protect you." Samm stood and Fynch followed suit, eager to be gone now. He took the sack and opened the door to where Knave awaited, stretching.

Together the three of them walked to the jetty.

"Take your pick," Samm said, gesturing toward the boats.

Fynch climbed into the nearest one, Knave following. "Bye, Samm. I won't forget your kindness."

"Be safe, Fynch, lad," the man said sadly, knowing the child would not return. He untied the rope. "Shar watch over you."

And they were gone, the stream's current pulling them toward the two huge willow trees whose branches intertwined to form a canopy. It looked like the archway into a dark tunnel. Fynch turned to wave as the willows gobbled up the boat into their shadows, but Samm had already gone.

26

AS FYNCH TURNED BACK TO THE WILLOWS, HIS FEAR OF THE unknown intensifying, Elspyth was doing her utmost to convince herself that Wyl had been right. She was not happy once again to be heading off on a journey toward a woman she did not know and was glad for Crys's company, despite his sorrow.

"Your mother is marvelous, so resilient," she said to him when she could no longer stand the awkward silence punctuated by polite conversation between them. Too much had occurred in the previous day and night for them to pretend otherwise, particularly as they would hit the Briavellian border within an hour.

"I never really think about it," he replied. "I think we all take her strength for granted, particularly Father."

She took the opportunity to touch on the hardest topic of all. "Crys, I haven't had the chance to tell you how sorry I am about your brother. I feel so awkward, not knowing him and yet feeling like I do somehow through all of you."

He smiled sadly at her. "Thank you. He was such a good lad—one of those rare people who can always see the positive side of life. Father had high hopes for him at Stoneheart—once Wyl made him his deputy, his future was secured."

Elspyth understood. "Fourth son, you mean?" Crys nodded. "How did it happen that he left your home for the capital?"

Her companion shrugged. "Bit of a long tale, really. Let me see if I can simplify it. Father and Fergys Thirsk go back a long way; they always had a lot in common financially and shared similar outlooks on life. Also, like Fergys, my father was intensely loyal to King Magnus. So the family connection to Stoneheart and the Crown was already strong. The King made a trip north not long after General Thirsk died and naturally stopped by Tenterdyn. I think my father must have mentioned he was not sure what to do for Alyd and the King suggested he send him south—said he knew another young lad around the same age who could use the company."

"Wyl?"

"That's right—and my father couldn't have been happier to keep the families close through another generation—although we didn't bank on Alyd falling in love with Ylena."

"I gather they were the perfect couple."

He nodded. "We only knew of Ylena, but her glowing reputation was known throughout the realm."

"I'm surprised the move to Stoneheart hadn't been discussed earlier, then," Elspyth mused.

"Well, Magnus and my parents hadn't seen each other in a long time. He was a little in love with my mother in their early years, I think," he said. "Perhaps father never trusted the King around my mother." He winked.

"Truly?"

"No, I'm teasing. It's true that the King had a terribly soft spot for my mother when they were all very young and to his death considered her with great affection, but he knew how much she loved my father. I think the reason for the length of time in their visits is that Felrawthy really holds the north for the Crown. Traditionally, Father had taken charge of the Legionnaires who guard the Razors."

"I see. So that's why Jeryb wasn't there for the tournament."

"Yes, and we were all furious. Mother desperately wanted to see Alyd and the tourney was a great excuse to pay a visit south. But the border in recent years has been threatened and Father would not risk it."

"You know Cailech and his men slip into and out of the Razors regularly."

He glanced at her. "We've suspected as much."

"I've seen them. No one minds them much in Yentro. They keep to themselves. Trade a bit and disappear almost as fast as they arrive."

He nodded thoughtfully. "They have excellent scouts. We can't even catch them in Morgravia, let alone track them into the mountains."

"You wouldn't want to. They know them too well." Elspyth frowned. "But why did our soldiers kill those children? It made Cailech furious. He's vowed revenge of the most horrible kind. It's why Gueryn le Gant was captured and tortured."

Crys slowed his horse. "Elspyth, it wasn't our men who killed those children, nor was it our men who traveled with Le Gant."

She pursed her lips. "It's always Celimus behind it," she said bitterly.

"He orchestrated all of it—through his own henchmen, of course. I've never seen my father so angry as the day he received orders to send in Le Gant with that scrawny bunch of men. They weren't even proper soldiers. Le Gant insisted my father stay out of it. He said in as many words that Celimus had planned to separate him from Wyl and that he suspected treachery somewhere."

"So I heard."

"Do you think he's still alive?"

She shook her head. "Gueryn was nearly dead when we left him. If an arrow didn't find its mark that night, then surely his fever would have killed him."

"I gather Wyl doesn't want to believe it?"

"It is the thought that Cailech saved Gueryn's life as bait for Wyl that keeps Wyl determined to go back to the mountain fortress . . . that and for another brave man called Lothryn."

"I've heard you mention him before. You always say his name tenderly." He glanced shyly toward Elspyth, who blushed.

"Do I?"

"Mmm." He nodded.

They rode in silence for a few moments.

She broke the quiet first. "I'm in love with Lothryn."

"I worked it out."

"Oh?"

"Most women can't resist me," he said archly, and then grinned.

"It must be your modesty," she replied, but liked him all the same for it.

"He's a lucky man, Elspyth."

"He's very special," she admitted softly. "It's taking all my courage to ride south and away from him."

"And all of ours not to wage war on the Crown," he added, bitterness strong in his tone.

"What will happen, do you think?"

"Wyl's beseeched my father to keep up the pretense. I hope he knows what he's doing."

"You must trust him . . . as I do," she replied. "He needs to be able to rely on us."

"But what's his plan?"

"Your guess is as good as mine. He's trying to find the father of the woman who cursed him with this magical life."

"It's all too strange—how bizarre to become a woman."

"Imagine how he feels! He was Romen Koreldy when I met him, then he became this Faryl woman, and now look at him." Elspyth shook her head. "His poor sister."

"What can he hope to achieve as a woman?" Crys wondered aloud.

"Don't be so sure!" she cautioned. "Women are far more cunning than you give credit. Wyl's new facade means different doors may well open that were closed to himself or Koreldy."

"You forget that Celimus is familiar with Ylena. If he has been chasing her, then he'll have her killed on sight."

"I'm sure Wyl's aware of that, which would explain why he's so determined to find Myrren's father. Perhaps he can demystify this gift of hers."

He interrupted their conversation by holding his hand up. "We've reached the border," Crys said, pointing to a sign.

"So I just guide my horse across the imaginary line?"

"Yes. Security between the realms has been stepped up since the death of Valor—they'll soon pick you up. There are guards everywhere."

"And not before?" she queried, referring to life prior to Valor's demise.

"Well, merchants could come and go fairly freely. But these days you need permits for trade or good reason for the crossing if you're not a merchant."

"And what's my reason?" she asked, worried now.

He grinned. "I can always get you past the guard from Morgravia's side. You just have to hope that letter from Wyl gets you through Briavel's scrutiny."

"Or?"

"You'll be coming back with me, and nothing would give me greater pleasure." He grinned at the innuendo in his own words.

Elspyth found his wit infectious. If not for Lothryn, she might well have fallen prey to this man's obvious charm. "You've been very kind to me, Crys. I hope I can repay you someday."

"Well, marry me, then," he jested, and pulled a face at her scolding expression. "All right, my apologies. Come now, let me get you safely across."

As he gestured for Elspyth to follow, he heard the sound of a rider coming toward them at a breakneck gallop. "Wait!" he hissed to her. "I can see my father's standard. Something's wrong."

The rider came into view. They could see the lather flying off the animal.

"It's Pil!" Crys exclaimed, jumping down from his horse.

Elspyth felt the chill of fear crawl up her spine and ooze throughout her body until every hair felt as though it were standing on end. No one rode this fast unless there was danger. She could see the wild look in both man and beast's eyes as they bore down.

Pil pulled the horse up too sharply and in pain and panic it reared, throwing him to the ground. As he gingerly stood up, the horse ran away into the nearby trees, terrified and exhausted.

Elspyth followed Crys, leaping from her own mount and running to Pil. "Shall I go after the horse?" she asked, knowing how the Donal family prized their animals.

"Leave it," Crys ordered through gritted teeth. "Pil, what madness is this?"

She could see the strength and leadership of the Duke now in his eldest son. It was an attractive quality. Its reassurance cut through her fear. "Take a deep breath, Pil," she urged.

His eyes were wide and scared. He rubbed at his newly bruised elbow. "Shar's Blessing, I found you."

"What's happened?" Crys demanded.

"They're all dead," the novice blurted. "Your family."

Elspyth felt Crys's body go rigid next to hers. "What are you talking about?" he growled.

Pil looked toward Elspyth. His words came out now in a rush, tripping over one another in his terrified eagerness to explain. "Brother Tewk wanted to pay his respects to the Duke and Duchess. I said I'd take him back to the estate. When we arrived—" His voice broke.

"Tell me it all," Crys said, pain spreading from his heart through his body.

According to the novice, Aleda had heard the sound of galloping horses first. She had wondered aloud to Pil and Brother Tewk if the men at arms her husband had promised to raise had arrived. It was not they, but by then it was too late—the men had entered the grounds. Aleda had admitted to Pil and Brother Tewk that she was afraid of these men, who were not of the Legion but seemed to be traveling under the King's authority.

" 'Go upstairs now. Hide!' she said to us," Pil said. "She was determined to hide all trace of any guests, especially after Daryn had come in to warn us that the men were looking for the woman resembling Faryl or any woman fitting the description of Ylena."

Pil explained that Aleda was angered by their audacity and had swept out of the house and across the courtyard to where her husband was talking with the leader.

"The man didn't even step off his mount," Pil recalled for his terrified listeners. "He just addressed your father from the saddle."

The young novice told them how from their hiding spot in the attic, he and Brother Tewk had watched as heated words flared up between the two men.

"The rider kept pointing at the Duke, issuing orders it looked like, but the Duke stayed calm. He must have invited them to search the house, but that's when it all went wrong. I have no idea what happened, but I suspect the man said something that your brother Daryn could not tolerate being said to your father," he said to Crys, whose stony expression did not flinch. "He bravely, or perhaps unwisely, reached up and grabbed the leader, pulling him down off his horse."

"Stupid boy!" Crys cried. "Daryn never could keep a cool head."

"Pandemonium broke out, my lord," Pil said, and the new title was not lost on his audience. "One of the riders fired an arrow into Daryn's chest. He dropped like a stone. Your mother screamed and fell to the ground beside him. He may still have lived for a few moments, my lord, but I could not tell. Your father had already drawn his sword. He didn't stand a chance. He fought bravely, but they brought him to his knees, my lord."

"Stop!" Elspyth interrupted, tears blinding her. "Crys—I—"

"I will hear it all," Crys growled, ignoring his own free-flowing tears. "Say it—all of it!" he commanded.

Pil shivered and nodded. Jakub had always warned him to stick plainly to the facts when conjuring up an important event. He told it precisely as it had unfolded, hating every painful word and its effect on Crys.

"They beheaded him, my lord duke. It was not clean. I

had to look away. They held your mother, made her watch. When it was done, they took her and tore off her clothes. They raped her one after another in the courtyard. Your other brother, Jorge, appeared from the stables but died also, fighting for her dignity."

At this, Crys fell to his knees and screamed, beseeching the heavens for deliverance from this nightmare. Elspyth threw herself on top of him, arms around him, weeping as hard as he was. She alone could understand his pain, wanted to absorb it for him. He cried in her embrace for a lengthy time while Pil sat, head bowed between his knees, in his own horrified silence.

Finally they heard Crys's voice, croaked and muffled.

"Pardon, my lord?" Pil said gently.

"I said how! How could they know?" the new Duke of Felrawthy screamed into the novice's face. He had moved so swiftly, Elspyth had fallen backward but Crys did not seem to care. He had the monk in a viselike grip, their faces barely inches apart.

Pil stammered out the final, crushing item of information. "Brother Tewk, my lord. He was a spy." He began to weep. "I led him to your family, asked them to make him welcome. I tried to keep up the pretense, stick to the story we'd all agreed to. But, my lord, I could not lie to a man of the cloth. I didn't mention about Wyl being Faryl, of course, but I admitted that I had brought Ylena to Tenterdyn."

Crys looked as wild and angry as an injured beast. He shook off Elspyth's touch and pushed Pil away as he dragged himself to his feet, running blindly toward the shadows of the trees where Pil's horse had fled to.

"Leave him," Elspyth said. She could feel the tension build in her own jaw until her temple throbbed, so frightened was she to ask the question. "The Duchess?"

"I don't know. I have no idea whether she lives or died."

She felt sickened. "You're sure everyone else is dead?"

He nodded, although a sob escaped him. "The Duke definitely. Jorge was hacked down and Daryn's body didn't move after Aleda was pulled from him. The arrow had hit in the region of his heart."

"Shar's Despair . . . all of them, all of them," she whispered to herself, shaking from the trauma of realization. "I led you to Brother Tewk. It's all my fault. Again. I did it! I am a curse!"

"No, Elspyth. How could you know of the impostor? I fell for it too. Anyone would have."

"How did you get away?"

"I fought him. I sensed him watching me closely when the first of the deaths occurred. Something about him suddenly felt wrong. It all began to add up—the fact that I sang a well-known hymn on the way to Felrawthy with him and he didn't know the words. Plus he said he'd visited Rittylworth, yet couldn't remember Brother Bors—everyone knew Brother Bors, he was over ninety years old." Pil shook his head. "I suddenly realized I'd been duped. When I saw them hurt Aleda, I began looking around for a weapon. I knew it was stupid; how could I fight them? But I needed to do something, but he grabbed me . . . and that confirmed his betrayal. So I fought him with everything I had, knocked him unconscious, through luck more than anything, and then I fled. I climbed out of the window and ran across the rooftops as I had done once before with Ylena. They never knew I was there, so I was able to get to the stables, steal a horse, and come after you and Crys."

"Did you kill him?"

"Brother Tewk?"

She nodded.

"No, I . . . I think he was just stunned."

"Then he will tell them about you and they will come after us," she said, newly panicked.

Elspyth leapt to her feet and walked to Crys.

"Go away, leave me!" Crys roared, rounding on her.

"Listen to me now," she begged. "They'll be coming after us, Crys—I'm sure of it—and they will slaughter what remains of Felrawthy. You are its duke now. You are all that's left. We will avenge them but not unless we get you to safety, now."

He laughed bitterly. It was a horrible sound. "Duke of Felrawthy, you say."

She looked around at Pil. "Get the horses readied, yours is over there," she said, taking charge. "Crys, look at me. We have no time for recriminations, not yet anyway. We must flee and save our lives."

He groaned. "Elspyth!"

His broken expression tore at her heart. "I know," she wept, reaching for him."I know. But you have to be strong now. You will get your war with Celimus, but you have to—"

She never finished what she was about to say. He took her into his arms and sobbed into her hair. She shook her head toward Pil and he obediently took the stray horse back toward the others. It felt frightening to hold this man so close. Elspyth felt a dangerous stirring spark between them. She pulled away, shocking Crys with her sudden movement of rejection.

Gazing directly into his hurt, dashingly handsome face, she spoke softly. She hoped he would recognize her affection for him, if not right now while he hurt, then later when he was rational and understood her heart was already claimed. "Come now—we must get you to safety."

"Where?" He looked lost.

"Briavel. They wouldn't dare follow."

He nodded, capitulating to her strength and suddenly glad to be led. He understood how it must have felt to be Ylena not so long ago. "Let's go," he said, a grimness to his voice Elspyth had not heard before.

27

ELIMUS SAT ATOP A CHESTNUT MARE, HIS NEW PRIZE IN THE royal stables. He called her Grace, which was befitting. She was light, elegant, and the swiftest horse he had ever ridden. He was still breathing hard from their gallop—

he had given her the rein and allowed her to let loose with her superb speed. Cooling her carefully, he walked her toward a tree where he would wait. Jessom and his falconer would be a while yet catching up. He bent to stroke her head and she tossed her mane, keen to be off again.

"Not so fast, bright one. There is business to be done yet," he cooed.

The King took a draft of water from his flask and surveyed the beautiful landscape about him.

"I must have an heir for all of this, Grace," he said, tapping her finely muscled neck. "I want him to have two thrones, at least"—and he laughed—"even better, three. I want him to be called Emperor . . . after me, of course. For good or worse, Empress Valentyna will be his mother and I shall teach him to mock the pretender, Cailech, whose head I shall have preserved on a spike outside Stoneheart for eternity."

He drank again, noticing the two riders finally appearing over the crest of a small rise.

They arrived panting. "Sire," the falconer said. "We are ready. I have your three favorite birds. We're positioned down there, your majesty." He pointed into the distance where two men could be picked out.

"I won't be long," Celimus said to the falconer, who dismissed himself with a nod to his king and a glance at Jessom, who was catching his breath.

"I think we should introduce a new rule, sire," Jessom commented once the man had departed and he felt more composed, "that you should not ride without at least one guard."

"Bah! This is Morgravia, man. I have my bow with me," the King said contemptuously.

"Nevertheless," Jessom replied somewhat imperiously. It was his favorite retort.

"I won't be babysat. I am a king."

"My very reason for suggesting the higher security, your majesty. Your status demands it."

Celimus nodded reluctantly, but it did not mean he would concede his position.

Jessom left the topic for now. "Did you want me to watch

you work your birds or shoot arrows at deer, my lord, or is there a reason I'm freezing my balls off in this thoroughly fascinating landscape?"

The King laughed. Jessom's sensibility about when to jest with his sovereign was always masterful.

"I'm meeting someone. Not for castle ears."

"Ah," his man replied knowingly. "Do you want me involved in the conversation or hidden, sire?"

"You may remain. Here he comes now," he said, nodding toward a lone rider.

"Excellent timing," Jessom noted, shivering at the bite of the spring morning. "Who is he, my lord?"

"His name is Shirk. He ran an errand for me."

"I see," Jessom acknowledged. It was all he needed to know. Shirk was clearly one of the King's newest henchmen, sent off to tackle unsavory tasks that could not be given to the Legion.

They watched him approach. "Lady Bench?" Celimus inquired of his chancellor while they waited, his glance not moving from Shirk.

"Having a large party in a few days, I gather, sire. Her husband is on one of his rare visits to Pearlis, though I imagine he won't remain long."

"He's a wanderer, that one. However, my father suggested I listen to his advice. Much as I detested my father, his advice was sound. I have found Eryd Bench, so far, to be reliable counsel."

Jessom nodded, remained quiet, waiting for his next instructions.

"So nothing out of the ordinary for Lady Bench, then?"

"Not that I can tell, your highness. I'm having her household watched day and night, as you requested. There have been no odd comings or goings."

"Good. Keep her under watch."

"Another week, sir?"

"That should do it. Ah, Shirk."

"Your highness." The newly arrived man bowed in his saddle.

"This is Chancellor Jessom. You may speak freely."

The man nodded at Jessom. "Thank you, sire. Shall I report?"

"Go ahead," Celimus said, looking down toward the falconers as if it did not matter one way or the other to him.

Jessom noticed the man's clothes were of sufficient quality to cost reasonable coin. A well-paid mercenary, then.

"We found no sign of the Lady Ylena Thirsk or the woman Leyen you described."

The Chancellor noticed his king's jaw clench in disappointment. He alone was sharp enough to see and read Celimus's subtle mannerisms. He dreaded to hear what was coming, wished once again that his king had asked him to handle this particularly delicate mission. It needed finesse and he could only imagine the damage he suspected he would be left to mend.

"But?" the King asked, his tone still deliberately casual.

The man nodded. "One of the sons became uncooperative when we questioned the Duke. He drew a sword."

"I see," Celimus said. "Something to hide, then. And did you handle it as I recommended?" he asked, choosing his words with care.

Jessom feared what was coming. Surely nothing had befallen the aristocratic Duke and Duchess?

"Yes, your majesty. Precisely how you required. The Duke, Duchess, and the sons are dead."

Jessom flinched. He tried to set a blank expression on his face but was sure he was unsuccessful. This was a dire revelation. He felt his normally controlled thoughts spinning frantically to imagine the consequences. How would they cover this new atrocity? This was well beyond even his slippery and dark notions of manipulation. He could not come up with a single scenario that justified the slaughter of the loyalists in the north who single-handedly shielded the southern half of the realm from invasion. In his short experience, Duke Jeryb had shown himself to be steadfast and true to the Crown. He had a bright intelligence and his information flow to the King could only be admired. He ran his legionnaires with a firm, fair hand, and Jessom, even from his much removed position, could sense that the Legion admired the Duke and his fine family in the same manner that they had admired the Thirsks. Killing the youngest son had been a horrific mistake—one that had occurred before his arrival, to be fair, but still he had been chilled to hear of it. And although it had been covered well, they were still dealing with the repercussions of the murder. The remains of the boy could still reappear and undo them all. He could not begin to imagine how they might explain away five new deaths in the same family and yet already his mind was racing toward how they might do just that.

"You're quite sure they're all dead?" Celimus asked, fixing the man with his unnerving gaze.

The Chancellor saw the mercenary blink. It was the first time Jessom noticed the man hesitate. It was a slow, nervous, and altogether telltale sign that perhaps all had not gone according to plan.

"Well, the Duke's head is no longer attached to his body," the man replied with an unsure grin. "His wife, well, she's dead, I'm sure of that. I know one of the men checked and the—"

"How did you deal with her?" Celimus asked, his tone innocent but his intense manner far from it.

"As you required, sire. We humiliated her."

"You raped her," Celimus said.

"Yes, your majesty. Each of the men took a turn with her. I think the last half dozen were riding a corpse, your highness . . . pardon my language."

Celimus was unfazed. "But someone checked her pulse," he said.

Again the man nodded, more dumbly this time, Jessom noted. The man was clearly not so sure of the Duchess's current state of health.

The King let it be. "The sons . . . three of them dead?"

The mercenary looked up sharply now, his eyes roaming desperately from his king and then with more of a beseeching expression toward Jessom.

Jessom helped him out. "There are three sons. The heir is

Crys—golden-haired, tall. Handsome, they say. The other two are darker, more like the mother. One is Daryn, the other Jorge." This was his first and only contribution to the conversation, but his words made the mercenary visibly pale.

"I see," the King said, understanding all too well. "Which one didn't you deal with?"

"The handsome one, your highness," the mercenary stuttered. "There was no sign of him."

Celimus kept his voice even, his disgust in check. Jessom felt a little sorry for the well-dressed man before them, for it was now very clear—to the Chancellor anyway—that his days were sadly numbered. "Is there anything else?"

"Yes, my king." The man tried to speak crisply but failed, perhaps already sensing his own demise. "Our spy . . . er, Tewk his name is, posed as a monk and was making his way to Felrawthy when he met a young woman. Her name was Elspyth. She was not important, according to Tewk. She was passing through the duchy and paying a visit to the family to give a message from her aunt, who apparently knew the Duchess. Tewk was careful to check that Elspyth did not resemble either woman we were following. The next day she sent a young novice by the name of Pil to return the donkey she had borrowed from Tewk."

"So, with this fellow, Pil, to interrogate . . ." Celimus began.

Shirk looked abashed, both for the interruption and what he had to say next. "The youngster escaped over the rooftops, sire."

"But you've caught him," Celimus said.

Jessom felt genuine pity for the cornered mercenary. The King's voice, so well controlled, managed to imbue a horrific sense of threat all the same.

The mercenary nodded eagerly. "We're giving chase, your highness. We should have him by now."

"A novice you say? What was he doing with your spy?"

The man began to shrug but shook his head instead to avoid offence to a sovereign known for his erratic moods. "I don't know the answer to that, sire, but he introduced Tewk into the family. Tewk felt he could learn more about whether the two women had been at Tenterdyn."

"And did he?"

"Yes," the man uttered triumphantly. "The women had been there. The novice, in fact, had brought the noblewoman to the family."

Oh, you poor fool, Jessom thought. This should have been the first item in the report. He feared for the man's next few minutes.

"Shar's Wrath, man!" Celimus bellowed, leaning in his saddle to strike the man hard across his face, toppling the mercenary from his horse. The King leapt down from his own mount, all feline grace, and in one smooth movement kicked Shirk so hard, he was unable to get back to his feet again. The man lay on the ground, coughing, groaning in pain. "Where are they?"

In obvious agony, the man spluttered his answer. "The woman, Leyen, goes by the name of Faryl, sire. According to the novice's information, she did not tarry long at Tenterdyn. There's no trace of the noblewoman and the young monk said he delivered her and departed the Duke's residence almost immediately."

"Lies!" Celimus roared. "Felrawthy protects her. I was right to suspect the Duke. He was not loyal to me."

Jessom thought otherwise. The Duke had given no reason to be considered anything but loyal to the Crown. The truth of the death of his son might have changed that, but so far he imagined that had all been kept secret. "Sire—" He attempted to speak, but was rewarded with a glare so fierce he closed his mouth and sensibly opted to remain silent.

"Get away from me," Celimus spat toward the injured man. "Crawl away from me, down that hill. Don't let me look upon your face again."

Shirk did as commanded. Not caring for his horse and despite his pain, he crawled away, no doubt eager to be far from the King's wrath. Unhurried, Celimus reached behind himself and brought his bow to his front. He lifted an arrow from the few he carried in the quiver on his back.

Jessom felt a moment of pity for the man retreating down the incline on all fours. He had not been disloyal, simply careless. But then Celimus suffered no fools about him.

He sighed. "Would you like to see me in your study, sire, after I clear up here?" Jessom inquired, knowing the answer, his mind already racing toward how he would tackle the damage in the north.

Celimus nocked his arrow and took aim. "Immediately," he said, and loosed his anger toward the crouching back of the man who had failed him.

Jessom watched his quarry alight from their carriage. He had decided to handle this particular item of business himself. Crossing the road, lifting his robe slightly so it would not trail in the general muck and damp of the busy market cobblestones, he artfully bumped the shoulder of the man.

"Do forgive . . ." Jessom began a solicitous apology and then feigned an expression of delighted surprise. "Lord Bench, what a pleasure. I'm so sorry for knocking you just now. I was in a hurry to cross the street."

"No harm done, Jessom." Eryd Bench waved off the apology.

"Lady Bench," Jessom acknowledged with a short bow.

"Chancellor," she said, nodding, her arm tightening ever so slightly around her husband's. "I'm so sorry you couldn't attend our recent evening."

"None more sorry than I, my lady," Jessom replied. "I'm afraid our king keeps me on a hectic schedule." He permitted a rare smile.

She felt its insincere touch, knew he suspected something. Also knew that so far he had nothing to level their way. "Oh, such a shame, Chancellor. I know how you like lamprey too—it was on the menu."

He made soft noises of despair at missing out. "Are you home for long, Lord Bench?"

"No, not this time. We're about to take a family trip actually."

"Oh?" Jessom inquired, already knowing the general

gossip. "Where are you off to—somewhere warmer, I hope?" and he chuckled, pulling his cape closer around his thin shoulders.

"No, indeed." Bench smiled ruefully. "I'm headed north, in fact, to meet a wonderful shipment of exotic goods coming into Brightstone. Helyn and Georgyana thought they might accompany me this time."

"Yes, I've decided it's high time I saw what my husband does on these trips," Helyn offered.

"And where will you stay?" Jessom asked, all politeness.

"Normally I'd stay at an inn, but with the ladies along, we have a small holding up north, not far from Yentro and Deakyn, in fact. Been in the family for donkey's years. I thought we might make them more comfortable in the house."

"Indeed," Jessom soothed. "A lengthy trip?"

Eryd knew he was being interrogated, as his wife had been just a few weeks back. "Not sure yet. With my family in tow, I suppose we can take our time. I thought we might travel up via the east. Perhaps catch up with that old rogue Jeryb and his marvelous brood before my shipment comes in."

Jessom was alarmed, but he did not show it. "Brr, it's cold out today. Can I offer you both a nip of Shorron to warm our insides?"

Neither of his companions cared to spend a moment longer with him.

"Of course," Eryd answered. "I'm never one to say no to a glass."

"We'll have to be swift, my love," Helyn warned, wishing Eryd had declined. "I've lots to purchase today for our trip."

Eryd patted her arm in reassurance and the trio headed toward the nearest Shorron counter, where the hot, bitter liquor was served in warmed glasses with a dollop of honey to sweeten its passage. Shorron was a local specialty of Pearlis, so there were bars and counters aplenty. In summer the drink was serve chilled, but its warming, softly aphrodisiac effect was best felt on a crisp, wintry day.

Jessom ordered three nips. "Do you mind, Eryd, if I suggest you don't travel to Felrawthy?" he said quietly as they waited. Helyn had already fallen into conversation with a friend at the counter.

"Why ever not?" Lord Bench asked, wondering at the sudden familiarity of the Chancellor.

"Bad news up north, I'm afraid. Our king will announce it to the court tomorrow. We only heard this morning."

"And what is it?" Eryd felt a chill crawl through him.

"We've received sketchy reports that the Duke might have been killed."

"Shar save us!"

Helyn turned back at the exclamation, excusing herself from her friend. "Eryd?"

"That's not all," Jessom said sorrowfully. "We haven't had anything confirmed yet, but the same source reports that all in the family are dead."

"This can't be right," Eryd blustered.

Jessom shook his head. "We're not sure, as I say," he said carefully. "I've sent some reliable men to check. It's shocking, I know. The King is devastated, as you can imagine. He relied heavily on the Duke's counsel regarding the north."

"Not to mention his protection. But how could such a thing have happened?" Eryd asked.

"Drink this," Helyn said, piecing together the disturbing news. She handed her husband his Shorron.

Jessom tipped back his head and downed the liquor, feeling its burning warmth. Eryd followed suit, genuinely appalled at the news. Helyn toyed with hers. She suspected—as did her husband—that they were being fed untruths here and yet the story was so shocking, it would have to be based on reality, which meant that the marvelous family up north had probably suffered.

"Everyone dead, you say?" Eryd asked.

Jessom nodded. "We await confirmation. The barbarian King's men apparently. The family was expecting reinforcements of their own and had left the gates open at Tenterdyn. We'll know more in a couple of days. I just think it's best you don't take your family into a region that is clearly dangerous."

"Cailech! Why would the Mountain King be bothered with Jeryb?" Eryd spluttered, signaling for a second shot.

"I think the self-crowned madman of the north decided that the Duke was his main obstacle. By dealing with Felrawthy, he probably believes he's effectively crushed Morgravia's northern defenses."

Helyn could hardly help the snort she gave. "You believe the Mountain King has actually raided and might head south?"

Jessom put his hand to his lips to signify that they must be careful about what they said. "King Celimus suspects as much. The Duke had confirmed many sightings of Cailech's men in our northern lands. I fear, madam, that it's only a matter of time before the Mountain King feels confident enough to try."

"Well, thank you for the warning, Chancellor," Eryd said, holding out his hand in farewell. "This is dire news indeed. We shall certainly steer clear of that region."

Jessom blinked slowly and nodded before he shook his companion's hand. He reminded Helyn of a vulture. "I'm glad, Lord Bench. Be safe on your travels." He bowed, turned to Helyn, and took her hand. "Lady Bench, my respects to your lovely daughter. Shar guide you all on your journey."

"Thank you," she said sweetly, pulling her hand away as quickly as she dared.

They left, Eryd's second glass of Shorron untouched. Jessom drank it, pleased with his morning's work. He felt quietly confident he could stop the permanent observation of the Bench family now. He would have their party followed on their departure for the north, and if they immediately took the westernmost road toward the port of Brightstone rather than the road that veered east toward Felrawthy, it would satisfy him, and no doubt his king, that this family was no threat.

Outside, Lady Bench hurried to keep up with her husband's long, angry stride. "Do you believe him?" she asked breathlessly.

"That Felrawthy has fallen. Yes. Not how it fell, though. Cailech is not that bold. Jessom forgets that I know the north better than most. No, this is darker work. I think your suspicion about our king and Leyen's warning is right."

"What do we do?"

"Nothing! Just observe for now—it's what you're best at."

King Celimus pondered all that Jessom had told him. "I'm inclined to agree. The Bench family is no threat. Their watchers can be released. Now, I want you to have a letter couriered to Valentyna for me—it's obvious Leyen or Faryl, whatever her name is, has not succeeded in dealing with Ylena and might not follow my other instructions to head to Briavel. We shall have to rely on Aremys to deal with the Thirsk woman. I'd prefer it if you copied this one yourself."

"Of course, sire." Jessom fiddled with parchment and stylo, searching for the right nib. "Ready, my lord."

Celimus strolled to his study window and glanced down into the courtyard. " 'My dear Valentyna,' " he began. "No wait! Make that 'Valentyna, my dearest.' " He listened as Jessom scratched away at the paper before continuing slowly. " 'I do hope this finds you in good health, although no doubt as busy with matters of the realm as I find myself. Perhaps you've made some time to spend with the exquisite filly I sent you? I gather she arrived in fine spirits and I know she has found the most generous and caring of owners. I would be interested to hear whether you liked the name I chose for her—she is the latest offspring of one of my finest broodmares. I'm sure you and she will enjoy good times in the beautiful woodland surrounding Werryl.' "

He paused, waiting for Jessom to catch up.

" 'Darling Valentyna'—I hope that's not too forward?"

"No, sire, it's perfect," Jessom replied.

" 'Darling Valentyna,' " Celimus repeated, " 'I hope you know that it is my heart's desire that we formalize our union without unnecessary delay. Since meeting you, I have thought of nothing but our marriage and the bringing together of our realms in peace and harmony.' "

Jessom scratched furiously. "And now a gentle threat, sire?" he prompted softly.

Celimus chuckled. "You know my thoughts too well, Chancellor," he said. "Indeed, we must spice this note with a warning. Let me see now." He pondered, watching the comings and goings below him in the yard below. "Ah yes. 'Time threatens our peace, my dear one. The upstart of the north—King Cailech, as he hails himself—has spilled the blue blood of Morgravia in slaughtering the Duke of Felrawthy and his entire family.

" 'I'm sure you know of them and grieve with all Morgravians at the tragic loss of this fine and noble line. We are taking steps to shore up the defenses of the north, but I sense Cailech grows too confident, and with the smell of Morgravian blood in his nostrils will now push south. My fear is that when he meets our resistance—and I promise it will be fierce—he will turn his attentions to Briavel. I cannot, nay, will not, permit this savage to threaten you, my darling, or your land. Once sworn enemies, we must now cleave together. Let me please help keep you and Briavel safe. I will pledge my entire Legion to the safekeeping of both our realms as soon as you confirm our marriage.' "

He turned and beamed at Jessom. The Chancellor wondered how Valentyna could resist that radiant smile. "Brilliant, sire. Perhaps we should suggest a date?"

"Yes! Read back the last line."

Jessom did so.

"Good. Go on and say, 'I have set a date of the last moon of the spring equinox. I see you only as a Bride of Spring when the land is bursting with life again. It is how you make me feel, Valentyna.' " He paused again to consider how to finish his letter. " 'My factor will deliver the necessary paperwork for your signature and I will begin to make preparations for our splendid wedding day—when all Morgravians and Briavellians will rejoice together . . . and our enemies will fear us, my beautiful one. No one will ever threaten our new empire.' " He clapped his hands gleefully. "And then you can finish as you see fit."

"I'll get this away immediately, sire."

"Have our factor await the reply. A few days' turnaround, no doubt?"

"Weather permitting, my king."

"See to it, Jessom."

The Chancellor began clearing his papers.

"What's happening at Felrawthy, by the way?" the King asked.

"I've sent some reliable men to clear all traces."

"The bodies?"

"Will be burned."

"Excellent. And you'll leave some signs that this was the work of the mountain dwellers."

"Already taken care of, sire."

Celimus felt happy and in control. In this mood he found it was appropriate to take his pleasure with a woman. "Have the Lady Amelia sent up after you."

"As you wish, my king."

28

HE MEN STOOD AROUND THE PIT, DEEPLY DISTURBED. SOME scratched their heads nervously, others fidgeted and tried to hold their breath. No one was sure what to say. There were supposed to be four bodies. They counted only three stinking corpses.

"Fetch someone who was here," their leader growled. A man was brought several minutes later. "How many corpses were there?"

The man looked surprised. "Four—three men, one woman."

"Well, we've got three bodies. The Duke and the two sons presumably, whom you *were* able to deal with. No woman here, unless she likes men's clothing."

The man grimaced at the sarcasm and responded with defiance. "The third son was *not* at Tenterdyn. The woman definitely was."

"Well, she's not now!" the leader roared. "Do you want to explain that to the man who is paying us a lot of gold to do this?"

"What are you suggesting?"

The leader of the party sneered. "I'm suggesting, you idiot, that the woman was never fully dead. Might have looked it, but she's gotten away . . . or someone helped her."

This time the man openly bristled at the insult, remembering how revolting it had felt to rape the dead woman. At the time it had been clear that she had breathed her last. "She was dead, I tell you," he snarled back.

"Well, you find her corpse and then you let the Chancellor know when you do. I shall be reporting that we disposed of three male bodies only, and I reckon it's not just your purses that you men should be worried about," the leader said viciously. "Burn them," he added, giving the order to dispose of the Duke and his twin sons. "I suggest you start searching Brynt and its surrounds for a dazed woman," he said. "Try the chapels, hospices, anywhere they offer succor without questions. She'll be hiding, for sure."

Not very far away, Aleda grimaced as she heard this conversation come to a close. If only they knew, she thought, that she was barely a few yards from where they did their ugly work.

Aleda had regained consciousness during the early evening of the attack. As she became fully oriented to her surrounds, she had realized she was lying in a pit covered by branches. Dusk allowed some dying light to filter through the leaves and twigs overhead and she had screamed to discover that Jorge lay beneath her. His eyes had been open and it seemed to his mother that he wore an expression of anger, even though she knew it was not possible to hold any last look in death. He had died fighting for her honor. She had begun to weep, scrabbling farther, discovering her other boy, Daryn, as cold and lifeless as his brother, and remembering how he had been cut down before her.

To her despair, she had noticed her husband's headless body at the bottom of the pit and she wept harder. She found his head tossed carelessly by his feet. The attackers would have laughed as they had thrown it in. Aleda had sat up, hating the sensation of sitting atop her fallen family, and cradled the bloodied head of her husband in her lap as she cried, losing hours in her grief as she stroked his dearly loved face.

When her sobs finally subsided, realization had hit and she had looked around frantically. "Crys!" she had shrieked. Not being able to find her eldest son had given her the courage to claw her way out of the pit. She had fallen several times, sobbing and scrabbling as the earth caved in on her repeatedly, covering her beloved men. Finally she had made it out and she had knelt at the lip of the pit, keening from her sorrow and trembling from her exertions. She had not even noticed her bleeding knees or tragically torn fingernails.

Perhaps Crys still lives, he had comforted herself, desperately pushing away thoughts that he might have been taken and tortured by their attackers. And then she remembered Pil and wondered why his body was not here among the dead. Aleda had pulled back the hair from her face, streaking it with mud, and only then had she permitted herself to realize that her body was badly hurt. The pain was not easily described. It felt deep within and with a woman's instinct she knew her internal injuries might yet kill her. Night had almost fallen, so she had only been able to see the blood on her skirts as a dark stain, but she knew it was there; remembered all too well how it had been earned. Death was not her fear. Time was. She was happy to die, would welcome the sight of Shar's Gatherers if not for the painful hope that Crys might still live . . . might still need her.

She had heard Jeryb in her mind, encouraging her to flee. Exhausted, she had re-covered the pit, and weeping only lightly, she remembered a special hide Crys had made just slightly uphill of this place. He had boasted that he could see the northern route, just in case the mountain people ever came raiding. He had been much younger then and she had laughed at him indulgently, but his father had praised him for his endeavor and foresight. "You can never be too well prepared for raiders, son," he had said, and ruffled the youngster's hair.

Over the years her eldest son had continued to use the hide and had kept it clean and dry. He had invited her to sit in it once and Aleda had marveled at the cozy comfort. It was sheltered, relatively warm for their harsh climate, and well stocked, which had amused her. Food had always been first on her growing eldest son's mind.

She had crawled toward that haven and lay in its safe womb for two days, trying to heal, thanking Crys silently for the water skin. Although she had no appetite for the food, it had been the water that had kept her alive and angry.

Aleda watched now as the men dragged the bodies of her beloved family toward a fire and without ceremony threw their corpses among the flames. They would not burn the memory of her fine family, though, Aleda thought, watching the fire exploding high into the air, fanning her fury. She knew who was responsible for this.

Celimus would be sorry his cold and beautiful mother had ever conceived him, she promised herself. She waited another half day in the hide, just to be sure the men had gone. It was too late to retrieve anything from the pyre. They had scattered it; gotten rid of as much evidence of the fire and its contents as possible. All her men were dead, bar one, she prayed. She clung to the hope that Crys lived, and as she crept back toward the family house to find fresh, warm traveling clothes and medicines to help kill the pain of her own injuries, Aleda tried to imagine where her son might find sanctuary. He was no longer safe in Morgravia; neither was she, for that matter. He had been escorting Elspyth to the border. Perhaps he had returned to Tenterdyn but seen the devastation in time and fled. But where to? He might be anywhere. She would have to travel to Briavel and find Elspyth. Perhaps the young woman's last encounter with Crys would reveal something.

It suddenly dawned on her that she was not just chasing the last remaining heir of Felrawthy but its new duke. Did he even know? She swallowed a draft of poppy liquor, diluted enough that it would not put her to sleep but just take the edge off the pain—enough to saddle the same mule Elspyth had ridden into Tenterdyn. She packed a small bag—water, a wedge of cheese and a knuckle of bread, proof of her identity, and a miniature painting of her family. It was not worth looking in the stable for one of their horses. The attackers had stolen everything; the house itself was ransacked of all valuables. None of it mattered.

As she approached the grazing mule to lead it from the field opposite the house, Aleda wondered what had happened to the round-faced monk whom Pil had brought here to meet them. The thought left her mind swiftly. There were more important matters on hand. She led the animal back to the stables, and after saddling it, she tied on her tiny bag of goods and a leather bag of Jeryb's, which now contained her youngest son's remains. Without looking back, Aleda Donal set off for the famed city of Werryl, for if Wyl Thirsk believed in the Briavellian Queen, so must she.

29

HE CURIOUS-LOOKING TRIO OF TRAVELERS WAS ESCORTED TO and then stopped at the magnificently ornate Werryl Bridge. Liryk was given the news that a novice monk, a noble from Morgravia, and a young woman from Yentro, claiming to have a special missive for Queen Valentyna, were awaiting permission to enter the castle walls.

Liryk recognized the noble's family name. It was not one to be ignored, but all the same, he shook his head. "Ask them to give us the documentation and we will consider their request."

"I've tried that, sir," his captain replied. "They're quite firm."

Liryk considered. The Queen's mood had plummeted into nothing short of despair since the death of Romen Koreldy. She masked it well for strangers, but those close to her could appreciate that their sovereign was emotionally scarred. She carried on her duties with vigor and dedication, but she was withdrawn and strangely detached from all of them.

"Tell them it is impossible. The Queen is indisposed and they can either pass over the letter and await instructions or they can leave."

His captain clicked a bow, and rather than leave it to one of his minions, he went out to meet with the Morgravians himself.

"I'm sorry, but I cannot permit your entry." He saw the woman's shoulders slump. "If you give me the paperwork you speak of, it will be reviewed and your request will be considered." The soldier could see how exhausted and disappointed they were.

As fate would have it, Valentyna chose that moment to

emerge from her private study and stroll out onto the battlements. She looked down and noticed the trio on the bridge.

"Who are those people?" she asked Liryk, who welcomed her with a broad smile.

"Morgravians, apparently, your highness. They seek entry to Werryl. They say they have a message for you. Captain Orlyd is finding out more information for us."

She looked down again. Their clearly fatigued body language raised her sympathy. "Do we have their names?"

Liryk nodded. "The young noble says his name is Crys Donal and I admit that surname is known to me. A proud Morgravian family, but for all I know this man could be an impostor. The woman is originally from Yentro and her name is Elspyth. The youngest is called Pil."

Valentyna frowned. "What an odd assortment to be carrying a missive."

"Quite! This is why I have asked Captain Orlyd to find out more for us." The Captain appeared. "Ah, Orlyd," Liryk said.

The man's eyes flicked warily toward his commander as he bowed to his sovereign.

"What news of those people, Captain?" Valentyna asked, the kindness in her tone irresistible to the young officer.

"Your highness, they beseech me to tell you that they are friends of General Wyl Thirsk. They . . . they mentioned Romen Koreldy," he stammered, embarrassed. He had been one of those entrusted with the secret of Koreldy's death and subsequent burial at Werryl.

Both men saw Valentyna's eyes widen and the flash of color suddenly erupt on her cheeks.

"Bring them to me," she ordered, flustered. "I'll be in my solar."

Liryk sighed, looked at Orlyd, and nodded. "Search them carefully."

Two soldiers escorted them across the famous Werryl Bridge. Kings and Queens watched them pass and Crys, despite his bitter sorrow, voiced his astonishment at the spectacular setting. He mentioned that he had heard about it from rare travelers who passed through Morgravia's north but no one had ever done its beauty justice. The men smiled, appreciating his sincere appreciation of their city's center-piece.

Their horses were led away and Elspyth, Crys, and Pil were relieved to be asked to follow the Captain beneath the huge gate that suddenly yawned open at the end of the bridge and permitted their entry to the famed Werryl. If El-spyth had not felt so disturbed by recent events, she would have marveled at its sparkling beauty and the soaring towers of the wonderful whitestone, exclusive to this region. Where Stoneheart was all dark and brooding majesty, its neighbor-ing palace was bathed in a light of its own, reaching toward the skies. She did not remark on it, though. Instead she low-ered her head and gratefully followed the man who would allow them an audience with Wyl's queen. She could think of Valentyna no other way.

"Let me do the talking, Crys," she cautioned.

He was so lost in his depression over his family that her warning was probably unnecessary. He nodded.

They ascended a superbly fashioned staircase at the top of which an older man met them. "Thank you, Captain," he said, and dismissed Orlyd.

The old man bowed slightly. Elspyth appreciated his gra-ciousness. "I'm Chancellor Krell and will escort you to meet her majesty," he said. Elspyth smiled and held out her hand, which he took. "Perhaps we should hold further introduc-tions until you're presented to our queen and Commander Liryk. Come now, you all look terribly tired. Let me organ-ize some refreshments." As they followed him he signaled to a page. "You look famished, too—we'll rustle up some food so none of you collapse at her majesty's feet," he said, and Elspyth grinned. She liked him straightaway.

"Why did she suddenly agree to see us?" Crys asked him.

Krell smiled benignly. "Perhaps her highness should an-swer that. We are here," and he knocked, then opened the door for them.

Elspyth knew for certain why the Queen had invited them

in—it was the mention of either Thirsk's or Koreldy's name. She had imagined Valentyna to be attractive and Crys had heard through his family connections that the former Princess of Briavel was a beauty, but nothing could have prepared either of them for the tall, statuesque Queen who turned to greet them as they entered.

"Your highness," Krell said, "this is Elspyth of Yentro, Crys Donal of Felrawthy, and Pil, novice of Shar and lately of Rittylworth Monastery."

Valentyna nodded thanks to her chancellor. "Be welcome, all of you. Krell, have we organized some refreshments?" She knew he would have done so, but making this sort of polite inquiry helped to ease introductions.

"On its way, your majesty."

"Thank you. Come in, all of you." She motioned as they all straightened from their various bows. "Do sit, please; I understand you've been on a long and tiring journey." A little stunned to be in the same room as this dazzling woman, who wore no finery attesting to her status, they sat. "Now, forgive my informal welcome," she said, smiling wryly at her garments. "These are the Queen of Briavel's working clothes," she added, arching an eyebrow and making Pil chortle briefly, which is precisely what she had been hoping for. They all looked so tense. She could hardly imagine what news was about to be delivered. "This is Commander Liryk."

Their gazes turned toward the man standing near the solar window. He nodded at Crys.

"I know your father," he commented. "A fierce soldier, a good man."

"*Knew* him, sir," Crys said. He had not meant it to come out quite so viciously, but he could not control his emotions. "He was murdered a few days ago, along with my mother and my two brothers."

Elspyth's shoulders slouched in a heartfelt sigh. She had hoped to handle this with a bit more diplomacy, but it was too late now. She risked a glance at the Queen, who threw a look of such sympathy toward Elspyth it was as if she sensed this was not how Elspyth had planned their meeting.

"What?" Liryk roared. "Felrawthy dead?"

Elspyth knew she had to take control; she could not let Wyl down again and allow Crys's mouth to run away with a story—truth though it may be—that the Briavellians would not accept. This had to be told right in order to win their help. She stood. "Crys, please. Your highness, we have a shocking tale to tell and perhaps if you'll allow me?"

Valentyna nodded. "Of course," she said, waving away what Elspyth knew sounded like an apology. The Queen, she could see, was very concerned for Crys.

"My companion has much heartache. Please forgive us this sudden intrusion and how odd I know it must seem. Commander Liryk, Crys Donal is the new Duke of Felrawthy."

The Queen sat, sensing the import of what she was about to hear. "Tell us everything," she said as Krell ushered in some serving staff with trays of food and drinks, both hot and cold. "But first eat." She smiled encouragingly at Crys, but it was Pil, utterly smitten, who beamed back.

In between mouthfuls, Elspyth told her audience their sorry story. When she had finished speaking, she could not help but lean over and squeeze Crys's hand. He had not eaten or drunk anything.

"All dead," Liryk muttered angrily. "You're quite sure?"

"Pil witnessed all that I've spoken of. He can confirm that the Duke and his twin sons are dead."

The young monk nodded bleakly.

"They would not have permitted my mother to live," Crys said, emerging from a silent stupor.

"And you're absolutely certain that these men were hired by King Celimus?" Valentyna asked, her voice as cold as the grave.

Liryk squirmed. This was everything they did not need.

"Your highness," he began, but she held up her hand and returned a penetrating dark blue gaze at Elspyth.

It was unsettling to have such intense attention leveled at

her. Elspyth felt as though no one else's opinion mattered to the Queen but hers. She recalled how Wyl had mentioned that Valentyna could make you feel you were the only person in the room.

"From what I gather, your majesty," she said carefully, "Celimus is capable of anything."

"That's not absolute certainty, though, is it?" the Queen replied, her gaze steady.

Elspyth blinked. "No, but Aremys and Faryl, each in the employ of Celimus, confirm it is his doing. Aremys defied the King and came to help us; Faryl came to kill Ylena Thirsk."

"Your majesty, we cannot trust the word of hired mercenaries. They would say anything, do anything, for gold," Liryk warned.

Elspyth bristled. "We did not pay them anything!" she said angrily, then pulled back her claws. "Forgive me, highness. Aremys can be trusted." She delved into her pocket. "I have a letter for you. It's from"—and she hesitated, almost saying Wyl—"from Ylena."

"Wyl Thirsk's sister?" The Queen frowned, taking the letter from her.

"Yes, your highness. Aremys took her to safety."

Krell stepped back into the room, gliding toward the Queen. He bent down to whisper something to her. Valentyna nodded.

"Excuse me," she said to her audience. "There's an urgent messenger here from Morgravia." She tucked Wyl's letter away. "I shall return shortly. Please make yourselves comfortable and eat more. We won't keep you long from your beds."

In her absence, Liryk felt obliged to continue the discussion. He was shocked to learn of the death of Jeryb Donal, a formidable enemy who respected the laws of war and, like his former general, Fergys Thirsk, had not been one to fight battles merely for the sake of fighting.

"I'm very sorry to hear of your loss, son," he said into the awkward silence.

Elspyth was glad that Crys was gracious enough to acknowledge the Commander's commiseration.

"Can you enlighten me as to how you know for sure these were men sent by your king?" Liryk pressed, hoping they could not.

"Well, sir, because, according to Pil, they said as much. They claimed to be trying to track down Ylena Thirsk, who had been removed from Stoneheart by Romen Koreldy."

Pil nodded. "That's right. Koreldy brought her to us seeking shelter and sanctuary. She had been abused by the Crown and I don't put that lightly, sir," he qualified, his complexion flushed as everyone's attention suddenly locked on him. He too had been sworn to secrecy about Wyl and was terrified he might slip up. "Romen left her with us."

"And then the King's men burned Rittylworth, you say—and its monastery too? Whatever for?" Liryk asked.

"My home!" Pil said, his eyes misting. "They were sent by the King, sir, on orders to raze the village and teach it a lesson for harboring Ylena Thirsk. They were calling her a traitor, presumably because of her brother's actions."

"None of which was traitorous, to my knowledge," Elspyth said, realizing too late she would have no reason to know Wyl Thirsk. Fortunately, the Commander was suitably confused and did not pin her down on this point. She suspected Valentyna might have done so and knew she would have to be still more careful.

"The King sent Faryl of Coombe as well," Crys added. "She had come to Tenterdyn, looking for Ylena, supposedly to kill her as per Celimus's orders. This we have learned through Aremys, who was meant to aid Faryl. I know it sounds like overkill, Commander Liryk, but the King is determined to murder Ylena and anyone who protects her."

"And this Aremys you speak of, if he is a hired mercenary, why does he want to help you?"

It was a good question. Crys hesitated. "He is a friend of Romen's," Elspyth cut in before either of her companions could form a response. "I gather they were both of Grenadyn," she added, recalling something Wyl had mentioned.

The Queen reentered. Both Liryk and Crys stood immediately and bowed. Pil leapt to his feet too late and Elspyth was not sure whether she should curtsy again—she did so, just in case.

"Relax, everyone," Valentyna said, pushing away strands of hair. "We have much to discuss. You people need a rest first, though. Duke, Elspyth, Pil," she said, "please follow Stewyt, who will show you to some rooms where you can sleep for a few hours and refresh yourselves. Commander, I have called a meeting of our senior nobles. Krell is gathering them now. We meet this evening. The news from Morgravia is extraordinary."

Elspyth lay restlessly on her bed in a small chamber that smelled of fresh herbs and offered a beautiful view of Briavel's orchards. She knew she would not sleep even though she was desperately tired. The refreshing bath and the generously left garments had made her feel all too awake, in fact, and so she welcomed the soft tap at her door when it came an hour or so after she had been shown to her room.

It was Stewyt again. "Her highness wonders if you would care for some company, Miss Elspyth," he said, nodding a small bow.

Elspyth was both surprised and delighted by the invitation. "Of course," she murmured. "I'll just fetch my shawl."

She followed the lad through the corridors and stairways she had passed earlier but soon realized that they were not headed deeper into the palace.

Stewyt must have read her thoughts, for he said, "The Queen will meet you in the herb gardens," and he held open a door for her that she realized led out toward the back of the kitchens and scullery.

They found Valentyna picking lavender. She had changed into a deep purple gown. Once again, no adornments. *She needs none,* Elspyth decided, admiring the Queen's fresh-faced natural beauty.

Valentyna looked up at the sound of their arrival. "Oh,

I'm so glad you came," she said to Elspyth, smiling warmly as if she were welcoming an old friend. She handed the stems to the page. "Thank you, Stewyt. Would you have these sent up to my chambers," and she turned back to her guest. "Walk with me—it's a beautiful afternoon and these gardens do wonders for my spirits."

Elspyth hardly knew what to say as she fell in with the Queen's graceful step.

"I thought you might find it easier to speak freely without the men," Valentyna admitted conspiratorially.

"Thank you, your majesty. Crys is having to face so much—it's certainly difficult talking about it all."

"I can't imagine what he's going through, losing his family in such horrific circumstances."

"Do you believe us, your majesty?" Elspyth asked in her direct way.

The Queen paused beneath a lemon tree. She inhaled its fragrance. "Yes," she replied softly.

Elspyth let out her breath, suddenly feeling tears of relief sting her eyes.

"Do you know that Romen Koreldy is dead?" Valentyna asked, just as directly.

Elspyth nodded. "Word travels fast."

"From whom did you learn this news?"

Elspyth felt trapped. This was clearly a test. She wanted to be as honest as she could with this woman, but she could not betray Wyl's wishes once again.

"From Faryl," she said, making a decision.

"And how did she hear of it?" the Queen asked, bending down to smell some basil. It seemed a nonchalant response, but Elspyth sensed an underlying tension.

"I gather she was in Briavel, your highness."

"I see. That's interesting. Would you describe her to me—I do have good reason for asking." She handed Elspyth a small bunch of mint to smell and smiled disarmingly.

Elspyth took a deep breath. "She's tall and strong looking; a handsome woman. She has a very direct golden-green gaze," she said, remembering Faryl in better detail as she concentrated, recalling those terrible few minutes after Wyl had arrived at Tenterdyn.

Valentyna put her hand on Elspyth's arm. "Ah, yes, her eyes have a feline quality, don't they . . . and her hair is an oddly golden-brown color, not unattractive but unfashionably short for a woman."

Elspyth blushed as the Queen turned her own hard blue gaze on her. "Yes," she stammered. "That sums her up rather well."

Valentyna's look darkened. "I believe, Elspyth, that this Faryl you speak of is the very same Hildyth who murdered Romen. No one else believes me here. It's not something that matters to them, but it matters very much to me to know who took his life."

"She . . . she is in Celimus's employ. Aremys confirmed that she is an assassin, your majesty, paid for by the King of Morgravia."

Valentyna raised her face to the sky in obvious despair. "I knew it," she said in a choked voice. "She killed him as he made love to her."

"Please, your highness, let's sit," Elspyth suggested, taking the Queen's arm and encouraging her toward a low stone bench surrounded by sweet-smelling bushes.

"Thank you," Valentyna said when they were seated. There was a slightly awkward pause, which she filled by snatching at the one stray tear that threatened to roll down her cheek. "May I tell you a secret, Elspyth?"

"Yes."

"I was in love with Romen Koreldy."

"He was an easy man to fall in love with," Elspyth admitted, unsure what was expected of her.

"How well did you know him?"

"We met each other in Yentro. We were captured together by men from the mountains."

"I know."

"You do?"

"He told me everything of his time in the north."

Not everything, Elspyth suspected. "Then you've heard him speak of me, highness."

"Yes, I know of you, Elspyth. It's why I do believe you regarding this terrible business at Felrawthy. But all of my advisers and the nobility of Briavel want me to marry Celimus so badly, I need to give them proof that he is as sinister and treacherous as you tell us."

"And the death of your father is not sufficient, I presume?" Elspyth said bitterly, and then, realizing what she had said, she grabbed the Queen's hands and swung onto her knees before Valentyna. "Oh, your highness, forgive me," she begged. "That was so cruel. You've been very fair with us—I just feel so frightened and desperate."

Valentyna smiled softly at the bowed head of Romen's friend, wondering how he had not fallen for this pretty, feisty woman who had come into his life before she had.

"You're forgiven, for it is a fair accusation," Valentyna replied. "But you need to understand that we cannot risk war with Morgravia, Elspyth. This is diplomacy at its most frustrating. It seems my father's death must be overlooked in order for peace to be won for Briavel." She paused before adding, "Romen mentioned a mountain man called Lothryn."

Elspyth flinched at the name and saw the recognition of that reaction reflected in the Queen's imposing gaze. Honesty was required here. She nodded. "A very brave person who put our lives before his own. He defied his king, probably paid for it with his life."

"Romen said that you and Lothryn are in love."

"I . . . we were . . . are, your highness," Elspyth admitted, deeply disconcerted that Valentyna knew so much about her. "I will never love another."

Valentyna's expression showed the ghost of a sad smile of agreement. "Then you will know how hard this is for me. I too can never love anyone else now that I have loved Romen Koreldy, but I'm being forced to marry the man who organized the death of my father, of Romen, of Wyl Thirsk—who tried to warn me about Celimus."

"Don't marry him, your highness," Elspyth warned. "Do everything in your power to avoid it. Did you read Ylena's letter?"

"I did. She wants me to wait for her. She claims that she will help me." The Queen gave a short, hollow laugh. "What can a young, helpless Morgravian noblewoman on the run from her own king do to help the cause of the Briavellian Crown?"

Elspyth agreed. It did sound futile. She desperately wished she could tell the Queen the truth. "Trust her is all I ask. She begged me to implore this of you and to offer my services to you."

"Yes, she mentioned that too. I'm glad of the friendship, Elspyth, really I am, but I'm afraid I can't completely understand her concern."

Elspyth nodded, returning to sit beside Valentyna.

The Queen sighed. "The worst of it is that I do want to trust her! Her letter takes the same tone that her own brother, the General, did in our only meeting. Romen made me feel safe and secure; Wyl Thirsk did too when he ordered me to accompany Fynch to make our escape from the mercenaries who killed my father. And now his sister conveys the same sense of strength." She shook her head. "I miss Fynch. He's gone too, you know. Did you ever meet him?"

Elspyth held her breath at what Valentyna had just said. Without knowing it, the Queen had already hit on the truth. Her senses served her well. "No, but Romen did speak of him."

"He's a very special person. Odd, most might think, and incredibly serious, but there's something about him I can't really explain. It's as if he's all-knowing, or at least more enlightened than I often feel." She turned to look at Elspyth directly. "Do you know what Fynch believes?"

Elspyth shook her head slowly; could guess what was coming.

Valentyna raised her shoulders in a gesture of helplessness. "He believes that Wyl Thirsk and Romen Koreldy are somehow linked. I don't mean through friendship. He claims there is a spiritual link, as though they could be as one. Are one, in fact, though he does stop short of saying that. Now what do you say to that?"

Elspyth squirmed, the truth aching to escape from her lips. She fought the temptation. "Queen Valentyna, I hope you won't be offended if I admit that I believe very strongly in spiritual connections. I never doubt that souls who belong together will always find one another again. Even after death they will be reborn and search for one another."

"Do you really?"

She nodded. "I do, your highness. And it's why I believe you and Romen will find each other again." Elspyth skirted the truth as closely as she dared.

"But not in this life," Valentyna admitted sadly.

"You never know, highness. There are those who believe that sometimes if a life is taken early—before it is ready to be gathered by Shar—it stays close to the ones it loves."

Valentyna smiled at her. "That's a rather lovely way of looking at life. It lifts my heart just to hear you say it, even if I can't believe it."

"Oh, you can believe it, your majesty. Allow yourself . . . take a risk and believe it." Elspyth seized her opportunity. She owed Wyl Thirsk this much. "I believe that some people are reincarnated. Perhaps you should listen more carefully to your friend Fynch. It's to this which he refers, I'm sure. And you must promise me that should another person look at you and perhaps touch you emotionally as Romen did, reminding you uncannily of the man you've loved, that you will permit it."

"Permit them to love me, you mean?" Valentyna said, her voice laced with gentle amusement.

Elspyth nodded. "Perhaps even a woman," she dared.

"Because it might be him?" Valentyna's dark eyes flashed with both embarrassment and bemusement.

"Yes." It was a risk, but she was glad she had taken it.

The Queen surprised Elspyth by leaning across and giving her a hug. "I'll remember that. Now come, I have avoided it long enough." Elspyth looked at her quizzically. "I've called a meeting of the nobility. It's serious and why I'm hiding here."

"Quiet time?"

Valentyna nodded, knew Elspyth would understand.

"Thinking time too. I feel as though I'm about to enter a chamber where I'm bargaining for my life."

Pil preferred to remove himself from the world of politics and asked to be excused to spend time in the palace chapel with Father Paryn, a man he took to immediately. Crys and Elspyth were invited to attend the meeting, which brought together the most senior people in Briavel. Respecting the sensitivity of the issue, Chancellor Krell made notes from the meeting himself, which he planned to dutifully copy out for the two important nobles who were not readily available in the capital. Couriers were already organized to carry the details of the meeting to their respective destinations across the realm.

The Queen arrived somberly. The feeling of tension was overwhelming. Krell dismissed all servants, and when privacy was assured, Valentyna addressed her inner sanctum of advisers, first introducing Elspyth and then the new Duke of Felrawthy to the muted sounds of shocked whispers, as most were familiar with Jeryb Donal's towering reputation.

"Gentlemen, these Morgravians are our guests and enjoy the full protection of Briavel. They risked their lives to bring us information, riding here in urgency, crossing their border and outrunning their pursuers, whom we are presuming had been sent to execute them." She allowed her words to sink in. "With them, Duke Donal and Elspyth have brought grave news from our neighboring kingdom." She waited for the hushed murmurs to die back and then outlined succinctly the torrid events that had unfolded.

The room predictably erupted as the shock of the Duke's demise was absorbed.

"We're not just talking about a very high-ranking noble, gentleman, but two of his heirs and his wife—innocents. If it wasn't for the foresight of Elspyth here, there might well be no heir to Felrawthy standing among us."

"There were three other heirs, if I'm not mistaken," someone said.

Crys cast a glance at the Queen and answered on his own

behalf. "Indeed, sir, there were four of us. My youngest brother was murdered at the King's pleasure in Stoneheart many weeks earlier. Reliable witnesses have attested to this fact."

Excited talk broke out and anything further that Crys had planned to say was drowned out. Elspyth noted that Crys had benefited from his rest and refreshment. He looked composed and very focused. Perhaps the gravity of this meeting had reminded him of the title he now bore. She chanced a small smile toward him and was thrilled when he cast a shy wink her way and lifted his strong chin. She loved him for it; knew how deeply within himself he must have dug to find such strength and composure in front of these critically important strangers.

The duchy of Felrawthy is in safe hands, Jeryb, she thought.

"Your majesty," a deep and distinguished voice said from the center of the room.

"Lord Vaughan." Valentyna nodded.

"With the greatest of respect to our noble guest, I must ask what the internal politics of Morgravia have to do with Briavel? Until you are married to King Celimus and formally link our two realms, I believe it may be unwise for us to meddle with Morgravia's domestic matters. Those whom the King's men execute on their soil, providing it is only Morgravian blood spilled, is surely his business alone."

"I appreciate your position, Lord Vaughan," the Queen said. "The problem is that Morgravia has brought this problem to us . . . in more ways than one. I have only outlined one side of this tale, sirs. As I mentioned, a man of Shar, albeit a novice, witnessed the shocking slaughter at both Rittylworth Monastery and at Felrawthy. He now seeks peace from these nightmares with our own Father Paryn and I do not, for one minute, doubt this young man's word about what he saw. Peaceful men of god were cut down as they tended the monastery gardens; the senior monks were crucified and burned.

"Pil escaped and with him took a woman called Ylena Thirsk, who would be in a position to attest not only to the bloodbath at Rittylworth but to the execution of Alyd Donal of Felrawthy, her husband of just one day. I'm sure the significance of her family name is not lost on any of you."

Angry mutterings broke out, which she hushed.

"Ylena Thirsk was brought to Rittylworth for sanctuary and safekeeping by none other than Romen Koreldy. I already knew this because he told me about it during his stay with us. The men who attacked Rittylworth were under the King of Morgravia's express authority to raze the village and its monastery, killing the holy men."

"How do we trust this information, highness?" Vaughan asked, sounding fractionally exasperated.

Valentyna ignored the tone and looked toward Elspyth, who had half hoped she would be spared such scrutiny.

She took a deep breath and begged her voice to hold firm. "My lords, I happened upon Rittylworth soon after the devastation. I saw the chaos of what the raiders had left behind, the cruelty and ruin of their work. I spoke with the dying head monk as he hung, still smoking, from the cross." Elspyth deliberately described the scene as viciously as she could and was pleased to see many of the nobles look away in pain at her words. "He could barely speak through his scorched throat, but he confirmed to me that his executioners were the King's men; that they were searching for Ylena Thirsk and would kill her if they found her."

"It seems the King could not risk an all-out revolt by the Legion, which remains loyal to the Thirsk name. Instead he sent assassins out on Ylena Thirsk's trail, gentlemen," the Queen continued. "Once again it seems she has escaped— this time with a man known as Aremys Farrow of Grenadyn. But the family who offered her safety did not escape the King's attention and was punished in the most dire manner." She paused and glanced at Crys, who took up the tale.

"My youngest brother, Alyd, was beheaded as punishment for marrying Ylena Thirsk. The other members of my family were murdered because they offered her a haven. King Celimus is mad," Crys said, eyes burning passionately.

Angry retorts from the stunned audience prompted Krell to give a warning glance toward his queen.

"Gentlemen, please." She held up her hand. "Let us take some wine together and calm ourselves."

The mood had not changed, despite the wine, but at least the gathered nobles were quiet.

Valentyna motioned to Krell, who handed her a parchment. "This arrived today from Morgravia," she said. "It is a firm offer of marriage from King Celimus. He has set a date of the last day of the spring equinox." She could feel the nobles' joy at the reality of the wedding like a separate pulse in the room. It nauseated her. "He continues by warning me of a very real threat from King Cailech in the Mountain Kingdom."

"Briavel and Morgravia are stronger united, your majesty. Celimus is right," a man from the northern province said.

She nodded without commitment to his sentiment. "Celimus goes on to explain that he has proof of this threat. He claims the Donal family of Felrawthy was slaughtered mercilessly by Cailech's men."

Crys stepped forward angrily. "That's a lie!" Elspyth reached toward him, but he shook her arm away. "Cailech is too wise to risk his people now. It's easier to let Morgravia and Briavel tear each other apart . . . can't you see?" he roared, looking around the room. "The Mountain King has never set foot in Felrawthy. Our men would have known about even the slightest incursion and we would have been well warned of any raiding party. The northern defenses of my father's were second to none. Believe me when I say this is Celimus contriving excuses, poisoning Briavel's collective mind, protecting himself so the marriage will go ahead."

The Queen nodded. Crys had summed it up perfectly. Valentyna looked around the room, trying to gauge the mood.

"My lords, Wyl Thirsk warned me of Celimus's more sinister intentions when he brought the marriage proposal to my father. He counseled that Celimus might not be so interested in peace as he is in acquiring the rich and fertile lands of Briavel. It's my contention that he wishes to rule us, gentlemen; paying lip service to our own proud sovereignty. He is empire building, sirs. Why else would King Valor have met such an ugly death? Celimus wanted us vulnerable and desperate for peace."

She hoped this subtle mention of her father might win the support she wanted, but instead eyes were averted from her own. There was uncertainty in the air.

"At least we might achieve peace, your majesty," one of the oldest, most senior men declared plaintively, and Valentyna's heart sank. She knew then—in that frigidly stark instant—that she would not escape marriage to the King of Morgravia. These nobles would accept rule from the usurper provided that no more of their brave, bright sons had to march toward hopeless war. She felt the tears of realization prick at her eyes and she blinked them away. How could she blame them? Her father had refused to risk her life—had given his own to save hers. Why would these fathers feel any differently for their own beloved children? Her marriage to Celimus would bring the peace they craved, give their children prosperity. She felt her gut twist at the thought.

"Peace at what price, my lords?" she asked the room, eyeing each of them with a hard blue gaze. "Is this what you have fought for all your lives . . . and your fathers and your grandfathers before you? Is this what my father raised me to believe? To marry peace and squander our pride and Briavel's name?"

She felt her heart hammering at her passionate words. It won the right attention. The men she thought she might have lost shifted uncomfortably at her accusation.

But it was the powerful and elderly Lord Vaughan who spoke for them all. "We need more proof, your highness," he said firmly into the silence.

"What proof, my lords, would satisfy?" she asked, her tone as sharp as a blade.

Lord Vaughan shrugged. "So far, your majesty, with respect we have heard hearsay and unreliable accounts. I acknowledge what Elspyth of Yentro has told us of what she saw at Rittylworth, but we need more. Bring us Ylena Thirsk . . . she, more than any, might convince us that Celimus's intentions are as dark as you suggest."

Valentyna watched heads nodding, knew her fate was sealed. Ylena Thirsk could not save her. No one could. She would be wed to the King of Morgravia in the same helpless manner that a baby lamb was led to its slaughter.

30

WYL AND AREMYS ARRIVED AT THE THICKET FROM THE VILLAGE of Timpkenny on the northeastern rim of Briavel. The village had struck them as an odd, almost nervous sort of place that suffered from being the closest clump of humanity to the place where the Darkstream presumably joined the River Eyle. Much quiet superstition surrounded the Darkstream. It was not a fear of the magic so much as a privately held belief among these northerners that the unknown beyond was enchanted and was not a place for nonsentient people to roam.

Although they inquired at several Timpkenny establishments, no one could give the pair the Darkstream's ultimate source or indeed destination, but everyone they spoke to nodded apprehensively and confirmed that to everyone's knowledge the Darkstream was the only way to cross over into the Wild once you had negotiated the Thicket. Aremys asked one man why he lived so close to a place that carried so much superstition and the man had shrugged, answering that the land of this region was uncannily fertile and the weather, though cold, was reliable. The rains always came and the summer never failed.

"Our animals and crops thrive," he had said, shrugging again. "My family eats."

Wyl and Aremys knew they should count themselves lucky for having experienced an uneventful journey north. They had traveled relatively swiftly and without incident from Brynt across the border, always heading toward the mighty Razors and then cutting east once the famed mountains began to rise up menacingly before them. Briavellian guards had picked them up soon after and did little more than smirk when they admitted they were hoping to find a quiet pass to enter the Razors and avoid Cailech's fortress. That was the cover story they had agreed to use if stopped by anyone.

The head of the guard was the only one of the Briavellian soldiers not smirking when Wyl and Aremys had stood at his checkpoint, brought to him by his men.

"There are several entries into the Razors from this part of Briavel, but you say you're headed for Grenadyn. Surely it would have been easier for you to access the mountains from western Morgravia?"

"Too much trouble brewing on the border over there, sir," Aremys had admitted. "It might be dangerous to take Lady Farrow via those routes."

The officer had nodded thoughtfully. "You've made your journey three times as long, though."

"Sir," Wyl had interrupted, noting how the man had instantly regarded him with softer eyes. He had wondered if he himself had done this when addressing a good-looking woman. In truth, he found it insulting that a woman should be considered with such instant sympathy—or was it desire? He had tried not to let his irritation show in his tone. "It's imperative that I return to my home in Grenadyn." The lie came surprisingly easily. "However, I wish to draw as little attention to myself as possible and I'm prepared to lose the additional week or so that it will take us by using this more circuitous route."

"And whose attention are you trying to avoid?"

"Why Cailech's, of course," Wyl had replied, adding a hint of irritation now. "I've learned on our travels that the Mountain King is moving toward the notion of summary executions for strangers."

"Morgravians only, as I understand it, my lady." He eyed her and stifled a smug expression. "You could have sailed more easily to Grenadyn, surely?"

"But we were nowhere near the coast, sir. I'm sure you don't need to know my life story, either, Captain, er . . . ?"

"Dirk, my lady."

"Captain Dirk," Wyl had said, "and I appreciate your concern for our long journey, but I have employed Aremys, who knows the mountain routes well. We shall be fine," he had added, avoiding blatant condescension but hoping to bring an end to the man's inquisitiveness.

"Well, Lady Farrow, it's none of my business where or how you choose to go but—"

"That's right, Captain," Wyl had interjected, but as gently as he remembered Ylena might admonish someone. "I understand that you are responsible for the security of the realm in this part of Briavel, and as you can surely tell, we are no threat to it. We are simply travelers passing through. I gather there's no law against that. I appreciate your concern for my safety. Aremys will see to it."

The man had shown amusement for the first time. "I was only going to say that I thought you were not dressed sufficiently warmly for the Razors, my lady. It will be rough sleeping in the mountains. Are you really up to such challenge?"

"No need to worry," Aremys had chimed in. "It's my intention that we'll make a stop at Banktown and buy what we need."

Wyl knew there was little more the Captain could do unless he wanted to detain them. Besides, it was now obvious that Aremys did know the region—perhaps the Captain had not expected him to know the local towns and villages and had been testing them. As it had turned out, he had finally nodded, wished them well, and allowed them to move on.

Aremys had seen to it that they left the patrol in a northerly direction as though headed deeper into the foothills and ultimately up into the Razors. He knew the terrain well enough and soon had them back on track heading east in the relative obscurity of the lightly wooded hillsides. They had arrived at Timpkenny—their real destination—just before dark, took a couple of rooms in a very ordinary inn, and in the morning sold the horses. Wyl knew the price they had managed to negotiate was just short of theft, but they had had no choice. It was on foot from here on, as the famed Thicket would not permit horses to be led through. After purchasing a few minor provisions, they had set off.

Aremys and Wyl stared now at the Thicket without knowing it had not been so long ago that a small boy and a large dog had sat and regarded the same scene in virtually the same position.

"It suits its name," Wyl admitted. "Have you been here before?"

"No. I've skirted around this region but never actually seen it."

"How do we get in?"

"Push in, I suppose, although the old stories say it lets you in once you've made up your mind to cross it."

"Lets you in, but not out?"

Aremys grinned at the beautiful woman who crouched next to him with the scowling expression. Strange as it was, he had thought of her as Wyl since Brynt—not that he had ever known Wyl Thirsk. He had witnessed the magic of Myrren's Gift with his own eyes and suddenly anything and everything seemed possible. He had never considered whether he believed in magical powers or not. It was simply not an issue that had come up through his childhood in Grenadyn. That far north, the old stories prevailed and were accepted as folklore. It was only when he found himself in the south of Morgravia that he noticed how wary of magic the people seemed to be.

Now, having watched Faryl change into Ylena, stories about the Thicket and the Wild seemed plausible. He suddenly realized how vulnerable Wyl was as Ylena. Who knew what lay on the other side of the Thicket or what was to come?

As if reading his thoughts, Wyl nudged him. "Don't stare at me like that. I know what you're thinking, and big as you are, you're no match for me, Aremys. I may look fragile in Ylena's body. I assure you I'm not."

"Did Myrren make you a mind reader as well?" Aremys asked, turning back to regard the incredibly dense line of trees and bushes that confronted them.

"No. You're as easily read as an open book. Didn't your mother teach you to mask your emotions?"

"I thought I had," Aremys said, feigning hurt. They grinned at each other, although with more anxiety than mirth. "To answer your question, no, apparently the Thicket only lets you travel from this side to whatever lies on the other side. That's my understanding, anyway. I believe legend has it that you can't turn around halfway through and change your mind. Once committed and once permitted entry, you have to continue."

"Extraordinary," Wyl breathed. "And we're not supposed to believe in magic," he added, somewhat sarcastically.

Aremys did laugh out loud now. "I think you and I know better. Come on, if we're going to do this, we should start now. There's rain clouds set to burst."

"I'll go first," Wyl offered.

"Are you scared?"

"Yes."

"Good." Aremys sighed. "I thought it was just me."

Wyl grinned. "Shall we hold hands, then?" he suggested with only a hint of sarcasm.

"Oh no. Ladies first," Aremys offered, in an overly polite tone.

Their banter was just another way of avoiding making the move. Wyl forced himself to approach, and as he stepped toward the Thicket, he noticed something to his right dangling from one of the low branches. His gaze slid past it momentarily as he scanned for the best entry point before recognition hauled his attention back. "Look at that!" he said, striding to the clump of bushes and untying the item, elation burning through him. "This is Romen's bracelet."

Aremys shook his head. "I don't understand."

"I do!" Wyl said fiercely, tying the oversize thong around his now-dainty wrist. "Only one of two people could have brought this here and I suspect it wasn't Queen Valentyna."

"Who then?"

"Fynch!"

"The gong boy you've spoken of? But he's a child."

"Never dismiss him as just a gong boy . . . or just a child. He's a gifted youngster and with enough courage for both of us. If we look hard enough, I reckon we'll find paw prints close by. Fynch and Knave have already come this way and left this as a sign."

"Brave lad," Aremys murmured. "Well, if a boy can do this, so can we."

Wyl nodded and bent over to push his way into the Thicket. Before he entered fully he called over his shoulder to his companion. "Can you whistle?"

"I guess that's a fairly important question and needs answering right now?" Aremys said, all but bent double to follow directly after Wyl.

"It's just that Ylena can't. One thing I couldn't teach her."

"Well, I really appreciate that critical and indeed relevant information," his friend grunted behind him.

"Aremys, whistle, damn you! I can't, so you'll have to do it for both of us!" Wyl snapped.

"Happy to indulge you, my lady. Just not sure why?" came the response.

"Because we don't know what happens in here. I don't want us to be separated."

"Oh," Aremys said, understanding now. "All right. Any requests? . . . I do a fine 'Under the Gooseberry Bush.' "

"Just get on with it, you fool!" Wyl said, daring a laugh through his fear. The Thicket's presence was ominous and he could not shake the feeling that danger lay ahead.

"Can I just mention, as we're on the topic of Ylena's

strengths and weaknesses, that she's got the best arse I've had the pleasure of being close to." Aremys's muffled voice came from very close behind.

"Whistle!" Wyl shrieked in her voice. He knew what Aremys was doing. He was forcing the lightheartedness to combat their fear, but it was not working; they were both frightened enough to feel their own hearts pumping hard in their chests. It felt as if the Thicket were drawing him in . . . but to what? He marveled at how Fynch had found the courage to enter the Thicket.

Wyl entered the gloom of the Thicket and was immediately struck by its eerie silence, which was sufficiently heavy to give him a sense of suffocation. He could not stand, either, for the branches were low and tangled. He breathed hard and loosened the button near Ylena's throat. He knew it was afternoon outside, yet it was so dark beneath the yews that Wyl could swear night was coming on. Nothing moved but he and Aremys.

At that moment he felt a terrible pressure on his chest. It felt as if all his breath were being sucked away; he could hear Aremys crashing into the Thicket behind and he momentarily heard his friend whistling all too brightly before the sound was suddenly cut off. And then he could breathe again. Wyl swung around, presuming the reason for his friend's quiet was that Aremys had been shocked by the silence and dark, but he could not see his companion.

"Aremys?" He listened. Nothing. "Aremys!" he yelled.

Only dread silence responded.

Valentyna finished dictating her response to the message from King Celimus, the couched threat in his letter burning in her mind.

It had taken much soul-searching to reach her decision, but now it was finally made. She knew it was the only way forward under the circumstances. The nobles were not going to support her without Ylena Thirsk, and even if she could produce her, she could not imagine what the young noblewoman could say or do to change their minds. Valentyna had seen it in their faces this afternoon, read it in their pained expressions, heard it in their voices, made awkward by the tension. The Briavellian nobles wanted peace with Morgravia above everything.

Above even her.

She was a pawn; the valuable key that might unlock the barrier that stood between Morgravia and Briavel living side by side as friendly neighbors and as allies. Valentyna understood clearly that whatever lip service the nobles had paid her this afternoon, the fact of the matter was that they did not care what Celimus was or what his intentions were. They did not want further proof of his treachery. If she were married to him, no more of their proud sons need die. Even if—Shar forbid—Celimus somehow contrived to make himself Lord High King of both realms, he would no longer wage war on Briavel, which meant their children were safe and Briavel was safe. And after decades of warring, peace is what the Briavellians demanded of their new monarch. Despite all the adoration, she was expendable. The realization was a deep pain in her heart. It made her momentarily breathless. Valentyna was a figurehead queen . . . her own people might well accept Celimus as their sovereign once the marriage had taken place.

All the talk of finding Ylena and considering new strategies to stall the marriage any further all of a sudden seemed futile. She must marry Celimus on behalf of Briavel and sacrifice her peace for its peace.

As these thoughts raged in her mind, Krell finished his scratchings on the paper and blew on it to dry the ink.

"I'll add the royal seal, your highness, once you've signed it."

He handed her the quill. She reached for it but did not take it.

"I'm doing the right thing, aren't I, Krell?"

He searched her anguished face, which so recalled the beautiful woman who had birthed her, and he thought of how proud Valor would be of his daughter right now. She was putting her realm before her own inclination and ensuring its prosperity in the future. "Your majesty," he said gravely. "Briavel will flourish because of the important decision you've made today."

Her smile was thin and wavered beneath the force of her will, pushing away tears or sentiment. "I don't want to marry him, Krell, but I know I must."

"If you'll permit me, highness . . . ?"

Valentyna nodded. She trusted Krell implicitly and needed his assurances. He had been close to her father and she knew how much he cared for her.

The Chancellor's rheumy gaze fixed upon her. "If you're strong from the outset, child, Celimus will never make Briavel bow to Morgravia. You are a queen in your own right; you must not lose sight of this. We need his peace, yes, but, oh, your highness, he needs your sons! The bluest of royal bloods mingling. It's a royal fantasy, highness, which both our dear King Valor and the great King Magnus dared imagine only in their wildest daydreams. Imagine your own blood reigning over two realms in years to come."

She nodded again, genuinely teary this time. "I agree. If my reign is remembered for nothing else, I will secure peace for Briavel and birth the heirs it needs to sustain peace in the region."

"That's the spirit, highness. Very few royal marriages are made by Shar, your majesty—most are pragmatic and highly strategic. This is no different. Your father, may his soul rest quietly, would advise the same."

The Queen smiled sadly. Krell knew what she was thinking. She had hoped to marry for love. Which princess did not?

She could not help herself. It needed to be said. "And I must forget that he designed the death of my father, the death of Wyl Thirsk, the murder of Romen Koreldy, the slaughter of those monks at Rittylworth and the noble family of Felrawthy . . . and no doubt countless others?" Her chest rose and fell with the anger she was holding at bay.

"My queen, we have no proof that his hand was behind any of those deaths."

"But we know it, Krell!"

"Yes, your majesty," he admitted truthfully. "But as diplomats, we must pursue the peace he offers or more of our young men are going to die. We stand to lose a whole generation if we go against him. Celimus, I fear, does not possess the honorable qualities of Magnus—he will fight us until the last man of Briavel falls and then he will dissolve the realm as we know it . . . wipe out its name, make it solely an annex of Morgravia."

Valentyna did not say that she felt in her heart that he would annex Briavel anyway. "And still you would urge this marriage, knowing I'm sacrificing myself to a man I could never love."

"Love is not the issue here, my queen," Krell said firmly. "This is politics now and your emotions must be set aside. Your decision is purely a diplomatic one . . . a sound one. You will be Queen of Morgravia as well as Briavel and you must use that status to high effect. This is not Celimus, King of Morgravia, and Briavel as his queen consort. You are both equal sovereigns with equal say in the running of both realms. You alone can carve a path for this marriage to work. Put aside what you feel you are losing and consider only what you are gaining, your highness." He surprised Valentyna by suddenly kneeling before her. "You must leave behind whatever has gone before. Cut yourself free of those bonds and those sentiments. Start a new life with Celimus and see if you can't be the one who makes the difference."

"To him, you mean?"

"To him, to Morgravia and Briavel. Both realms crave this union and the harmony it will bring. Work hard for peace in the marriage, your highness, and you may well bring about surprising changes."

Valentyna felt entirely trapped. There was nothing more she could do. All of the warnings she had heard—from Wyl, from Romen, from Fynch, and even more lately from Elspyth—haunted her, yet Celimus's messenger had been ordered to wait for her response. Time was the enemy. The King was both impatient and impetuous—who knew what he might do if she did not answer in the affirmative? How long could she wait for Ylena and what difference could Ylena Thirsk make anyway? she asked herself, filled with frustration.

She made a small sound of despair before grabbing the quill and quickly signing her name, accepting Celimus's proposal of marriage on the last full moon of the spring equinox.

"There," she said, unable to disguise the disgust in her voice. "Get it away with the messenger."

"Yes, your highness," Krell said, rising and feeling a sense of loss at his part in forcing this young woman to act against her instincts. But the alliance was necessary for the well-being of Briavel. He and Valor had discussed on many occasions how insecure Briavel might be if faced with a battle on two fronts and Krell firmly believed that the threat from Cailech in the near future was real.

Wyl felt a cold tremor pass through him. Aremys had gone. Disappeared. There was no sign that he had even followed Wyl into the Thicket. Somehow he knew it would be pointless to search. If the Thicket was as enchanted as he had been led to believe, it had made the decision to separate them.

He shivered. Magic.

As that thought passed through him, a black dog melted out of the darkness and sat huge and still before him.

"Knave."

The dog leapt and Wyl felt a moment of exquisite fear. He should have known better, for although he found himself winded and flat on his back, Knave towering above him, the dog merely licked him enthusiastically.

"Where's Aremys?" Wyl asked, pushing him away.

Knave growled low. It was an answer but not one Wyl could understand.

"Is he all right?"

This time Knave barked once. Wyl convinced himself the animal had answered affirmatively. Thin though his premise was, he had to believe that Aremys was somewhere safe and not wandering aimlessly through the Thicket.

Knave growled again and turned. Wyl knew the dog

wanted to lead him somewhere. They set off, the black beast at a trot and Wyl behind, crouching, blindly following. There were moments when he felt convinced that the branches were reaching out to touch him. None did. The silence was oppressive; there was only Knave's presence and his own pounding pulse to reassure him that life existed in this strangest of places. It felt to Wyl like they had been moving for a long time and he could hear the rushing of water nearby.

Images echoing his fears began to rush at him. Aremys lost in the Thicket calling to him. Valentyna being raped by Celimus. Elspyth screaming for Lothryn while the man she loved begged Wyl for help. Romen, Faryl, and Ylena walked toward him, their expressions showing the same confusion they had felt when death had claimed each of them. And then that vision disappeared, to be replaced with blood and gore surrounding Tenterdyn. He could almost smell the carnage, and just when he thought he might have to scream for the dog to stop, that he must go back, they burst through the other side of the Thicket, emerging into gray daylight and a soft drizzle of rain.

He dragged a lungful of the damp air, not caring that his cheeks were wet from his own tears. Knave was gone. Instead, through the murkiness he saw a small cottage on the other side of a short bridge. Its chimney smoked cheerfully through the gloomy afternoon and light glowed through the windows; like a magnet, the dwelling drew him to its warmth.

31

LEDA WAS DYING. SHE KNEW IT AND SOMEHOW IT WAS ALL right, provided she could cling to life long enough to learn the whereabouts of her eldest son. That knowledge would allow her to pass over with the grim happiness that the

Donal name was not completely stamped out. Each heavy step of her faithful mule hurt her and all her waning energies were focused on simply remaining on its back. If she fell off now, she would have to lie on the ground and hope that the Briavellian Guard would find her before she took her last breath.

Shar was guiding her passage that day. A tinker, selling pots and sharpening knives from village to village, came across the blood-spattered, bedraggled woman with the torn fingernails. He leapt from his small cart, calling to his horse to be still as he reached for a water skin.

"Drink," he said, offering it.

Aleda did so. She had not taken water in hours. Perhaps she had forgotten to—she could no longer remember. "Thank you," she croaked.

The tinker looked around anxiously. There was no help nearby; they were in the middle of nowhere. He himself had crossed the border at around midday yesterday—although Brackstead was not far away, he was sure.

There seemed little point in taxing the woman with questions. She looked too ill to speak anyway. "Come on," he encouraged. "We have to get you to Brackstead."

Aleda did not complain—she too wanted to keep moving. Who this kind stranger was mattered not. If he was going to help her get another step closer to Crys, she would take it. "Thank you," she whispered.

"Don't talk. Save your strength."

They set off, Aleda feeling stronger just for the presence of another person. They had traveled less than a mile before rounding a bend in the road to see the cheering scene of a large village laid out before them.

The sight of Aleda brought several people running to help.

"I don't know her," the tinker replied to their queries. "I found her just a mile back. Can we get her to a doctor?"

Someone sent a young boy running for a traveling physic.

"You're lucky he's in our village today," the woman said.

"Is there an inn?" he asked.

A man nodded. "Yes, the Lucky Bowman. Shall we go there?"

"Please. She says she has money."

Three burly men carried Aleda into the inn, which was run by a kindly-looking woman.

"Shar's Mercy," she cried as they bundled Aleda and her few belongings past her.

"The physic's coming," one said as he nodded to the others to head upstairs.

"Room four," she called to their backs, before turning back to the tinker, who looked thoroughly uncomfortable.

"They've just arrived, Nan, in terrible shape," the woman who had rushed in with them said, clearly excited by all this activity. "I've sent Rory after that traveling physic who was here today."

"I don't even know her name. I . . . I just stumbled across her on my way here," the tinker admitted.

Nan nodded toward the door. "Here's the physic—we can sort out her food and board later," she said kindly. "Take them up, Bel, I have to keep a watch on things down here."

Bel was only too glad to remain a part of the day's intrigue and she bustled past and called to the physic, a middle-aged man with gray at his temples and a soft-spoken voice, to follow her. He stopped to chat briefly with the tinker, who then took his leave, glad to be gone from all the attention and activity.

Later, alone with his patient, the physic learned the full horror of what the severely injured woman had gone through and, even more distressingly, who she was.

He gave Aleda a draft of something crimson in color. "Rest now, Lady Donal," he said, taking her hand. "We'll get word to Werryl for you."

At those reassuring words, Aleda sighed and closed her eyes.

The physic went downstairs to speak with Nan, who in turn called for Bel.

"She needs a carer," he explained. "You will be paid."

Bel nodded. "You want me to stay with her until you return, right?"

"She will not recover from her internal injuries," he said.

"But yes, I need someone by her side. I've stanched the bleeding for now and she will sleep for several hours. When she wakes, I want you to brew up these leaves." He handed her a pouch. "They will give her strength."

"Food?"

He shook his head. "Furthest thing from her mind. Keep the water up to her, though. She'll die of her injuries before she dies of starvation."

"How long can she hang on?" Nan asked, not at all happy about having a potential corpse cooling in one of her beds.

"She's got courage. That alone will keep her going twice as long as someone with a weaker disposition. A day or so perhaps."

"And where are you going for help, Physic Geryld?" asked Bel, ever curious.

"I will ride back to Werryl and bring help swiftly," he answered, determined to keep the patient's identity a secret. He knew they had guessed her status as a noblewoman, but he did not wish to give away private details to these village folk. "Your job is to keep her alive until then with the tea and your voice."

Bel frowned. "My voice?"

"Talk to her. Keep this woman alert when she's awake. She'll need her wits about her. I'll leave immediately."

"How long will you need?"

"I hope we'll have help back here by tomorrow if I ride through the night."

He returned to the room and was surprised to see that Lady Donal was not sleeping . . . was, in fact, agitated.

"I told you to rest," he said sternly.

Her eyes were glazing from the effects of the sleeping draft, but she was fighting it. "Not until I give you something to take to Werryl. You must show it to the Queen, sir," she said emphatically, pointing to the leather bag that had been attached to the mule.

He frowned. "What is it?"

"The proof she needs that she's contemplating marrying a madman."

32

AREMYS CAME TO SLOWLY. WAS SOMEONE KICKING HIM? HE could not be sure just yet. In fact, he was not sure of anything other than that he breathed. And that there was pain everywhere. Concentrating hard, he determined that there were also voices—men's voices—and then he made out the familiar sounds of horses. He risked opening his eyes, trying for the life of him to remember why he would be lying down in the open in such a freezing temperature.

"Ah, so you're alive, then?" someone said.

He grunted. "Just."

"Get Myrt," the voice said, and Aremys heard footsteps retreat, crunching on fresh snow. It was a lovely sound, a sound he thought he remembered fondly from childhood. "Can you move?" the man asked.

"Let me just open my eyes," he replied, squinting through them to discover a fantastically sharp brightness and a big scowling man, tall enough to match even his substantial height. He closed them again hurriedly.

More footsteps. A new voice, deeper this time. "Well, help him up, Firl."

Aremys felt himself hauled roughly to his feet. His legs were unsteady and leaden, his mind clouded. He forced himself to open his eyes again, but he ignored the man called Firl and regarded the older fellow with knowing gray eyes. Blinding pain sliced through his head as he did so. "I'm sorry." He smiled crookedly. "My head aches."

"You must have fallen and hit it," the man, presumably Myrt of the deep voice, suggested. "What's your name?"

Aremys reached up to scratch his head. Everything hurt. "I'd tell you if I could. I can't remember a thing right now."

Myrt sighed. "Get a blanket on him, someone. You, Firl, double with him. Let's go."

Bruised and feeling sorry for himself, Aremys was helped, none too gently, onto a horse with the surly man called Firl—who clearly did not want to double with him—and began a journey he knew not why or where to . . . or even where from. What he did know was that he was high in the mountains and there was only one enormous range to his knowledge. It could hardly be anywhere else . . . or could it?

Firl ignored him for the first hour or so. This did not bother Aremys; he was too concerned with keeping his balance and trying to remember his name. He was grateful for the blanket, though.

"Where are we?" he finally asked.

"Razors," the man bluntly responded.

Aremys never could suffer fools. "Yes, I think I've worked that out. But where exactly?"

The sarcasm seemed to have little effect on the young brute. "East."

He could tell he was not going to get much more out of the chatty fellow, so he delved back into his own mind, which felt like tangled skeins of wool. Ignoring the growing headache, he forced himself to concentrate on recalling anything about himself. Nothing surfaced and he growled in frustration.

"Who are you?" he asked.

His companion spoke again in the same disinterested tone. "Firl. I thought we'd already established that."

"And the others?" Aremys asked, struggling to keep his irritation in check.

"Did you want me to list their names?"

"Not if they're all as uninteresting as yours." He felt the man's body stiffen and was glad he had struck a blow. "I meant, what are you doing out here?"

"We're a scouting party."

"For Cailech?"

"Who else?" the man said, and Aremys, sitting behind him, imagined him scowling.

"Am I a prisoner?"

The man snorted. "Why don't you make a run for it and see what happens? I'm a great shot."

"Is your conversation always this scintillating, Firl? I'll bet the other men in the party just love it when they know you're coming along because of all the witty repartee they're going to enjoy with mighty Firl and his equally huge ego. Do you understand what 'repartee' means, Firl, or is it one of those words that are just too big for your minuscule brain?"

Myrt overheard Aremys and the threatening tone that had crept into his voice. He steered his horse over and lifted his chin in inquiry. "Anything wrong?"

"No," Firl mumbled.

"Actually, yes," Aremys countered. "I want to know if I'm a prisoner and why. I'd like to know where we're headed and why. I'd appreciate knowing why I've been seemingly captured by a scouting party, sitting with this oaf of few syllables, and I'd love to know my own name!" he roared, his headache pounding in tandem with his blood pressure and anger.

"Hop up with me. Firl, you go on ahead," Myrt ordered. There was something of an admonishment in the man's expression and it was not lost on the sulking Firl.

Aremys was more than glad to clamber up behind Firl's superior. "Thank you," he mumbled. "And for the blanket. I'm sorry for the outburst. I seem to have lost my manners as well as my memory."

"So I gathered," Myrt said, clicking to his horse and moving forward again. "Either that or you're a clever spy."

"Shar strike me! Is that what you all think?"

"Why wouldn't we? You're Morgravian, aren't you?"

"I . . . well . . . I don't know," Aremys blustered.

"You dress like one and curse like one."

"Then perhaps I am. I have no idea who I am. Mind you,

I understand the Northernish you were muttering with your men earlier. Does that mean anything?"

"Is that so? And what were we saying?"

Aremys told him.

"All right, stranger, I'm impressed," Myrt admitted. "Most Morgravians wouldn't understand a word of it, which is why we used it in front of you. Anything else?"

"No, not really," Aremys admitted. "The Razors are familiar, although I can't tell you why or how I even knew their name. No horse, no belongings, save my sword," he said, and shook his head. "No memory," he added mournfully.

"Well, perhaps pulling out your toenails will help your memory," Myrt said, and felt Aremys start behind him. He let out a deep rumbling laugh, enjoying his own jest.

"Shar's Wrath, man! Will it come to that?"

"Be easy. Did Firl tell you our business?"

"Oh yes, we enjoyed a long and cordial chat." Myrt waited, unaffected by the biting wit of their new guest. "Only that you're a scouting party," Aremys grumbled.

"That's right. Do you know Morgravia has all but declared war on the mountain people?"

"If I do, I don't remember."

"Then you'll forgive us our suspicions," Myrt said. "Well, if you're from Morgravia—which you probably aren't—you'd know about our problems with King Celimus."

The name was familiar and its mention sounded a distant series of alarm bells in Aremys's mind. He pushed at them but had no success. "Why do you think I'm most likely not from Morgravia?"

"Because we've picked you up on the Briavellian side of the Razors and your accent isn't right. It's Morgravian all right, but it's covering something else. If I didn't know better, I'd think you were from the northern islands."

Again, a prick of familiarity, but it was elusive. "I see. Maybe I am. I wish I could dredge up something to help my cause."

The man called Myrt nodded. "It will come. To answer your question, yes, you are our prisoner, but we shall treat you honorably until the King has decided what to do with you. I'm afraid relations with Morgravia are strained, but your odd accent may save you yet. What shall we call you until then?"

Aremys pondered, unhappy at his situation but fully aware that he had no option other than cooperation. He had no mount, no food, almost no memory, and was somewhere in the Razors, where a single night could be deadly. "What's a good mountain name?"

"How about Cullyn? It's one of the oldest."

He shrugged. "Fine."

"No such thing as free meals in this troop, Cullyn. We'll be on the ridges for a few days yet. What can you do to earn your keep?"

Aremys shook his head, feeling suddenly grateful to the big man of the mountains. "I have no idea. You tell me."

"All right, then. We're about to make camp here. You can provide the entertainment for tonight. How about you take sulky Firl on with the sword. I think he'd quite like a go at you."

"And me at him, I assure you."

Myrt laughed. "I like your arrogance. Hope you haven't forgotten your skills, Cullyn. Our Firl is one of the best in the Razors with a sword."

"Just promise me some ale and worry about your mountain boy over there," Aremys said, grinning hungrily despite his pounding head.

A camp was settled and the horses corralled in a small copse of fir trees that also provided the wood for the men's fire. Myrt ran a tight troop and gave orders briskly. Some men were designated to prepare the food, others to gather the wood, some to take care of the animals, and the younger ones to restock the water skins. He took Aremys and another man to hunt down some meat. Aremys pleased his host by shooting four hares without wasting a single arrow. Each man returned with a small brace of game, which was quickly skinned and gutted and before long roasting over the coals.

They did not speak Northernish, a language no longer in

use except for reasons of disguise and the odd word here and there. If Aremys's memory had been intact, he would have known that the language only survived because of King Cailech's love for the mountain culture. He had passed an edict that Northernish would be taught from elder to grandchild in order to keep the language alive. In daily life, however, the mountain people spoke the language of the region, the common tongue from Briavel in the east to as far west as Tallinor. Aremys did not know that he recognized the Northernish because his wet nurse, an old woman of the isles, used to sing to him in the old language.

Sadly, right then he could not even remember as far back as the previous day, when he had been clambering through the Thicket, one moment following the shapely bottom of Ylena Thirsk and the next overcome by a sudden wave of magic. He could not recall the air thickening to a dull, almost solid wall and the powerful blast of the magic that had opened the cleft through which his prone, unconscious self had been pushed . . . in this case on a northeastern ridge of the Razors into the path of Myrt's scouting troop, all memory blurred deeply within his subsconscious.

While the meat cooked and a hearty vegetable broth simmered in a pot, Myrt posted lookouts and then called the remaining eleven men around the fireside for the early evening's entertainment. There was fifteen of them in total; all strong-looking men but none of them, other than Firl, tall enough to go eye to eye with the giant stranger.

"How you do feel, Cullyn?"

"Like hurting someone," he mumbled, and a roar went up from the delighted audience, ready for sport.

"All right, then. Do we have a sparring partner to go up against our huge guest here?"

Firl stood, cutting the air with his heavy sword. He held it two-fisted and snarled, "He's mine."

Aremys shook off the blue blanket that had been lent to him and drew his own sword. As he did so, the movement of the dyed wool reflected off the blade and he momentarily staggered under the fleeting blaze of memory.

"Koreldy," he whispered, remembering a sword with a blue tinge to its edge.

Only Myrt caught the word and he too was forced to pause in recognition of a name known all too well to the senior members of Cailech's circle of trusted supporters. This was not the time to confront the stranger with it, he decided, and instead stored it away. It would be brought to light when it counted . . . before the King. Suddenly this man among them was important.

He cleared his throat. "Firl, Cullyn, this is not to the death. If either of you should mortally harm the other, I shall kill the perpetrator myself—do you understand?" Aremys nodded. Firl just snarled. "Firl?"

"I understand, sir."

"Good. This is sport, for our entertainment. Don't forget it, either of you. First blood declares the victor—then we shall eat in his honor."

Both men touched their blades before Firl adopted the two-fisted stance of the mountain race, one leg placed wide diagonally behind the other, knees bent, ready to strike. But it was Aremys who surprised all, including himself, by holding the sword upright before his face, fist upon fist on the hilt. This was a stance unique to one region alone. Everyone recognized it as the formal Grenadyne salute before combat.

Myrt, more taken aback than any, wanted to halt the proceedings immediately, but it was too late. The combatants hurled themselves at each other.

Firl gave away much in bulk, but he fought like a savage. Myrt could see straightaway, however, that his own man was no match for the stranger. Cullyn, or whoever he was, was clearly a superior swordsman, with the moves and speed that came from a soldier's experience. Firl was young and headstrong. He might feel invincible, but his skills had been tested only among the mountain men, and courageous though he was, he knew none of the finesse of the southerners, who prided themselves on grace and speed rather than brute force.

Myrt could see Cullyn was merely blocking rather than

attacking. He was allowing Firl to wear himself out and this was precisely what the youngblood was doing all too fast. His heart was generous and spirit keen, but the older soldier was virtually playing with him. Aremys looked over at Myrt and winked. It was all Myrt could do not to laugh, particularly as he watched Cullyn backing away and supposedly defending his life as the enraged Firl stomped forward, blustering and roaring his anger, slashing with the heavy sword like a battering ram.

Despite his dislike of Firl, Aremys felt sorry for the youngster. He was brave, but would almost certainly lose his life young if he were to be caught in any serious fight with a Morgravian. He could tell the young man wanted to impress his companions in his fight with the arrogant stranger and it struck Aremys that it would not do to humiliate Firl—he would make no friends among the mountain men should he do that . . . and he could, quite easily.

And so, although Firl was no match, Aremys allowed him to feel like a genuine combatant. He felt surprisingly good about such generosity. After all, Myrt had been fair. Considering that Morgravia was an enemy of the Mountain Kingdom, they could just have easily run him through as he lay in the snow, but they had given him warmth and transport, food and company, as well as safety. Not humiliating Firl—as much as he would have liked to—was the least he could do, if just for the leader, Myrt. And so he winked and the message was understood.

The fight continued until Aremys felt the pain of his headache beginning to weigh heavily on him. He had been able to set it aside, but hunger and the exertion of the sword contest had brought it pounding to the fore again. Seeking the right opening, he feinted all too obviously, so that even the less agile Firl could see it coming. He slashed. Aremys felt the welcome, if painful wound, open on the top of his nonfighting arm.

He yelled appropriately and the audience roared appreciative applause for the youngblood who grinned awkwardly but regarded his fighting partner with unease. Both stood before each other breathing deeply.

"Good fight, Firl," Myrt said. "We eat in your honor tonight."

Aremys nodded at Firl. "Well done," he said, but the younger man just stared. Others had risen to thump him on the back, which meant Aremys could turn away from the unhappy stare. The lad was no idiot. He knew he had been allowed to win.

"Come. Let me bind that for you," Myrt said to Aremys. "And don't say no, it's too awkward for you to do yourself."

Aremys gladly followed the leader toward a tiny spring that skirted the copse.

"That was bravely done," Myrt said, kneeling beside his guest. "A lesser man would have felt the need to impose his superior skill."

"Nothing to be gained but an enemy."

Myrt nodded. "A soldier with wisdom."

Aremys looked at him. "What makes you say 'soldier'?"

"You fight like one. You've had experience—even you must have felt that."

It was so frustrating not to know. "A soldier?" he mused. "The sword felt comfortable in my hand, I'll admit it. He's your best, you say?"

"I said it for his benefit. Firl's a good man, but he's young and hotheaded."

"He'll die quickly, Myrt."

"Then teach him."

"What?"

"You've got nothing else to do right now. Teach him, teach the others."

"How to kill Morgravians, you mean?"

Myrt grimaced as he cleaned the wound. It was a surface cut, nothing serious, and even the victim wasn't complaining. "Your loyalty is not there."

"And you know this?" Aremys muttered.

"Cullyn, I think I'm right in saying you're from Grenadyn originally."

Aremys shot him an angry look. The naming of that place seemed to jolt some memory from long ago. It made him think of children . . . a young girl in particular. He could see her. All curls and chubby smiles. She threw herself into his arms and kissed him. "Serah," he breathed, the sorrowful memory of a sister slotting into place.

"What?"

"I am from Grenadyn," he declared, knew it was right.

"You remember?"

Aremys nodded. "I think so, yes. It would explain why I understand Northernish."

"And why you hold your sword in the formal Grenadyne manner."

"Hmm . . . now you're just showing off."

"I miss little. Who's Serah?"

Aremys was not ready for this man, even though he could not help but like and trust him, to know too much. He suspected his lost memory possessed secrets, and although he could not remember them just yet, if his memory was going to come back in dribs and drabs, he would rather be in control of what he revealed. "I don't know," he lied effectively. "Her name just drifted across my mind."

"You see, I said your memories would come back—give it time," Myrt said, pleased. "There, it's just a nick. My thanks for your indulgence with the lad."

"He needs encouragement," Aremys admitted.

"And training," Myrt said. "Perhaps we all do," he added sagely before returning the wink.

The meal, out in the open and the cold, with the man huddled around a campfire, was the best Aremys felt he had ever eaten. Although they were hardly friends, the men were convivial enough. Even Firl had relaxed and treated him with a new cordiality, remarking that he might like to learn some of Cullyn's moves. The songs they sang he knew somehow, reinforcing the idea that he was from Grenadyne stock and not Morgravian. That was reassuring—and yet why did he feel the pull toward Morgravia, or more keenly toward Briavel, where he was now sure he must have been relatively recently? He had no explanation for why he was in the Razors, alone and without a horse.

The men explained that the horse had probably bolted; all were sure they would come across it dead soon enough, but Aremys had felt all over his head. There was no bruising, no lump, and still it hurt badly enough at times to make him feel nauseated. The pain he felt was not external, had not been caused by a fall from a horse. This was internal pain. He could not explain it. And the worrying fact was the tingling sensation in his fingertips. That was odd. He had felt it immediately on regaining his wits but had paid no attention initially. It was not painful, not even that uncomfortable, but it was definitely there and he had no idea what it was, why it was there, or even if it had been there before.

The night closed in around them as they sang more mournful ballads, and it suited his mood. Serah haunted his thoughts. She and the name Koreldy. Were they the key to who he was?

For now, though, he was Cullyn. It would have to do, he thought as he drifted off to sleep.

33

WYL STOPPED WALKING TOWARD THE CHEERFUL HUT. HE FELT empty and angry, suddenly lost without Aremys, who had disappeared without a trace. And now Knave had gone. Late afternoon was reaching across the small valley in which he found himself, and Wyl shivered. He watched a man lighting candles in the cottage. There seemed to be no others around. No family, then. Just this fellow, living alone on the outskirts of a place of fear. Wyl cast a glance behind at the black of the Thicket. It did not look so menacing from this side, but he knew it held secrets. He had felt the thrum of its magic.

Where could Aremys be? He turned back. It was no good. He would have to satisfy his anxieties by at least trying to find his friend. He could not just leave him.

"No, don't do that, my lady," called a voice.

Wyl swung around to see a large man stepping toward him across the bridge. "Er . . ."

"I'm Samm. The Boatkeeper. I saw you just now hesitating and thought I should come out and provide a welcome. It must be hard for a lady traveling alone," he said, looking about him. "You are alone, aren't you?"

"I . . ." Wyl wavered between the truth and a lie. He opted for the latter. The fewer people who knew the better. "Yes, yes I am. Apologies, I'm Lady Rachyl Farrow."

"Would you like to come in?" Samm said kindly, gesturing toward his cottage.

"Um, well, I think what I need is a boat, to tell the truth," Wyl said.

"I understand. Come in. Let me at least fix a pot of tea and then we can discuss your requirements."

After one last searching glance at the Thicket and another roving look for Knave, Wyl accepted that he was alone on this journey and he nodded to Samm to lead the way.

"Why did you say that I shouldn't go back into the Thicket, Samm?"

"I felt something a few moments ago. Just thought it best to let it be. The Thicket can be contrary and I've got used to its strange sighs and movements. There are occasions when it feels quite alive."

"And this was one of them?" Wyl queried, crossing the bridge behind Samm.

"Yes," the man replied simply, but offered nothing more.

Inside, Samm went about the business of making a pot of tea. "Why are you here, my lady?" he asked gently.

Wyl opted for honesty. "I'm following someone. A boy."

"Ah, the lad, Fynch."

"That's right!"

"And his strange black beast."

"Knave. He's my dog, actually." Wyl felt a surge of relief that Fynch had passed through safely.

"Is the lad in trouble?"

"No, not at all." He thought quickly. "He's my brother."

"So you're from Briavel too?"

"Yes, that's right," Wyl answered, desperately wondering how much deeper the lying might get. Already he was no longer from Grenadyn, which had been the original plan.

"Your brother was seeking someone."

"Mmm, yes." He did not want to answer these questions. "Do you need any help with that?"

"No, my lady. Here we go," Samm said, putting down a mug of tea. "Honey?"

"Please."

"Family?" Samm was not going to be put off, Wyl could tell.

"That's right," he answered, sipping, desperately hoping he could escape further interrogation. "How much for the boat?"

"One crown. Is there anything I can do to dissuade you from going, my lady? Your brother is sadly not returning from the Wild. No one does."

"I must try, though, Samm. He's so young," Wyl said as plaintively as possible.

"It's a one-way journey, my lady. People leave and empty boats return. His has already found its way back to its mooring outside. To lose two fine people, well, it disturbs me. I always hope I can stop someone going."

"Not this time."

"That's what Fynch said."

"I must leave before I lose the light. Thank you for your tea." Wyl stood and held out his small and pretty hand.

"Why not go in the morning. Sleep on it?"

"No, Samm. I really must get going."

Samm sighed heavily and went foraging for his great black book. Following the same routine he had with Fynch, he droned out the terms and conditions of his visitor's departure, his normally genial face heavy with regret that another young life was to be lost.

"Thank you," Wyl said, having clearly spelled out his name for recording in the book. "Just out of interest, Samm, who was the previous person to enter the Wild before Fynch?"

"Funny, I had the same conversation with the boy, miss. It was a young lady like you. Her name was Emil Lightford, a scholar from Pearlis."

The name meant nothing to Wyl, but he nodded and smiled.

"That was two decades and four years ago," Samm said, counting back. "And now two of you in such short time."

"Here's my money," Wyl said, holding out the coin. "Do I just take a boat?"

"Whichever you like, my lady. Let me escort you. And don't worry about steering. It navigates itself."

Wyl smiled nervous thanks and followed Samm down to the jetty. Just as Fynch had done, he took the nearest.

"That was your brother's choice too," Samm said. "All I can offer now is good luck."

Wyl waved once and then turned to face forward. Two overhanging willows looked as though their hanging branches were tentacles, waiting to grab him and pull him into their darkness. Aremys's absence played heavily on his mind—another person who had trusted him, gone. Hopefully not dead, but perhaps he was.

Why would the Thicket be selective? he wondered, and then forgot the thought as the darkness of a thick canopy of overhanging trees enveloped him. His eyes adjusted to the murky darkness and he risked sitting down on the small plank in the boat. There were no oars. It was cold too. Wyl hugged Ylena's arms about him as the boat rounded a slight curve in the Darkstream and a sheer rock face came into view.

It was huge—most likely part of the Razors, with that granite. A narrow low arch was hewn out of the face, just large enough to allow a single boat through. Wyl held his breath, wished goodbye to all that he recognized as familiar, and reflexively closed his eyes as the mountain closed its lips around the little boat and swallowed him up.

Initially when he opened his eyes, he saw only depthless black. It was disorienting and he held the sides of the boat to give him a sense of up and down and his position in this dread place. If it had been cold just before he had entered, it was now freezing beneath the thousands of tons of granite and he felt his teeth beginning to chatter. Ylena did not have sufficient flesh on her body to keep herself warm in such conditions. Shivering uncontrollably now in her body, Wyl wondered whether Samm had been right. A one-way journey from which no one ever returned. A never-ending tunnel whose travelers died of the trauma of being alone in the dark for too long or froze to death?

These macabre thoughts were his only companions as the journey through darkness lengthened until any sane person would have felt the first flutterings of panic. Wyl could not tell whether he was imagining it, but the ceiling of his narrow tunnel began to lower. He felt too frightened to loosen his grip on the boat and reach up to confirm this. He felt a curious battle going on internally. Wyl knew he was not one to be afraid of the dark or enclosed spaces, but given his increasing agitation, he recalled that Ylena liked neither. Even as an adult, she had always kept a single candle burning through the night, and her worst childhood nightmare had been dreaming of being locked in a cupboard. Was some residue of Ylena's fears surfacing? Whatever it was, it was getting worse. His pulse had quickened to the point of panic and his breathing was coming in shallow gasps all of a sudden. He did his best to quell the fear, to rationalize it, but the tunnel was surely closing in and the thick silence was working against him.

Ylena's fear took full flight and Wyl began to scream and scream. He stupidly tried to stand and instantly lost his balance. His hysterical shrieks were cut short suddenly by a new sort of darkness. A wet and drowning sort of darkness. He gulped the Darkstream as it swallowed him, much faster, of course, and farther into its fathomless depths, down toward death, where perhaps he would come to rest next to Fynch and Emil whatever-her-name-was . . . he could no longer remember. All he could focus on now was letting go of this life. Finally he would die, and mercifully at no one else's expense.

Perhaps it was for the best. His life—if he could call it that—was too dangerous. It was a weapon. Who needed swords or arrows when one could simply claim the lives and bodies of his killers? He hated himself. Death felt good. Wyl sank farther still. It was freezing and silent . . . and easy. No life to be claimed but his.

He let go of the last ounce of breath in his lungs and his hold on life.

Wyl was being pulled. Nothing gentle about it. A savage, angry yank bit through his shoulder and reawakened him to his struggle. *Survive, damn you,* he cried to himself as something big with teeth and strength hauled at him. Wyl had no idea which was way up and his thoughts were too dizzy for him to think in any straight pattern at all. Death was indeed close. Just moments before he had anticipated seeing the friendly, welcoming faces of Shar's Gatherers, assuring him all would be well once their outstretched arms laid hands upon him.

No faces, no welcome. Just a fight for air and a monster that dragged at him. They burst through the Darkstream's surface.

"Here, Knave!" a voice called. It was Fynch and next to him stood a figure. "Quickly," Fynch urged. "Drag him here."

Wyl was pulled, unconscious, from the black, icy water.

"Let me see him," the other person said.

"Her," Fynch corrected, shocked. Ylena's body lay inert and pale before them. He helped Knave from the water and gritted his teeth as the huge dog shook his shining black fur free of the Darkstream. "This is Ylena Thirsk," Fynch said sadly.

His companion shook his head. "Let me help him."

Moments later Ylena's body shuddered, before spluttering with a heaving cough, bringing up the water she had swallowed, sucking in lungfuls of life-giving air. Her eyes flew open.

"Fynch?" The coughing began again.

The boy nodded. "Hello, Wyl. We thought we'd lost you."

Ylena's expression was confused. She was shivering uncontrollably while she was coughing. "Who . . . ?"

"It was Knave; he dived so low for you and was gone so long I worried for his safety too." Knave took this moment to loom into view and lick Ylena's face while Fynch took Ylena's slim, delicate hand. "Wyl, this is Elysius. Myrren's father."

Wyl opened his sister's eyes, glad that he had finally rid himself of the dregs of the Darkstream, and regarded the strangest-looking person he had ever seen.

"Don't talk yet," Elysius said softly. "You're shivering. We need to get you warm and dry very quickly."

When Wyl woke he was lying in a small cot. He had no idea where he was, although he could see that it was a small, stone cottage. His mouth was dry and he felt weak. As he stirred, Fynch came to his side and it all suddenly came back to him; he remembered seeing the boy momentarily after being dragged from the Darkstream. He had been drowning.

Fynch noticed his confusion and answered the obvious questions in Wyl's mind. "Knave saved you. You were given something to sleep."

"Where are we?" Wyl asked.

"We're with Elysius—where he lives . . . in the Wild," Fynch said. Wyl could see he was struggling with his emotions.

"Well, it's certainly good to see you again, Fynch," he admitted, and sitting up, he opened his arms.

"What happened?" Fynch wept. "How come you're Ylena?"

"It's a long and horrid story. I can scarcely believe it myself and hate even thinking about it. It only happened a few days back, so I'm not very used to being her." He smiled awkwardly with her face and held Fynch away so he could look at him. "You're amazing, do you know that? To get yourself all the way here?"

Fynch risked one of his rare smiles. "I got a fair bit of help from my four-legged friend over there."

Wyl looked over to see Knave settled by the side of the bed, regarding him with those dark, knowing eyes. Knave barked once and Wyl grinned. "Thank you for coming after me, Knave, I was all but finished down there," he said, flinching in memory of the Darkstream. He turned back to Fynch. "I'm glad he keeps you safe. Where's Elysius?"

"Preparing food." Fynch chuckled. "He's a terrible cook."

Wyl shook his head. "I'm not sure I really caught sight of him properly back there."

Fynch grew serious again. "You did. He's . . . well, he's strange to look at."

"What do you mean?"

"See for yourself," a voice said. Elysius had arrived.

Wyl regarded what looked to him to be one of Shar's jests. The sort of creature one might glimpse at Master Jensyn's Freak Spectacular, which roamed the realms terrifying and amusing people with the tallest man, the ugliest woman, the boy with no face, and suchlike. Elysius, however, struck him as being one of those freaks who would normally never be permitted to take a second breath past birth.

"Which explains why I live in the Wild." Elysius read Wyl's mind, breaking the awkward pause.

"Wyl!" Fynch admonished under his breath.

"You're not what I was expecting," Wyl finally said, a little at a loss for the right words.

"Neither are you," Elysius admitted, a crooked smile breaking across his strange face. "I'd heard from your friend here that you were someone called Faryl of Coombe."

Wyl was fascinated by the person talking to him. Elysius's head was too large for the small, dwarfed body. Big through the abdomen, his torso sat atop legs that were ridiculously short. It struck Wyl that Elysius's arms were not the right length either—everything about him was out of proportion, in fact, and although Wyl had once worried about his red hair and freckles, here was someone to make him feel ashamed of such a sentiment. Elysius was ugly beyond imagining. A massive forehead swept down toward a heavy, jutting brow and a wide, flat nose. And when he smiled, as he was doing now, his lips seemed to stretch forever, revealing huge, horse-like teeth. As if this were not enough, his face was covered in unsightly lumps and both Elysius's eyes were milky white—blind. The latter feature was probably the most shocking. Lank, dark hair was carelessly tied back behind his enormous troll-like head. Seemingly, Elysius's only attractive feature was his voice. It was all warmth and mellowness—that same voice that had soothed Wyl when his nightmares had threatened to overwhelm him.

"It's not polite to stare, you know," Elysius said in his lovely voice.

"I . . . I'm so sorry," Wyl said, wondering how the man had known.

The curiosity standing before him, barely reaching above his bedside, stopped smiling. He took Ylena's birdlike hand in his stupendously oversize one. "No, I think I'm the one who should be sorry, Wyl. You've suffered plenty at my whim."

There was another awkward silence for a moment as the gravity of what had just been said sat between them.

Wyl took a slow breath. It was all in the past. Romen and Faryl and Ylena were dead. Even he could surmise that the magic of Elysius could not bring those people back. Keeping Valentyna safe and securing her realm was the only thing that mattered to Wyl now—that and keeping his promise to Elspyth to track down Lothryn. His own life felt inconsequential. He cared nothing for it.

"Tell me about yourself . . . please," Wyl finally said.

"Over some food. Come, join me at my table. Do you feel better?"

Wyl nodded. "Did you make me sleep?"

"I did. Your body needed a rest after its shock. I'm afraid you've been out for many hours. It's night outside—too dark to see anything."

Fynch led the way.

"I'm not much of a cook," Elysius admitted, waddling after Fynch in his strange manner on his fantastically short legs.

"So I've heard," Wyl said, and then grinned Ylena's warm, assuring smile when Elysius feigned hurt at the suggestion.

"Fynch is plain ungrateful," he grumbled. "Starling-and-fish pie is delicious."

Wyl threw a troubled glance toward Fynch, who could only shrug.

The so-called starling-and-fish pie was not nearly as bad as Wyl had imagined. He munched hungrily on the breads and delicious cheeses that Elysius had laid out too.

"Drowning must give you an appetite," Elysius commented, enjoying seeing his guest eat so heartily.

Wyl grinned, feeling immeasurably better for the rest, food, and convivial atmosphere. "I shall have to stop soon. Ylena will never forgive me if I ruin her figure."

His jest was mild, but it struck a blow at Elysius. "I do owe you some explanation," he admitted as he reached to re-fill the mugs.

"Start from the beginning," Wyl said, swallowing a mouthful of the refreshing ale on offer. "I want to know everything."

Elysius sighed, sat back in his comfortable chair, and began his story.

34

ALENTYNA WAS PICKING OVER A LATE SUPPER WITH HER MOR-gravian guests and her two most trusted counselors, Commander Liryk and Chancellor Krell. A friendship had formed between the two women, and the new Duke of Felrawthy had, to all outward apperances, battled through the worst of his horror. The wound no longer showed so openly on his face, although Elspyth, who had known him, albeit briefly, before the trauma, could see he was already a changed man. The pain would never leave his heart. He would hide it, bury it well, but Elspyth grieved that the bright expression that had come so naturally to Crys now held a haunted quality. Another reason for her to hate Celimus. Still, the Briavellians who were just getting to know the new Duke could see the intelligence, integrity, and humor that the young man possessed—testimony to his fine parents.

Krell had deliberately driven the supper conversation to a less controversial subject than his young queen's impending marriage, which was clearly on everyone's mind. He felt sure she had enough of her own misgivings and fears to want not to be subjected to the weight of the Morgravians' despair when they learned of her decision. Krell had taken it upon himself to speak quietly with the young woman from Yentro, who was the most vocal; he had tried to make her understand the fragile and highly complex position the monarch of Briavel found herself in. Elspyth had listened, but he saw the pity and no little disgust she felt on behalf of her new friend and he knew he must do everything he could to dissuade this fiery girl from convincing the Queen that her marriage was doomed.

Supper had been his idea. Since the Morgravians' arrival, the atmosphere around the Queen had become tense. He felt a light meal, late at night in Valentyna's private chambers, might help alleviate some of the tension. It would be an ideal opportunity for himself and Liryk to help these guests understand Briavel's precarious position.

It was his firm hope that they could discuss the Morgravians' departure, for as long as they were around Valentyna, their talk of Celimus served no purpose other than to poison any chance Briavel had of achieving peace.

The novice monk, Krell noted, had closeted himself away with Father Paryn, choosing to share his meals and time with the elder man of Shar. Perhaps he would even remain in Briavel; this was less disconcerting for Krell than Pil being more visible around the palace.

All was going well until Liryk was called away by the head guard on duty for the night. The Commander returned to whisper something in Krell's ear and then both men disappeared.

"Chancellor?" Valentyna had inquired when Krell had reentered, looking decidedly sombre.

"A very exhausted and disturbed Physic Geryld, your majesty, asking specifically for an audience."

"Good grief," she said, standing. "He attended my father on occasion. Permit him, immediately."

"Perhaps, your highness," Krell said cautiously, "I might bring him to your study?" He glanced toward the Morgravians.

Her gaze narrowed. "This is urgent, I gather?"

He nodded.

She thought of the solar—there was no fire burning in it this evening. "I think you should bring him here. If he's exhausted, the man needs warmth and food. I can't imagine why he would ride in so late."

Krell did not look happy at her decision and disappeared.

"Something's wrong," Valentyna surmised.

"We can leave if you wish, your highness," Crys suggested.

"Please stay," she said. "I imagine this is some small domestic matter that we can sort out quickly. No need to disrupt everyone's supper." She cast a smile his way.

Elspyth, in turn, gave him a wry expression. It was clear to her at least that Crys was entirely captivated by the Queen.

Krell and Liryk reappeared and bowed, bringing behind them the fatigued physic, who trailed a leather bag. Valentyna wondered why no one had offered to carry it for him, but her chancellor interrupted her before she could speak.

"Physic Geryld," Krell announced unnecessarily, but then he was a stickler for detail.

Elspyth and Crys had already withdrawn to the back of the room to stand within the shadows. They felt like intruders even though Valentyna had gone to such lengths to make them feel the most welcome of guests.

"Your majesty," the doctor murmured, struggling to bow in a genteel fashion. "Forgive my intrusion."

Valentyna threw a glance of concern toward Krell, who hurried to help the man to a chair. "Please, Physic Geryld," she said. "Sit by the fire and warm yourself. You look half frozen, sir."

He shook his head and remained standing. "No time, your highness. I bring grave tidings. May I speak freely?"

"You may," she said, holding her breath. This felt suddenly ominous.

"A woman is dying in our village of Brackstead, majesty. She has but hours. No ordinary soul, mind. She is of noble rank—a Morgravian no less—who begs your help. She tells a tale so horrid, my queen, that I could not trust anyone but myself to deliver it."

Elspyth and Cry both stepped forward from the shadows. A Morgravian! This concerned them as it did much as it did the Queen.

Liryk muttered something under his breath but cut it short when he caught the warning glance from his queen. "Go on, sir, please," Valentyna urged.

The physic shivered. "Actually, I will take that seat, highness, if I may. I'm not used to such wild rides at night." He smiled nervously and sat, feeling the fire's heat.

"And a cup of something, Physic, please," she replied, motioning toward Krell, who obliged.

The doctor took the cup and swallowed its contents; the powerful liquor offered an almost instant revival. He cleared his throat and looked back to his sovereign.

"She is the Lady Aleda Donal of Felrawthy."

A stunned silence claimed the chamber before Physic Geryld found himself lifted in a firm, unshakable grip.

"Where is Brackstead?" a young man implored, his tone just short of threatening.

"Who, sir, are you?" the doctor asked, confused and still a little dazed.

"I am the Duke of Felrawthy, the dying woman's son."

Valentyna restored some measure of calm to the chamber. "Let him finish, Crys, please," she cautioned.

"My apologies, Physic Geryld," Crys murmured, setting the man back down in his seat.

"It's all right," Physic Geryld assured, taking the young Duke's hand. "Son, it's for you alone that she clings to life. She needs to know that you are alive . . . safe. We must go, now." He struggled to his feet. "Highness, there is more to tell."

Valentyna steeled herself. She was not sure how many more shocks she could handle after the last few days. All of them led back to the hateful man she was to marry. The notion threatened to overwhelm her again—as it did every time she permitted it space in her thoughts. She fought it back. There was time still . . . for what, she did not know, but time anyway before she would have to face him again, say his name, take her vows.

"Tell us, sir, and then we must make immediate arrangements to leave for Brackstead."

Physic Geryld nodded. He was beginning to think more clearly now that the liquor had worked its special enchantments. "Yes, yes, at once, your highness."

"Celimus will know she has survived," Elspyth muttered.

Both Liryk and Krell individually wished they could silence the woman of Yentro. She was too poisonous to have around the Queen. This whole situation was turning more dangerous by the minute.

"Your majesty, please," Krell counseled softly.

She nodded. "Everyone be still," Valentyna demanded. "I need to think." She looked toward the doctor. "Is that all you have to tell us, sir?" she said kindly, not wanting to push him too far.

"One final item, your highness, which I am charged by Lady Donal to bring to you."

Valentyna nodded, deliberately expressionless so her anxieties would not betray her. "What is it, Physic?"

"I know not, highness. She would not say. Her words were for me to tell you that what she has sent is proof that you are marrying a madman . . . or words to that effect," he said awkwardly, embarrassed now.

Liryk rolled his eyes and Krell shut his with despair.

"Where is this proof?" Valentyna asked, angry herself. The physic's harsh message touched a nerve.

Physic Geryld leaned down to pick up the leather bag he had carried in. "This is what she gave me, your majesty. I have not looked inside it."

They heard Crys gasp as he recognized the bag that had belonged to his father. Valentyna stilled him with a glare.

Liryk could not help himself. "Well, tip it out, man," he said irritably.

Crys felt sorry for the doctor, who was the cause of everyone's frustration at this moment. Crys knew precisely what was in that leather bag. They had not had time to deal with the contents during the chaos that had occurred at Felrawthy.

"Allow me, sir," Crys said. "Although I could tell you now what it is."

The Duke of Felrawthy reached inside the leather bag and pulled out the head of his most beloved brother.

"This is Alyd Donal, your highness, what's left of him anyway after Celimus had his pleasure."

Pandemonium broke out.

Supper had come to a hasty close and Valentyna had mobilized to leave immediately for Brackstead. She insisted on meeting with the Lady Donal. After the shock of seeing Alyd Donal's remains, she felt compelled to offer her sympathies and promise this family that she would offer protection to the Donals' remaining son.

"Are you absolutely sure, Physic Geryld?" Valentyna urged on behalf of Crys.

"I am. She has only hours for this life. I will only hold you up if I come with you now, your highness," he replied

"Thank you, sir, for all you've done on my family's behalf." Crys reached down from his horse to shake the man's hand. "I won't forget you."

"She'll go to Shar happy, son, for seeing you. Just hurry and get there in time." Physic Geryld bowed to his queen who was dressed in her riding clothes and sat atop her favorite horse, who happened to be a gift from Celimus. She would need Bonny's speed tonight. Against Chancellor Krell's most earnestly delivered counsel, she was determined to ride to Brackstead.

"I beg you to leave this to our soldiers, your highness," he had beseeched earlier.

"No, Chancellor, in this matter I cannot agree," she had countered, and then said more intimately, "Krell, this woman has almost certainly given her life in order to reach me. She had no idea her son was here, so her intention was to speak with me. I am not, as perhaps you suspect, scavenging for excuses to renege on my decision. But let me tell you this, I will reconsider my position if I have firm proof that King Celimus is directly responsible for all of these deaths."

He had noted the set of her jaw. Precisely the same as her father. Nothing was going to change this decision and he was better off leaving the battle to fight another day. If he persisted now, he would surely lose. "As you wish, highness."

She softened her manner. "I am a sovereign, Krell. I musn't be closeted away and wrapped in fine linen simply because I am a queen. My father raised me to rule. Rule I will, as I see fit, and it would be imprudent of me to leave this woman to die without making an effort to grant her the audience she has given her life for."

He nodded. "Be safe, my queen."

"Liryk is bringing enough manpower to take on the Morgravian army," she said, trying to lighten his mood.

There was no smile in return. "Don't jest, highness. I hope you never face such a thing," and he bowed and removed himself.

She considered stopping him but left it. Krell was showing rare anger here, and whether or not he couched it in polite words, he was most unhappy with her. So be it. "Be true to yourself first," he father had always said. "Follow your instincts even if counsel wishes otherwise."

And that's what I'm doing, she reminded herself, *following my instincts.*

O ne small consolation for Krell and Liryk was that the Yentran woman was not riding out with them. She had taken herself off to check on Pil, muttering something about waiting for Ylena.

"I don't care what she does," Liryk had admitted privately to the Chancellor. "Just as long as she's not around to whisper in the ear of our queen."

"I can't agree more," Krell said. "I don't doubt she's been through plenty, but none of it is our concern. We must keep the Queen focused on her marriage, and this Elspyth is a serious threat to it."

Liryk snorted. "And you don't think riding off to Brackstead to hear more of Celimus's savory activities isn't?" he scoffed.

Krell ignored the sarcasm, accepting that both his and Liryk's nerves were frayed. "I can't stop her in this, Commander. Just keep her safe and bring our queen home as fast as you can."

The soldier nodded. "Hopefully the Morgravian noblewoman's already dead," he whispered. "Nothing more for her majesty to learn."

"Yes, but we still have the business with the head and if Lady Donal is still alive she's no doubt brimming with some sordid story," he said, disgusted. "This is none of our business," he added, more to himself than anyone else.

Liryk sighed. "Time to go."

"Shar guide you," Krell muttered. He did not mention to the Commander that an idea was forming in his mind. It was one laced with its own perils, but the Chancellor was feeling uncharacteristically ruffled by events. He was a man used to being in total control—both of his own emotions and of his office. Suddenly all of the activities of recent days were spinning beyond his normal reach. The Queen was making firm, independent decisions, and although she still looked to him for counsel and indeed friendship, here she was riding off impetuously, he felt, on behalf of Morgravians.

When the messenger from Celimus had first brought news of Wyl Thirsk's imminent arrival, Magnus had risked saying to Krell—when neither could imagine what in Shar's name the enemy might be doing in making a diplomatic mission—that this might indeed be an offer of marriage to Valentyna from the Prince of Morgravia. The King had said little more upon seeing Krell's startled expression, although he added that as much as it galled him to face the thought of giving Briavel's most prized and beloved jewel to Morgravia, he considered it the most inspired move either monarch might make in his reign.

Krell had not forgotten that conversation, or the look of awe on his majesty's face at the notion that peace might be possible . . . that Briavellian sons might live to old age without facing battle and that their sons could be raised never knowing the threat of war or of defeat. Krell, who had been a close friend and confidant to the King as well as a counselor, wanted to see Valor's vision come true. He did not like Celimus; for all his easy charm and grace, his honeyed words and grand style, the man was sly. His eyes were cold and calculating and something dark lurked within. In spite of this, and as much as Krell loved Valentyna, he also knew she must make this sacrifice for her people. Unlike Thirsk and the other critics, Krell did not believe Celimus would seek to destroy her majesty or her realm; he truly believed she had the ability to affect Celimus, change him . . . and begin a mighty dynasty that embraced both realms.

Krell had taken up Valor's vision and was determined to bring it to reality. The fact that he had won the Queen's cooperation and acceptance that this marriage was her duty, that he had been able to see her signature on the bottom of the parchment on its way back to Morgravia, was a balm to his troubled soul. But these new events unfurling threatened to damage the pledge of marriage irrevocably. He could not let it happen. He, Krell, would have to do something . . . at least make an effort to save the situation.

His mind was made up. Another messenger would be sent. A private one. The recipient would surely assist in easing the passage toward marriage, perhaps help him put out these fires that kept threatening to burn down the two realms' plans for peace.

As the Queen and her entourage thundered across the Werryl Bridge in a bid to reach Brackstead before the Lady Aleda breathed her last, Krell summoned a page.

"Have a courier readied at once."

"Yes, Chancellor Krell," the wide-eyed lad said. "What message shall I give him, sir?" the boy asked.

"Tell him it's a letter to Chancellor Jessom of Morgravia."

35

WYNCH WAS AS FASCINATED TO HEAR ELYSIUS'S TALE AS WYL was, and even though he felt himself fading quietly into the shadows while the conversation between his two companions continued, he knew he would drink in the details as if he were parched.

"I am Myrren's father," Elysius began "but my story begins much further back . . . when I was a youngster growing up in the far eastern province of Parrgamyn."

"Where Queen Adana was born?"

"That's right. And the cruel, cold streak that ran in that woman also ran in the bones of my younger brother. I don't know where he is—he's somewhere in Morgravia, I suspect—but I feel the malevolent swell of his magic and its dark activities."

"How did you both come to be here?"

"Our parents migrated as part of Adana's retinue when she was sent to Pearlis to marry Magnus. My father was one of her father's most trusted advisers. The King of Parrgamyn asked him to accompany the young Adana on her journey to the far southwest. My father didn't want to go—he despised the woman for her determination to wipe out those gifted with magic—but in the end he had no choice. His family was his secret, you see."

"Because you were empowered," Wyl finished.

Elysius nodded. "Yes. It came from my mother's side, but it was very strong in us boys, which is odd. It normally transfers powerfully through women, not men, but my mother told me once that there was a wildness to our magic she could not account for."

"So you came to Stoneheart."

"We didn't live there, though. Adana quietly set up a household for her own people in Soulstone."

"Oh . . . of course." Wyl said, remembering the story now. "Did she prefer the country palace of the south?"

Elysius snorted. "No. She never had a kind word for anything Morgravian. But she preferred to have her own people away from Stoneheart itself. She hated Pearlis and Morgravia's king. She had grand ideas of running separate courts; it was very obvious to all that she could hardly bear to spend any time near the King. Then Celimus came along unexpectedly and that changed her life dramatically. As I understand it, even though Magnus didn't have much time for the boy, he certainly wouldn't agree to his heir being carted off to Soulstone. He wanted him in the capital. From what I gathered from my father, this enraged Adana and life between the two royals became strained enough for us to feel its chill even all the way south."

"And how old were you by then?" Wyl asked, trying to work out Elysius's age.

"We were lads. I was sixteen, my brother fourteen." He sighed softly. "Myrren's mother was so much older than I. In light of what it has cost me, I wish I had never set eyes on her during one of those rare visits we made to Pearlis with our father. He was often called upon to advise Adana, but he did not like us boys coming into the city with him."

"Was he worried about you?"

"Not about me. About Rashlyn." Wyl sat forward, his mouth suddenly dry. Elysius saw the change in his guest's demeanor immediately. "What's wrong?"

"You said Rashlyn?"

The man nodded.

"I've met him."

It was Elysius's turn to be surprised. "I lost trace of him when I was banished."

Wyl ignored the startling statement. "He works for the King of the Razors."

The man's eyes narrowed. "Cailech!" Elysius declared, quietly shocked. "So that's where he is. What use is he to the Mountain King?"

"Plenty, apparently. He bears the title of barshi, I gather, which means wise or magic man in the old tongue of the north. He and the King are close. But more than that, I sense your brother has a somewhat unhealthy hold over the King."

Elysius bared his horse teeth in a grimace. "My brother will work out a way to control him. Rashlyn is very dangerous. He is the reason I appear to you in this guise."

"Guise?"

The Manwitch smiled ruefully. "There's so much to tell you," he said, realizing his tale was disjointed, leaping from one amazing fact to another. "I was actually quite a handsome sort once. Tall and strong. Myrren's mother, Emil, was a fine-looking woman whom I met while running a couple of messages to her husband, who was physic to Adana. He was older than her by a number of years and I think she found herself lacking in amorous activity, you could say." He grinned. "She was attracted to me from the moment we met—I could tell." He shrugged. "And what young man would say no? She possessed a brilliant scholar's mind too."

Wyl's eyes widened with understanding and he glanced

toward Fynch, whose attention was riveted on their host. "And she became pregnant," he stated.

"Immediately. It only happened once," Elysius admitted. "But then she became obsessed with me. It was sad. I do believe she actually loved me and in a way I her, although there was no future for us. My father discovered the truth and was horrified—not just because of my indiscretion— but there was the threat of passing my abilities on to a child, you see."

"Which you did."

"Only marginally. Myrren was not a witch in the true sense, Wyl. She had some powers, mainly of the healing sort, and if she'd had the chance to follow in her father's footsteps—I mean the man she called father—she would have been very talented at medicine."

Wyl was astonished to hear this. "Not a witch! But the gift?"

"Is all my doing. I channeled through Myrren."

"As you channel through Knave?" Fynch chimed in, his first words in such a long time that his host had all but forgotten the quiet lad.

Elysius nodded. "Yes, son. That's right, as I use Knave to be my eyes and body elsewhere."

Wyl sat back, speechless. He had truly believed Myrren to be a witch, and ever since Knave had revealed his mysterious powers, Wyl had convinced himself that Myrren had possessed magics she had managed to keep secret for years. He said as much.

Her father shook his head sadly. "She was innocent, poor child."

Still trying to absorb this revelation, Wyl pressed on. "But why me?"

Elysius shrugged. "You were the only one who showed her any pity that day. She did not deserve to die, especially not as she did. That young woman never exercised her weak powers on anything but doing good for others. If not for her eyes, which she unluckily inherited from her great-grandmother, no one would have been any the wiser. I was angry, Wyl. She wanted revenge on those who hurt her and I wanted to give her that."

"So you used me."

He nodded. "I could tell you were the only person in that chamber who possessed nobility in the true sense of the word. I could count on you."

"To do what?" Wyl asked, his voice rising in rare anger.

"To kill the man who crafted her death," Elysius answered quietly.

"Lymbert?" Wyl said, aghast.

Elysius shook his head. "Lymbert was only the instrument."

"As I understand it, then, Lord Rokan called for her death," Wyl continued, his anger still high. "And Magnus permitted it."

Once again the Manwitch demurred. "Neither of them. Yes, they were responsible, but they were not the key to Myrren's suffering. One person alone encouraged the King to sign her warrant. One person alone enjoyed her agony more than any."

"Celimus," Fynch whispered from the corner.

They both looked toward the boy and Elysius nodded. "Yes, Celimus. I heard him talking, boasting about how he had coerced his father into allowing the torture and trial."

Wyl's mind felt like tangled threads. "How did you hear it?"

"Through Myrren. You were there also, Wyl, but I think you were too young, too alarmed, perhaps, to concentrate on the prince bragging to those gathered."

"No . . . no, I do remember now. The priest was saying a final prayer and above it Celimus was boasting that the trial had been his idea," Wyl recalled, frowning.

"That's right. And then Myrren singled him out, demanding to know why a prince of the realm would be present for such mummery."

"And he said it was in the name of education, using me as his excuse," Wyl followed up despairingly, remembering it all again as if it had been yesterday.

"Myrren sensed your hatred for the Prince, Wyl. She might not have been endowed with pure magic, but her powers gave her a highly developed perception of others—it allowed her to see you, look into you. My daughter knew you were true and that you despised the young man who had forced you to watch the ugly proceedings. She learned who you were that day and knew that you had the ear of the King and the status that could wield power. She chose you. But it was I who used you, son. Forgive me. If I could take it back, I would."

"You can't?" Wyl asked plaintively. He had secretly harbored the hope the Manwitch could reverse the gift.

Elysius shook his large head with deep regret. "No. It must run its course."

"What course?" Wyl cried, not understanding, Ylena's voice ascending in tone. He hated to hear himself.

Their host pursed his wide lips and stood, clearly upset. He began clearing the table. Wyl's temper flared and boiled over.

"Leave it!" he cried, reaching for the man's curiously elongated arms. "I must know!"

Elysius looked down at where Ylena's fingers dug cruelly into his arm, where the pressure of her anger had chased away the blood to leave blanched spots.

Wyl pulled her arm away as if stung. "Forgive me, Elysius. This is a burden . . . a . . . a curse," he moaned, feeling the full strain of Myrren's Gift.

The little man returned to his clearing and silence spread uneasily about the large room in which they ate, punctuated only by the clank of dishes. Wyl sat glumly while Fynch maintained his quiet. Elysius busied himself making a pot of tea and soon the silence eased itself into something less awkward and more comfortable. Elysius sat himself closer this time when he returned to the table and surprised Wyl by taking Ylena's uncared for, yet still-elegant hands between his two enormous palms. His eyes, now sightless, seemed to regard Wyl all the same.

"There is nothing to forgive, son. The apology is all mine.

I deeply regret all the terrible events that have occurred and wish I could change the magic that is within you, but I can't. Once cast, it is its own master. No one controls it."

"But how do I stop it?" This time Wyl's voice held nothing but helplessness. Fynch had to look away, unable to bear the look of defeat on Ylena's face or his own sense of loss at this news.

"It will stop," Elysius answered gravely.

Fynch held his breath at the words and watched Wyl lift Ylena's head to search his host's face. "Tell me how," he whispered.

It was Elysius who could not hold his guest's gaze this time. "It will stop when you become the person you are meant to be. Who Myrren wanted you to be." Wyl swallowed. He thought he already knew the answer; did not want to believe it. Elysius spoke the words Wyl did not want to hear. "The sovereign of Morgravia."

Wyl's emotions were not his to command at this moment and he let out a long, shrill cry of such deep despair that Fynch began to weep softly in his corner.

"No," Wyl begged. "Please, Elysius."

The man of magic held his large head low. "I'm so sorry."

When Wyl pushed the chair away and disappeared out of the chamber's door, Elysius told Fynch to let him be. "The dog will go with him. Wyl can come to no harm in the Wild with Knave nearby."

It was hours before Wyl returned, subdued but composed. Elysius knew he had not gone far, barely steps from the small dwelling he had built himself many years ago. He understood Wyl's need to be alone, to come to terms with the confusion and the terror.

Fynch had long ago been carried to bed, sleeping in the same cot Wyl had used earlier. It was still not dawn.

"I imagine you have questions for me," Elysius said gently. "Put on the pot, we'll have another jar of tea each, I think." And as Wyl silently moved to oblige, Elysius added, "I'll tease up the fire again."

Knave padded up quietly to steal a warm spot. Water was set to heat while the embers were prodded and encouraged to flame again. New kindling erupted into larger flames and a fresh log was thrown on. Satisfied, the Manwitch made himself comfortable in the creaking rocking chair he had also crafted.

"Ask me," Elysius said. He could feel the barrage of queries stored up in Wyl's mind.

"How do you see?"

"I use others. Knave is my favorite, but I can use birds or other beasts. I am deaf, too, Wyl. Others are my ears."

"People?"

"Only if I'm prepared to open my magic to them."

"Which you aren't, I gather."

"Rarely. It's too dangerous. Animals take nothing from me."

"But you used Myrren for this purpose," Wyl accused.

"Only during her incarceration, so on two occasions, and yes, I had to relinquish some of my powers to her. She took just enough to dull the pain of her torture."

Wyl nodded, seemingly satisfied with that line of questioning. "Your brother. I gather from what you've said that he has made you look this way," he said, trying hard not to give offense with his words.

"Yes."

"Why?"

"Because I believe he hated me."

"Why?"

"I would not share the secret of communicating with beasts or birds. It was evident to me from a very young age that Rashlyn was unstable." Elysius scratched his large chin. "More than that, in truth. I knew Rashlyn was mad. And he was cruel beyond imagining as a child. As he matured, he became worse."

His curiosity piqued, Wyl could not help but ask more about the strange, dark little man in the mountains. "Why didn't he possess the secret you did?"

"We have different skills. Mine are based in nature and living things. He has . . . well, other talents. His magic is what I would call black. It is frightening, and with his twisted mind wielding it, it would be the darkest of weapons."

"But he could learn your magic?"

"Oh yes," the Manwitch answered. "As I could his. He offered me all of it—every answer to every question—if I'd give him the secret of the beasts."

"Why did he want this so badly?"

"To command them, I suspect."

"To do what?"

Elysius smiled, but there was no mirth in it. "He would rule the land if he could."

Wyl looked at him incredulously. "You mean as a sovereign . . . a usurper."

"Beyond. Why not Emperor? Why not Lord High King of the three realms, just for a start. He would look to Parrgamyn and further. With all that power at his disposal, he could control all of us."

"Why hasn't he tried to do something like this already. Surely if he can call up storms, he can wreak all sorts of havoc."

Elysius nodded thoughtfully. "I think my brother is losing his wits. I noticed it all those years ago when we were still together. There would be periods when he was not lucid."

"He's mad—is that what you mean?"

"Insane. I sense his madness is getting worse. And he will know this, of course, so I suspect he will seek to influence instead and this is perhaps why we now find him in the Razors working with Cailech. You said you sensed that he had an unhealthy control over the Mountain King. This is likely Rashlyn beginning to exercise his dark influence over a powerful man. If he can control Cailech, he can wreak havoc."

"Was he like this as a younger man?"

"He could not control me—my mind was closed to him. Rashlyn always did crave power but never had it. Youngest son, you see. And as much as my father was uncomfortable with our powers, he loved me and I him. His relationship with Rashlyn was strained from early childhood. My father sensed the darkness in his youngest son, often talked to me about it and whether I could somehow work my powers on my brother to stem his powers."

"Why didn't you?"

Elysius cringed somewhat. "It seemed cruel at the time. He had so little going for him and I seemed to have it all. But as we got older I realized my mistake and by then it was too late. He was far too suspicious of me. I'm surprised he took as long as he did to exercise his power over me, to tell the truth. We had little love for each other."

"Could you not"—Wyl searched for the right words—"prevent him from using his magics on you?"

"Shield myself from his powers, you mean?"

"I don't know what would be the right expression," Wyl admitted.

"It has taken me years to learn his 'scent.' That's how I describe magic, being able to sense the wielder's characteristics."

"And so you can—what, feel him using his powers?"

"You could describe it that way, yes," Elysius replied. "He is up to dark things, Wyl, and it bodes badly for all of us . . . all of Morgravia and Briavel, even for the Mountain Kingdom he ostensibly serves."

"Can he sense you?"

"Perhaps. I don't know. He thinks I'm dead, remember, and I use my magic fleetingly these days. I also suspect that the use in my magic out in the Wild is somehow masked. The Thicket filters sentient activity. I can sense him, in other words, but he can't sense me."

"Why wouldn't he have recognized me in Koreldy's form?"

"Because of the Thicket . . . it has subtle powers, most of which even I am not privy to. It is my belief that it has protected you."

Wyl had the feeling that Elysius was not being entirely forthright but decided it was more urgent to focus on the central details of Elysius's story. Rashlyn was not important to Wyl—or so it seemed to him—and he pressed on to get the full tale of Elysius's finding himself in the Wild. "So tell me what happened after your father asked you to stem your brother's magic."

"I lied and said that I couldn't. I was too young and stupid to realize how that would come back and bite me. My father's relationship with Rashlyn was nonexistent by the end."

"The end?"

"Yes, sorry, we've been jumping about, haven't we? After my father discovered my relationship with Emil, he banished me to Parrgamyn, to live without my family. Leaving Morgravia, our home, was punishment enough, but to be without my family—he knew how much it would hurt. My parents did not know that Emil was pregnant, of course, but Rashlyn suspected as much. He also guessed that I wouldn't return to our place of birth permanently. I rather liked Morgravia and I especially enjoyed the south, where it's green and filled with meadows and woodland. Parrgamyn is more arid, you see." Wyl nodded. "Anyway, in my anger I carelessly boasted to Rashlyn that I would jump ship and escape back into Morgravia. I recklessly thought he might help. Quite the opposite, he began to blackmail me. He threatened to tell our father of my intention unless I gave him the secret of the beasts." Elysius laughed, but there was little amusement in it. "I refused to relinquish the secret, despite his threat."

"So what happened?" Wyl prompted.

"I had given my parents the promise that I would return to Parrgamyn, but I had every intention of returning to Morgravia after a suitable period. I think my father knew this but chose not to acknowledge it. And so I dutifully took the ship home from Brightstone, but we'd barely gotten out of the port into the deeper waters to sail around the Razors toward Grenadyn when Rashlyn wove a brilliantly dark and evil concoction of spells to capsize the ship I was on. I imagine he hoped I would drown with the rest of the unfortunates on that sailing—ninety souls were lost that day—but I miraculously remained afloat, although the freezing waters of the north would have surely killed me. With my last remaining strength,

I summoned a wind and cast my luck with it. I remember very little of that wild night, but when I regained consciousness, I had washed up on a tiny beach in the far north.

"But this is how cunning Rashlyn is, Wyl. He took the precaution that should I survive, I would never be able to live in a normal society again. He cast his second devastating spell." Elysius sighed. "Death would have been easier and my brother knew this; he understood my love for poetry and literature, knew I would suffer without the social contact I thrived on."

"And this is the result of his work . . . this guise you wear?"

Elysius nodded. "A sea eagle showed me through her eyes how I now appeared. And I had lost my sense of sight, hearing, taste, smell." Elysius fixed his nonseeing gaze on a faraway spot and recalled that difficult time. "With the sea eagle's help, I navigated my way into the foothills of the Razors, and then using a variety of animals for my lost senses, I skirted the mountains for several weeks. I was in shock—I had nowhere to go and was so terrified of being seen that I had to avoid all humanity. My friends, the animals, whispered to me of a place—an enchanted place—called the Wild, where no person dared go. I begged them to take me there . . . and so they did. I've lived here since."

"The spell cannot be lifted?"

"Not with any magic I own," he answered ruefully, "though I have tried, Wyl, I have tried."

"We are both cursed, then."

"You speak true," Elysius admitted. "You are only the third person I have met since I came here."

"And Fynch is the second, so that means . . . ah, yes, of course, Emil. I remember now, the Boatkeeper gave me her name, but I didn't make the connection . . . so Myrren's mother came to you?"

"Yes. She braved the Thicket and the Darkstream to find me."

"How did she know where to find you if everyone thought you were lost?"

"I shouldn't have but I used a seer I knew to seek her out."

"Widow Ilyk!" Wyl cried, hushing himself for fear of waking Fynch.

The Manwitch nodded. "I knew she was safe to use because her powers were weak. Whatever enhancement I added by opening myself up to her would not make her dangerous—I believed she would take only what she needed to make herself more skilled in her craft."

Wyl wrapped Ylena's thin arms about her elbows and shivered. "Tell me about the widow."

"Well, she and I had met on several occasions during a couple of her visits through the southern region and once in Pearlis. I had always liked her and so I took the chance. I cast myself wide and was able to reach out and find her. Naturally, she was amazed to hear my voice in her head, but she was a believer of magic, so I suppose she overcame her fright rapidly. She agreed to find Emil and give her a message. And in return she took some of my power—not very much, she was not greedy—which allowed her to become very gifted with her sight."

Wyl sipped the strongly brewed tea. "Extraordinary."

"Emil came. She was shocked, terrified, of course, by the state I was in. I learned of my daughter and she learned that the child she bore me might be cursed with the same magics. She could neither bear to look upon me nor stay longer than the hour she already had. All my hopes of finding some love or companionship again evaporated the moment I saw the revulsion in her face. With some help from me she was able to navigate her way back through the Thicket safely without the Boatkeeper noting her return, and I have had no further contact with her. I'm presuming she never told anyone that I was still alive."

Wyl shook his head. "I imagine not. How did Myrren react to learning the man she called father was not her real one."

Elysius grimaced. "It was as if she'd suspected as much all her life and yet how could she have? Nevertheless, she took the news calmly when I finally found the courage to speak with her in the dungeon—it felt almost like relief, in fact, to tell her the truth. The next time we spoke, it was very brief, and occurred after her torture, so she was near enough dead anyway. She told me she wanted vengeance on the Prince through you. I think she believed you might relish it. I could not refuse her."

"Her gift seems to be more suited to her uncle's magic, if you don't mind my saying so, although I'm presuming you both share some powers."

"You're right on both counts. There are certain skills we can both wield. And it might be that Myrren did inherit some of our combined magic and that when she took my power, she corrupted it with the sort of dark twist Rashlyn would use. She made the conditions of the gift, not I. I simply channeled her the power to achieve her desire."

"And so I have no choice in this. My destiny is mapped out," Wyl said into the gloom of the dying embers.

"You also have no choice in making it happen, Wyl. Remember this, you cannot force death. It does not work that way. Myrren's Gift has its own momentum, its own force, you could say. You do not control it; it controls you."

Wyl shook his head. "So if I asked Celimus to stick his blade in my belly, the gift won't work."

Elysius shook his head slowly. "What's more, it will make you pay a penalty. Those were my conditions—I couldn't have you running around begging influential people to kill you. Now that I know you, I realize you would never do such a thing. Power is not what you crave. You cannot welcome death through someone else and thus maneuver it to your own ends. The gift is subject to the whims and fancies of the world around it."

"What do you mean?"

"Well, I do not use my power for dark purposes, and this vengeance—which I was obliged to provide—had a blackness to it that went against the spirit of my magic. So I made sure that although you could not control the gift yourself, it was subject to choice."

"Other people's choices, you mean?"

"Exactly. Death must visit you because the perpetrator decides it, not because you or the gift does. People will influence how the magic applies itself, in other words."

"And that made it all right in your mind?" Wyl asked, aghast, his tone leaden with disgust.

Elysius felt his anger and frustration. "It made it easier, Wyl, that's all. I thought that if others had some choice in the matter, you might be spared."

Wyl laughed humorlessly. "And as you can see, I've been spared a lot of suffering."

Elysius remained quiet. He had no words of comfort to offer.

"And it will stop when I rule Morgravia?" Wyl said into the thick silence.

"Yes. This I do know; it was Myrren's greatest desire that Wyl Thirsk rule the realm that caused her death."

"Because she knows I'll stop the persecution of witches once and for all?"

"Because you'll stop torturing any souls, including the persecution of empowered people," Elysius said softly.

Wyl sighed. "Of course she wouldn't have known that the same King who permitted her death would campaign to stamp out the Zerques and the persecution. She could have saved me a lot of trauma."

Elysius nodded. "Magnus was a good king even though he allowed my daughter to die."

"Elysius, is there anything good about your daughter's gift to me?"

"Only one thing—an odd one, too. Myrren was determined that any child of yours would truly be yours."

Wyl frowned, confused.

"I think she was understandably feeling very sorry for herself in that dungeon, realizing that the father she had grown up loving was not her father and her true one was some sort of freak living in the fabled Wild. Her head was probably spinning. Anyway, she threw it in as an afterthought and I respected her wishes when I crafted the magic."

"But what does that mean?"

Elysius shrugged. "It means that when you father an heir to the throne of Morgravia, no matter whose body encloses you, the child will truly have Thirsk blood running in its veins."

It was a cold comfort for Wyl but a comfort nonetheless in an otherwise cheerless tale.

36

ALEDA HAD SLEPT AS DEEPLY AS THE DOCTOR HAD PREDICTED. When she surfaced it was into a dulled confusion; she did not recognize where she was, but there was a woman staring at her.

She felt weak; knew her time was upon her.

"Welcome back," the woman murmured, her expression one of relief.

"Where am I?"

"Safe. In a town called Brackstead."

"Briavel?" Aleda asked anxiously.

The woman soothed her. "Yes. My name is Bel. Let me help you to sit up. You need to drink this—all of it." She held out a mug.

"What's this?"

"A special tea. Physic Geryld insists. I'll tell you about him."

Images flooded back as her mind cleared. "Did he go to Werryl!"

"Hush," Bel said. "Physic Geryld rode to Werryl for help."

"I have to find my son," Aleda whimpered.

"You're in no state to do anything." Bel did not want to

tell her that she probably would never leave this bed. "Let's wait for news from the capital."

Aleda already knew her fate. She was too weak to sit up. "If I can last that long. I can feel that the bleeding's begun again."

"You must hold on," Bel urged. "Please. Drink."

Aleda struggled with a few sips and then let her head fall back onto the pillow.

"You must keep drinking the tea if you want to live," Bel urged, terrified of losing the woman and being blamed for a noble's death.

"I have nothing to live for. My family is dead, murdered." Aleda groaned.

Bel fell into an awkward silence and hoped it would encourage the noblewoman to sleep again. She might even have dozed herself until a noise disturbed her.

"Riders!" she said, sitting up.

There was a cacophony of voices, excited ones from below. Then footsteps, a man's tread, heavy and eager, thundering up the stairs. The door burst open.

"Mother!" Crys cried, his voice thick with emotion, and then he was across the room in a few strides, his head buried in his mother's arms as a smile of pure joy stretched across the older woman's face.

"My boy." She was so weak, she could only whisper. "You made it."

Valentyna was not far behind Crys. Bel, in her excitement and confusion, did not recognize the Queen. She was summarily excused by Liryk, who also pushed into the room.

Crys wept into Aleda's chest only momentarily, sensing that he would lose her very soon. He looked up into the face that had always made him feel safe and loved. "Pil found us, told us . . . Elspyth made me ride to Briavel rather than home."

She could see his despair at having to make that decision, wondering whether he could have saved his family if he'd ridden in the other direction. "You chose right, thank Shar for Elspyth's clear head. You live, Crys, and you are now

Duke of Felrawthy. Make that count." She refused to dissolve into the tears she felt were determined to fall. "They never gave us a chance, were sent by Celimus to slaughter us. You would be dead too. But you must fight back now, son. Rally an army, as Ylena advised, and make that treacherous sovereign of ours pay for what he's done to this family and to the Thirsks."

Crys heard the fighting words and marveled that his mother could set aside all her pain and loss in her final moments of life to talk to him about duty. He could almost hear his fine father's voice joining hers, urging him to live up to the family name of Felrawthy, this time fighting against, rather than for, the Crown. It was a chilling thought.

"I love you," was all he could say to his mother, and then she died with the bittersweet joy that her son lived and Celimus might yet face retribution.

At first the commotion was only about the sudden arrival of Briavellian soldiers. The folk of Brackstead were thrilled to see the purple and emerald colors so rich and bright on a murky early spring morning. Then word got around that no less than Commander Liryk was in town. Whatever was happening at the Lucky Bowman was obviously of great import to have the highest-ranking soldier in the realm descend upon it without warning.

"It's to do with the stranger," Bel offered knowingly to any who would give her an ear. She had been thanked soundly for her time and paid handsomely, then asked to leave. "I should know, I was asked to look after her. She's noble for sure and with a Morgravian accent. What she's doing traveling alone is anyone's guess, although that youngblood who suddenly appeared was apparently her son," she said, nodding as if she had solved the puzzle. It became obvious that Bel knew very little more when she was unable to answer further questions; nonetheless she enjoyed far closer attention than she was used to as the locals clamored for news.

When an observant onlooker suggested he was sure it had

been their young queen riding into town and leaping off her horse with long-legged agility, the tempo of the conversation increased to near-boiling point. Such high excitement had not been experienced in Brackstead since King Valor himself had dropped in for an ale on his way back to Werryl from the north three years back.

Confirmation had to be sought. Bel considered it her duty, now that she had been elevated to such stellar heights, and she accosted the irritated keeper whose inn had been suddenly cleared of its downstairs patrons by soldiers and official-looking people storming room four upstairs.

"Just tell us, Nan," Bel urged. "Or I'll never be able to get them to leave this place," she added, conspiratorially, as if she had immense sway over the townfolk.

Nan remained tight-lipped only for a moment longer before realizing that her friend was right. A crowd would keep gathering and would disrupt the proceedings if she did not come clean. "Yes, yes, all right. It is her."

Bel swung around to the waiting people. "It's true! Our queen is here!"

A roar went up and Nan understood all too clearly her mistake. The frenzy was too high, no one would leave. Her admission had only made it worse, as runners were sent off to take messages to more of the townfolk.

She sighed. "Reduced-price ale for everyone, but it's served outside," she said to Bel. "Anyone not drinking will have to leave," she warned. "I might as well make myself a penny or two if you're all going to clog my path." More cheers as Bel passed on this news. "But, Bel, you'd better keep them still for now. They've asked for quiet and that's from the top."

The woman's eyes widened with excitement. As she turned to relay the instructions to an eager audience, Nan stomped back inside and dropped a curtsy to Commander Liryk, who happened to be blocking her way.

"Sir, I've done my best, but they're not leaving until they see her . . . er, sir. I've offered some ale and they in turn have promised quiet."

"Thank you," he said gruffly.

He had no doubt Valentyna would oblige the crowd and took one more look around to ensure that all entrances were guarded and all windows blocked by burly men. Once satisfied, he turned his attention to the inn's common room, where he watched the sovereign of Briavel nod at something the Morgravian Duke had said to her. She was resting her hand on his arm, no doubt offering condolences, and he appeared composed—stoic, in fact—Liryk noticed, which was to be expected from a duke of the realm.

"Please, Crys, be at ease. The regret is mine that I did not have the chance to meet her, offer my thanks," Liryk heard her say. "She brought proof, that's enough," she added, and the Commander of Briavel had to wonder what this new turn of events would mean for the realm and its hopes of uniting with Morgravia.

Crys Donal was hiding his grief admirably. His father would be proud. Hearing himself named Duke of Felrawthy was still a bitter sound to his ear and he reminded the Queen to address him by his given name rather than the formal one, even in this company.

He was glad she had obliged so readily and could hardly believe how adeptly Valentyna had turned the awkward situation of finding herself in an inn in rural Briavel, with a Morgravian duke in her company, into something easy and comfortable. Her ability to put people at ease was a true skill. She had used it well with himself, Pil, and Elspyth when they had turned up so unexpectedly with such shattering news, and she was using it again now to ensure that everyone remained calm and talking.

He watched her stretching out stiff limbs and yawning, issuing requests for food and warm drinks, making everyone relax. It was a very deliberate and calculated move and he admired her judgment and stored it away as something he must acquire. His father had tended toward a more authoritarian style of managing his people. Crys appreciated the pragmatic way Valentyna dealt with those around her. She remained very much in control—she was a sovereign, after all—but she listened to people, and even in the short time he had known her, Crys could tell that she strived to ensure that everyone's needs were attended to. He listened as the older soldier stepped up to mention to her majesty about meeting with the townfolk; she nodded and said something back before the man moved aside, and Crys knew that she had agreed to do what would please her people without considering her own fatigue.

She turned toward Crys. "I haven't yet told you how sorry I am," she said, taking his hand.

"At least I saw her . . . had the chance to hold her as she died," he said bravely. "Which is more than I could do for my father or brothers."

"Don't torture yourself," the Queen said sagely. "I'm speaking from experience. It makes no difference and doesn't bring them back. You must now take up where your fine father has left off."

He smiled. "As you had to."

He sensed the sadness in the soft smile she gave back. He felt as if he were the only person in the room with her. "Yes. And his boots felt very large indeed at first. Allow yourself to make mistakes; forgive yourself when you do. And follow your instincts, Crys. I have no doubt your parents have groomed you all your life to take on this challenge, as my father groomed me. The know-how doesn't come easily, but we're more ready than either of us admits, I'm sure."

It felt to Crys as though something snapped into place in his mind. Valentyna knew precisely what to say. She made him feel strong when the detracting voices in his head were doing their best to weaken him.

"Thank you," he said, wishing he could kiss her, and not just out of gratitude. The same voices told him to get that idea out of his head immediately.

"You're welcome," she replied. "And no matter what happens, Briavel will always be a friend to the duchy of Felrawthy."

And with that final comment, which lifted his spirits and

filled his heart with hope, Crys watched the Queen of Briavel release his hand and call for a hearty breakfast to be served once she had had the opportunity to say hello to the people of Brackstead and apologize for the lack of warning about her visit.

Her comment regarding the need for food made people nearby grin. It was a well-known fact in Briavel that their Queen, despite her lean figure, possessed a fierce appetite. The Guards loved her for it all the more, for on many nights she would stroll onto the battlements and never failed to show interest in what was on for supper. Moreover she was happy to crouch with them and share a small bite of whatever they were eating or drink a mug of ale with them. And somehow it never felt unseemly; she had the knack of making everyone feel comfortable about her presence while never relinquishing her grace or regal bearing.

Later, over breakfast, they spoke of the horrid tale Physic Geryld had related.

Crys shook his head. "The hide, the timing . . . it all fits. That area would also be the logical place to do the ugly work of burying my family in the pit and later burning bodies." He did not want to say that not so far away was buried the corpse of Faryl of Coombe—a spot especially chosen for its remoteness. It seemed Celimus's mercenaries had selected well.

Valentyna put her face in her hands. From behind them she sighed. "You're quite sure it was the King."

"I wasn't there, highness, so I cannot be absolutely sure. However, all the shocking events that led up to this—from Alyd's death to Wyl Thirsk's death, the slaughter at Rittylworth, the pursuit of Ylena, even the sending away of Gueryn le Gant, and now the destruction of my family, seem to be rolling together into one nasty campaign from a new king determined to stamp out any threat to his power. He must be demented if he feared my father—there was no more loyal subject to the Crown than Felrawthy, other than perhaps Argorn. And yet Celimus has done his utmost to destroy both the great loyalists. He thinks he's achieved his desire, but I live to fight on and this time it won't be for him. It will be against him."

And herself, Valentyna thought miserably, should she marry Celimus? "So your mother brought the—pardon me for mentioning it again—the remains of your brother to me. Who gave them to your family?"

"Alyd's head was left with the monks by a man called Romen Koreldy." He saw the Queen react to the name. "Do you know him?"

Valentyna nodded. "I do. He's dead, though, no use to any of us." She tried to make her words sound offhand, but they came out forlornly. "I'm pleased he rescued Ylena Thirsk."

Crys dared not explain Ylena's fate.

"Where is she now, do you think?"

The lie came easily, as Wyl had instructed. "As we said, she was taken away at the same time as we left by a man called Aremys Farrow, who promised to get her to safety. He's a Grenadyne . . . knew Koreldy apparently." He saw the Queen's brow furrow in thought and knew her next question. "Apparently Koreldy asked Farrow to look in on Ylena at Rittylworth." Crys shrugged, hoping he was being convincing. "I suppose when he saw what had happened, he came looking for her. Presumably Koreldy had mentioned that she'd married one of the Donals."

"So where do you think he would he have taken her?" Valentyna persisted.

"Aremys cautioned that it would be too dangerous for any of us to know where they were headed. Celimus might target yet more death and destruction."

The Queen nodded. "It seems so." She was thinking of the note Elspyth had brought, but her thoughts were disrupted by a new voice joining the conversation.

Liryk cleared his throat nearby. "I don't think we should jump to any conclusions, your highness."

"No?" the Queen said. "How can you look me square in the eye, Commander, and tell me otherwise regarding the man I'm supposed to marry?" She instantly regretted her barb, knowing it was wrong of her to belittle this good Briavellian in front of strangers, Morgravians especially. "I'm sorry, Commander Liryk," she hurriedly followed up. "You're right, of course. I must think about what I've heard." The damage was done, though. The old soldier looked mortified and did not acknowledge her contriteness. Valentyna could do nothing to repair his injured ego at present. Instead she stood. "Well, there is nothing more we can do here. We travel for Werryl immediately. Liryk, please make arrangements for the Lady Aleda to be transported into the palace chapel, where Crys will have the opportunity to pray to Shar for his mother's soul."

"Thank you, your highness," Crys murmured.

"I wish I could do more," Valentyna responded, standing to make arrangements for departure.

37

REMYS WAITED OUTSIDE THE GREAT DOORS THAT LED INTO Cailech's private rooms. He had finally remembered his identity, but not much else, although tantalizing glimmers of further information teased at his mind. He believed it would be only a matter of time before his memory was fully restored; until then, he decided he would feign full amnesia.

For now he was Cullyn and he would need his wits about him. Myrt had cautioned him not to play the innocent victim with the King. Aremys, despite his damaged memory, retained sufficient knowledge to remind him that Cailech was known as the Fox of Grenadyn . . . and for good reason. He would heed his new friend's warning.

Myrt emerged. "The King will see you now. Remember what I said."

Aremys nodded and followed the mountain man into the vast, light-filled chamber, warmed by an open fire at one end. He was entranced by the view.

"This is Cullyn, my lord, although that is not his real name," Myrt said, nodding toward a yellow-haired man who sat at the end of a table, eating.

Aremys turned back from the breathtaking scene beyond the tall windows and bowed low. Royalty made him feel anxious, but this King looked anything but regal. No pretentiousness at all about the man. He wore no outward signs of his status as he stood to greet Aremys, wiping his hands on his breeches,

"Welcome, Cullyn . . . or whatever your name is," he said.

"King Cailech, I'm honored," Aremys replied, straightening from his bow.

He had height and width on the King, but then Aremys had these on most men. This one, however, was not in any way cowed by his size. If anything, he was amazed.

"Haldor's arse, but you're huge, man," Cailech admitted good-naturedly. "A Grenadyne, I hear?"

"Yes, my lord. We think so." Aremys grinned. "Apparently my accent gives me away. Plus, I held my sword in a Grenadyne fashion. It seems I understand Northernish and . . . well, I just know I'm not from Morgravia or Briavel."

"So what were you doing in the Razors just north of the Briavellian border?" Cailech inquired, going straight to the point.

Aremys shrugged, genuinely baffled. "I cannot tell you, my lord. Not yet anyway. I'm hoping my memories will not stay blurred for long."

Cailech held his gaze, granite-faced. It was a test, Aremys knew, and much as he felt inclined to look away from that searching scrutiny, he forced himself to hold the penetrating stare.

"And you fight like a soldier. You're good, I hear."

Aremys was not sure how to answer. "It's instinctive, my lord. I don't remember any training, although I suspect there must have been some in my past. Yes, sire. I am good."

"A mercenary, perhaps?"

He nodded this time. "That's probably true," he agreed. "I've been thinking as much myself."

"Join me," the King said.

Aremys was taken aback. One moment Cailech was interrogating him, the next inviting him to eat with him. He sat. "Thank you," he replied, confused. "But I'm not hungry."

The King gestured that it was of no matter. He resumed his meal and nodded to someone who immediately poured Aremys some wine. "Try this, it's my favorite," Cailech encouraged.

He did and it was delicious. Aremys told the King as much. "I'm fairly certain I haven't tasted white wine of such a crisp, fresh flavor in years. The south favors the red grape."

The King nodded. "It was also Romen Koreldy's favorite," Cailech said conversationally.

"Oh? Koreldy . . ." Aremys frowned. "Who is he, my lord?"

"I thought you knew him," Cailech replied, not looking up from his baked water fowl. "Myrt tells me you mentioned his name."

"Did I?" Aremys asked, looking around, and even Cailech believed his confusion was genuine. "When?"

Cailech looked toward Myrt, who stood back near the window.

"Wait!" Aremys interrupted. "I do remember now. I said 'Koreldy' when I was preparing to spar with Firl."

Myrt nodded at Cailech.

"So you do know him?" the King continued, pleased that this newcomer was being honest.

"I must, but I can't dredge up from where or how I know him. It was . . ." He searched for the answer. "That's right, it had something to do with a sword that reminded me of him. Is he a Grenadyne?"

"He is," came the reply.

Aremys shrugged. "That's how I know his name, then. I have no other recollection."

"He carries a sword of a bluish hue, my king," Myrt said softly.

Cailech said nothing in response, but Aremys nodded. "I'm not remembering anything at all about him, sire. Is this man important?"

"To me, yes."

"May I ask why?"

"We have unfinished business to settle," Cailech said, unfathomable eyes glinting over the rim of his goblet. "To your full health returning, Cullyn," he said, raising that goblet now.

"I'll drink to that, your majesty," Aremys replied. "What is your plan for me?"

Cailech resumed his eating. "Well, as you have no memory to draw upon, I presume you're in no hurry to be anywhere right now, so why not remain with us? Myrt tells me you can help with teaching my men some sword skills."

Aremys could see no harm in it. He rather liked the mountain dwellers. He could not help but rather like the direct man who ruled them. "I'll be glad to. Do I remain on as your prisoner?"

Cailech smiled now. "I think 'guest' is a nicer word," he suggested.

Aremys understood. It was true. He had no idea where he should be or why, so he might as well accept the hospitable imprisonment of the Mountain King and make the best of it until his memory returned fully.

"Oh, and Cullyn. With regard to the Morgravian King. Do you have any thoughts on him . . . any memories coming to mind?"

It could not hurt to be honest with this question, Aremys decided. He knew within himself that he hated the man called Celimus but could not remember why . . . not yet anyway. "I hate him, sire . . . I think. When Myrt mentioned his name, my hackles rose. It must mean something, though I've yet to learn what."

The King nodded thoughtfully. "That makes two of us. I hate him enough to do battle with him. But I fear a war right now would only waste my men."

Aremys looked startled. "I'm sure my limited recall serves me faithfully when I suggest that to take on the Morgravian Legion would be suicide for your men. The Legion are well-drilled soldiers. I know your people are hard and don't lack for courage. But I would avoid out-and-out war with Morgravia."

"Unless, of course, we could bring them into the Razors. If we fought on our own territory, we would win."

"Undoubtedly," Aremys agreed, and believed it. "But Celimus would not be lured, sire. He's too smart."

"You have met the man, I presume."

Aremys scratched his head and frowned. "You must be right—I suppose I must have met him to feel so assured of his ability." There were thoughts niggling at the fringe of his mind; they were just out of reach, which was frustrating but Aremys reminded himself to hold faith. His memory would return.

"Do you have another suggestion?" the King asked, more in conversation than with genuine expectation that the injured man could offer sage advice.

"Yes! Parley. As long as you're talking, no mountain dweller is losing his life."

Cailech fixed Aremys with a hard gaze again. There was humor in it this time, though, because the stranger had taken him by surprise. "Go on."

"Why fight? For what reason? Do you truly want Morgravia?"

"I might," Cailech said, not prepared to share his thoughts.

"No, sire. Why would you want Morgravia? Your people belong here among the mountains. But what if trade was free and your people could come and go across the border without fearing an arrow. That would be worth striving for—not dying for, though."

Myrt smiled to himself in the background. Cullyn was turning Cailech's own creed back on the King. He had preached negotiations all his early life and, in so doing, had united the tribes of the mountains.

Aremys pressed on. "And by the same token, sire, Celimus might think he wants the Razors, but in truth, why would he want the Mountain Kingdom? What is he going to do with it? No Morgravian would survive easily up here, save a few hardy northerners perhaps. And he certainly isn't going to move his palace up here, my lord. It's pointless. From talking with Myrt—and I mean no offense, sire—I believe this situation is just two obstinate Kings, neither prepared to give ground. Why not get together and work out a solution? Spill no blood. Who knows what good might come of it." It was a long speech for Aremys, but as much as he knew he hated Celimus, he did not for a moment believe the mountain dwellers were a match for the Legion. A new thought struck him. "And should you escalate these skirmishes I've been told of, my lord king, if I were Celimus I would unite with Briavel to crush you. Between the Morgravian Legion and the Briavellian Guard, I don't care how brave your people are, sire, they will die and in numbers. You are a nuisance, for want of a better word, and Morgravia might well put its differences with Briavel behind it temporarily if it meant getting rid of the nuisance from the north." He had no idea where his assurance had come from and could only assume that his knowledge was returning at a rapid rate now.

He expected a harsh reaction from Cailech. But the King nodded. "You speak sense, Cullyn. I just want to teach the upstart King a lesson, let him know we are not the simpleton barbarians he believes us to be. In truth, I could not leave my beloved mountains."

"But that's precisely what you would have to do, sire, should you conquer him. And anyway, there are many ways to skin a rat, sire."

At this old northern adage, the King laughed, green eyes twinkling with his mirth. "You mean there are other ways to teach the southerner a lesson."

Aremys nodded. "Precisely. It doesn't have to be by proving you are mightier. Intelligence is the key here, sire. Prove you are the King with the vision for peace."

"Do you think Morgravia and Briavel will unite?"
Cailech asked suddenly.

Aremys could not guess at this. "It was a theory, your
majesty, but one with merit." He shrugged. "If I were the
Morgravian King and faced war with you, that's what I
would seek to do. I think I'm right in saying that the Briavellians are less warlike people, but they have their own
suspicions about the mountain dwellers. Faced with fighting
you, yes, I think they might strike up a tentative bargain as
neighbors to work to defeat you."

"And that's precisely what he is doing, Cullyn. Your instincts are sharp, but your faded memory has not told you
that Celimus is petitioning Queen Valentyna of Briavel."

At the King's words, old memories resurfaced and slotted into place. A man called Wyl suddenly came to his mind.
He could not see him, but he was thinking orange-haired . . .
a general. Morgravian, no less. Try though he might, he
could not put a face to the memory. He kept seeing a
woman's eyes . . . feline and sensual. The naming of the
Queen had prompted this memory of the Morgravian—were
the two connected? He shook his head to rid it of the disjointed thoughts; he would have to consider them later.

"All the more reason to parley, King Cailech. Seek
friendship, seek trade, seek peace. You will be the winner;
it's your people who will benefit more than the Morgravians,
in truth."

"I like your style," Cailech said, after draining his goblet.
"What do you suggest?"

Aremys thought about it and the King did not seem to
mind the pause. "Don't be too proud," he finally said. "Lead
the talks—show his people and your own that it was you
who had the vision rather than he. Celimus is not trustworthy, so you must tread carefully. And should the talks fail,
then no one can accuse the Mountain King of acting in anything but a chivalrous manner. They will know you held out
the hand of peace."

Cailech stood, impressed and a little startled. He needed
to think this audacious idea through; perhaps have the

Stones read. "I like you, Cullyn of Grenadyn. We shall talk more. Join me later for a ride. You must see Galapek, my new stallion."

Rashlyn moved the Reading Stones about before him. He was alone and he was baffled. They spoke to him of change. Big change, but he could make no sense of it. He cast again, specifically looking for any indication that might spell his greatest fear—the death of King Cailech. He had saved his life once previously, when Koreldy had threatened it all those years ago, and he now regularly searched the Stones for answers with regard to Cailech's longevity.

Alas, change, once more, was all the Stones would yield. What did it mean? Without Cailech he had no power. He must not allow the King to be threatened in any way and yet here was Cailech murmuring about escalating his dislike for the Morgravian King to out-and-out war with Celimus.

Rashlyn moved restlessly to the window of the stone chamber he liked to work from, well removed from the hustle and bustle of daily life in the Cave. In his increasingly rare lucid moments, such as now, Rashlyn himself knew he was losing his mind, but it was a slow and tormenting process and he hoped this inability to get more out of the Stones was not part of that disintegration. He pulled angrily at the wild beard he hid behind and admitted to himself that his periods of lucidity had shortened significantly while the time spent in the prison of his dark thoughts had increased until he wondered if each sane period would be the last. Only he knew that spells that were once so easy for him to concoct and use were now challenging him. Oh, he was still brilliantly skilled, but the talent was beginning to elude him. Stranger still, he was beginning to recall, in vivid detail, memories of his childhood playing with his brother.

Elysius! Curse him! Rashlyn felt sure he was dead and felt no remorse for causing his brother's death.

Emil had met Rashlyn first and flirted recklessly with the plain young man. And she had done so just because she could, picking her target perfectly, for it was obvious Rashlyn was starved for female attention. As much as Rashlyn desperately wanted to touch, to kiss, to lie with a woman, none would have him willingly, so Emil was a revelation for him. Even the whores of Pearlis thought twice about taking his money. There was something about his wild eyes and disturbing manner that frightened them. And they were right to be scared. Rashlyn's insecurity had caused the death of two prostitutes on separate occasions when he had been unable to see their brief, paid couplings through to their normal close. Neither woman had laughed or made him feel in any way inadequate—if he'd known the truth of how frequently this happened in their work, he might not have overreacted. Instead, embarrassed to the point of anguish, he had lashed out with his powers and murdered both cruelly and painfully.

This was not his first taste in killing, of course, and since tasting its feel of power, he wanted more, needed more. He loved the sense of power that death brought. He wished he had killed his brother sooner so Elysius would never have met Emil, for as soon as she had clapped eyes on his handsome brother, the humiliation for Rashlyn had been complete. Her passing interest in him was done. *So be it,* he had decided, *I will find my pleasures in other, darker ways.* And he had.

He had hated his brother for his looks and his easy manner with others, but mostly he had hated him for his ability to work magic with animals, for as helpless as they seemed to Rashlyn when he had them pinned out or trapped, he had no control over them . . . no relationship with the natural world at all.

He hoped Elysius had fought death hard before the sea consumed him, and if by chance he had cheated the waters, he hoped his brother had died a pitiful death as a freak in some corner of the realm.

He had not felt his brother's magic since that dark day of death, but then Rashlyn could not be confident that his waning power could still detect something as subtle as Elysius at work. He had always pretended that he found it easy to trace his brother's magic, but in truth it was the opposite. Elysius's magic was artful and delicate while at the same time so potent it took his breath away. He had feared that as Elysius matured, he would learn the key to cloaking his magics. Perhaps he had . . . perhaps he was alive and practicing his art right now?

Since his brother's presumed demise and his own defection into the Mountain Kingdom, Rashlyn had devoted his energies to unlocking the secret to achieving power over the animals and birds, the mountains and the trees. One could rule the world with that sort of power at your call. His own sort of skills simply made him a sorcerer; he knew this, which is why he had attached himself to the far-thinking, highly intelligent King of Mountains. Using him as his cover and indeed his tool, Rashlyn could imagine himself manipulating power . . . and not just in the Razors.

But right now Cailech was being rash. He was howling for Morgravian blood too soon. Rashlyn knew the King had this notion that Rashlyn's magics and prophetic ability would serve to keep him utterly secure. It was on this confidence that the King was riding, believing that even in war, his barshi's magics would ensure as few casualties as possible among the Mountain Dwellers.

Rashlyn needed more time to shore up his defenses, work new spells. Recently he had come to the startling realization that death was easy to inflict, but crafting a spell to prolong an agonizing life was the challenge. Changing Lothryn from man to horse was the culmination of years of practice in his wing of the mountain fortress where no one could hear rabbits and squirrels scream. And now that he had at last harnessed these new powers, his magics were failing him. He remembered how he had only just managed to hold on to that glamour of Elspyth.

A few moments more and the vision would have crumbled. The breathtaking spell on Lothryn—which so impressed his king—had been achieved brutally. There was nothing subtle or beautiful about what he had done, even though the result seemed so miraculous. It was an abomination. Elysius would never do something so tainted with wrongness . . . but he was not Elysius.

He considered Lothryn, wondering at the pain he was probably in. If Elysius had conquered the spell to shapechange, Rashlyn knew in his heart he would have achieved it effortlessly and without the smashing and distortion of limbs and breaking of the mind, and without the torturous pain, both mental and physical, he had put the courageous man through.

Rashlyn did not mind Lothryn suffering the pain, in truth. His despair was all selfish—he wanted his magic to be subtle . . . more like the magic of Elysius. Instead it was messy and clumsy.

Would Lothryn die? Rashlyn had no idea if the man's spirit would survive the trauma and keep the beast alive, or whether it would wither and kill Cailech's beautiful new stallion. The anxiety of not knowing the answer infuriated the barshi, but Rashlyn comforted himself with the belief that this time of discomfort would be brief. The madness would descend any moment now and his mind would once again swirl itself back into its dark and twisting pathways that held no questions about his work, no remorse, no sympathy, no love for anything but power and corruption.

Next to the shapechanging of Lothryn, being able to tap into Cailech's mind was his most recent diabolic act. He had learned how to roam the King's thoughts and influence his decisions to suit his own base ends. But he could not wield this magic unless the King stood near him and was receptive to that manipulation. There were times when Cailech was utterly closed to him. And without direct and undivided attention, he had no hope of influencing the King through magic. That was his weakness.

The door opened and Cailech, as if acting on some silent signal, entered. He pulled Rashlyn from his musings and the sorcerer felt the familiar drag downward from rationality into his other, deranged self. No one but the King ever came to his rooms.

"My king," Rashlyn said, not turning yet. "I was just admiring the day out there." He used the moments to compose himself.

"How serene for you," Cailech said, clearly agitated. "We must speak. I want you to do a reading for me."

"I just have, my lord king."

"And?"

"The Stones predict change."

"Oh? What sort of change?" Cailech asked, his body language suddenly intent and eager.

Rashlyn turned now and noticed the flush on his king's cheeks. Something had created high excitement. "This they don't tell me. I have cast the Stones several times, your highness. Each time a prediction of change is prophesied."

Cailech surprised his barshi by clapping his hands and laughing. It was a cheerful response to something that would normally disturb his king. Rashlyn frowned, unsettled by this reaction.

"Perfect!" the King muttered. "Do you have any wine here?"

"Er . . . why yes, of course. Let me pour you some," Rashlyn offered, intrigued. He poured for both of them and waited for the toast he sensed was coming.

"To change," Cailech obliged, holding out his cup before swallowing it contents.

Rashlyn copied his king and put his cup down. "So you are happy with my prediction, your highness?"

"Yes. It confirms what I must do."

"And what must you do, my lord?"

"Go to Morgravia!" the King said. "For a parley with King Celimus."

"This is a jest, surely? The Stones suggest no such thing," Rashlyn spluttered, all politeness deserting him.

Cailech hardly noticed. He put a gleeful finger in the air. "Ah, wait, hear me out," and he told him of the capture and subsequent meeting with the man known as Cullyn.

"And you trust this man . . . this stranger!"

"Oddly, yes," Cailech replied, unpredictable as always in his responses.

"Wait," Rashlyn cautioned. "Say no more until I read the Stones about him."

Cailech nodded and settled back with a second cup of wine while his barshi set about casting the smoothed rocks with their odd assortment of engravings. He remained silent as Rashlyn threw the eleven Stones across the floor and squatted to read them. He stood up again after a long time.

"Well?"

Rashlyn shook his head slowly. "The Stones are confused. They tell me that he speaks the truth, but—"

"Ha!" Cailech interrupted, delighted.

"But . . . he holds back on things. I can't tell what these are."

"He has lost his memory, man . . . that would explain it. And anyway, we all have secrets . . . even you, Rashlyn."

Not you, though, sire. No secrets. I can read your mind as if it were an open page, the man of magic thought sourly, knowing this was not wholly true. "I would recommend caution, my lord."

"The Stones themselves predict change. Change of scenery, change of heart, change of ideals, change of plan. Not war with Celimus, Rashlyn . . . but equals, trade, prosperity together. I'm ashamed I wasn't the one to think of it first. It is inspired—I can't wait to tell Lothryn about it. Do you think he hears me . . . understands me?"

Rashlyn sighed inwardly. The King's mind was made up. He would go right into the lion's den. So be it. "I think there's enough of his spirit still left that the horse remains Lothryn despite his appearance, though I cannot promise it will remain so."

"Excellent," Cailech replied, ignoring the promise, "for he would approve of this plan."

"My lord king, may I ask how you intend orchestrating such a delicate parley?"

"Not me. Cullyn, or whoever he really is. He will make it happen."

Rashlyn nodded and changed the subject to something he

could control. "About the prisoner, my lord—the Morgravian soldier."

"I'm not planning to give him back as a peace offering, if that's what you're leading up to."

"No, sire. I have an idea for him. A rather entertaining one which I think you'll approve of," the barshi said, reaching out with his probing spell and entering Cailech's mind.

Later that afternoon Aremys met with the King on horseback, Myrt, Firl, and a couple of other mountain men, including Maegryn, in attendance.

"Isn't he magnificent?" Cailech said to his guest.

Aremys had to admit, intact memory or not, he did not believe he had ever set eyes on a finer horse. "Fit only for a king, my lord," he admitted, and could see this comment pleased Cailech. "May I?" he asked, so impressed he wanted to touch the sleek, black coat of the stallion.

"Of course," the King replied, and Aremys hopped down from his own chestnut mount.

He walked around the black horse, which tossed its head. Aremys whistled. "I have never seen a prouder stallion," he said, stepping gently toward the animal in order not to startle it.

"Here, Cullyn, give him this," Maegryn suggested, tossing an apple toward Aremys, who deftly caught it. "He's picky, he doesn't like the green ones, they make him sicken," and the men laughed.

Aremys held the apple in his flat palm and raised it toward the horse's mouth. He was captivated by the animal and enjoyed watching it take the fruit greedily. As its velvety lips brushed against his hand, Aremys felt a tremor of shock pass through him. In his mind a dam had burst and a river of information—his memories—flooded in. He staggered backward, holding his head.

It was Cailech who reached him first, leaping down agilely from Galapek. Again Aremys was struck by the man's lack of pretension. He could just imagine Celimus caring enough even to look his way!

"Cullyn, man! Are you ill? What's happening?" the King asked, reaching for Aremys while holding the reins of his horse.

Aremys was not ready to reveal too much. His cautious nature forced him to take stock of his situation first and consider his position fully. "I . . . I'm sorry, my head suddenly hurts." In this he was not lying; it throbbed.

"Take him back," Cailech said to one of his men. "If he's well enough, he can ride with us tomorrow."

"I'm sorry," Aremys repeated, stunned from the shock, not just of his memory returning whole but of something else, something frightening affecting him. He straightened, deciding to give the worried men something genuine of himself. "My name is Aremys Farrow," he admitted, hoping it was not an error to admit as much.

Cailech scrutinized him, then nodded. "We know of your family, then. You are from the northern isle of Grenadyn. Anything else?"

Aremys shook his head miserably. "Just that. It came to me just as this pain did," he lied. "I'm sorry about the ride."

"No harm done," the King said affably. "I'm pleased your memory returns. Are you able to ride back on your own horse?"

"Yes, of course." Aremys reached again toward the horse known as Galapek, bracing himself this time. He needed to be sure of something. He touched the animal's neck as if in farewell to the riders. The tremor of knowledge that passed between him and the horse was genuine. It was there. Magic! How he knew this, he did not know; how he could sense it, he had no idea. But it existed. The stallion was riddled with a huge and tainted spell he could feel passing through his hand and resonating throughout his body. It made him feel like retching. He almost did. "I'll rest, thank you, my lord," he said as evenly as he could, not daring to say more.

"We shall see you later, Aremys Farrow," Cailech said, something unreadable in his expression.

Alone at last in his chamber, Aremys remembered everything about himself, and it was terrifying. The Thicket had risen up against him and, using its magic, had hurled him into the Razors. He could recall, understanding, as it had occurred, that the Thicket did not want him to pass through with Wyl.

One moment he had been whistling and admiring Ylena's rump, the next he had found himself separated from her. He could remember now how the air had become suddenly chill—freezing, in fact—and then he had felt it gathering about him. The air had begun to thicken behind and before him and it was as if invisible hands had shoved him through that thickened air to blast him into a different place.

The Thicket's magic had knocked out his memories for a while. Hence no blow to his head, he realized. It had all happened internally. He felt his insides twist with fear for Wyl, traveling as a helpless young woman—although in truth, he knew Wyl could easily hold his own against others, but perhaps not against magic. What if the Thicket had done the same to Wyl as it had done to him? Perhaps it had not wanted either of them there and now Wyl was lying in some corner of the realm without memory, also trying to piece his especially strange life back together. Aremys's thoughts began to travel rapidly now. He needed to get out of the Razors and back south to Wyl. He must find him, help him. If, by some stroke of luck, Wyl had found Elysius, then no matter what had occurred between them, Wyl would still head toward Briavel and Valentyna; of this he was sure. However, if Wyl had not made it to Elysius and the Thicket had treated him with similar disdain, then he might be in Morgravia and not the mountains, for Cailech's scouts would surely have spotted him by now if he had also been thrown into the Razors.

Thoughts and plans swirled, but once the initial panic had settled, Aremys began to think more clearly. Perhaps he could be of some use to Wyl while he was here. His friend had spoken of the soldier Gueryn. In his heart, Aremys believed Wyl's mentor was dead. There was just no reason to keep the man alive, and from what Wyl had told him, Gueryn was a thorough nuisance to the Mountain King.

However, Wyl believed the man was alive . . . would be kept alive as bait to lure Romen Koreldy back into the Cave of the Mountain King. Aremys grimaced. He wondered how Cailech would react to learning that Koreldy was long dead and that Ylena of Argorn was yet another host to Wyl Thirsk. What would he think of her arriving to claim Gueryn, if he lived? Plus there was the other man—Cailech's man—who had turned traitor to help Wyl and Elspyth escape the mountain fortress. Wyl had told Aremys often enough that he would return, come what may, to find out the fate of brave Lothryn.

"I must find them for Wyl," Aremys muttered, swinging his legs over to sit up on the bed. "As long as I'm captive here, I might as well make myself useful."

He turned his mind to the strangest of all experiences—the fact that he could suddenly detect magic. It had pulsed through the stallion Galapek, and his head still pounded from the ferocity with which that magic had spoken to him. He could only assume that the huge jolt of magic from the Thicket had somehow made him vulnerable to sentient matter around him.

It was a revelation. And he had not imagined it. He had touched the horse a second time to ensure that he was not making this notion up. Aremys shook his head. He understood none of it, but one thing was sure: He had to get into the dungeons. If Wyl's friends were alive, that was as good a place as any to start looking for information on them.

A knock at the door disturbed his thoughts. Aremys looked out of the window and noticed the sun lowering. He must have been wrestling for a long time with his confused thoughts.

"Who is it?"

"Messenger. The King wishes to see you."

38

WYL WAS ADMIRING ELYSIUS'S HANDIWORK. "YOU DID THIS?" HE asked, his gaze sweeping across the breathtaking landscape before him. They were standing on a rise amid a copse of tall trees whose leaves shone a fantastical lime color as the sun slanted through the translucent canopy to the gently moving stream. Beyond the copse was a rugged cliff face over which water flowed direct from the Razors, Wyl presumed. They had already walked through sweet-smelling meadows from the modest dwelling Elysius had built for himself on a hill overlooking an equally panoramic view. Wyl could hardly believe how incredibly beautiful the Wild was.

The little man took a few moments to reply. "In Parrgamyn we believe in our god, Mor. In Morgravia and Briavel it is Shar who holds the spiritual power. In the kingdom of the Razors, Haldor is the god whom the mountain dwellers pray to. My belief, Wyl, is that we're all praying to the same god. And I think that god is Nature. Anything that can create such beauty as this," he said, sweeping an elongated arm across the vista, "or craft such sophistication as you or I, such grace as a deer or such majesty as an eagle—this is a power worth worshipping. What you see before you is Nature's work . . . I have simply embellished some of it," Elysius said, "because my skills adhere to all things natural. The waterfall's theatrics are my work, but in truth, the framework had been in place for centuries. Shar had seen to it."

"So this wild beauty was already here? Harmless and gorgeous . . . and feared."

Elysius nodded. "And I seem to be the only one who enjoys it. It suited my purposes in the early years to live a hermit's existence, but I have since found my loneliness to be a curse. I would add that it would be a pity for Briavel to discover how harmless the Wild is, for it to become an annex of that realm—just imagine its trees cut down, its streams dammed and diverted, its sheer wildness harnessed. But, on the other hand, I do miss people. Sometimes I fly with the birds so I can look through their eyes over Briavel or Morgravia and get a sense that I am back within a community."

"Then go. Can't you cast a glamour about yourself and leave?"

The Manwitch smiled. "I cannot work magic of that kind on myself, no. Irritating but true."

Wyl frowned. "So if the Wild is not enchanted, why did people of old fear it?"

"There is magic here, Wyl—be very sure of that. I can't explain it, I simply accept it. The Thicket, for example, is something rather extraordinary that, from what I can tell, has no reason for being other than to keep people away from the Wild. Perhaps if we were to delve back into history, the scholars might throw some light on why no one has explored the region . . . what exactly they feared so irrationally or perhaps knew to be true."

"Old superstitions, I'd guess."

"More than that. The Thicket is real and thinks for itself. It allowed me through all those years ago, as well as Emil and then you and Fynch, but I suspect it actually does frighten away many who might attempt to cross it. It certainly dealt with your friend." He saw Wyl's expression fall at this comment. "I'm sorry, that was clumsy of me. I don't believe your friend Aremys has been hurt. I feel sure the Thicket has never injured anyone, but it does have the power of choice and it chose for him to be repelled."

"What has it done to him?"

Elysius sighed. "You are the first person I have shared this with . . . you won't be the last, though. One other must know," he answered cryptically. "My belief is that the Thicket is more than just a barrier . . . it is a gate."

"To what?"

"I don't know. Other regions, I imagine." Elysius shrugged. "Perhaps other worlds."

Now Wyl was astonished. "What!"

"I don't know enough about it. I have never made use of it, nor will I."

"So you're saying Aremys might be in a different world," Wyl replied, aghast.

"No, I'm not saying that. I understand it so little that I would never suggest such a thing. I think it has the ability to be a gate to other places . . . to travel . . . is all I'm hazarding."

Wyl paced. "And Aremys has been pushed through that gate?"

Elysius shrugged again. "I'm sorry, Wyl, regarding Aremys I can't enlighten you. For all we know, he could be on the other side, taking an ale in Timpkenny. It is not important."

"Not to you, perhaps," Wyl said tersely, moving to check on Fynch, who was playing in the nearby stream with Knave.

"And that was clumsy of me again. What I mean to say is that I believe he is safe, wherever he is, and that what's of importance right now is you and the decisions you make."

"I came here for an answer, Elysius, and I have it now." He scowled, spoiling Ylena's pretty face. "There are no further decisions to make. I must leave for Briavel."

"You know she must marry Celimus, don't you?"

"It doesn't have to be so," Wyl countered. "And how could you know that so surely while you're stuck out here?"

"I know many things, Wyl, and I've explained that I travel with the animals—I see and hear all sorts of things."

Elysius's calm countenance was frustrating. "How! How can you know with such certainty that she must marry the madman of Morgravia?"

"It is prophesied."

"By whom?" Wyl demanded, his tone just slightly mocking.

"The Stones tell me so. They always speak the truth."

"The Stones! The same sort of pebbles that your brother uses to advise Cailech on how to roast people alive?" Wyl was just short of yelling.

Elysius was wise enough to understand Wyl's sense of helplessness and his fears. He did not react to Wyl's wrath. "The Stones don't advise. They simply give answers to questions. Their answers are not always clear, I grant you, but in this they are firm. Queen Valentyna of Briavel will marry King Celimus of Morgravia, come what may."

"Then we had better hope he kills me first," Wyl said bitterly, "for I won't allow it. I'll use everything I have within myself to prevent such a marriage taking place," and he hated the sympathy in the Manwitch's expression, as if he knew it to be a hopeless cause. "I'll take my leave, Elysius. I thank you for your hospitality and your explanations."

"I'm deeply saddened, Wyl. I wish I could offer more comfort, at least more guidance, but the way ahead for you is not clear—other than Myrren's choice for your final destination. Your journey there is shrouded."

Wyl nodded, too depressed to respond, and then walked away.

Elysius called to him and reluctantly Wyl halted and looked back. "We will not meet again, Wyl Thirsk. The Thicket will permit you through. Take food from the cottage and leave before dark. Remember my warning. Myrren's Gift cannot be manipulated. If you try, it will punish you in ways you cannot imagine. She insisted you rule Morgravia. Rule you must."

Wyl felt a tremor run through Ylena's thin body at such prophetic words. He could not speak, simply raised a resigned hand in farewell.

"Trust Fynch, although he has his own path now," Elysius called after him somewhat cryptically. He wanted to say more, but he feared it might persuade Wyl that the Quickening could be foiled. Elysius knew better. He watched the retreating back of the only person in the land who could save Morgravia, Briavel, and the Mountain Kingdom. He watched until Wyl was long gone and his own ugly wet cheeks had dried from the tears he had shed.

Fynch sat between Ylena's legs, her thin arms hugging him to her chest. Knave had positioned himself so close that he was touching both of them.

"I don't mind that you'd like to remain here awhile. It's so beautiful, I could live here for ever," Wyl admitted.

"But why can't you stay longer?" the small boy asked.

"I must go to Valentyna, Fynch. I have to get a grasp on what's been happening." He scratched his head. "I don't even know if time passes the same in the Wild—who knows what could have occurred since we were last in Briavel."

"It does," Fynch assured. "And you're sure you don't mind if I stay here a little longer?"

"I promise," Wyl said, meaning it. "Is there a reason beyond the peace and solitude, though?"

Fynch nodded. "I can't explain it, though. I feel compelled to remain."

Wyl noticed Knave was staring at him. He wondered if Elysius was with them, seeing through the animal. The dark eyes seemed to be imploring Wyl to trust the boy.

"Come straight to Werryl once you leave here. I hope I'll be there, but you know you have friends there, no matter what."

Again Fynch nodded, his mind already turning to more practical matters. "How will you travel?"

"I'll buy a horse at Timpkenny."

"I have plenty of coin if you need."

Wyl chuckled. It was the first time in a while that he had heard Ylena's tinkling laughter. "And I suppose you have Knave so you don't have to worry about transport."

"That's right," Fynch said, turning in Ylena's arms. "Be careful, Wyl . . . please."

Wyl nodded. "I promise to try to remain Ylena," and was rewarded with a smile from his friend. "Although you know this thing isn't over yet. Elysius says it will continue—"

"Until you rule Morgravia," Fynch interrupted. "Yes, I know. But who knows what might happen yet."

"He says it must happen."

"Then he's ignoring the bit about free will. Remember, Myrren's Gift is still bound by the will of others, if not your own."

Wyl hugged the boy again. How odd that no adult could bring the sort of comfort that this child could. Fynch always seemed to say the right thing at the right time.

"I must go." They stood and Wyl leaned down and kissed Fynch. He looked toward Knave. "Bring him safely to me."

The dog growled softly in answer.

Wyl wasted no further time. He packed a small sack of bread and dried meat together with some hard biscuit and a bladder of water. It would do. He left the cottage with a single glance behind in case Elysius had come to add something heartening. Only Fynch stood there, his hand on Knave, his other arm in the air waving.

Leave soon, Fynch, he suddenly thought, even though an hour earlier, with the boy hugged close to him, he had felt the lad was safer in the Wild than in any of the neighboring realms. He could not put his finger on the reason for this about-face, but Wyl had a sense that Fynch would be changed next time they met. As he raised his hand in farewell, he took a moment to fix the picture of the innocent, serious little boy and the large, mysterious dog in his mind because he somehow knew both would be different next time he saw them. He felt an urge to warn Fynch, but he was already too far away. It would mean climbing back up the hill and the small boat was bobbing invitingly just steps away on the Darkstream.

Against his inclination, he made the decision to press on. As much as he felt a fear for Fynch, he knew it was irrational, based on no fact, and Wyl was the first to admit that both of them were caught up in something so dark and strange that no one could predict the outcome. He wanted to believe he could stop Valentyna uniting Briavel with Morgravia through marriage, but there was something about the sorrowful look on Elysius's face that told him the prophecy was true and he was fighting a hopeless cause. Still, he must try . . . die trying, and he smiled grimly to himself, for death was all that was ahead for him until he became the person he was destined to be.

As for Fynch, he was on his own path of destiny. Wyl would just have to hope nothing untoward leapt into Fynch's way, although with Knave at his side, Wyl doubted anything—even magic—could deter him from his journey . . . whatever that was.

He lowered himself into the boat and undid the small rope. Immediately the craft set off against the current. It moved through the dark waters effortlessly toward the great mouth of the mountain that had swallowed him once already.

He sent a prayer to Shar that he would hold his nerve this time, make it through to the other side without succumbing to the Darkstream's invitation to drown.

39

FYNCH SAT QUIETLY WITH ELYSIUS OUTSIDE HIS SMALL MUD cottage, watching the birds darting in and out of the trees and swooping across the picturesque meadows. He made a chain of daisies and looped it around Knave's neck; the dog did not seem to mind—he was more intent on snuffling around for a smooth, round stone he could use in the absence of his red woolen ball. In the comfortable quiet, while Knave thought about a game and Fynch plaited flowers, Elysius considered, with a heavy heart, how to approach the frightening topic that needed to be discussed.

"How long will you stay here, Fynch?" he asked, finally breaking into the silence.

"As long as it takes," the boy replied, stringing a second daisy chain over Knave.

"For what?"

"For you to tell me what it is that is burning at your lips and making you so anxious."

Elysius was stunned. He was right about the child. "How do you know?"

Fynch shrugged. "I sense it. Near to you, it's easier for my senses to tap into your mood. And Knave's magic is strong because you are so close. I think he helps me to understand all sorts of things. And then there's the Thicket. Even through the rock face it seems to whisper to me."

Elysius nodded, amazed. "You sense right, child."

Fynch scattered the flowers he held. "Then tell me. Don't be scared."

"Have your senses told you what it is that sits between us?"

The boy shook his head. "It's important, though, isn't it?"

"It's also a secret."

"You didn't tell Wyl?" This obviously surprised Fynch because he frowned and then sighed as if accepting something unpleasant.

"No. Trust me when I say it would endanger him if I had."

Fynch accepted this without further question. "Should I be scared?" he asked, eyeing his companion now.

Elysius did not know how to answer. Fynch was such a sharp child, it would not be right to give him anything but a direct answer. "Well, I am scared about sharing it with you."

Fynch nodded gravely. "Tell me, then."

Elysius wasted no further time in hesitation. "I am dying. It will happen soon."

The boy did not react other than to stare at the ground. Elysius saw him lace his fingers together as if to steady himself while Knave stopped his search and lay down silently next to Fynch.

"Have you read it in the Stones?"

"Yes," he said. "But they assure me, in their strange roundabout way, that the magic need not die." He leaned forward. "Must not die, in fact," he added emphatically.

Fynch sighed heavily and lifted his gaze to look directly

into the whitened eyes of his dying friend. "And you can pass it on to me."

Elysius felt an enormous outpouring of gratitude and pity toward Fynch. The brave little boy had worked it out for himself. He could hear the regret in the child's voice; wished he could avoid giving this terrible burden to a youngster who had already given more than enough to Myrren's cause. This was not for Myrren, though. This was another sort of gift, a terrible, heavy gift of responsibility to entrust to a child. But he was the right one and Elysius had known it from the moment Knave had encountered the tiny gong boy at his work all that time ago.

"Fynch. Will you accept it?"

"I fear it," Fynch replied without committing himself.

Elysius was surprised that the boy had not balked. "It depends only on how you wield it."

"I don't understand how I can use magic," Fynch said, shifting to touch Knave, stroking the large head and fondling the dog's velvety ears.

"Yes you do, child. You have always known in your heart. You told me your mother was fey. She passed her talents and her own susceptibility for sentient ability on to you. In truth, I do believe you chose me."

Fynch took no notice of the gentle accusation. "And I must use it to protect Wyl. See to it that he rules Morgravia. Is this right?"

Elysius hesitated and Fynch heard it, his gaze flicking up from Knave's eyes to stare at his freakish friend. "You will help Wyl—of this I'm sure—but Myrren's Gift has its own momentum. It will take him to his destiny, come what may. You . . . well, you have a much more complex task, son, and I wish I could spare you it."

"What is it that I must do?" Fynch asked, dread in his voice.

"There are two parts to your task. One is dictated by the magic itself. The other is a plea I personally make of you as custodian of this magic," Elysius explained, feeling similar dread.

Again Fynch did not hesitate. "What is the first part?"

It was not a time for further apology or placations. Elysius knew this weight of responsibility must fall on the narrow shoulders of this small child. "When I first came to the Wild, guided by the birds and animals, they called me the Gate Wielder. It took me a long time to understand it and then I spent years trying to ignore it before I accepted what it meant. The rest of my life I have devoted to avoiding it. I never believed I was strong enough."

"Gate Wielder," Fynch said, testing the words on his tongue. "And what does it mean?"

He told Fynch about the Gate as he had detailed it to Wyl the previous evening.

"Has there always been a Gate Wielder, then?"

It was an astute question and Elysius acknowledged this with a smile. "No. In past times there have been, I suspect. But I was the first in a very long time. The Thicket takes care of itself and can ordinarily keep people out through its own means. Those who may are allowed to pass through for whatever reason then have Samm, and before him his predecessors, to contend with."

"Samm is persuasive," Fynch agreed. "So why now? Why did the Thicket need you?"

"My guess is that until fairly recent times it hasn't needed someone of magic for all that time."

Fynch looked at him confused. "Your guess?"

Elysius shrugged. "Fynch, the Thicket has never spoken to me in the manner I'm gathering it speaks to you. My communication with it has been through the birds and animals. From the few things you've said, it sounds to me as though the Thicket itself talks to you. My feeling is that you are no ordinary Gate Wielder, if there is such a thing." He laughed briefly, sadly. "I believe that you are someone very special, not just a Gate Wielder."

"What do you mean?" Fynch asked, scared afresh.

"I don't know what I mean. I'm speculating. Perhaps the Thicket needs you for more than simply watching over a Gate that almost never gets used."

That notion hung heavily between them for several long moments.

"If the Thicket has its own powers, why does it need you?"

"Well, again I can only surmise. My hunch is that it needs to channel its magic through someone to achieve change outside of itself."

"You mean change in the world beyond its own borders."

"Exactly." Elysius reached for a flask of juice he had squeezed that morning. He gestured to Fynch, who nodded. As he poured them a cup each, he tried to make this difficult notion more clear for the child whose burden suddenly felt so much heavier than his own. "I think it needs the wilder magic which my mother spoke of and it seeks someone whose talent revolves around Nature. It found that combination in me and I presume any previous Gate Wielders offered similar qualities. I am passing my nature magic to you, so that would answer one part of this strange equation, but the other is how and why the Thicket speaks to you. I can't imagine how it will use you."

Fynch had never felt more frightened in his life. He took the cup from his friend and drained it. "So Aremys went through this Gate?"

Elysius nodded, surprised by the sudden switch in topic. "I pushed him. It was the first time I have ever used that unknown magic."

Fynch's eyes widened. "Why did you push him?"

"He was a complication. You and Wyl were the only ones I wanted to come through and perhaps the Thicket sensed this. It has the ability to make up its own mind, but it is firmly linked to the Wielder. Normally it can repel people with the greatest of ease, but Aremys was strong—his friendship with Wyl very real—and I realize now that he was somehow protected by Wyl and the magic that Wyl himself possesses. The Thicket summoned me to open the Gate."

"Where did you send him?"

"I was careful not to push too far. I hope he's in Briavel or Morgravia."

Fynch addressed another question niggling in his mind. "So I must stay here after . . . after you leave?"

Elysius finished his drink and sighed. "Yes. For a while anyway. This is why I've asked you not to follow Wyl, although I'm sure he asked you to come to Werryl." Fynch nodded. "Stay here until you've learned more about the Thicket and its intentions."

"How?"

The little man looked at Fynch sorrowfully. "I'm hoping it will tell you."

Fynch bit his lip in thought. "And the second part?"

Elysius sighed. "Wait, there is more connected with the magic of nature. I'm sorry that it must exact this from you, but each time you unleash your magic, for whatever reason, you will sicken."

"Is this what has happened to you, then?" Fynch asked, and once again Elysius was struck by the boy's ability to see through to the core of a topic.

He nodded. "It will take my life shortly. In fact, son, I suspect that passing the burden to you will herald my end." He saw the misty look in the child's eyes. "No, don't be sad for me. I wish I could spare you the same burden."

"Will I die too?"

"Perhaps," Elysius answered honestly. "This is why I must counsel you to use your magic sparingly," he added.

Fynch nodded, looking suddenly older for this terrifying knowledge. "And the favor for you?" he asked.

Again Elysius resisted the urge to try to soften the blow, offer up empty words of comfort. He pressed on. "I want you to track down and destroy my brother, Rashlyn."

The boy visibly shook. "Elysius! I could never kill anyone."

"I know what I ask of you is difficult."

Fynch shook his head rapidly, as if trying to shut out the placating words. "No. No!" he said, forcing Elysius into silence. "I will not kill another living being for yours or anyone's personal revenge."

"Not even Celimus, after all that he's done?"

At this, Fynch's mouth hung open. He wanted to respond

but could not. Then he held his head, miserable. "I don't believe I'm capable of it . . . not even Celimus."

"Fynch," the mellow voice said softly. "I don't ask this of you out of personal need. I ask it for the sake and safety of those and that which you love . . . Wyl, Valentyna, your family—Morgravia, Briavel. I'm daring to think that this is why the Thicket is becoming involved."

"What do you mean?"

"Now that I have discovered where he is, I realize that Rashlyn has the ability to plunge all the three realms into war. If, as Wyl says, Rashlyn can manipulate King Cailech, then there's only bloodshed ahead."

"Why should the Thicket care if we all kill each other?"

"I don't know. You need to seek those answers for yourself. I think it does care, though."

"Why me? Why not Wyl, who is a soldier and knows how to wield a sword and kill a man?"

Elysius shook his head. "Dear Fynch, I wish I could spare you this. Wyl is a wandering soul trapped in helpless flesh and bone."

"You have never seen Wyl fight! He might walk as Ylena now, but he is still Wyl Thirsk."

"Child, you miss my point. Rashlyn is far superior to Wyl. He could snap a sword from fifty paces, deflect an arrow, smell the poison . . . he cannot be killed by conventional means. Wyl is no threat to him. No one is, in fact."

"How can I do it, then?"

"I am giving you the means, son. Shortly you will be a sorcerer—but far more fearsome is the fact that you also possess whatever power the Thicket deems to lend. Find out what it can do. Use it."

A dawning expression moved across the small boy's face. Elysius pressed further. "Rashlyn is a madman. A destroyer. No one can stand up to the sort of power he wields, except you. You alone can stop him. You and Knave and the secret of the Thicket."

Whether Fynch was filled with uncertainty and misgivings or felt frightened and alone, Elysius would never know.

A dread silence sat around them as the former gong boy considered all that he had just learned. Suddenly the memory of being a hardworking child, coming home to his parents' tiny cottage with its meager belongings, seemed like the best time of his life.

But even he could appreciate that there was nothing random about his relationship with Knave, which connected him to Myrren through Wyl, and thus to Elysius and his mad brother. His part in saving the life of Valentyna was not coincidence. His own life was being shaped, orchestrated. He had been chosen. He looked at the strange, mysterious dog who sat beside him and only now acknowledged the curious tingling sensation between them that had only occurred after they had moved through the Thicket.

He made his decision.

Fynch finally spoke. "I wish I could stay here in this serene place without taking on this terrifying role, but then I think about Wyl's suffering. He too is on a strange path he didn't asked to journey upon. It seems to me we're both being asked to do things neither of us wants to, and yet we must. I know I have to be brave and accept the burden of becoming a manwitch even if it does mean an early death. I'll help Wyl all that I can and I'll face Rashlyn for you. I can't promise I'll overcome him, Elysius, but I will die trying."

Elysius felt a rush of love and admiration for the selfless, bright, brave boy. He hardly trusted his voice to speak without trembling and he fought back the water that sprang to his eyes. "Fynch, one more thing." Large, trusting eyes turned to look at him. "You cannot, under any circumstances, allow Rashlyn to seize your powers. He will try, believe me. You must never lose sight of the fact that you will be weakened each time you wield magic, and this is why I urge you to make for the Razors first. Don't try following Wyl. He must follow his own path now . . . and you yours. You will need all of your strength to match Rashlyn; you cannot risk being compromised in any way. I beg you to heed this warning, for if he defeats you and takes your powers—as he can—then the world is doomed."

Fynch hugged Knave close. The dog licked him as if to say he understood the import of what was being discussed.

"Wyl left very upset," Fynch commented, wanting to leave behind talk of death and destruction.

"I brought no peace. He came seeking answers and I gave him the wrong ones," Elysius said, filled with regret.

"It occurs to me that the reading of the Stones is open to interpretation—would that be fair?"

"Of course. They never provide a clear answer."

"So perhaps Wyl's fear of having to become Celimus is also open to interpretation," Fynch prompted.

Elysius did not answer immediately. He had learned even in the short time he had spent with Fynch that he was a serious, deep-thinking person. He might be young, but he was sharply intelligent and perceptive. "How would you interpret the notion, then?" he asked gently.

"I wouldn't. I don't trust the Stones or what they predict in their misted way. I trust only what I see or hear and what I feel in my heart."

"Do you think they lie?"

"No, I'm not saying that. I'm simply saying that there are many scenarios that we might not be considering. The Stones have put a notion into your mind and you're trusting it, but you yourself built into Myrren's Gift the aspect of free will, didn't you?" Elysius nodded. "We don't know what might happen or who might influence the future. Celimus could die tomorrow in a riding accident or from disease. That's the randomness of the world, isn't it? And then Wyl would not have to answer to Myrren's Gift any longer."

Reaching for Fynch, Elysius hugged him hard. "You are the most extraordinary person I've met in my life, Fynch. You alone will give our world hope, and I go to my death relieved that it is you who takes over my power and proud that I've known you. You are right, none of us knows anything for sure."

It was Fynch's turn to feel choked. He did not feel brave and he did not want to be a savior of the world. He hugged the little man back with affection and sorrow that both of them would suffer for his magic.

"How much time do we have?" Fynch asked after a long silence.

Elysius regretted it but knew he had no choice. "Time is short. I must channel all my magic into you."

"And then you'll die?"

"Yes."

"When shall we begin?"

"Now, son," Elysius replied softly.

EPILOGUE

The corpse of the former Duchess of Felrawthy had been
laid out in the small chapel at Werryl where those who had
known her—only four of them Briavellian—could pay their
last respects. Father Paryn was muttering a final gentle
prayer to commit her body to a peaceful rest. He was aided
by Pil, who lit small candles at given moments in the prayer.
One for her head, one for each limb, one for her soul. They
would burn until they snuffed themselves out and presumably Shar's Gatherers had collected her.

Physic Geryld, Commander Liryk, and Chancellor Krell
sat behind the Queen, who had, on her right, a composed
Duke Crys of Felrawthy. On her left side was Elspyth, the
only one weeping. Elspyth had liked Aleda immensely and
could not contain the sorrow she felt at this fine woman's
shocking end and her courageous, desperate bid to see her
son alive and to warn the Queen.

Valentyna reached to put an arm around her petite companion. "I gave Romen an identical kerchief," she whispered, handing Elspyth a beautiful square of embroidered
linen. "You keep this. Now both my best friends own one."

Elspyth was touched by the sentiment, which made her
lack of composure worse, and she could only nod her thanks.
Later, when the prayers were done and the candles glowed
softly around Aleda's body, Elspyth was sufficiently calm to
whisper back to the Queen. "I'll stay on with Crys for a few
moments."

Valentyna smiled and nodded. "Forgive me, I have business to attend to," she whispered.

Everyone bowed for the Queen's departure, and once she

was outside the chapel, her counselors had to run slightly to catch up with their monarch's long stride.

"I don't need to remind any of you, I'm sure, that no one is to discuss these events outside the nine of us who know. The death of Aleda Donal as well as the presence of the Duke and Elspyth are to remain a secret to the best of our ability." She saw Krell balk and surmised what he was about to say. "I understand that the folk of Brackstead are the weak link in this plan and that the nobility has met Crys and Elspyth, but we can say they have departed. The gossip in Brackstead will die away soon enough and we must protect this secret to the best of our abilities."

Krell had gone pale now. She frowned at him, but he said nothing and so she continued. "The Morgravians will remain as our honored guests as long as they choose. No one is to discuss their presence outside the palace. Is that clear?"

Everyone nodded except Krell.

"Thank you, gentlemen," she said, effectively dismissing them. "Chancellor Krell?"

"Your majesty?"

"A word please, in my solar."

With the agreement of both sovereigns, Jessom had set up a system of couriers, which made the mail journey between Briavel and Morgravia much faster. Special huts for overnighting had been established in recent weeks. These huts always had a rested man and fresh mount ready to go, as well as a supply of dried foods and watered ale. By handing over messages at these courier points, the journeying time for written correspondence—and less sensitive verbal messages, if need be—was more than halved.

And so it was that Krell's communication to his counterpart in Morgravia was received quickly at Stoneheart and now King and Chancellor were standing together in Celimus's study, both seething.

"Read it again!" Celimus ordered.

If it had been anyone else, Jessom would have suggested that reading it once more would not change the contents, but he sensibly held the acid-tongued comment and did as his king demanded. "He was right to tell us, my lord king," Jessom said after he had finished.

"Obviously Valentyna doesn't know he has. She wouldn't have sanctioned him writing to you like this. No, he's taken this entirely upon himself because he's frightened."

"Of the consequences, do you mean, sire?"

The King stroked a hand through his dark, lustrous hair. "I think it's more simple than that. Krell and that Commander of theirs seemed determined that the marriage be a reality. They said as much during our visit. Their people want the peace as much as our own do, but those two, Krell, in particular, appreciate that Briavel is in no position to fight a war with us. Diplomacy is their one weapon."

"Yes, I understand," Jessom said, even though he had grasped all that he needed on the first read. He knew he had to get the King to calm down, then Celimus's thoughts flowed smoothly and in a more cunning fashion. Jessom had learned this the hard way. When the King was angry, people got hurt.

"And that sniveling bastard son who should have died," Celimus spat, "but who somehow escaped our clutches is now walking tall as the new Duke of Felrawthy. Not to mention some stupid woman from Morgravia poisoning the Queen's thoughts. They know everything."

"Not everything, sire. They are piecing together various stories," Jessom soothed, though he knew the King's words had a horrible ring of truth. Valentyna might be young and inexperienced, but she was the daughter of a canny sovereign, and if his own first impressions were correct, she possessed an intelligent head on her shoulders. And that is no doubt why his counterpart in Briavel had reacted so swiftly and done the unthinkable in sending a private communication into Morgravia. It seemed obvious that the Queen would be appalled by what Crys Donal and this female companion of his—Elspyth of Yentro—would surely be telling her.

Jessom walked to a nearby cabinet to pour his king a goblet of wine. "We don't know the full measure of the young Duke yet, your highness. He might be useful to us in ways we cannot anticipate," he said, thinking aloud.

"True," Celimus replied, taking the proffered cup. "But my inclination is to believe that at this point Valentyna has no intention of marrying me. You must agree?"

Jessom nodded gravely—the King was right. "I do, highness."

"Then if she won't unify willingly, we shall take Briavel the hard way."

Chancellor Jessom was not ready for such a leap forward. "War, sire?"

"Threat of it, anyway, Jessom. She has understood all the couched words of intimidation. Valentyna is far from dull. She knows precisely what's at stake here. I freely admit marriage would be easier and certainly a more economical method of bringing Briavel under our rule, but if she won't see the sense of unification this spring, then I shall teach her that she never was an equal . . . no matter what she has been raised to believe."

Jessom unhappily had to agree with the King. "Your orders, sire?"

"Summon my general and his captains. War with Briavel is now on the agenda," Celimus said, before swallowing the contents of his wine cup and slamming it down on the table. "And while we're at it, I might as well deal with the barbarian of the north," he added, glee lacing his tone.

Valentyna's hand was at her throat, alarm spreading through her every fiber at hearing Krell's admission. "You did what?" she said, tone icy, turning on her faithful servant, hoping somehow she had misunderstood him.

Krell had never before felt so unsure of himself. "Someone had to, your majesty," he said, his voice small and filled with dismay. Suddenly the letter to Chancellor Jessom seemed like a rash move.

"Someone had to what, Chancellor Krell? Betray me? Don't you think I'm dealing with enough here without my

own people working against me? Wouldn't it have been easier to take out a knife and just plunge it straight into my
heart?"

"Your highness," Krell beseeched. "It was for the good of
Briavel . . . for your reign. You father—"

"Don't you dare, Krell!" she snapped. "Don't you dare
cite my fine father. Yes, he craved peace. He did not want his
daughter fighting endless, pointless wars with Morgravia
just to keep a tradition alive. But he would have trusted me.
You never would have gone behind his back in this manner."
She could see Krell moving to explain, but she held her hand
up. "What possessed you, Chancellor? What was going
through your head when you sent that letter?"

He swallowed hard. He had never seen her like this. Suddenly the young Queen appeared possessed herself. Such
wrath; her dark blue eyes blazed bright with anger and it was
all directed at him. Surely he did not deserve this? "I thought,
your highness, that Chancellor Jessom might shed some light
on the strange series of events. That he might explain
whether there was some misunderstanding and prevent us
leaping to wrong conclusions and making hasty decisions."

"Chancellor Krell," she snarled. "The only person making
hasty decisions is you, sir. You have presumed too much.
Your office and your familiarity with this family and with me
does not permit you to send secret missives to our enemies."

"Enemy," he echoed softly. He looked completely baffled. "Me confer with an enemy?" The accusation was too
much for him to bear.

Valentyna stepped forward. "Yes, enemy, Krell. Celimus
wants Briavel, not me and not peace and not for the good of
Briavellians or even Morgravians, for that matter. He simply
covets the realm. He is empire building. He is also a madman, although I didn't think I'd have to explain that to you.
His latest actions speak a thousand words."

Krell tried to resurrect some measure of his former composure. He forced himself to stand straighter, to stop cringing before the angry monarch who towered above him. "My
queen, if you don't marry him, he will make war upon us."

She closed her eyes momentarily, as if to gather her patience. "And you don't think that's precisely what he will be ordering right now . . . as we speak?"

"But, your highness, I had to do something. What was I supposed to think you were doing—"

"I was stalling, you reckless, interfering old man. I am trying to find the solution," she said. Tears welled, but she fought them back. "I wanted this whole business kept quiet so I could have time to think, to carry on diplomatic relations, and to keep the King of Morgravia at arm's length until I knew how to go forward. I don't know yet what the answer is. If you hadn't interfered, Celimus would be none the wiser. He would still think I had intentions to marry him and I would have time to plan . . . and perhaps I still would have had to marry him, sir, but I would have been able to do it on my own terms. Not yours! You have now committed us to war. How does it feel to have so much blood on your hands?"

Krell wept.

Valentyna despised herself for reducing this good man to such a state, but her anger was burning white-hot with fear. "Get out of my sight. Leave the palace."

"Highness, please, let me help."

"Help?" She gave a bitter laugh. "I don't need your sort of help, Krell," Valentyna said cruelly. "What I need is people who are faithful and true to Briavel and its ruler above all else. You have betrayed both and I will never forgive you. Now go."

Valentyna waited until her heartbroken chancellor had left her alone before she buried her face in her hands and cried like a child. Through her tears all she could think about was her beloved Romen Koreldy and how badly she needed his strength and his arms around her now. He would have known what to do. She had nobody. Not even her friend Fynch and his strange dog, Knave, were near to offer their usual solace. And then her father's face swam before her and reminded her once again of whom she was. She could never depend on anyone but herself.

The Queen of Briavel's resolve crystallized, and by the

time the startling news was delivered that Chancellor Krell had jumped to his death from the battlements, her heart was hardened. She shed no tear at the tragedy, for it was because of him that Briavel might go to war and she would be held responsible for leading more of her young men to their deaths.

It must be avoided. She searched her mind for ideas. What could she give to Celimus as a sweetener? The answer was the same bleak solution she had arrived at many times before. She would give Celimus herself. No more stalling or hoping for deliverance from her fate. Perhaps she could suggest bringing the marriage date forward? Yes, it made sense and would please the King, prove her commitment to this union.

Valentyna called for a secretary. Arrangements needed to be made for Krell's funeral . . . and for a wedding.

Read on for a preview of the stunning
conclusion to The Quickening trilogy

BRIDGE OF SOULS

in which Wyl Thirsk, trapped in a body not his
own, must walk his most dangerous path yet—
straight into the brutal clutches of
King Celimus—in a desperate attempt to save his
nation, his love, and himself.

It felt like an eternity to Fynch.

There was brightness, unbearably sharp, and combined with a hammering pain. He squeezed his lids tightly but the dazzling gold light hurt his eyes all the same as he helplessly relinquished control of his small body to the vast agony exploding through it. He believed he felt his body writhing uncontrollably, but in truth he was rigidly still, his teeth bared in a grimace as the force of magic gifted from Elysius radiated painfully into him.

At one point he thought he glimpsed the sorcerer passing through him to his death, like a distant memory he could not quite bring into focus. Elysius appeared whole again and he was smiling. Fynch vaguely sensed him offering thanks but was unable to lock on to it as the pain claimed all of his attention.

The sickening throb of power began to pulse through his body in time with his escalating heartbeat, each push harder, each more breathless in its intensity, until he lost all sense of himself. He no longer knew who he was or where he lay; he had to relinquish all to the excruciating pain until, finally, he glimpsed its end. The agony ebbed gradually but steadily until he realized he was bearing it. His pulse was fast but his heart no longer felt as though it might explode through his chest. The blinding light had dimmed to flashes of gold, as if he had been staring at the sun too long, and his breath was no longer panicked and shallow but came in deep, rhythmic drafts.

His wits returned. He had survived.

Trembling from the chill that now gripped him, Fynch opened his eyes to slits. He registered a new layer of pain and closed them again; this time it was a headache that prompted instant nausea. He felt like crying. But where other youngsters might have had the comfort of a mother's voice and love, there was no such consolation for Fynch. He was alone. Wyl had gone.

Fynch hated the way they had parted. He knew Wyl had wanted him to leave the Wild immediately and he had watched his friend battle his inclination to say as much. Ylena's face was too expressive to mask what her brother was thinking. And yet Wyl had said nothing, had permitted Fynch to make his own decision and remain a little longer. Fynch felt a profound sadness for his friend who had suffered so much loss already and would suffer more yet, he sensed. He wished he knew of a way to spare Wyl more pain, or at least to share some of it with him.

He sighed. The nausea had passed. His eyes were still closed and he realized the pain had dimmed considerably. But the loneliness remained. There would not even be Elysius to offer solace. No. The boy suspected he was alone in the Wild, save for the four-legged beast who was his constant companion.

Full consciousness sifted through his shattered nerves and Fynch became aware of a pressing warmth at his side. Having sensed he was alert again, the source of warmth moved and growled.

"Knave," Fynch croaked through a parched throat.

Never far, a voice replied in his head. The unexpected sound made him flinch.

The boy turned toward the great black dog. "Did you speak to me?" he asked, tears welling. "Can I finally hear you?"

Depthless eyes regarded him and again he heard Knave's reply in his mind. *I did. You can.*

The friendly voice—one he had never thought to hear—

was too overwhelming. Fynch managed to command his reluctant arms to obey him. Slowly, painfully, he wrapped
them around the big animal's neck and wept deeply and
without shame.

Elysius? Fynch asked after a long time, testing his newly
acquired power.

The dog's response was instant. *Dead. It was quick. And
he was glad to go.*

Where is his body?

*Everywhere. He became dust. The massive transfer of
power disintegrated his physical being and then dis-
persed him.*

Did he say anything before . . . before he passed on?

*That you are the bravest of souls. He agonized that he
might be wrong to force this burden upon you,* the dog admitted. *He regretted the pain you would experience and the
journey ahead, but he believed there is no one else who can
walk the path but you.* The dog leaned closer and spoke very
gently. *In this I know he is right.*

Fynch pulled away from his friend, eyes still wet. There
was so much yet to learn. *Knave, I don't know how to use
this power. I have no—*

Hush, the dog soothed. *That is why I am here.*

The boy took the beast's huge head between his tiny
hands. *Who are you?*

I am your guide. You must trust me.

I do.

The dog said no more, but Fynch sensed that he was glad,
even relieved.

But there is something I must know, he went on, his tone
almost begging.

Ask it. Knave's mental voice was so deep that Fynch suspected that if the dog could speak aloud, he, Fynch, would
feel the sound rumble through his own tiny chest.

Who is your true master? Where do you belong?

Fynch sensed Knave's smile. *I have no master as such.
But I do belong.*

Where? Please tell me.

I am of the Thicket.

Ah. Fynch's tensed muscles relaxed as understanding flooded through him. The neatness of the dog's answer pleased him. *Are there others like you?*

I am unique, although there are other enchantments within the Thicket.

So Elysius didn't send you to Myrren?

Elysius did not know me by flesh until we both came here, although he knew of me. And Myrren was not the person I sought.

This was a revelation. Fynch pressed his hands against his eyes in an attempt to ease their soreness and clear his swirling thoughts. *Then why didn't you just search out Wyl?*

Because Wyl was not the one I sought either.

Fynch looked up sharply. *Who, then? Who must we now search for?*

The search is over. It was always you, Fynch.

What? The dog's unerring gaze told Fynch Knave would never lie. *But why?*

You are the Progeny and I am the Guide.

I thought I was the Wielder, Fynch asked, confused.

That, and so much more, Knave said reverently. *You are many things.*

The Thicket sent you to find me?

The Thicket sent me to find the next Gate Wielder. It did not know that would be you.

But it must have known Elysius was dying in order to send you in search of his replacement?

Yes.

So your role has never been about Wyl or Myrren . . . or protecting Valentyna? Fynch sent wonderingly.

Knave's response was measured. *My task is to protect you. When the magic of the Quickening entered Wyl, the Thicket believed he was the next Wielder. Elysius wondered the same.*

Are you saying that it was pure coincidence you came

into Myrren's life? Fynch asked, desperately trying to piece the puzzle together.

Not exactly. She was Elysius's daughter. Magic was part of her even though it was not strong in her. It was she whom the Thicket decided to keep a watch over. When Myrren made such connection with Wyl, we thought he might be the one. It was only when I met you that I realized it was you we searched for.

How can you tell?

There is an aura about you, Fynch. Unmistakable, and invisible to all but those of the Thicket.

Fynch sighed. *I was born with this aura?*

Yes. Your destiny was set.

Elysius never mentioned it.

Elysius didn't know. The Thicket told him who you are only as he died.

It talks!?

Communicates, the dog corrected.

Fynch held his head and groaned. These revelations were causing fresh gusts of pain to surge through his already aching mind. *It hurts, Knave. Will it always be so?*

You must control the pain. Don't allow yourself to become its slave. Master it, Fynch.

Is this how it will kill me?

The dog held a difficult silence between them.

I would know the truth, Fynch insisted. *If you are my friend—my Guide, as you say—then tell me honestly.*

He sensed the dog's discomfort as he began to explain. *This is the beginning. You must use your powers sparingly. Talk to me aloud whenever you can, although hearing my response in your mind will not sap your energies. The pain and other weakenings will only occur if you send the magic yourself.*

How long have I got, Knave?

The dog raised his head to look Fynch directly in the eye. *I don't know. It depends how strong you are, how sparingly you use this power.*

If Knave expected despair it did not come. Fynch wiped his eyes and, using his companion as support, raised himself wearily on unsteady legs. *I must rest,* the little boy said gravely.

And then we must go to the Thicket, Knave said, equally somber. *It awaits you.*

EXPLORE THE REMARKABLE
UNIVERSE OF

KAREN TRAVISS

CITY OF PEARL
0-06-054169-5/$7.50 US/$9.99 Can

Environmental Hazard Enforcement Officer Shan Frankland agreed to lead a mission to Cavanagh's Star to check on the missing Constantine colony. But her landing, with a small group of scientists and Marines, has not gone unnoticed by Aras, the planet's designated guardian.

CROSSING THE LINE
0-06-054170-9/$7.50 US/$9.99 Can

War is coming again to Cavanagh's Star—and this time, the instigators will be the troublesome *gethes* from the faraway planet Earth. Shan Frankland has already crossed a line, and now she is a prize to be captured . . . or a threat to be eliminated.

THE WORLD BEFORE
0-06-054172-5/$7.50 US/$9.99 Can

Those who are coming to judge from the World Before— the home planet, now distant and alien to the *wess'har*— will not restrict their justice to the individual humans responsible for the extermination of a sentient species. Earth itself must answer for the genocide.